S0-AZL-269

NIGHT OF THE HIDDEN FANG

LYCANTHROPE TRILOGY — VOLUME ONE

NIGHT OF THE HIDDEN FANG

by

T. JAMES LOGAN

BEAR PAW PUBLISHING
DENVER

Copyright © 2018 by T. James Logan

ALL RIGHTS RESERVED
This novel is a work of fiction. Names, characters, places, and incidents are either the product of the author's imagination, or, if real, used fictitiously.

No part of this work covered by the copyright herein may be reproduced, transmitted, stored, or used in any form or by any means graphic, electronic, or mechanical, including but not limited to photocopying, recording, scanning, digitizing, taping, Web distribution, information networks, or information storage and retrieval systems, except as permitted under Section 107 or 108 of the 1976 United States Copyright Act, without the prior written permission of the publisher.

Illustration and Cover Design: Holly Heisey

PAPERBACK EDITION

ISBN 978-1-62225-418-7

Bear Paw Publishing
Denver, Colorado, USA

www.bearpawpublishing.com

DEDICATION

For the boyz:

Jace, James, Garion, and Logan

FOREWORD

The publishing industry is a strange beast. A few years ago, this story was published under another title, under another name, by a publisher that is now defunct. For many reasons outside of my control, that book never achieved its full potential. I'm delighted to present the story to you now in a re-envisioned package, in a form more in line with what I originally intended, and with two more books on the way. This edition of the story is the doorstep to a larger, darker world, a trilogy of stories about a world that will be irrevocably changed.

Things there are among us, things that might look like us, but they are things that are *not us*. And we don't know who they are until it's too late.

T. James Logan
January, 2018

PROLOGUE

arvey Roach groaned. "Oh, crap, not again."

The spot of mustard stain on the front of his uniform looked like a little dollop of dried vomit next to his Pinkerton Security Services badge. He rubbed at it with a napkin, succeeded only in smearing it around, then gave up and shoved the rest of the cold hot dog into his mouth, washing it down with warm Mountain Dew.

He leaned back in his chair and sighed, rubbing the grain out of his eyes from the incessant flicker of the surveillance monitors. The hard, wooden office chair—circa 1940—creaked with his weight. Fortunately, Beeckman wasn't scheduled for a site check tonight, and, conscientious supervisor that he was, he always made sure to let Harvey know when he was coming. Harvey rubbed at the mustard stain again. No one would likely see it except Shelly when she did his laundry, but it still made him look like a slob. He crumpled up the food wrappers on the desk and tossed them away, then picked up his dog-eared copy of *The Maltese Falcon*.

A shade of movement on one of the monitors caught his eye. Father McManus walking alone down the hallway from his office, at this time of night, probably going to the rectory, likely a few glasses of hooch closer to bed. The camera paused in that view for fifteen seconds, then cycled to the interior of the gymnasium, then the industrial arts shop, the entrance hallway to the original Saint Sebastian's orphanage, the area surrounding the security shack, an adolescent boy in pajamas shuffling toward the second floor bathroom of the boys' dormitory. The boy scratched his head and disappeared into the bathroom.

Harvey considered texting Katrina again. Might be nice to line up a woman on the side, for contingency purposes. Trina liked his gun. Shelly rode his ass too much, kept telling him he should have higher aspirations than being a "rent-a-cop." God, he hated that term. He was a *Site Security Specialist.* But *nooooo,* that wasn't good enough for her. "Why don't you apply to the police department again?" she would whine. "Why don't you go back to school and finish your criminal justice degree? You could even apply to the F.B.I. then!" As if he could ever get into the F.B.-frickin'-I. Besides, someday, after a few years of experience, he would open his own private investigations office. Private dicks were way cooler than Feds. The idea of working for the government gave him a case of the shudders.

He leaned back into the ancient chair, feeling that moment of doubt where he might fall over backwards if he weren't careful, then eased into the chair's rearward limit and flipped through the Hammett novel. He would be finished with it before morning.

Shelly could go pound sand. Where else could he get on-the-job training *and* time to read detective stories?

The monitor flicked through its sequence of cameras again. The worst that ever happened here at Saint Sebastian's School for Children was the occasional glue-head sneaking into the bathroom at night to sniff himself into a coma, or scampering off to some midnight skateboard rendezvous. This place was the end of line for most of these kids. Next stop, living under a railroad trestle or in juvenile detention. At least Father McManus gave them three squares, a roof, and a school, a place on the fringe of the city, surrounded by farmland on three sides, away from the black and Hispanic ghettoes or white-trash trailer parks, away from gang territories, hookers, pimps, and drug dealers.

The human eye detected movement more than shapes, especially at night—he knew that from training—and it was movement that caught his glance again. The boy was standing in the dormitory hallway, staring at something in the bathroom, backing slowly away. He was speaking, but the cameras had no audio pickups. Then he spun and tore down the hallway, his eyes gleaming with fear in the dim light.

"Crap," Harvey sighed, tossing down his book. He pressed the button to hold the monitor on that camera feed. Damn kids.

The lights in the hallway went out, but the kids weren't supposed to be able to access the switches. The light from bathroom spilled out and formed a bright smear in a sea of electronic black. A low-slung shadow appeared in the hallway, like someone bent over. The silhouette of a face suddenly filled the screen, and the camera went black. Those cameras were near the ceiling. What had that kid been standing on?

"Dammit!" Harvey jumped to his feet, checked his gun and pepper spray, and rushed out of the security shack, heading for the dormitory. He hoped it wasn't another suicide attempt. Some of these kids showed up with their psyches scarred by abusive adults, either relatives or foster parents. A real variety of real pathologies. Pathology was a technical term. Harvey just called it "effed-up." It happened once six months before Harvey started here. One belt, one shower head, and one young meth-head, done.

He whipped out his massive ring of keys as he ran, searching for the right one.

Somewhere, a fire-door slammed. Where had that come from? The back of the dormitory? Somebody making a run for it? Somebody too stupid to realize that this was their last shot at avoiding juvenile detention? What had the kid in the hall been running away from?

A few seconds of fumbling at the door with the five-pound jumble of brass and zinc and steel, and he was inside, running for the stairwell to the second floor, where that camera was mounted.

The hallway was still dark, and the heavy puffing of his breath echoed down the empty, tiled corridor. The light from the bathroom still spilled a skewed rectangle onto the floor and wall. He ran for the bathroom, certain he was going to see some emo junkie hanging from a shower head by a bedsheet or left in a beaten bloody pile.

But when he reached the bathroom, he saw no such thing. Nothing at all in fact. Empty. Spic-and-span. Not even a dribble of errant urine on the floor, even though the kid who had run looked like he had practically peed himself. But what was this? Two long parallel scratches gouged into the paint of a toilet stall door, about two feet from the floor, so fresh that flakes of paint still hung from the edges. Why would someone want to deface the door so close to the floor? Most graffiti or vandalism happened at eye level.

Somewhere a door slammed, then a strange scratching-running sound. He pulled his Maglite and ran toward the noise. Sounded like it came from the door to the far stairwell. This building held three floors of boys ages six to eighteen, with the oldest boys on the top floor. At the far end of the hallway, the plastic box covering the light switches and thermostat controls were shattered, as if by a hammer. Shards of plastic littered the floor.

He flipped the switches, and the hallway lights flickered on. Another slamming fire-door, this one far below, drew him in a gasping rush into the stairwell. Looking over the banister down well, he saw a flicker of shadow disappear through the fire door. He charged down the stairs two and three and a time. Shelly would kill him if he fell and broke his neck. Seconds later, he plowed through the fire door back out into the night air. The rattle of the chain link fence snagged his ears. A trio of shadows landed on the other side of the fence, shapes barely glimpsed in the darkness before they dashed into the cornfield beyond with the rustle of leaves.

Harvey sighed and pulled out his cell phone.

Father McManus picked up on the second ring. "Good evening, Harvey. What can I do for you?"

"I think we have some runners, maybe three."

Father McManus sighed. "Did you see them?"

"Not clearly, no."

"Thank you for letting me know, my son. I'll call the teachers."

Harvey stood up straighter. "I'll start investigating and find out who's missing."

"I'll come over to the dormitory in a few minutes."

"Yes, sir."

Father McManus hung up, and Harvey went back inside. He pressed a special alarm button on his keychain. The alarm bell erupted through the building. By the time he made it back into the hallway, packs of boys—wearing expressions of varying ratios of sleepiness, fear, and annoyance—were shuffling from their rooms, waiting beside their doors, rubbing their eyes.

Harvey's first task was a head count. A storage locker on each floor held the room rosters. Starting with the youngest first-grade boys, he systematically worked his way through them, checking names off the list. Four boys to a room, with a handful of empty slots here and there. When he reached the top floor, he sensed an immediate increase in the tension. Downstairs, he had seen a lot more fear and uncertainty in their eyes. On the third floor, the eyes were downcast, subdued. He sensed secrets being hidden.

A deep scratchy voice from right behind jerked a yelp of surprise out of him. "Harvey, what's going on?"

Harvey spun, clutching his chest. "Where the hell did you come from?"

"You were preoccupied. What's up?"

Harvey cleared his throat. "Well, seems we got some runners, Mister Slade." The wrestling coach's sharp blue gaze burned into Harvey like propane flames. Thick shoulders and muscular chest, hands on narrow rippling hips. What Harvey wouldn't give for a physique like that. "I was just about to do a head count."

"I'll give you a hand."

"No need for that, Mister Slade, I—"

Slade turned away, oblivious. "I'll do some looking around." He walked away with a swift but strangely careful stride.

"Right. You do that," Harvey sneered to himself. "Arrogant prick." The way Slade moved creeped Harvey out a little.

He returned to his task. The headcount revealed three boys missing. Now for a check-off to determine who they were.

As he worked his way down the lines on both sides of the hallway, he soon recognized the pajamas he had seen on the video, the kid from the bathroom. The kid's skin was sheened with sweat, and his face was as pale as a boiled egg. Harvey couldn't remember all of the kids' names, but this boy's was on his list—Carlos Moreno.

Carlos glanced up at Harvey, saw Harvey's distinct attention, then looked away again, fidgeting.

Harvey took Carlos by the shoulder. "C'mon. Let's go talk down there."

The boy's arm tensed like a bundle of steel cables. "I didn't do nothin', man!"

"You're not in trouble."

One of the other boys jeered. "Maybe he oughta be!"

Harvey took Carlos to an empty dorm room at the end of the hall, sat the trembling boy down on the mattress, and said. "You're not in trouble, Carlos."

"Then what's this about, man?"

Harvey suddenly felt like a real P.I., starting a *real investigation*, and pride ballooned in his chest. He'd have this solved before the police even got here. "You saw something. I want to know what it was."

Carlos' hands became fists between his knees. "No way, Harvey. Forget it. You wouldn't never believe me anyway."

"That's 'Officer Roach' to you. You went into the bathroom. You came back out again in an awful hurry. What did you see?"

According to the roster, Carlos was fifteen, a freshman. He played junior varsity running back. According to Harvey's own eyes, Carlos looked ready to cry. "What did you see in the bathroom? When I looked in there, it was empty."

"You're lucky."

"What did you see? Did someone attack you? Are you hurt?" There was no visible blood or bruises on the boy.

"You wouldn't believe me."

Harvey loomed nearer, frustration tightening his jaw, his fists. This punk kid was holding out on him. "Tell me!"

Carlos swallowed hard, shoulders sagging. "They was monsters, man! Three of 'em! Big, hairy, goddamn monsters. With teeth like this and—"

"Cut the crap, Carlos!"

Carlos clamped his mouth shut and he sighed. "See? I told you you wouldn't believe me."

Harvey had to admit that the kid looked too terrified to make this up. "You sniffing anything? Any drugs?"

"Naw, man. I don't do that crap."

"Yeah, you're squeaky clean, I'm sure. This'll do for now."

Harvey caught Carlos shooting him a look of contempt as the boy left the room, but the terror in that boy's face...that had been real. This kid wasn't smart enough to be that kind of actor. But seriously? Monsters? He scoffed and shook his head.

What about the scratches on the toilet door?

CHAPTER ONE

Mia O'Reilly's face grew warm, and her heart flipped over. Mrs. Vanderweg crossed her arms at having to repeat herself. "Dalton, I said, you're up."

In the four weeks since school started, Mia had watched him from the opposite side of the classroom, hoping every day for a chance to speak to him. He wasn't the cutest guy in school—most of the jocks had locks on sheer hotness—but there was something about his shoulders and big brown eyes.

Dalton walked to the front of the class room, stood before the chalkboard where Mrs. Vanderweg had written "POETRY SLAM: Keats and Yeats and Byron, Oh, My!", cleared his throat, and ran his fingers through his long brown waves.

A boy hooted from the back of the room. "Nine point oh!"

The class snickered.

Mrs. Vanderweg, "A little premature on the judging, Scott."

Another boy snickered. "He's premature a lot!"

The class tittered, and Dalton pointedly cleared his throat to gain their attention.

Mia could see his nervousness at war with his natural confidence.

He took a deep breath and raised his note card. "'Never Give All the Heart' by William Butler Yeats."

Every female eye in the room trained upon him like a pink laser. He cleared his throat again. When he spoke his voice was quiet, but full and deep, and he spoke with a carefully measured cadence.

Never give all the heart, for love
Will hardly seem worth thinking of
To passionate women if it seem
Certain, and they never dream
That it fades out from kiss to kiss;...

Mia's heart revved. She squeezed the edge of her desk. Twelve other girls were staring as if heartthrob Zack Jackson from Alpha Children had just sprung into existence in eleventh grade language arts class. Dalton lowered his note card, spoke the words of a long-dead Irish poet, and Mia's toes *curled*.

...For everything that's lovely is
But a brief, dreamy, kind delight.
O never give the heart outright.
For they, for all smooth lips can say,
Have given their hearts up to the play.
And who could play it well enough
If deaf and dumb and blind with love?...

Dalton looked out into the imaginary distance like a mournful lover alone in a field of Irish heather.

...He that made this knows all the cost
Because he gave all his heart, and lost.

Hoots and whistles and applause erupted, and he struck a bow. Mia clapped furiously. He grinned around the room to his buddies, then bowed again. "Thank you! Thank you very much!" He returned to his seat. His eyes flicked toward Mia once, and her ears heated.

Mrs. Vanderweg interposed herself in the front of the room. "Judges, what say you?"

Six students held up little whiteboards with their scores. Mrs. Vanderweg tallied up the results. "Well, it seems we have left the best for last today. In first place for today's Poetry Slam is Dalton, with a total score of forty-nine point six. Second place goes to..."

Mia zoned out as she whipped open her notebook and tried to scribble down as much of the poem as she could before it evacuated from her brain. Her hand somehow turned her normally looping swirls of purple ink into jagged geometric shapes. Mia, you're an idiot. He doesn't even know who you are.

The bell rang, and Mrs. Vanderweg dismissed the class. Mia could only get a glimpse of his tall back, swathed in leather jacket, as he disappeared into the hallway with his buddies. As soon as she had a few minutes, she would Google the poem and write it down properly, but right now she had to hurry to chemistry lab. Oh, wait. She didn't have a laptop anymore. It had mysteriously disappeared during the second week of school. She suspected someone had stolen it, but she couldn't prove anything. Writing everything by hand felt so Old School.

As she merged with the freeway traffic of students in the hallway, she wondered who had broken Dalton's heart. He had read the poem with too much emotion for it not to be *real*. Words like that came from somewhere. On one hand, Mia wanted to kick that girl's ass, whoever she was. On the other hand, Mia wanted to make it all better.

She hurried down the hallway, alone in a sea of people a full head taller than her, all these beefy corn-fed boys and blonde Amazon girls, all these broad shoulders and big boobs and here was Mia with her little skinny butt and—

SLUT

Scrawled in red marker on a color photo printout of a nude Asian woman. A few choice dabs of red had been added to the woman's genitals. All nice and bright and taped to her locker.

She froze, unable to even look around, feeling eyes on her from every direction. A few people were taking notice, looking at the photo, then at Mia, smirking, their eyes traveling up and down.

She snatched the paper off the locker with her fist, crumpling, crushing, stuffing the paper into her pocket, wishing she could do the same with the pain that just punched into her gut. Her eyes scanned the passing throngs. Who was standing around? Whoever did it would want to see her reaction.

Suddenly her armful of books went flying. They splatted against the floor with the sound of cracking spines and tearing pages. Big blunt features around a pug nose and a heavy brow. The cave man stepped toward her, his Size-14 Nikes falling upon her notebook, where her hastily scribbled poem lay hidden. "Oh, sorry! Didn't see you there!" the cave man said with exaggerated sincerity. His sheer size, looming over like an entire football team, set her back a step. It would take three of her to make just one of him. He spun his foot on the cover of her notebook, tearing it free and rending the spine, and sauntered away. All that remained was a shoe print amid a snarl of savaged pages. Purple ink bled from between the tears.

Mia mumbled through gritted teeth as she knelt to gather it up, along with the rest of her books. "Neanderthal douche bag!"

A long, tan leg slid into her field of vision and kicked her binder fifteen feet farther down the hallway. "Oh, sorry! I didn't see you there!" The voice dripped with contempt and patronizing superiority.

Anger flared up, heating her face, tightening her muscles. Eyes bored into her from every direction, sizing her up, probing for weakness like a pack of wolves, circling. With only four weeks in this new territory, if she showed any weakness, she was finished.

Mia jumped up with her fists clenched, coming face to breast with Chelsea Cole. She shouted the first word that came to mind, a uniquely Japanese word with multiple levels of insult. "*Baka!*" Chelsea stepped closer into Mia's anger. Mia swallowed hard but held her ground. Wow, those things were huge—compared to Mia's—and pointed right at her face, as if asserting dominant womanhood.

Chelsea tossed back a lustrous ponytail of spun gold and walked away.

Her cohort, Brittany Something-or-Other, loomed over Mia. "What the hell, don't you even speak English? Go back to China."

The shock froze Mia, and her brain went blank, but tears welled up.

A third girl, Tara Anderson, shuffled beside her taller friends. Her face showed pity, but she hung back.

Mia's ears burned, and she stared at their long, smooth legs still tanned from summer. The trio moved away into the river of students.

Only after they had disappeared did Mia's throat unclench. She yelled after them, "Were you *born* a cliché?" But it was no good; they were out of hearing. Why couldn't she ever formulate a scathing, soul-shattering retort when she needed too? Always too late to let her keep her self-respect.

"Yo, dude," said a familiar voice. Nate stood over her, looking down with an expression of mixed apology and pity. "Here." He handed her binder to her.

"Thanks." She yanked a handful of papers from under a passing shoe.

"And to answer your question, yes, Chelsea and Brittany were born clichés."

She gave Nate a wry smile.

"Seriously, dude," he said, "I can't have them messing up my Chem homework. I'd be lost without you."

"I appreciate your confidence in my amazingness, but I'll be amazed if I get through that class with a B."

"That would be a *bonus*. Most of my grades spell *dickhead* or *fool*."

The growing number of red flags appearing in her grades so far this semester might belie that assumption.

She shuffled her ravaged notebook carefully, carefully back into something she could recover later, then finished gathering the rest of her papers and books into an unkempt wad.

"Shall we?" he said.

She sighed and they headed down the hallway in silence. They rounded a corner, and the caveman who had sent her books flying now stood chatting with Chelsea and the other two girls. Mia couldn't hear them, but she saw the coquettish wiggle Chelsea gave him. He leaned in and gave her lecherous leer.

Nate saw it too, and paused to give Mia a pained look. "Wilcox is a festering douche nozzle."

Mia fought down the sour lump forming in her throat.

Wilcox threw Chelsea another lascivious, drool-ridden look and went on his way.

After he lumbered away, Chelsea rolled her eyes and stuck her finger in her mouth to mime a gag. Brittany giggled. Tara gave a half-smile, but mostly looked uncomfortable. Chelsea then spotted Mia. Their gazes locked for a long moment, Chelsea's eyes burning into hers with icy contempt. Then she tossed her ponytail and led her cronies away.

Nate said, "In the dictionary under *cliché bitches*, see Chelsea and Brittany. Once more, with feeling."

Mia watched them disappear. "You didn't include Tara in your assessment."

"That's because..." He sent a long, yearning gaze down the hallway.

Mia rolled her eyes. Oh, no.

He blinked and returned his attention to Mia. "Because high school is suppurating pustule of social dysfunction and animalistic compulsions."

"Somebody has been reading the dictionary."

"No, H.P. Lovecraft, but kind of the same thing. Anyway..." He shrugged, sending another longing gaze down the hallway.

She almost said, Oh, man, you have a crush on a girl who's out of your league.

He elbowed her. "Maybe if things don't work out with Tara—"

She held up a palm. "Don't even." *Thanks, now you want me to be your second pick.* Boys were so damned stupid sometimes.

He poked her shoulder. "Hey, it's not completely hopeless. Did I tell you?"

She sighed. "Tell me what?"

He looked like his head was going to pop off his shoulders and fly around the hallway, skidding along the ceiling. "Tara and I are going running tomorrow night. Cross-country practice."

"Good for you." Mia started toward the chemistry lab again. "That's almost, like, a real date." Tara hadn't even acknowledged Nate during this interaction. This did not bode well for him.

"You forgot to ask me how I managed it. I mean, she's out of my league, right?"

She flushed. Was she such an open book? It wasn't a very nice thing to think about the only guy who talked to her on a semi-regular basis. "No, I mean—That's awesome. It's just—" Open face, insert leg, Mia.

He went on as if she hadn't spoken. "I used my immense scoundrel-like charm and charisma and wal-lah, I'm hanging out with a homecoming candidate." He did have a kind of nerdy adorability, an endearing goofiness about him, along with a cute crooked grin. He rubbed his chin. "You think she'll want to play with my light saber?"

Mia choked.

"Oh, did I say that out loud?"

"Uh, yes. Chain up your hormones and come on."

They walked in silence toward chemistry lab, and Mia was conscious, just as she was most days, of the sheer ubiquity of Midwest suburban uber-whiteness, which mostly meant closed-minded, parochial mediocrity. Her father had sworn to her that Omaha was a real metropolitan city, but a nice place, a safe place. He didn't have to say that he hoped it would be a place where their family could forget.

She had always blended in, everywhere they had lived. Even Kadena Air Force Base back in Okinawa had been more culturally diverse, with the wide cross-section of ethnicities in the military, not to mention the Japanese and the native Ryukyu. Here, she felt like a diminutive *koi* swimming among a bunch of hulking catfish.

A familiar voice came up from behind her. "Hey, G.F., wait a sec."

Mia turned. "Hi, Nicki. What's up?"

Nicki gave Mia a cute, freckled grin. "You doing anything tonight?"

Mia tried to contain her surprise. "No, not really. Want to hang out or something?"

"Well, I don't have time tonight, but I wanted to ask if you could help with my algebra homework again."

Mia restrained the snarky comment that had almost popped out. "Well, I kind of have my own stuff to do..."

"There's twenty bucks in it for you. I'm *desperate!*"

Mia shrugged. "Okay." Twenty bucks was twenty bucks, and she needed a new laptop. If she could find more 'clients', she might have a new laptop by the end of the semester. If only Chelsea and her sycophants would quit sabotaging her at every turn.

"Awesome." Nicki handed Mia a worksheet.

Mia took it hesitantly. "Tomorrow?"

"Yep. Thanks! You're awesome!" Nicki then bounced down the hallway.

Nate snickered. "She asked *you* to help her?"

"Hey, I can do algebra, buddy."

"Sorry."

"I just choose not to."

"Sorry."

"Most of the time."

"Yeah, twenty bucks. I should put up a flyer or something. If Tara doesn't work out, maybe I could meet babes that way..."

Mia rolled her eyes.

Even after almost four months in Omaha, she had yet to find a group of friends to hang out with. These kids thought Kansas City was wild and exotic. One of them had even asked her, in all seriousness, if she routinely ate raw fish, and if so, would she eat a goldfish. She could barely stomach five minutes of conversation—hello, Nicki—much less develop any real friendships. Not that she'd ever had many friendships. Her father's years in the Air Force had torn too many dear friends away from her when she was little. She reminded herself not to be too harsh; they had intended to stay settled in Los Angeles after he retired from the Air Force and joined the F.B.I.

And then Sho.

God, don't let her heart get started on that now.

Then they pulled up stakes and moved as far from the ocean as they could. Here, no saltwater within twelve hundred miles.

Nate elbowed her. "So what do you think my chances are?"

Mia sighed and rolled her eyes. "Approaching zero, because if you don't quit stressing about it, you're going to just blow it anyway."

Nate deflated. "Yeah, but I can't help it."

She patted his arm. "Just use your smooth, sexy man-charisma on her, and she'll be like Play-doh in your hands."

Then she spotted a girl leaning against the wall, sobbing uncontrollably, phone squeezed against her forehead. Mia did not know her, but the sight so much raw pain made her pause.

One of the girl's friends laid a hand on her shoulder. "Geez, Cassie, what happened?"

Sobs tumbled between the girl's words, and she held the phone before her staring at it as she could not believe what she had just heard. "That was my mom! My dog was missing this morning, I looked and looked, but we couldn't find her, and Mom said she'd keep an eye out, but she was gardening and found her!"

"That's good, right?" the friend said.

"No! She was dead, half-buried in mom's garden! Something had eaten her! Mom said there was just some fur and bones left, and I just saw her last night!"

"Oh, god!" The friend tried to hug away Cassie's sobs, but it was no good.

Mia's wanted to hug Cassie, too, even though they had never met. If something happened to Deuce, Mia would probably lose her mind.

But she held back for a long moment, torn, until Nate took her arm. "Come on, we're going to be late."

Cassie cried and cried. "I just saw her last night!"

CHAPTER TWO

When Mia rode her bicycle into the garage, that old familiar dread formed a cold lump in her chest. Moving hadn't made that go away. She had hoped the change of scenery would help things, but the scenery here was so unremarkable—utterly nondescript suburban neighborhoods hemmed in by an ocean of grass, fields of corn and soybeans, and endless low hills undulating to the western horizon—that it gave her little else to think about.

Her backpack felt like a full military field pack, complete with lead bricks and anvil, as she dragged it into the kitchen through the garage entrance. She stepped out of her shoes and left them neatly beside the door.

Deuce lay under the under the table. The shar-pei peeked out at her with one eye, his spiky, stubbly tail wagging faintly. Deuce never hid under the table, except when he had been scolded, which never happened except when...

Mia's warning bells clanged. "Mom?"

Her mom's voice sounded from the living room. "Here."

Mia peered around the corner and saw her mother's narrow back and short black hair, just visible over the back of the couch. The room was silent and dim, filled with furniture, but yawning with emptiness. "*Tadaima.*" I'm home.

Her mother wrung at something in her hands. "*Okaeri.*" Welcome home. Her reply was toneless, rote.

She knew what her mother was holding. Something in Mia built up suddenly and popped. "Mom, why don't you put the baseball away? You're not trying out for a team are you?"

Her mom sighed and half turned. She spoke in Japanese. "I need some things for dinner. Please go to the market. There's a list and money on the table."

"But I just got home and—"

"Just do it, please."

"You've been home all day! Why can't you go? I have to call Nicki!" She didn't, but any excuse—

"Mia!" Her mother's voice shrilled, and she half-looked at Mia over her shoulder. "Can you manage this simple thing? Or when your father comes home there won't be anything to eat!"

"I manage a freaking lot!"

"There's a letter from school on the table. What are you doing, Mia? Skipping school? Doing drugs? Slutting around with boys?"

A rod of cold fury slid up Mia's spine. "No, I'm not! But if I was, I'd be having a lot more fucking fun!" If her mother wanted a fight, an F-bomb would certainly raise the threat level straight to DEFCON-2. Angry Mom was bad enough, but it was preferable to the Mom of Relentless Black Emptiness on days like today.

Strangely, Mia's escalation didn't have the usual effect.

Her mom sighed and looked down at the baseball, worn smooth and stained. Her voice was quiet. "I'm sure your father will want to talk about your grades when he gets home. Just go to the market, please."

The lack of reaction chilled Mia even worse. "Fine. Fine. I gotta get out of here anyway."

Deuce looked up at her with sympathy.

She scooped up the shopping list and handful of cash. American money was so boring compared to yen. Doubtless the cash would equal the bill to within a dollar. Mia wouldn't even be able to buy a Pocari Sweat to drink without contributing from her own allowance. That was one of the things she hated about the Midwest so far; she had to make a special trip to the Asian Market to find her favorite soft drinks. This thought stoked her resentment into a searing coal. With her hand on the doorknob to the garage, she yelled back over her shoulder, "Mom, Sho's gone! I'm sorry having me around is such punishment!" She flung open the door and slammed it behind her.

Her legs pumped the pedals like burning pistons, sliding past parked cars and endless curving rows of colorless suburban houses, one after the next. Her vision fuzzed, tears cooling in the wind. Her mother's words swarmed in her brain like a murder of crows, mixing from arguments past, a swirling, black cacophonous cyclone, harsh words building up in the two years since Sho—

That was it.

Two years today.

Mia squeezed the brakes, swerved and jumped onto the sidewalk, skidding to a halt. She let her bike crash onto the concrete, and plopped down on the curb, hugging her knees. She let the tears come.

Sho's mischievous giggle scattered the crows in her mind like a warm updraft. The hard leather of a baseball in her own hands. His relentless pain-in-the-ass-ness. "*C'mon, let's play catch, you big, fat loser!*"

I hate baseball.

"NOBODY hates baseball! Please?"

No, really, I hate baseball.

"I'll do your Japanese homework!"

Okay, but just for a while.

And she was standing on a brilliant, white Okinawan beach, with sapphire-blue waves stretching to infinity and warm foam lapping over her toes as the hard, useless object they threw back and forth evoked smiles and giggles from him that she had seen nowhere else.

Soon he would hoot at her, "Let's go swimming!" It was such a beautiful day, and they weren't in Okinawa anymore, but L.A. with its beautiful California ocean.

But oceans hide things.

She hated baseball.

Mia had done her best to sop up the tears before she arrived at the market. She already felt stupid for breaking down. Crammed between the drab, strip-mall storefronts of Joe & Luigi's Pizza and Ashley Vixen Tanning, Cornhusker Asian Market smelled like a fish market even on the outside. She wondered if only Asians found that smell to be comforting, familiar. Did anyone who grew up near the ocean? The two cashiers greeted her with an English, "Hello!" then returned to chattering to each other in Cantonese. The aisles were cramped, too tall for her stumpy self to easily reach the top shelf. Nevertheless the ubiquitous noodles and sauces and uniquely Japanese snacks evoked a nostalgic sigh. She doubted there were many Omaha kids who thought *nori* or *wasabi* were acceptable snack flavors.

With her basket hooked over her elbow, she strolled the aisles, looking for the things in the shopping list—Chinese cabbage, *daikon* radish, *soba* noodles, Japanese-style mayonnaise, and few other things. The shelves were packed with a mish-mash of Asian foods—Chinese, Japanese, Korean, Vietnamese, Thai, Malaysian, Indonesian, and Filipino. A cooler with a variety of fish and crustaceans laid in rows on the ice filled the back wall.

A smattering of Japanese syllables from the next aisle over caught her attention. Omaha did have a Japanese immigrant community, but Mia had no idea how large. How many of them were wives of American men, now congealed here near the military base, like her mother? Just like all groups of immigrants she had ever seen, both in Los Angeles and in Japan, they tended to keep to themselves. A couple of weeks after the move to Omaha, her mom had gone to a few meetings and organizations to meet people but had since stopped.

Rounding the corner brought Mia face to face with two middle-aged Japanese women dressed in stylish skirts and Prada boots. Their Kansai dialect was so thick and rapid-fire that Mia could only understand half of what they were saying.

Mia bowed to them and said, "*Konnichiwa.*"

They smiled with surprise and returned her gesture. One of the women was taller, with fashionable glasses and a confident square to her shoulders. Despite the fact that the woman was *old*, maybe forty, Mia wished her mom looked half that good with a fraction of the fashion sense. The woman looked down at Mia with appraisal. On one arm hung a Louis Vuitton handbag and her shopping basket, which contained a few trifling foodstuffs, as if she mostly shopped elsewhere.

An urge to speak to them, to have a civil conversation, even if it was Japanese, swept over Mia. "*Nice day, eh?*"

"*A lovely day*," the tall one said.

Mia appraised the supple leather sheathing the woman's calves. *"Awesome boots! Where did you get them?"*

The woman gave her a half smile. *"Rome."*

"Wow, I bet that was nice. I've been a lot of places, but not Rome. I want to go someday, though." Did every word that came out of her mouth have to be utterly, inescapably, mind-numbingly lame?

The other woman, slightly older than the first, with her hair in a bun, bowed and gave her a friendly smile. *"You speak Japanese very well."*

Mia's mouth froze. The woman had intended it as a compliment. But it was given as a compliment only to gaijin. A native speaker would never say such a thing to another, anymore than a kid from California would tell one from Nebraska that his English was excellent. Mia spoke Japanese with native fluency. A sour taste formed in her mouth. What, did she not look Japanese enough? She forced her mouth to start working again. *"Uh, that would be because I'm half-Japanese. I grew up there. My mom is from Tokyo."*

She felt eyes on the conversation, and happened to glance at the cashier. The cashier's face went blank as a stone and turned away.

The tall woman tittered, switching from Kansai dialect to standard Japanese. *"Of course, we should have known. You have some Okinawa twang, too."*

The older woman's face hardened almost imperceptibly. *"Mm. Okinawa, yes."*

Now Mia felt herself getting angry again. On mainland Japan, Okinawa was largely considered a hopeless backwater, home primarily to much of the U.S. military presence, not even real Japan. Okinawa was the unwanted step-child, treated with little more than tolerance. Suddenly she wanted to spout a few choice Ryukyu epithets at these two women, but she clamped the words between her teeth.

The tall one bowed with a faint smile. *"Enjoy the lovely evening. Take care."*

The older woman bowed as well, and the two of them walked away before Mia could return the gesture.

The sick emptiness in Mia's belly returned, and she sighed. She blurred through the rest of her shopping. Fortunately the two women were gone when she lugged her full basket up onto the cashier's counter with a half-smile. "I got a lot of stuff."

The cashier started ringing it all up as if Mia had not spoken. Bitter anger simmered off the woman in almost visible waves. She threw Mia's things into the bag as if hoping to crush the *soba* noodles and bruise the cabbage.

"Hey, take it easy. That cabbage didn't hurt anybody." Mia gave a half-hearted laugh.

The cashier ignored her. She was older than Mia's mom, round-faced, blunt-featured, streaks of gray pulled into a loose bun staked in place with an upright chopstick. Mia had never seen this woman working here before, but this was only Mia's third visit.

Then Mia spotted a book behind the counter, propped open with a jar of Tiger Balm. The pages were splashed with grainy black-and-white photos of Japanese soldiers from World War II, rifles and katanas and bayonets, screaming civilians, weeping women kneeling in a row, a flamethrower. Since the Japanese and Chinese languages shared so many characters, she could discern that the chapter heading said something like, "Japanese Massacre Nanking - 1937".

Mia sighed again, wanting to yell at the woman, *Are you seriously blaming me for something that happened way back then? You weren't even alive then! Neither was I!* But instead, she gave the woman a fistful of cash, snatched up the shopping bags, and fled, leaving her change on the counter.

CHAPTER THREE

Mia sighed as the bell finally rang. She had spent the last twenty minutes of English class drawing endless curlicues around the text of Dalton's poem in her new notebook; hot pink, purple, and green now made an ornate frame around the poem with intertwining versions of his name. She had found the full poem on the internet last night, read it over and over, and had gone to bed thinking about it. It was one of Yeats' more famous poems, and, as she wrote it in her notebook, she had an unexpected sense of the vastness of human knowledge and endeavor, nearly all of it available at the touch of a few keys, nearly all of it still unknown to her. God, she didn't know anything about anything. But maybe someday she would; and then maybe people would take her seriously. Other kids in school talked like they knew everything there was to know. Somehow, glimpsing the breadth of her ignorance made her feel a little smarter.

She snapped her notebook shut, in case anyone might see her idiotic doodling, then gathered up the rest of her books as the other students sifted out the door.

"Mia," Mrs. Vanderweg said, "Come here a minute please."

A pile of cold pebbles settled in Mia's belly and started sloshing around. She approached the teacher's desk.

Mrs. Vanederweg said, "How are you doing in school?"

Mia shrugged. "Okay, I guess. I'm surviving."

"How about outside of school?"

Another shrug. "Same story there."

"You're new here this year, right?"

Mia nodded. "Moved here from L.A. this summer."

"It must be quite a change. Are you having trouble adjusting?"

Her shoulders were apparently infested with shrug-bugs. "I don't know."

"Do you like it here? Do you have any friends?"

No, and No. "I guess so. Why?"

"There's an exam coming up. How do you think your quiz grades are?"

Mia eyed the door. "Okay, I guess."

Mrs. Vanderweg held her hand horizontal at chin level. "This is 'okay.'" She moved her hand to chest level. "This is 'bottom of the barrel.'" Her hand dropped to belly-button level. "This is you."

Mia's eyes bugged out, and she squeezed her books to her chest. "I didn't know it was *that* bad!"

Mrs. Vanderweg sighed and tried to sound comforting. "Okay, maybe it's not that bad, but I'm trying to make a point here. I'm worried that you're not doing any of the homework I assign. All you have to do to pass those quizzes is read. If you can't pass those, the exam is a foregone conclusion. I wanted to talk to you. You look like a smart girl, but my sense is that you're having some problems that don't pertain to my class." She brightened her tone. "Boy troubles?"

"A little." An enormous throbbing ton.

"Got a crush? You looked like you enjoyed our little poetry-reading contest."

Mia couldn't restrain a little smile. "Yeah, I liked that."

"Well, I'm sure you'll get his attention. Maybe try some poetry yourself?"

"I might."

"Good. There's plenty of hope for you. Make sure you read the sections on Emily Dickinson and Sylvia Plath. You might like them."

"Okay."

"See you tomorrow."

Mia nodded. "See you." She had expected a real chewing-out. Mrs. Vanderweg wasn't such a bad sort.

Nate was waiting for Mia at her locker. "Dude. Chem quiz today. You ready?"

"As ready as a zit to be popped."

"That's attractive. I'll bet you got guys swarming around you with that attitude."

"Sorry, I'm just in a really crappy mood today."

"How come?"

"Long story."

"We have a long walk."

"Let's just say that yesterday was a very unpleasant anniversary."

"Bad break-up?"

"No."

"Good break-up?"

"No."

"Somebody die?"

A searing-cold bolt shot through her heart. She bit her lip. This was *not* the time and place to start talking about Sho. Two sentences into that story, she would be blubbering like a baby.

He raised a hand. "Okay, sensitive subject."

They rounded a corner, and she almost walked into the back of someone's leather jacket. "Oh, sshhh..." Her voice trailed off liked a punctured beach-ball as Dalton turned around.

She caught her books at her waist, before they tumbled onto the floor.

"Hi," he said.

"Hi," she said.

Nate stared as if someone had just smacked him in the face with a cold tuna.

Tara edged out from behind Dalton. "Hi, Nate."

Nate's mouth opened and quavering "Hi" came out.

Tara glanced up at Dalton, smiling a beautiful smile, big brown eyes stroking his face. Mia's guts heaved. Part of her wanted to be sick all over Tara's LOVE PINK hoodie. Tara slid closer to Dalton, under his arm leaning against the wall.

Nate looked like a toad wearing a tire-track.

Mia took Nate by the arm, then cleared her throat. "Sorry, we're gonna be late for Chem lab." He offered no resistance as she tugged him down the hallway.

Dalton called after them, "Hey, you're Mia from Language Arts class right?"

Mia glanced back at him. "That's me!" *Mia, the hopeless idiot.* Then she allowed herself to be swept up in the tumult of flowing students.

In chem lab, all Nate could talk about was Tara, his face stricken as if he had just seen the worst horror of his entire life. Mia did her best to console him.

His hands were shaky. "Should I text her and make sure we're still on for tonight? I want to text her."

"No, don't."

"Why not?"

"Trust me. I'm a girl. Act like you don't care that they were almost making out in the hallway."

"Oh, god! Thanks, Mia! Jesus Christ!"

"Sorry," she said. The pebbles in her belly had formed a lump of black lava rock, much more coarse and painful than a pep-talk from a teacher. "Just send her a text an hour or so before and tell her where to meet you, as if it's a foregone conclusion that she'll be there."

"But—!"

She thumbed her chest. "Trust the *girl.*"

Nate sighed. "Okay. But he's such a cool guy!"

"I know that."

"But he doesn't have the greatest reputation."

She raised an eyebrow.

"We've been in the same school since seventh grade. You hear a few things sometimes. He had to miss a few days of school last year."

"Why?"

"Community service for a minor-in-possession citation."

Oh, great. She was crushing on someone her parents would immediately disapprove of. Still, fooling around with alcohol wasn't a deal-breaker. "You sure it was him?"

"Yeah, and there's another story that he put a North kid in the hospital, stabbed him."

"What!"

"Hey, they're just stories. Who knows what's true? He was dating a couple of girls from Central this summer, cheerleaders."

Mia felt sick. How could she compete with cheerleaders?

"Lucky bastard. I hate him. He probably just wants in her pants!" Another spike. "Don't you?"

"Well...yeah! Eventually. But I want the whole package. I respect her."

Mia sighed again. "Good luck." He was doomed. And so was she.

She trudged into the house that night, let her backpack plunk down in its customary place next to the kitchen table, and sat down. Her mother was chopping vegetables.

"*Tadaima*," Mia sighed.

Her mom's voice was carefully monotone. "*Okaeri*."

They had not spoken to each other since the previous evening. "Dad home?"

"He's working late again tonight."

"Wow, that's like every night for the last two weeks."

"Three weeks. He tells me he's working on an important case. Apparently the Omaha police asked for F.B.I. assistance."

"Why hasn't there been anything on the news or in the paper? Bringing in the F.B.I. is a big deal."

"He won't tell me, and they're keeping it out of the media for now, until they have something to go on."

A wet nose poked into Mia's hand. She rubbed Deuce's stubbly head and velvety ears. His loose, shar-pei skin slid back and forth as she stroked.

Her mother kept slicing cucumbers. "*Why don't you ever speak Japanese?*"

"*I speak Japanese sometimes.*" Just not to her mother. "I feel like I haven't seen Dad in forever."

Her mom sniffed. "Me, too."

Then Mia's tears came. She got so tired of having to take care of her mother, prop her up on the days when Sho's absence was too much to bear. Her chair jumped back as she stood.

"Where are you going?"

"I have to go study."

"Yes, you do."

Mia hurried upstairs to her room, shut the door, and flung herself on the bed. Soon a scratching at the door made her get up and let Deuce in.

Later, she lay on her bed with her rainbow-colored toe-socks against Deuce's warm, stubbly back. She could feel his snuffling snores through her feet, but her ears were crammed wall-to-drum with Alpha Children's "Love Hurts" crooning from her iPod.

The smells of cooking filled the house, but Mia wasn't hungry. All she could think about was Dalton's arm around Tara. If only she had *curves*, and a few more inches of height, and blonde hair, and blue eyes like Dalton liked, and...

Dammit dammit dammit.

Mia's phone buzzed against her leg. She pulled it out. An exultant text from Nate: "SHE'S COMING!!!!!!"

All she could say in reply was, "good luck n have fun. dont blow it."

Moments later: "I AM SMOOTH LIKE HAN SOLO."

Mia chuckled, then sighed again. "Oh, my god, you're such a nerd! Don't you dare blow it." If he succeeded, by some freak of universal chance, Mia's life might be just a little bit easier.

CHAPTER FOUR

Nate grinned as Tara gave him a withering look.

Tara huffed through carefully controlled breaths as she jogged alongside him. "Yeah, sexy uniforms are totally why the girls' team gets more medals than the boys' team." She rolled her eyes at him.

A crescent of moon hung above the purple eastern horizon, over the distant lights of the downtown skyline. Ah, how romantic, he thought. He poked her with his elbow. "Yeah, totally. You know, tighter. Less wind resistance. Over three miles, that adds up."

Her blonde ponytail bobbed behind her. "Then the boys' team should start running in Speedos."

He laughed for a moment, until he envisioned himself actually running in a Speedo. A cool September wind rustled across the soybean field on one side of the trail and into the trees and undergrowth hedging the opposite side.

"There's the mile and a half marker." Their running shoes pounded in arrhythmic disarray.

"You want to shoot for five miles?" Her voice carried a challenge.

"Five?"

Her stride was long and even and graceful. Another image flashed in his mind of stopping to rest on one of the benches along the path. Of trying to kiss her for the first time. He imagined what her lips would taste like. His body tingled and his ears grew hot. He shook the image clean, imagining his brain was an Etch-A-Sketch. Any more thoughts like that and his running shorts would show her what he was thinking.

Five miles? He could do it, but it would suck. After a mile and a half, he was feeling the burn.

"What's the matter?" she said. "Can't do it?"

"Sure I can. Just not sure if I want to."

"If you want to bail, I understand. I'll pick you up when I come back." She glanced at him, testing.

"No way. You're on."

She nodded and pulled away from him. He increased his speed. She pushed harder. He responded. Soon they were both running full out. Nate's heart pounded, and he adjusted his breathing to the rhythm of his stride. Notions of a kiss fell away as he was forced to concentrate on his breathing, putting one foot in front of the other, over and over again, chewing up the distance.

"Nice!" he panted. "You run pretty good."

"Thanks!" she puffed.

"For a girl!" He flashed a grin at her as he lengthened his stride, taking advantage of his longer legs to outdistance her.

She gasped at the challenge, but fell behind. From thirty yards behind him she called out, "You run pretty good for a girl, too!"

He laughed with exhilaration.

They neared the two-and-a-half mile post, their turn-around point. The dark smudges of trees and neighborhoods, sprinkled with streetlights and houses, surrounded them in the distance. The distant downtown skyline, speckled with multi-colored lights, rose above miles of intervening suburbs. The air smelled of impending autumn, of grass and earth.

Suddenly he felt a tightening in his calf. "Oh, crap." He looked over his shoulder. Tara was still thirty yards back. The tightening in his calf seized into a knotted ball of pain. He ground to a halt.

Tara was beside him instantly. "You okay?"

He gritted his teeth and squeezed his calf with both hands. "Cramp."

"I knew you'd find a way to wuss out."

"Gee, thanks." He massaged his calf muscles, grimacing.

The jibe on her lips melted away, and he saw real sympathy in her eyes. He liked the idea that she cared about his pain, but he didn't want her to feel bad. "Go on and finish. I'll catch up."

"You sure?"

"Yeah. I figure I'll have half an hour to rest."

"Half an hour my butt!" She took off down the path again.

His leg burned, but somehow he couldn't take his eyes off of her as she ran away. Her brilliant yellow running shorts hugged her in the dusky light, revealing all that leg.

The cramp in his calf loosened as he stood. He bent and lunged and pulled, trying to stretch the leg. The path behind him wended its way back toward the lights of his neighborhood. Before him, it disappeared around a bend. Tara was out of view now.

He had to do *something*. After what he had seen in school today, he had to do something now or she would fall into Dalton's clutches and Nate would lose his chance forever. What was it with girls and poet geeks anyway?

Where the path curved out of sight, a clump of bushes nudged out toward the concrete. Then it came to him, a stunningly brilliant plan. He would leap out, scare the crap out of her, then she would move closer and punch him or something, and he would move closer to her and voila. Instant romantic moment. Genius. He mopped the sweat off his face with his white cross-country team practice shirt. It wouldn't be cool to drip sweat in her face.

He limped toward the clump of bushes, where it extruded from the line of woods bordering the path on the left side. The cramp continued to dissolve as he ran. When he reached the bushes, he crouched down behind them and waited for her to come back. It shouldn't be long now. She could run that distance in less than a minute.

He counted thirty seconds, and she still had not come by. Had she missed the turnaround point and kept going?

He sneaked around the bushes and looked down the path past the curve.

There she stood, perhaps fifty yards away, peering into the wooded undergrowth at the edge of the path. In the diminishing light, shadowed by the encroaching trees, her white tank top and bright running shorts gleamed. God, she was hot.

"Oh, hi!" she said with some surprise, speaking to someone he couldn't see. He could just make out her voice over the drone of the crickets and cicadas. "Are you all right?"

He listened for a reply, but heard nothing, only the breeze and the crickets.

"Here," she said, moving off the path toward the darkness, "let me help you."

Nate suddenly felt he should be there beside her. She was so nice, always willing to help people, but the fact that it was dusk and they were more than a mile from the nearest help struck home. She stepped into the dark underbrush.

He ran toward the spot and stopped there, keeping his eyes on the underbrush. "Tara! What's up?"

The deepening night made it difficult to distinguish details in the gloom of the trees and undergrowth, but he thought he saw a gap she might have passed through.

"Tara? Quit messing with me."

The gap between the clumps of sumac and plum thicket yawned black. He listened. Leaves rustling? Something moving in there? He swallowed hard and stepped into the gap, spreading the foliage with his arms.

"Tara, you're pretty funny. Now quit messing with me. Please." Deeper into the gloom, he emerged into an open pocket amidst the foliage. Dapples of dying sunset filtered through the trees ahead of him, providing the only meager coins of light. His hands were pale smears against the shadows. Twigs and dry grass crackled under his feet. He caught the scent of Tara's perfume, fresh and powdery, laced with vanilla, along with clean sweat, lingering, mingling with the smells of old vegetation. And something else, something animal.

The hairs on the back of his neck rose and his body tensed. "Tara?" His voice quavered. "Where are you, dammit? Quit goofing off!"

He pushed further into the darkness, snapping twigs and crushing dry leaves underfoot. The coarse branches raked his face and legs. He kept shouldering through the undergrowth until, after perhaps fifty yards, he emerged. The dying light of dusk bathed him and the open prairie to the west. He stood thirty yards from the lip of a concrete canal, the man-made course of Spearhead Creek that ran through the city's outlying subdivisions. He looked up and down the creek bank, and cupped his hands to call out. "Tara!" He ran for a hundred yards in both directions, calling her name. The creek was an inhospitable ditch swathed in shadow and choked with filthy debris, with a thin ribbon of water reflecting the darkening sky.

This was bad. He felt his pockets and cursed. He had left his cell at home on the kitchen table.

He threw himself back into the underbrush, forcing his way through the animal paths and fox runs until his face and limbs bled from dozens of scratches.

Dusk diminished into night, and his voice grew hoarse from yelling. Finally, he stopped and pushed out of the brush onto the path. His gut was a roiling knot. Something terrible had happened to her, and he needed help. As fast as his legs would carry him, he ran back the way they came, toward the nearest homes.

He felt eyes on the back of his neck, and looked over his shoulder. The path was empty, but his legs found fresh speed. His breath pumped in and out of him, hoarse and dry with exertion.

A sound filtered through the undergrowth, a heavy rhythmic breathing, matching his, pacing him, leaves and branches pushed aside for the passage of something he could not see. Was it his breathing or something else that he heard? Fear bloomed like ice, and he kept looking over his shoulder for signs of something he *knew* was chasing him. How many of them were there? His legs and arms pumped, pounding his sneakers, stretching the naked flesh of his legs, the largest portions of meat.

Desperate speed poured out of him. It was the first and last time he ever ran for his life.

CHAPTER FIVE

Mia opened her locker and threw her chemistry book onto the pile inside, sighing. Nate hadn't shown up for chemistry lab today, which meant she had had to partner with Olive Mac-Gruder, the single dimmest bulb in the class. It was strange. Nate never missed school. She thought about texting him, but Nicki came running up, skidded to a halt, and bumped into the locker door, slamming it shut onto Mia's fingers. "Omigod, Mia! Did you hear?"

Mia faced her, shaking her hand. "Geez, watch it!" Ninety-five percent of the sentences that came out of Nicki's mouth began with "omigod."

Nicki's eyes were wide, and she clutched her backpack to her chest. "Did you hear about Dalton?"

Mia's ears perked up and her heart clunked into the back of her rib cage. "No, I just got out of chem lab—"

"Omigod, Tiffany heard it from Jackie who heard it from Scott. Dalton likes you!"

Mia's face grew warm, and her heart went ka-lump. She had not told a soul about her own feelings. She didn't dare. If she told someone about it and then nothing happened, no one would know she felt like a complete moron. She had always kept herself far removed from the flittering females who wore their bleeding, thumping, oozing hearts on their sleeves and then changed them with the laundry. She was pretty sure at this point that her crush on Dalton would last forever. God, what a hopeless dork she was.

She cleared her throat. "Really? What did they say?"

"Well, you know. He said that you're kind of cute, and kind of smart, and he likes that."

"I saw him yesterday with Tara Anderson glommed onto him. Are you sure?"

"Just telling you what I heard."

Mia's attention rambled to the passing hordes of enormous Midwest Caucasian girls, like Tara, with their LOVE PINK sweatpants, their long legs and big boobs and blonde hair. So separate and distant from Mia that she must be on an alien planet and they were all aliens speaking an incomprehensible language.

Nicki was practically vibrating. "Isn't that exciting?"

Mia leaned back against her locker and took a deep breath, let it out. "Well, it'll be exciting if he asks me out." If he didn't ask her, having this information would now be like a punch in the stomach.

"Oh, check this out." Nicki shoved a dog-eared paperback novel into Mia's hand, *Surrender to Passion*. On the cover a half-naked man embraced a woman with enormous cleavage exposed all the way to her navel.

Mia grimaced. "A smutty romance novel? Seriously?"

"Instructional material." Nicki winked. "Pages fifty-two to sixty-three." She rolled her eyes and wiggled. "Ooo la la."

Mia thumbed through the book to that section and spotted phrases like "gasping breath," "feathery hot touch," "lips like warm cherries," a "burning sword yearning to be quenched"— She snapped the book shut.

Nicki giggled. "I told you!"

Mia shuddered away the images in her mind so close on the heels of a conversation about Dalton. She spotted Kenji making a beeline toward her in the hallway. He looked a little lost, but then he always looked a little lost. His English wasn't good enough to understand even half the words zooming past him at any given moment. He bowed to her, and she wished he'd stop that.

"Hi, ladies," he said. "What happens?"

Nicki said, "Hi, Kenji." Then she edged away. "Well, Mia, I gotta go. Let me know how it turns out, okay?"

"Sure."

"Oh, I almost forgot! Homework. Is it done?"

Mia took out the worksheet. "Done."

Nicki beamed and took it. "Awesome!"

Mia held out her hand expectantly.

"Oh, sorry, I'll catch you with the dollahs tomorrow. Want to help me some more tonight?"

"Sure." Mia had her own homework to do. How was she ever supposed to finish hers *and* Nicki's?

"How's tonight?"

"Okay."

"I'll call you." Nicki waved and bounced down the hall.

Mia turned to Kenji and gave him a meager smile. She said in Japanese, "*Your English is getting better.*"

"Not at all. It's terrible."

"Well, you know, keep at it. It just takes time."

"Your friend is very cute. *I like her golden hair.*"

Mia was the only other student in West High who could speak Japanese, except the mega-lame *anime* geeks who took Japanese class and occasionally tried to practice their Japanese on her and ended up sounding like idiots. Cute attempts at social interaction, but lame nonetheless. Okay, maybe they weren't total geeks. She liked *anime*, too, but she'd never admit it to anyone. Poor Kenji had only been in the U.S. for a month.

"What means 'homecoming'?" he said.

"Well, it means a big football game with Central High, and there's a dance afterward."

"A dance!" He grinned. "Do you dance to a song?"

"No, I mean a dance is like, a dance. They play music, and you have a date, and you dance."

"Oh." He nodded a little too long. "Homecoming is soon, yes?"

"Yes, in a few weeks."

"So, do you need a ride home?"

"No, thanks. I have my bike."

"You are very cool."

Mia smiled, but suppressed a laugh. Kenji's social skills were so inept, it verged on adorable.

Then another presence loomed next to her bringing a familiar scent.

"Hey, Mia," Dalton said. "What's up?"

Her chest and neck grew hot. "Hey." She tucked her Dalton-riddled notebook behind her.

"Hey, Kenji," he said. "*Konnichiwa.*"

Kenji bowed. "*Konnichiwa.*"

Dalton grinned and glanced at Mia. His scent, after-shave and mint and leather, drew her closer. He put his long arm around her. She looked down at her new notebook, praying that Dalton didn't have X-ray vision. Kenji looked away conspicuously. "So you know I'm having a pizza party at my place tonight, right?"

Gulp. "You are?"

"Yeah, my parents are going out tonight. Some fund-raising dinner that's supposed to go long. I'm just having a few friends over. Want to come?"

"I don't know. I'll have to ask my mom."

"Is she strict?"

"Well, she just hasn't been in a very good mood lately." Like for the last two years.

"Okay, fair enough." He handed her a slip of paper. "Here's the address. If you can make it, all you have to do is show up."

Blood rushed in her ears so loud she could barely hear. "Mm-hmm," she said, just a little too quickly. How long before she made herself look like a goofy idiot and blew it? The address was in a neighborhood a couple of miles away, but she could bike that easily.

"See you," Kenji said, shuffling his feet uncertainly.

Mia smiled at him. "Bye."

"Later, dude."

Dalton took her shoulder, and guided her into step with him, closer than she had ever been to him. The sensations within her went to double-overtime-sudden-death, tingles and fuzziness and warmth.

Then she spotted a familiar face leaning her forehead against a locker, and her heart thumped again.

"Tara!" Dalton called. Mia found herself walking farther away from him.

Tara turned at the sound of her name, and Dalton waved. She smiled wanly.

Dalton gave her a big grin. "Rough night?"

Tara's eyes turned cold, defensive. "What do you mean by that?" She looked awful. Dark circles under bloodshot eyes, and her hair looked like it had barely been brushed.

Dalton raised a hand. "Hey, nothing at all."

"Oh, okay."

"So, you coming tonight?"

Mia's sick feeling came back.

Tara turned back to her locker, barely glancing over her shoulder. "I...don't know."

Mia said, "Um, you haven't seen Nate today, have you?"

Tara's voice darkened. "Why are you asking me? Why would I know?"

Dalton stiffened beside her, drawing back.

Mia stumbled over the words, suddenly wanting to get away from Tara. Had something gone horribly awry with the running date with Nate? "Uh, because I know you guys hang out a little and—"

"Well, I don't know where he is. I was sick this morning myself."

"Okay, never mind," Mia said.

"Yeah," Dalton said, "you don't look so good."

Mia had noticed Tara's cheeks were shadowed. "You need a doctor?"

"I'll be fine," Tara said, pressing her forehead against the locker, hard. The pressure increased until the steel flexed inward.

Dalton didn't appear to notice. "Well, take care of yourself. Maybe I'll see you later."

Mia said, "Bye."

Tara's body was as tense and rigid as a metal rod. The locker door creaked.

Dalton ushered Mia down the hallway, and the tension between Mia's shoulder blades—tension she hadn't known was there—loosened. "Damn," Dalton said, "something's up with her."

Mia nodded. Something serious. Romantic rivalries aside, Tara looked like she needed a doctor.

CHAPTER SIX

"Will boys be there?" Mia's mom said. Her face was sour, solid, like an old lemon. When had her mom gotten so many wrinkles? The carving knife slid through the slab of raw tuna. Rice cooled on a cookie sheet nearby.

Mia said, "Sushi? Is Dad going to be home for dinner?"

"I don't know. I was making this for you. Will boys be there?"

Hello, sweet, sweet guilt. "Well, yeah, I mean, it's Dalton's place. We're studying."

"And this Dalton. Tell me about him."

"Well, he's this guy in my Language Arts class. My teacher said I need to work harder, so...this is working harder."

"Do you like him?"

Her body betrayed her with a deep, warm blush. Her mother noticed this with a brief, pointed glance. Mia moved to the sink, washed her hands, wet them in a small bowl of vinegared water on the counter, took up a handful of sticky rice, and began to form a ball. Her silence hung over them like an anvil. Mia felt like Wile E. Coyote, waiting for it to fall on her head.

Finally, her mother said, "Does he like you?"

Mia blurted, "I have no idea."

"Does he drink alcohol, do drugs?"

"Mom!"

"I have to ask. I'm your mother."

The rice ball was exactly the size and weight of a baseball in her palm. It was too big. She almost spat back, *Yeah, he's probably a total stoner!*, but she bit those words back. Her mother sounded almost reasonable right now; saying such a thing would send a torpedo straight into the middle of Mia's tenuously afloat romantic raft. Instead, she said, "Well, not that I know of. I barely know him at all. That's the point of going to a party, isn't it? But he's a nice guy."

"How are you getting there?"

Mia's heart slammed into her breastbone and started to flutter. "It's not that far. I can ride."

"Be home before nine-thirty. *School night.*"

Mia almost rolled her eyes. Nine-thirty! Instead, she put her arm around her mom's shoulders. "Thanks!" It was a like hugging a board.

"Leave me the address and phone number."

The lights on the house were on and cars were parked outside. Through gaps in the curtains Mia could see people moving around, and here she was, all wind-blown and sweaty from the ride here. She stood in the dark outside, smoothed her hair (her best feature, she thought, thick and black and glossy), applied fresh lip gloss and a dab of powder.

Then she took a deep breath. Another one. Okay, time to go in and make Dalton putty in her hands.

At her ring, Dalton answered the door. She gave him her best humungous beaming smile. "Hi!" Mia, you're such a dork.

He gave her a little head nod and stepped aside. "Hey. Come on in."

A rush like Mia had never experienced swept over her. She was in his *house*! Where he *slept*! Where he took *showers*— Stop it, Mia! He was talking to her. Listen!

"...should be here in about twenty minutes. There's pop on the counter. You thirsty?"

"Mm-hmm."

A series of eyes followed her, boys and girls from school, most of whom she recognized, but none of whom she knew. Their eyes appraised her with every step she took through them. And, thank god, no Tara. Dalton led her through the nicely appointed living room into the nicely appointed kitchen. The place smelled clean, with hints of wood and earth and cat. Philodendrons draped knick-knack shelves, fireplace, bookcase. Miniature palm trees—real ones—filled corners and other potted plants nestled in various nooks and crannies. The living room almost felt like a jungle. In the spacious, faux-brick kitchen, an enormous Siamese tomcat, like a fuzzy gray mushroom, draped with half-lidded eyes over a stool near the central island. Several two-liter bottles of soda sat on the countertop. People from Nebraska called it 'pop.'

"Don't mind Dobby," Dalton said. "He just looks mean, but he's more like a big Totoro."

Her eyes widened at the mention of one of her favorite *anime* characters. "You know Totoro?"

"Yeah, I must have watched that movie a hundred times."

Her face felt like it had just been dipped in warm water. "Me too."

"What kind?"

"Diet Coke."

He affected a French accent. "Good choice, Madame." He held the bottle across his forearm like a waiter. "An excellent vintage."

She giggled as he poured her a plastic cup. As she took it, her fingers brushed his, and an electric shock went up her arm.

"Dude!" A head wearing a Minnesota Vikings cap protruded through a doorway. "We've got *American Werewolf in London* queued up. You in?"

"In a sec. Vince, you know Mia?"

Vince looked her up and down and grinned. "Sure, I've seen her around. Hey, Mia."

"Hi."

Dalton turned to her. "You like scary movies?"

"Not really." Maybe if they were in a dark theater, alone, so she could jump into his—internal face-slap! *Stop it, Mia!* "I'm a big scaredy-cat."

Dalton pointed at Dobby. "No, he's a big scaredy-cat."

Dobby looked up at him as if to say, *Stop talking about me.*

Dalton petted her shoulder. "I'll bet you're tougher than you think. But if not, you can hang out up here."

Oh, *hell* no. "Well, I—"

The doorbell rang.

Dalton went to answer it. "Sorry, just a sec."

Mia sighed. She didn't like to be scared. Why, because it was frickin' scary! But she took a deep breath and went downstairs after Vince.

Vince took up a seat next to her on the couch. Halfway through the movie, she realized he was very close to her. Not so bad in other circumstances—he was kind of cute—but she felt Dalton's eyes on her several times, and maybe on Vince, too, watchful.

The special effects were so gory that she could barely keep her eyes on the fifty-two-inch plasma screen, dripping with shredded flesh and lurid, crimson detail—appearing at times not unlike the stretched mozzarella and sauce littering the pizza boxes around everyone—but seeing David's transformation into a werewolf transfixed her. She felt so awful for him, falling in love with the beautiful nurse, even as he would become a werewolf at the next full moon.

Vince leaned forward. "Dude, is that C.G.I.?"

Dalton said, "No, man, this was 1981. They didn't even *have* computers then."

"Wow, trippy!"

At one point in the movie, the werewolf leaped out and attacked a man in the London subway, and Mia almost splatted against the ceiling.

Then she realized Vince's breath was in her ear. "You're choking me," he said.

"Sorry." Mia released his neck, sheepishly, then slid away from him.

She watched the climax of the movie from between her fingers, heart pounding, the grotesque howls and strange British police sirens grating across her spine, her body squirming at the ridiculous porno theater where the murderous werewolf David began his last rampage, the final moments when the beautiful nurse Alex tried to save him.

Mia wiped tears away. The credits rolled to a sappy doo-wop song, "Blue Moon."

Vince said, "That was a dumb ending!"

"What are you talking about?" Dalton said. "Wasn't that some scary shit?"

"Yeah, I guess, but they killed him too easy! Didn't they have to use silver bullets or something? That woulda been cool if he'd have gotten her, too."

Dalton said, "You're sick, man."

Mia's heart slowed its stampede, and she checked her watch. She jumped up. "Oh, god!"

"What?" Dalton said.

"I have three minutes to get home! Sorry, everyone. It was nice meeting you all. Gotta go!" She hurried upstairs. Her mother had barely let her come to this party. If Mia was late, the chances of getting to go out again before her thirtieth birthday were somewhere akin to spontaneously growing fur.

Dalton caught her in the living room. "Hey, thanks for coming over."

She stopped at the front door and faced him. "Thanks for inviting me. It was nice." Her ears heated again. She couldn't meet his eyes.

He stepped forward, and his hand was warm on her arm. "Hope the movie didn't freak you out too bad. See you at school tomorrow."

"If my mom doesn't lock me in the basement for being late."

He chuckled. "You're kidding. I hope."

"Mostly."

An awkward moment hung between them. *Kiss me!* her mind screamed.

He cleared his throat and put his hands in his pockets and shot her a slanted smile. "Have a good one."

"Good night." Then she turned and fled.

CHAPTER SEVEN

James Matthews sat in his Toyota, engulfed in silence and pitch-black garage, his mind flitting through a dark web of pitch-black thoughts. The passenger-side window pinched the garden hose in place, poking into the car. He had done an adequate job of duct-taping the other end of the hose to the car exhaust.

The engine was off, for now.

He heard them outside, snuffling at the cracks, padding through the grass, driving the neighborhood dogs into frenzies of barking. He had been smelling their presence for weeks as they left invisible scents in his back yard, an open invitation to join them. For weeks they had called to him, and the call tugged at every strand of his D.N.A., now yearning to be something else, something that was not a middle-aged insurance salesman comfortably ensconced in suburban life, something that was far more alive than he had felt in more years than he cared to consider. How long before the invitation became a challenge?

The call was like the breath of new love. He tried to recollect the heady days when he and Shae had first come together. The endless, timeless hours of conversation and sex, every sense heightened by the intensity of their passion, their happiness, every moment feeling so alive that his skin was on fire, his brain aflame with desire and the endless striving for possibilities, to make a life. To start a family. The settling down that raising Brittany required. The job one must have to make sure that family was cared for, *safe*, with a house in a good neighborhood, with good schools, with insurance, with vacations, with benefits, with all the obligations, pressures, necessities that such comforts demanded. A parade of incompetent asshole bosses, glimpses of unethical business practices perpetrated by said bosses, clamped in the soul-crushing grind of working within an enormous, greedy bureaucracy, the relentless pressure of trying to live the life everyone expected him to live, his parents, his wife and daughter, his neighbors.

He had the house (needed new shingles and sod), the picket fence (except his was six feet tall and made of plastic), the car (ten years old, because he had been a little too happy with the credit cards in his twenties), the lovely wife (now, forty pounds overweight), the beautiful daughter (good at sports but would be lucky to get through junior-college algebra, and treated her father with a sort of vague tolerance), the dog (who didn't like him anymore).

No, not even Dutch liked him anymore. Not since what happened.

Now, they called to him. As if he could simply walk away from everything he had built. Everything he loved. Everything he told himself he loved. It was like he was seeing the cracks between dreams, within the dream he had been taught to love, like there might be something on the other side, if only he had the courage to reach for it, something pure and uncomplicated by insurance premiums and mortgages.

But to reach for it meant leaving everything behind. Shae, Brittany, his house, his job. And worse, reaching for it might put his family in terrible danger. Even if he had to walk away from his family, he would not put them in danger. They had no idea what was coming. No one did.

The choice was impossible.

He groped for the key in the ignition. In a few minutes, he would just fall asleep, and not wake up.

Brittany was staying at her friend Chelsea's house. Shae was at a business conference in Chicago. He would be long dead before anyone found him.

Dutch was in the kitchen, growling and barking at something outside.

Why had James gone running on that trail on that night those weeks ago? What design had placed him in that situation? Did God want that to happen to him? He had grown up going to church—as his family and society expected him to—but in recent years, he only attended with his parents when they visited and on the religious holidays like Easter and Christmas.

Where had that thing come from? Did God design for this to happen to him? Or was he simply a moth, caught at the height of its life in a random spider-web, doomed by fate or coincidence to feed the spider's hunger?

He sighed and twisted the key. Even after a decade, the Toyota still started up and ran like a Rolex. He would never sell enough insurance to own a Rolex. Seconds later, warm exhaust roiled into the cabin. He covered his nose with a handkerchief, and then laughed at himself. Self-preservation ran deep.

His olfactory sense was so strong now that the stench of the exhaust made him retch. He retched again and again, heaving dribbles of spit and bile into his lap. He hadn't eaten any normal food in days. Nothing tasted good anymore. Even the best pizza in town tasted like gooey cardboard. His eyes watered and burned.

"Dammit!"

He turned the car off and got out. Time to clean up the evidence. He couldn't do it this way. Trouble was, he had no idea what would kill him anymore.

CHAPTER EIGHT

Fifteen minutes late coming home and her dad's car was not in the garage. Mia steeled herself.

Mia's mom sat at the kitchen table, reading a novel in Japanese by the light of a candle.

"Hi," Mia said. "Sure is dark in here. How can you read that way?"

Her mother glanced at the clock, then regarded her for a long moment. "*How was the party?*"

Mia's ears burned. It was like her mom was psychic or something. She considered standing behind her earlier lie, then thought better of it. "Fun. It was nice to finally meet some people. No Dad yet?"

"He came home for dinner, then went back to the office."

Mia sighed. She hadn't seen him in days. "'Night, Mom."

"*Oyasumi-nasai.*"

Mia went upstairs to her room. Deuce was already snoring softly on her bed. "Geez, Goon. People might wonder whose room this actually is." He looked at her with sleepy eyes, tail wagging.

Her phone buzzed in her jacket pocket. The screen said "2 MISSED CALLS." Both from Nicki. "Oops!"

Mia called her back.

Nicki answered. "Hey, Mia. Where you been all night?"

Mia couldn't help a heady giggle. "Dalton's place. He had a little pizza party."

"Really! That's awesome! Did you make out?"

"No. And none of your business anyway."

"Omigod, yes, it is! You're my best G.F."

"If something happens, I'll be sure to tell you."

"Awesome. Hey, did you get my homework done?"

"Hell-o! Par-ty!"

"Oh, yeah. Well, it's due tomorrow."

Mia sighed. "I'll see what I can do."

"Awesome. And, hey, read that book I gave you. Ooh la la, that's hot stuff."

"Okay."

"Later, tater."

Mia put down her phone and looked at the pile of her own homework sitting on the desk. She sighed. Twenty bucks was twenty bucks. If she did enough homework, maybe she'd be able to buy herself a new laptop, and not have to beg for a new one from her parents after she had been stupid enough to let someone steal hers. She could only imagine her mother's withering look.

Mr. Freeze was deserted, which made Mia's heart leap. Cool air-conditioning and cold fog emanating from the ice-cream counter.

She and Dalton sat side by side at a table outside, the sun warm on her naked shoulders. She was wearing her cutest tank top, even though she had never seen it before. The wind sent napkins flying. He held the banana split, and they shared it with two spoons. She had been strangely okay with him insisting on coconut sauce, and she tried it, and it tasted like strawberries.

The spoons dipped and scooped, and the ice cream helped chill the twittering in her belly. Would he or wouldn't he? Over and over in her mind. Her thoughts raced forward toward what it might be like to kiss him. Part of her mind warned her not to jump the gun, but her heart couldn't help it.

Nicki and her friends were sitting nearby, telling and retelling make-out stories, watching Mia and Dalton, laughing. Were they laughing at her? She didn't care if they were because she was right now sitting *next to the sweetest guy in school and*—Cool your jets, Mia. Calmness. Calm City. Relaxitude. Be cool. Would he or wouldn't he?

She couldn't call the fluttering in her belly entirely pleasant, kind of like a trapped two-pound butterfly flopping around. At the same time, each flutter sent waves of tingles up and down her arms and legs. Iridescent butterflies fluttered away from her arms into the afternoon sun.

Dalton leaned closer. "So, are you free Saturday night?"

She bit back the *Oh, hell yeah!* that almost came out. Instead, she said, "Well, you know, me and Nicki were planning on getting together and watching some movies."

"Ah, that's too bad."

"Why?"

"I was going to ask if you wanted to go to a movie."

"Yeah, that's too bad." She turned her face toward him, and found his only inches away. His eyes looked deep into hers. Her mouth went dry. "Um." A brain-freeze was coming on, and it wasn't from the ice cream. "Um, what did you want to see?"

Was he closer now? "*American Werewolf in London*. It's showing at the Dundee."

A butterfly landed in her hair, tangling itself, trapped. "I don't like scary movies."

"Don't worry. I'll protect you from the monsters." His breath brushed tingles of warmth across her cheek. Then he kissed her, and the world exploded into butterflies.

Her eyes opened with the warm, soft, wetness of the kiss still on her lips, her entire body tingling. She heaved herself onto her side, and *Surrender to Passion* slid onto the bed from her chest. Deuce snored softly against her feet, twitching at her movement.

She leaned over and switched off the bedside lamp, then leaned back and clasped her hands over her heart.

"Wow."

Where the hell was Nate? Mia flung her books into her locker. Another chem class with Olive MacGruder. Someone had definitely short-changed her at the Brains counter. Nate must really be sick or something. Mia should probably call him and give him the homework for tomorrow.

A body piled into her from behind and she almost smacked her forehead against the open locker door.

"Hey, watch it!" she snarled, spinning.

Chelsea and Brittany laughed. "Oh, sorry!"

By the time Mia had done Nicki's homework—and her own for a change—not to mention reading the first four chapters of the romance novel, she had probably passed out around 2:00 a.m. Her eyes still felt grainy *and* Nate was not here *and* she had not seen Dalton yet today. She felt decidedly surly. "You're such a bitch!"

Chelsea's face darkened and she stepped closer. "Say what?"

Mia's mind screamed, *Chelsea, you're such a bitch!* Her mouth opened. However, getting sent home from school or put in detention for fighting was just what Mia needed to smooth things over with her mom. Her mom would take it as simply more confirmation that Mia was a hopeless human being and probably should be euthanized. She deflated, but the anger still simmered. "Nothing."

Chelsea sneered. "I thought so."

Dalton emerged from the passing crowds. "Hey, ladies."

Brittany beamed a smile at him. "Hi, Dalton!"

He stood next to Mia and looked at Chelsea. "Don't you have gaudy eyeliner practice or something?"

Chelsea's brow wrinkled. "Huh?"

"Well," he continued, "if you don't practice putting make-up on, how are you ever going to get better?"

Mia suppressed a snicker.

Chelsea stabbed him with an icy Nordic gaze. "Screw you." She took Brittany's arm and stormed away.

Brittany called back, "Yeah! Screw you!" apparently just grasping what he had said.

Mia turned toward Dalton. "My hero. You saved me from the evil giraffe mafia."

"Milady, 'twas my pleasure to put such vacuous wenches in their place. Was your mom mad at you?"

"I don't think so."

"Is she really that strict?"

"She didn't used to be. We've—she's been through a lot."

"I'm glad to hear you didn't get yelled at. My parents are pretty laid back about stuff. My dad just says, 'Be careful, don't get caught, don't get anyone pregnant, and if you end up in jail, I'm not bailing you out.'

Seems like a reasonable philosophy for parenting to me."

Mia couldn't imagine her mother saying any such thing. Since transferring to the Omaha field office of the F.B.I, her dad hadn't said much of anything. She barely saw him.

"So, if your mom's not mad, do you think she'll let you go out on Saturday?"

Mia almost collapsed into a puddle of warm pudding, but she caught herself. "Um...are you asking me out?"

His face reddened, and he cleared his throat, "Well, you know, not really. Well, sorta. It's just hanging out, you know. Maybe Mr. Freeze and a movie?"

The mention of Mr. Freeze almost made her knees buckle. Maybe this wasn't the time to ask, but it fell out of her mouth before she could stop it. "I've heard you and Tara were a thing?"

He cleared his voice again. "Where'd you hear that?" He said it with a strange mixture of more curiosity that dismissal. Too much curiosity. The warm pudding cooled.

"I saw you."

"Well, you know, she's been acting really weird the last few days. So, want to hang out Saturday night?"

So that made Mia into second fiddle. Too much curiosity in his question, and she still remembered how close he and Tara had been in the hallway. The puncture in her ego started to bleed self-respect. "Sure. I don't have any plans except brushing my dog's teeth and applying to N.A.S.A., and those things can probably wait."

He smiled and her discomfiture evaporated. "Sweet. See you later."

CHAPTER NINE

"Hey, Deuce, you big hulking goon," Mia said. The shar-pei's claws clicked on the tiles as he met her at the front door. She rubbed his wrinkled, velvety soft ears and then patted him on the thick-muscled shoulder.

He looked at her quizzically, as if to say, *A bit rambunctious there, aren't you?* Then he huffed a greeting at her and wagged his spiky tail. She giggled and reached her face down to nuzzle the top of his bristly head. His tongue came out, and he licked her. His breath smelled like a combination of dog food and slobbery gym sock, but she didn't mind.

Mia took a deep breath and tried to slow her pounding heart. Calm, calmness, calmity, calmousness. She had *not* just been asked out on a *date* by the single hottest, sweetest, coolest guy in school. At least not as far as her mom would ever know. Her mom would never agree to a real date. Some sort of contrivance was in order. Another deep breath, let it out. Then two quick ones. She called out to her mother in Japanese, "*Tadaima.*" She took off her shoes and arranged them carefully beside the door before she stepped further inside. The savory, delicious smell of *sukiyaki* boiling in a pot filled the house and made Mia's mouth water.

Her mother responded in kind from the kitchen, "*Okaeri.*" Her mother sounded almost chipper! "*Your father will be home in about half an hour. Dinner will be ready then.*"

"Cool. I have time for a bike ride." Maybe she could avoid her mother noticing that something was definitely up. Her mother *always* noticed.

"We have a visitor!"

Another female voice called out from the kitchen in English, "Hi, Mia. Come give your Aunt Sarah a hug before you run off."

A spasm of joy shot through Mia, and she ran into the kitchen. Sarah rose from one of the stools beside the island. Mia buried her face in Sarah's blonde hair. Sarah laughed warmly and hugged her back. Aunt Sarah's tall, willowy stature was quite a contrast to Mia's mother. It wasn't the first time today that Mia had noticed that kind of disparity.

"I didn't even notice your car. Is that your Jeep parked out front?"

"A rental."

"When did you get back in town? You smell different. New perfume?"

Sarah hesitated a moment, taken aback. "Yes, new perfume. I got back last night late. So of course, as soon as I got settled back in, I had to come over and see you and bring your mom some real green tea from Shizuoka."

Mia mimed a gagging reflex. Her mother had been trying to make Mia like green tea forever, but green tea tasted like dirt.

"Someday, you'll appreciate it," Mia's mom said. "Everything you drink has too much sugar."

"Yeah, maybe when I'm *old*."

Her mother's eyes narrowed, and she threw a towel at Mia.

Mia laughed and caught the towel. To purge her mind of the imagined taste of green tea, she leaned over the *sukiyaki* pot in the center of the kitchen island and breathed deep. Her mouth watered like a fountain. Sarah sat back down, and Mia hooked an arm around her neck. "You'll be here when I get back, right?"

"Your mom says I'm staying for dinner."

"Good. I gotta run. See you in a while." She dashed off through the house to grab her shoes before heading toward the garage.

"*Wear your helmet!*" her mother called.

Mia rolled her eyes as she stepped out into the garage and raised her voice to sound like a sweet little *anime* girl. "Haaaaiii!" She grabbed her bike, left the helmet hanging on a peg, threw a leg over the seat, and pedaled down the driveway, out into the neighborhood, plugging her ear buds into her ears and cranking the new Alpha Children album to concert volume.

She had to burn off some of this giddy energy or her mom would know something was up.

A few blocks away lay the entrance to Spearhead Trail, her favorite stretch of bike path, and it was a perfect night for a ride. She breathed deep of the dusky, cooling air, and pumped her legs to build speed, belting out lyrics as she rode.

Sarah sipped her green tea and pondered the strong resemblance between the mother and the departed teenager. "She certainly is growing up. She's going to leave a trail of broken hearts in her wake." Unlike Sarah herself at that age, when she was too thin, too gangly, and too smart for her own social well-being.

Kyoko held her cup of green tea in both hands and took a sip, nodding. "Yes, mine. She's growing up fast. Too fast for mama."

"Her Japanese is pretty good."

Kyoko smirked behind her cup. "I make her practice."

Sarah took a deep breath, drawing the earthy fragrance of her own cup of tea into her nostrils. "It doesn't seem like I've been away six months."

"No, it seems like six years."

Sarah smiled. "You know I missed you, too."

"Why didn't you write? Or e-mail? Or call? You weren't in Japan for six months."

"*I'm sorry,*" Sarah said in Japanese, laying a hand on Kyoko's arm. She sighed. "*It's for the government. I can't tell you.*"

"Ah, that stuff." Kyoko took another sip of tea.

Sarah suppressed a frown. She and Kyoko had been best friends since their university days in Shizuoka, when she introduced Kyoko to her brother, Marcus. Lying to her friend felt awful.

A car door slammed shut in the garage, and Deuce growled an alert from his place on the couch and got up to investigate, waiting at the door to the garage, his tail wagging. The door opened and admitted a tall, familiar figure in a dapper business suit.

Marcus reached down and rubbed the dog's head. "Hey, buddy."

Sarah stood, arms outstretched. "My, my, but don't you look snazzy. Give your stunning little sister a hug."

His eyes brightened. He set down his satchel, came forward with a hug, and she squeezed him tight. Then he turned to the dog and pointed at Sarah. "Shame on you, Deuce. I can't believe you actually dragged this in the house. Smells like you should have left it buried."

Sarah gasped and punched him in the chest.

He laughed and rubbed the spot. "Damn, woman, you been working out?"

"Hot personal trainer at the gym. He motivates me."

He looked her up and down and grinned crookedly. "Well, it looks like you still have some work to do."

Sarah gasped again, but while she was formulating a scathing retort, Marcus turned to Kyoko. "Where's Mia?"

"Riding her bike," Kyoko said.

"Of course she is." His lips pursed.

"What's up?"

"A kid from her school is missing."

Mia's tires made invisible S's on the pavement as she drove a serpentine pattern, lackadaisically bopping her head and singing with the music. The wind lofted her black hair into a halo around her head, tickling her face. On another day her hair would have annoyed her, but her face still felt flushed. So what if he liked Tara? He was going out with *Mia*. Her memory lingered on that amazing dream, that amazing kiss. It felt like *forever*, like all of time and space had just gone away. Warm, soft, wet lips touching, molding, sliding, her heart exploding in her chest, her skin on fire. She had kissed a couple of boys before, but nothing like that. And it might very well happen in real life. She could barely suppress giggling like a goofy idiot all the way home from school.

If her mom knew what was up, the freakage would be legendary; it would show up on radar on the military base, and they would tell the F.B.I., and then her *dad* would know, too.

Energy crackled through her veins as the cooling wind blew across her face with the coming dusk, and she sang along with "Primal Love Howl" at the top of her lungs.

The neighborhood receded behind her as she passed the two-mile marker. On the side of a hill off to her right, four deer grazed in the belly-deep grass, dim tan smudges that still managed to look graceful even at that distance.

A couple of miles out, her cell phone buzzed against her leg. Dalton perhaps? She squeezed the brakes and rolled to a stop, pulling out the cell phone. The screen said, HOME. Probably Mom calling to tell her dinner was ready.

She answered it. "Hello, Mia's bicycle ride speaking."

Her dad's voice. "Hey, where are you?"

Uh oh. He sounded *really* serious. "Spearhead Trail, a couple of miles from home."

"Turn around and come home. There's something we need to talk about."

"Uh, okay."

"Okay." He hung up.

Oh, crap. This sounded bad. What could this be about? It was completely irrational, but what if they knew about her and Dalton? How could they? Her stomach started spinning like a washing machine.

The dread spun through her body out of her stomach and made her legs feel like lead. She had some fudge time. She threw her leg off and pushed the bike toward home. A night like this was just as good for walking as riding a bike. Crickets chirping, cicadas droning their rhythmic chant.

After a couple of hundred yards, she caught a strange smell. Like when she had found a dead squirrel in the back yard, but worse.

Much worse.

Dead squirrels don't stench up that badly. Morbid curiosity aroused, she slowed her walk and peered into the shadowy bushes alongside the path. Nothing in there but spider webs (eww!), rabbit trails, dead leaves, bugs, and—

A flash of something white.

She peered closer.

Something white and red. Cloth. Her school colors.

With a Spartan logo.

She lowered her kickstand and approached the bushes. Shadows pooled around her. The smell grew stronger. She cupped her shirt over her mouth and nose. Invisible flies buzzed in the dimness.

A T-shirt or something, a practice shirt that the athletes wore. Who would throw one of those away here? This one was covered with rusty-brown splotches.

Splotches that looked like bloodstains.

"Oh, my god!" She clamped a hand over her mouth.

Were those real?

She crept closer, then stopped to chide herself. "God, Mia, don't be an idiot. You're sneaking up on a T-shirt." Comforted by the sound of her voice, she took a deep breath and let it out, then eased closer to the bushes.

Her eyes flicked onto the spider webs misting through the branches, and a horrid chill pulsed the screaming heebie-jeebies through her neck and shoulders. Spiders. She hated spiders. Hated hated hated them. The very thought of webs brushing against her skin practically made her throw up. The thought of a spider falling onto her bare skin and *crawling* made her almost weep.

But the bloody T-shirt was still in there.

"Don't be such a baby." She pushed through the bushes, clenching her teeth and willing her anti-spider bubble into existence. She knelt down. It was a West High Cross-country practice T-shirt. And those were definitely stiff, crusty blood stains.

Okay, this was serious. She watched enough cop shows to know this could be a crime scene, and that she shouldn't disturb it. As she turned, her foot rolled to the side, and pain shot up her ankle.

"Ow, ow, ow!"

Sitting back on her haunches, her hand fell through a spider web. A strangled cry erupted from her throat. She thrashed spasmodically scrubbing the web from her hand, all but forgetting the pain in her ankle.

Then she saw what had rolled under her foot, half-covered by fallen leaves.

A dirty bone smeared with rusty-red stains.

She wondered later if she had screamed as she scrambled out of the bushes, back to her bike. Perversely, her brain ran off to biology class and recognized the bone. The largest bone in the human body. A femur.

Her hands were shaking so badly she could barely hold her cell phone. Her heart was trying to explode in her chest, her ankle still hurt, and her breath came in short gasps, as if someone were squeezing her chest too hard.

"Get a hold of yourself, Mia," she said as she dialed the phone.

The voice came quickly. "Nine-one-one emergency. What is your emergency?"

"Uh, I think I just found a body." Then her voice broke, and the tears came.

CHAPTER TEN

It took Mia a few minutes to explain her location to the police, and when she thumbed the disconnect, she no longer felt like she was going to vibrate herself into little sobbing Mia pellets. She sat on her haunches beside her bike, hugging her knees, squeezing her cell phone just a little too hard.

Was it really someone's body? Could it be some kind of joke? Maybe the police would arrive and tell her that everything was okay, that she was just being silly but they were glad she had called so they could check it out. Maybe they wouldn't laugh at her for being just a silly girl and freaking out over nothing. But what if it was real? What if that bone belonged to someone she knew? Who could it be? Who was missing? Who?

Her thoughts picked up speed, and a moment of dizziness unsteadied her.

A sound on the path snatched her attention, and she started.

A man came jogging toward her. Running shorts, black T-shirt, close-cropped curls of salt-and-pepper hair. Chest and shoulder muscles stretched the T-shirt tight, and his legs rippled as he came to a halt a few paces away. He was short for a man, maybe only five-feet six, but his shoulders were broad, his face hard and blockish, with a coarse shade of whiskers on his cheeks and throat.

His icy-blue eyes seemed to pin her to the concrete path.

She stood.

"Everything okay?" he said.

She squeezed her cell phone with both hands and hugged it to her chest. "Um, I'm okay, but..."

He sniffed the air and looked around. The smell of death found its way back into her awareness. He peered into the dimness. "What's your name?"

"Mia."

"You find something, Mia?"

"I think so."

"Something bad?"

"I think so."

He stepped toward the bushes, sniffing, raising his nose to the breeze. "Something stinks."

"I think it's a body." Her throat clenched.

He knelt fluidly at the brink of the foliage, his gaze scanning like a laser.

"I called the police." She shifted on her feet.

He slid into the space, easing onto all fours like a sprinter. His head turned back and one eye fixed on her again for a long moment, two.

She swallowed hard, and the hair stood up on the back of her neck. Her heart sped up, blood rushing in her ears. Thumbs worked the buttons on her cell phone, and she held it to her ear.

It rang once, then clicked.

"Dad," she said, holding her voice barely steady like a waitress with an overladen platter.

The man's head turned back into the darkness, and he nudged farther in.

Her father's voice was stern. "Where are you, Mia? I thought you were on your way home."

"Something happened."

"What do you mean? Are you all right?"

"I'm okay, but...I think I found a dead body. And the police are coming and—"

"Hold it right there. Where are you?"

"On the trail, maybe a mile and a half."

"I'll be there in five minutes."

"Wait! Dad!" Her eyes fixed on the man in the track shorts. He was built like a body-builder, a competitive wrestler. The man picked up the blood-smeared femur she had stepped on.

"What is it, Mia?" her dad asked. He sounded like he was already half-way out the door.

"Let me talk to Mom."

The man sniffed the blood-smeared bone.

"Um, sir," she called to him.

The man's eye snapped back over his shoulder.

"Shouldn't you leave that alone? It might be a crime scene." She swallowed hard. "The police told me not to mess with anything." The last part was a lie, but for some reason she couldn't just let this weirdo mess something up.

That could be the thigh bone of someone she knew. And this man was touching it. Her hands started shaking again.

The man laid the bone back in its bed of fallen leaves.

The voice of Mia's mother came over the phone. "Are you okay, Mia-chan? Your father told me what you said."

The man rested his hands on his thick-muscled knees, still surveying the scene. Something in the arch of his back showed anger or annoyance rather than horror or even curiosity.

Mia switched to Japanese. "Yeah, Mom, I'm okay, but there's this weird guy here."

"Is he threatening you?"

"No, but he just came along, and now he's checking out the...things I found."

"Your father is coming."

Mia could not remember the last time she had felt such relief. The tension in her shoulders loosened, and her eyes teared. "*Just stay on the phone with me.*"

The man backed out of the foliage and faced her. "That your parents?"

Mia nodded.

"Good," the man said. "So your dad's coming?"

Mia nodded.

"You live near here?"

"Not too far," Mia said.

The man nodded. His gaze traveling over her felt like the sharpened end of a pencil, applying just enough pressure to make an indentation in her flesh.

Her mother said, "*Is that him?*"

"Yeah. He's talking to me."

"Well, you keep talking to me, okay?"

Mia sniffed and wiped her eyes. "*Okay. What do I do?*"

"Um, think about sukiyaki?"

Mia couldn't help but snicker at the absurdity. "*How can I think about eating at a time like this?*"

Her mom snickered back. Mia couldn't remember the last time she had heard her mother laugh. "You have to eat, don't you? Keep your strength up."

The rumbling in her belly before she had left the house was long gone. If those bones in the bushes belonged to somebody she knew, she doubted she would ever feel like eating again.

The man's gaze was still fixed solidly on her. Another chill whispered up her spine. She turned away, hugging her chest. "*He's creeping me out, Mom.*"

"You're just scared. But be careful. Your dad is coming and I hear sirens."

Mia heard them now, too, but the bike path wasn't exactly accessible to four-wheeled vehicles.

"Cops are coming," the man said. "Hang in there, little girl."

She glanced back at him. Was he standing closer now? She turned away again and took a few steps farther away. Her dad was in great shape. With his own bike he could cover this distance in less than five minutes.

Five minutes.

What could somebody do to somebody else in only five minutes? It took over three minutes for a strangling victim to die.

She looked down the path. Was that speck her father? Too dark to see for sure.

Another glance over her shoulder found the man standing the same distance away from her, even though she had moved. She spun to face him. His eyes glinted. His hands rested on his hips, appearing casual, relaxed, but it was only façade. Every one of those lean, hard muscles was poised to act, like a leopard preparing to spring.

"My dad is going to be here in about one minute," she said.

"Good for you," he said, holding her gaze.

Her mom's voice. "Mia, what's happening? You've been quiet."

"*This guy is really creeping me out, Mom.*"

"Tomorrow I'll buy you some pepper spray."

"*Great idea.*" But what good would that do her right now? If this guy meant to harm her, there was nothing she could do. Nothing at all.

When the dark shape of another rider emerged from around a bend in the path, she practically melted with relief. She choked back a sob and covered her mouth with one hand.

"Dad's here, Mom."

"Okay, good. I'll keep dinner warm for you."

Mia disconnected. As the bike drew nearer, her feet started dancing of their own accord, and as her father braked beside her, she flung herself against him, almost bowling him off his seat.

Her father's arm encircled her, and he kissed her on the hair. His strong hand patted her back. Comforting words sounded in her ear, but she didn't hear them. She was too happy to hear anything. Tears streamed down her cheeks.

When she finally released him, the other man stepped forward, extending his hand. "Jack Slade."

Her father shook the man's hand. "Marc O'Reilly."

"You have a brave daughter there."

Mia didn't feel very brave at all. She felt like she had just watched a hundred scary movies in a row, by herself. In the dark.

Her father met the man's gaze. "Yes, she is. She's got a little grit. Takes after her old man that way."

The sirens grew louder.

Mia thought that Slade would back away from her dad a bit—her father had that command presence that she had only ever seen in military people—but Slade didn't back away. For some reason, Mia felt that if Jack Slade intended to hurt her, the presence of her father wouldn't make an ounce of difference. Another chill tickled her neck, not as strong, but still present.

Slade smiled at her father. The tension in his muscles disappeared. "You military?"

"Until a few years ago. You?"

"A long time ago. Semper fi."

"Air Force Intelligence."

Slade cracked a sharp grin. "Now there's a contradiction in terms."

Her father grinned back, but there wasn't any mirth in it. "Once a jarhead, always a jarhead."

"That's true. But I've been out a while. I coach over at Saint Sebastian's."

Mia wiped her nose. No wonder he looked so tough. The students at Saint Sebastian's School for Children were all orphans, stoners, thieves, gang members, the hard cases the rest of the schools simply couldn't handle. The Saint Sebastian's water tower stood just visible over a rolling hill, perhaps two miles away, glowing against the darkening sky.

"Tough job," her father said. "Wrestling?"

"Not so bad. I handle it fine. Soccer and wrestling."

Mia reached around her father's arm and squeezed it. What was her dad doing talking to this guy? A minute ago, Slade had been giving her the shrieking willies, but now his demeanor had changed to smiling affability.

Flashing lights in the distance snagged Mia's gaze. Apparently, the police found a way around the barriers that kept motor vehicles off the bike path. Two police cars and an ambulance snaked their way nearer.

A sick tightness settled in Mia's belly. Reality congealed around her. "Thank god."

Slade smiled broadly at her, revealing strong white teeth. "It's a good thing you found this, Mia. Who knows how long before anyone else would've? Maybe the cops will be able to catch whoever did this."

Mia leaned her head against her dad's chest, wishing Slade would quit trying to talk to her. She pulled away and walked down the path toward the approaching police cars, hugging her arms, realizing that she had been squeezing her cell phone so hard her fingers ached. She shoved it into her pocket. Her dad chatted with Slade while she walked away.

The blood on the T-shirt was dried, but not old. The bone looked fresh.

Who was on the cross-country team? It was one of the T-shirts new this year. Names flicked through her mind.

Her thoughts snagged on one name, but she refused to let it stop there. It couldn't be Nate. She pulled out her cell phone and called him. Why hadn't she called him when he hadn't shown up for school today? She was a horrible friend. His ring tone sounded in her ear, the "Imperial March" from *Star Wars*. Nate was such a dork that way.

"Come on, pick up."

The "Imperial March" continued to play, until the line clicked and Nate's voice came on. "Turn to the Dark Side and leave me a message."

After the beep, she said, "Nate, it's Mia. Call me, please. Right now. It's important."

A police car rolled around the bend in the path, carefully keeping its tires on the concrete. The strobing red and blue lights struck splashes of white into her vision, and the car's headlights bathed her.

The black and white cruiser stopped, and an officer jumped out, a dark silhouette behind the glare of the lights. A badge gleamed on his chest. "Are you Mia?"

"Yes."

"Are you okay?"

Mia nodded. "It's over there." She pointed, and her finger had ceased shaking.

Her dad stood nearby while the police officer asked her a bunch of questions. On one hand, she wanted to help, so she was happy to answer the questions, but on the other hand, every minute that ticked by without Nate returning her call twisted the knot in her belly just a little tighter. The police officers were surprised when her dad showed them his F.B.I. identification. He would help them in any way he could, but he reassured them this was all local jurisdiction.

The police questioned Slade, too, but he seemed to be more attentive to the conversation Mia was having rather than the questions the police were asking him. But he stood too far away to hear the personal information she gave the police. She didn't want him hearing her address, or phone number, or anything about her.

Yellow tape now encircled the area around the bones. Another car joined the line of vehicles. A man and a woman wearing jackets that read "Crime Lab" got out of the car, crossed the police line, and made their way into the bushes.

When the officer had finished asking her questions, he asked a few of her dad, and Mia's attention wandered back to Slade. The officer asking Slade questions looked soft and portly, the kind of guy who spent a lot of time reinforcing the donut shop stereotype, unlike the lean, serious officer who was still talking to her dad. The plump officer looked nervous, sweaty. Something about the way he was standing. He would scribble an answer to a question, then check his pistol in its holster. Slade faced the officer much the way he had faced her, appearing to be at ease but poised to act. She wondered if this guy had the ability to relax at all, ever.

When the officer finished with her dad, the officer said, "You can go ahead and take your daughter home now. If we need anything else, we'll call."

"Of course," her dad said.

Slade walked up and extended his hand again. "Nice to meet you, Marc." They shook hands. "Mia, take care of yourself." His eyes blazed ice-blue again.

Mia nodded and averted her gaze. God, why didn't he just go away?

When she mounted her bike again and pedaled toward home beside her father, her legs felt squishy and weak. And still her phone did not ring. It was the longest mile and a half she had ever ridden.

Her mother was waiting when Mia and her dad walked in. Her mother threw her arms around her and hugged her, and she wasn't sure how to react. Mia had already broken down once tonight; once was enough.

She put on a good face. "Thanks, Mom. I'm okay."

"Dinner is still warm..."

"I don't think I can eat tonight. At least not now."

Her mom rubbed Mia's arm and dabbed at a tear on her own cheek.

Mia sighed. "Sarah still here?"

"She had to go."

Mia shook her head. "Oh, geez! If only I had been back sooner."

"She said she'll be in town for a while."

"Good. Dad, I have to tell you about that guy you were talking to, Slade."

His eyes narrowed. "What about him?"

Her mom said, "He was scaring her to death before you get there."

The memory of it sent a chill across Mia's shoulders. "Yeah. Totally creeping me out. Like a serial killer or something."

Her dad twitched slightly at her last sentence. "I've known a couple of those. I didn't get that at all. Seemed friendly to me, stand-up guy, if wired a little tight. But then ex-Marines often are."

Her mom said, "Maybe you imagine things, Mia. You were really scared."

Mia's voice rose and anger flared. "No, I was not imagining it! He was *trying* to scare me!"

Her parents glanced at each other, that look they used when they thought she was acting like a drama princess.

Mia's voice shrilled. "So what was that on the phone, Mom? You believed me then."

"You were scared. I was scared for you," her mother said in Japanese. "And now it's all okay?"

Her mom hugged her elbows. "You're home now. Your father says that man was nothing to worry about."

"But it's not okay! Somebody is dead!" What if it was Nate? "Why don't you believe me?"

Her dad said, "Of course we believe you, Mia."

Mia clamped her mouth shut. Anything else she said would make her sound like a baby.

Deuce nudged her leg. She rubbed his bristly head. "Hey, Goon." He licked her hand. "I think I just need to go to my room for awhile."

Something passed between her parents, but whatever it was, they kept silent and just nodded.

In her room, she threw herself onto the bed and stared at the ceiling. She considered putting on some music, but silence was more appealing, so she just lay back and listened to the sound of her heart beating, her breath. She turned toward the full-length mirror near her dresser, and let her thoughts turn toward those that until today had occupied much of her mental energy. Maybe thinking about the regular stuff would distract her from bones and death and scary blue eyes and the fact that her parents thought she was a child.

She wondered if Dalton liked big boobs. Why weren't hers bigger?

On one hand, she wanted more feminine curves, like Sarah, but on the other, as she imagined herself with them, she wondered if she would then think she looked fat. Stick-thin or Porky Pig? She just couldn't win. At least these were familiar worries.

She pulled out her cell phone and called Nate. No answer.

Her mind started to pick up speed again, like riding a bike downhill without any brakes.

Wasn't Nicki supposed to have called her? She called Nicki. While she waited for the ring tone to be replaced by a real voice, her heart sped up. No answer, just voice mail.

She threw the phone down. "What the hell!" Was there no one on this planet she could talk to? Kenji wouldn't understand. He was so timid that all of this would just scare him.

Dalton.

No. She didn't know him well enough to make him the first one to talk to about all this. No, no, no. He'd think she was a clingy freak.

The phone rang with Nicki's picture appearing on the screen. Gum chomped out of the ear speaker. "What up, G.F.?" Her voice was barely intelligible over the background noise.

"Hey, um, what are you doing?"

"I'm at Caffeine Dreams with Toni and Kate. We're 'studying.'" She giggled. "They just made varsity cheerleader."

Mia said, "Oh, okay. That's good."

"So what's up?"

"Oh, nothing. What about your algebra homework?"

"Screw it. I don't feel like homework tonight."

"Oh, okay then. What about—?"

"Omigod, there's a cute guy giving me the eye. I gotta go. Talk to you tomorrow."

"Sure. Tomorrow."

"Keep it real!"

The connection went dead, and Mia let the phone slide away from her ear.

All the emotions and thoughts and gravelly bits of angst inside of her suddenly drained away into nothing, leaving her hollow, cold, numb, and alone.

Hours later, she awoke in the same position, unaware that she had finally fallen asleep, lying flat on her bed, with a warm, bristly lump of muscle warming her feet, awakened by her father's head poking through the half-open door.

She rubbed her face and blinked. "Hey, Dad."

"Hey. Anything I can do?"

Besides making Nate call her to tell her he was all right? Besides making her blonde, athletic like Tara, and popular? Besides making Dalton fall head over heels in love with her? "I'm fine."

"You know, I'm proud of the way you handled yourself tonight. You kept it under control."

"Yeah. Thanks." Why couldn't she just explode and have someone else pick up the pieces? The bones... Enough of that kind of thinking. "And thanks for coming to get me. I think you saved me."

He came in and kissed her on the head.

"Geez, I'm not seven."

"You'll always be my little girl."

She sighed. How would she have handled this situation differently if she was an adult? On one hand, she missed being able to let her parents handle all the serious matters for her; on the other, part of her was pretty darn proud of herself for tonight. She had crossed some sort of threshold. Had Nicki found those bones, rather than Mia, Nicki would have likely melted down and had a cerebral hemorrhage, and they would have found her drooling in a heap beside the bike path, nestled in a mound of tissues.

"'Night, Mia."

"'Night."

He let himself out, and she was alone again.

A chill breeze ruffled in through the curtains, and she shivered. She got up to crank the window closed when the sound of coyotes filtered in. Her hand stopped on the crank. A chorus of howls and yips drifted through the night like ghosts, fading in and out from different directions. She had heard a few disparate coyote cries before, but nothing like this. It sounded like a coyote town meeting.

Deuce got up and dropped to the floor with a meaty thump, then joined her at the window, his short loppy ears pricked, sniffing, listening.

He looked at Mia and ruffed.

Even though the coyote songs seemed to sing to each other in some long-distance community, they felt like songs of loneliness, isolation, yearning for closeness, for a mate. She hugged Deuce and rubbed her cheek against his velvety ear.

CHAPTER ELEVEN

Mia woke up the next morning and checked her cell phone for messages.

Nothing. Maybe someone at school would have heard something of Nate.

Her mom waited for her at the kitchen table, drinking a cup of green tea, with a breakfast of rice, egg, and miso soup. Her mom's gaze followed her around the kitchen. Mia didn't feel like speaking. Her mom meant well, but god, did she have to hover? She was the only person in the world who could hover without getting up.

Her mom handed her a lunch bag.

If Mia knew her mother at all, inside was a rice ball, wrapped in cellophane, and a plastic container full of sukiyaki. Mia loved sukiyaki, but why couldn't her mom cook like normal people? How many times had her mom said to her, *It's much healthier than American food.* How about pizza once in a while?

How about some comfort food?

Mia felt like an insect in a jar, with an enormous eye looming over her. "I'm fine, Mom. Really."

Her mom nodded and sipped her tea. "Please call or text me when you get to school. Let me know you're okay."

Mia resisted rolling her eyes. Her mom was just worried and trying to help at the same time. "All right." She grabbed her backpack and lunch bag.

"Study hard."

Mia sighed. "I always do."

All the way to school, Mia squeezed the rubber grips on her handlebars to keep her hands from shaking. Nate still hadn't called her back. Even for a goofy male nerd, he was more conscientious than that. Her legs still felt squishy, wobbly, as she remembered the imbalance of the femur turning under her foot, the brush of the spider webs, that she had touched the leaves that might have someone's blood on them.

Inside the school, Nicki caught her coming down the hallway toward the lockers. "Hey there, G.F."

Mia tensed and kept walking. "Hey."

Nicki felt in to step beside her. "Sorry, you know, for last night. Toni and Kate called me and stuff, and you know how it goes."

Mia nodded. "Yeah, it's no big deal." Her voice sounded colder than she had intended. She imagined vast torrents of fresh gossip flowing back and forth among the three of them, building and building until someone surely had to burst from the sheer volume. She wasn't sure she wanted to tell Nicki about what happened.

"No, really, I'm sorry."

"No problemo." Part of her wanted Nicki to go away, and part of her wanted to sob on her shoulder, the only female pseudo-friend she had.

"Sweet then. Hey, omigod, did you hear?"

"Hear about what?" Mia froze.

Nicki stopped. "You haven't talked to Nate have you?"

Mia covered her mouth. "No, why?"

"I heard the principal talking. They're looking for him. Like he's missing or something."

Mia's fingers clutched her mouth. Something tried to surge out of her belly. She cast about the nearest bathroom, a moan of desperation slipping between her fingers. She ran.

Nicki chased her. "What is it? Hey!"

Please do not let me spew all over the hallway! She made it to the restroom just in time to fling herself into a stall and hurl her breakfast into the toilet.

Nicki rubbed her back. Nicki's voice kept coming, but Mia wasn't receiving any of it, wasn't comprehending the words. A couple of other girls appeared behind Nicki, more curious than concerned.

She knew it. Those bones belonged to Nate.

In the principal's office, Mia told her story again, with surprising calmness and clarity. Mister Becker sat behind his desk in his suit and tie, clasping his plump hands on the blotter before him, and listened with his full attention, which was unusual considering that he rarely listened to anything that any student had to say.

When she was finished, he called the police, and then he called her mother.

Mia waited, her mind swirling, her fingers clasped into one white-knuckled, rock-hard fist. If those were Nate's bones, and he'd only been missing for three days, where was the rest of him? Why just bones?

Two officers and Mia's mother walked into the principal's office as if they had come in the same car.

Her mom sat beside her as the officers asked Mia another long series of questions, most of them exactly the same as the night before. She found her lips twisting downward, her teeth clenching. Why weren't they out there looking for who killed Nate? She explained that she had tried to call Nate the night before and several times today, but without success.

When she was finished answering their questions, she had some of her own. "What can you tell me? He's my friend!"

"His parents filed a missing person's report on him two nights ago. When they last saw him, he left to go running."

"He liked to run Spearhead Trail."

The officer nodded.

A memory snapped into focus. "You might talk to Tara Anderson." Tara's strange behavior could mean something...

"She's a student here?"

"Nate had a crush on her. They were supposed to go running together."

The officer wrote something. "We'll talk to her."

"How long before you know for sure? If the body is Nate's, I mean. You have to check dental records or something?"

The officer looked away. "We'll have to run blood tests and D.N.A."

"But I've heard that takes weeks."

"It does."

"So, don't you have other ways? Dental records?"

"We can't check dental records."

"Why not?"

"I really shouldn't say."

A surge of anger boiled up, and she rose out of her chair. "I'm not a baby!"

"I know that, miss, but—"

Her mom laid a hand on Mia's arm. "Mia, maybe we shouldn't—"

"He was my friend! I want to know!"

The officer sighed. "We can't check dental records because we haven't found the head."

She sank back down. "Oh."

The officer stood briskly and smoothed himself. "Well, that's enough for now, Mia, Mrs. O'Reilly. You can go. We'll be in touch. If there's anything else, please call me." He handed Mia's mother a card.

Mia's mother stood and took the card, then Mia's arm. "Thank you, officer. Come on, Mia."

Her mother led her out into the deserted hallway.

Nate without a head.

Nate without a head.

Nate without a head.

Her mother led her down the hallway toward the exit, and then outside.

They stopped beside the bike racks, and Mia unchained hers to load it into the minivan. As she pushed her bike along beside her mother, a figure stood in her path.

Mia stopped. "Tara."

Tara looked even worse today that she had yesterday, her hair unkempt, no makeup, her eyes hollow and haunted. Her blue eyes met Mia's, and Mia's knees went weak. She could read nothing in Tara's eyes, as if walls twenty feet thick blocked Tara's soul from the rest of the world. Her eyes were the eyes of a fish.

For several seconds, their eyes locked. Mia sensed thought and movement—restraint—behind the walls, but nothing else.

Her mother broke the spell. "Come on, Mia. Let's go home. Deuce needs to go for a walk."

Tara lowered her eyes and hurried past.

Mia didn't need a D.N.A. scan or dental records to know. She just felt it. The last time she had seen Nate, he gave her a big, goofy grin after chemistry lab. He was such a total lech, but he was good-natured about it. He didn't leer like so many of the other guys in school. She had liked the sparkle of mischief in his eye.

She sat in the passenger seat, leaning her forehead against the cool window glass. The street drifted past, cars, people, a kid in a white T-shirt.

A bloody white T-shirt flashed in her mind. She stifled a sob.

Dammit, Mia, hold yourself together!

She found herself in the garage at home, with her mother turning off the key. The garage door descended like a portcullis. Dragging her backpack inside felt like a chore. Taking off her shoes felt like a chore. The idea of taking Deuce for a walk felt like a chore.

All this stuff was too mundane, too normal, too *useless*. She found herself yearning to do something real, something that mattered. She wanted to help the police.

She stood in the foyer, backpack dangling from her hand, one shoe off. "Mom, I need to go for a ride or something."

"Are you sure? I don't think—"

"I'll take Deuce with me, so I won't be gone long. You said he needs to go out anyway." Mia had to get *out*.

Her mother nodded. "Okay."

When Mia came back after several useless circuits around the neighborhood, after each of which she returned to the same set of problems, Sarah's Jeep was parked in the driveway. Mom had apparently decided to call in the big guns. Sarah would have a banana split for Mia and would want to take her shopping or something. Sarah greeted her with a hug and when they separated laid a warm hand against Mia's cheek.

Mia's mom opened the refrigerator. "Sarah brought you something." She pulled out a banana split that on any other day would have made

Mia drool like a shar-pei.

Mia gave them both a wan smile. "Thanks, but maybe later, okay? My stomach is just not up for it."

Sarah settled back into her chair, tense, as if poised to do something. "Things like this can have a tremendous effect on people. Some handle it better than others."

Mia glanced at her mother, who sat clasping her fingers into a knot at the counter. What happened to a parent that lost a child? What were Nate's parents going through?

Sarah said, "I'm worried about you, Mia. How are you doing?"

"I want to help. I don't know how."

Her mom said, "The police are doing everything they can, I'm sure. Your father said he would look into things, too."

"Maybe, but *I'm* not! I want to do something."

Sarah said, "You feel helpless."

"Yes."

"Scared a little."

"Yes."

"Like maybe it's your responsibility to help your friend."

"Yes."

"And you feel happy that *you're* still alive."

"What? No—"

"And that makes you feel awful, guilty as hell."

Mia sighed and sank into a chair beside her. "Yes."

Sarah put an arm around her. "And you want them to catch the scumbag who did it."

"Yes!" Mia went rigid. *Yes.*

"Well, you've already told the police everything you know, right?"

"Maybe I'm missing something."

"As long as you're wracking your brain like that, whatever that 'something' is will not show up. You need to take your mind off of it for a while. How does that sound?"

Mia sighed again. She had been wishing she could forget all about this since last night.

"I took the day off from work."

She and Sarah hadn't hung out together in forever. "Really? Isn't that hard for your job?"

"I called the President. He said it was okay."

Mia elbowed her, unable to suppress a snicker.

"So, what'll it be? Manicure? Movie? Shoe shopping?"

"Well, there is a place..."

The zoo was practically deserted on a Wednesday afternoon. Summer was over. Schools were in session. A few young mothers pushed their toddlers in strollers. A gaggle of Chinese tourists walked in a close group and spoke Mandarin among themselves.

Mia was silent for most of the ride. As they passed through the front gate, Sarah said, "It's a nice day for walking."

"I suppose."

Sarah's warm hand squeezed Mia's shoulder.

They set off walking past the Desert Dome toward the Big Cat Complex. As they strolled past the cages and Plexiglas windows containing some of the world's most dangerous predators, Mia couldn't help but feel a quiver. A tiger lying on its side, sleeping. A leopard, resting on a fake tree branch, its wide paws dangling with a relaxation that belied its tremendous speed. A cougar rested in a corner of its cage, its head erect but eyes barely open, so much like just a big muscley house cat.

The lions were gathered in the sun in the center of their enclosure, sprawling over each other with a family intimacy that always surprised her. To be so close to those like you. To have a *place*. The male lion's impassive gaze made her feel like little more than a morsel of meat on a stick. Its golden eyes tracked her, the only thing between them a plate of clear Plexiglas. A lioness paced back and forth along one side wall, her muscles coiling and releasing, coiling and releasing, like ropes twisting under a sheath of supple fur. The lioness stopped near the glass and regarded Mia. Mia had not realized she had frozen. The lioness's nose almost touched the glass, little more than four feet away.

Sarah stopped beside Mia, but the lioness did not take her gaze from Mia. Mia imagined herself a chimpanzee, strong and clever, but unable to withstand the raw power of a three hundred pound predator, caught and dragged away in the cat's jaws to feed the pride. What must it feel like to have your flesh stripped away while you're still alive, your bones cracked and the marrow sucked out, your lungs still breathing but with a fanged snout buried in your innards? She shivered.

Sarah touched Mia's arm and broke the spell. Mia shook herself, and they moved away. The lioness followed them on the other side of the glass.

They continued around the perimeter of the zoo, past the timber wolf cage, where the pack sat together, much like the lions, some asleep, some panting like dogs in the warm sun.

As Mia and Sarah walked past, one of the wolves took notice of them. Like lightning, it jumped to its feet and lunged to the edge of the pit that kept it away from the bars. The wolf's tail stood upright, its body in a half-crouch, its yellow-green eyes burned, and a low growl emanated across the twenty feet separating them.

"Thank god for the bars," Mia said.

Two other wolves slunk forward on the leader's flanks, bodies slung low, ears back, tails sticking out straight behind them.

Mia edged closer to Sarah. "What is with these animals today?"

Sarah pointed to the middle wolf, the biggest one. "That's the alpha male. He's feeling a bit territorial today, it seems."

"You think?"

"Don't look him in the eye. He'll see it as a challenge."

Mia gulped. "Too late."

"Come on. Let's not get them too worked up."

Mia nodded, and they shuffled away quicker than she would want to admit. Being so nervous was just silly. She was perfectly safe. "How do you know so much about wolves?"

"I know about a lot of things. That's the kind of thing that happens when you go to school." Sarah smirked.

"Oh, yes, Miss Adult. I'm just a dumb kid who thinks school is a waste of time."

"Sorry."

Mia wished that someday she might know half as much as Sarah did. Besides, school beat hanging out at the mall with wastoids like Chelsea and Brittany, at least most days.

The air smelled of coming autumn, and wind gusted through the leaves of the oak trees.

She stopped beside the gazelle enclosure, putting her hands on the fence. She didn't see any gazelles. "Have you ever had a friend die?"

Sarah stood beside her. "I was in the military, like your dad. A lot of my friends died, or got hurt very badly."

"Does it hurt every time?"

"It hurts a lot. Always. When it happens, you have a hole in your life shaped like that person."

"I can't go through it again."

"Everybody dies, Mia."

"But it's not fair! Nate was a good person!"

"Lots of good people die, and it sucks. Every single time." Sarah hugged her close, and Mia shrugged away.

"Some holes never go away, do they."

"Some don't."

"How do you stand it?"

"I don't. I just get through it, try to ignore the hole. Some days it hurts less. Then something will remind you of someone, and you'll feel like crap because you miss them. It never really goes away."

"Some holes are so big, people can fall into them and never get out again. Every day, I try to—"

Sarah sucked her top lip for a moment. "You're not talking about Nate, are you."

Mia let the tears come. "I miss Sho." She couldn't look at Sarah.

Sarah's voice cracked. "Everybody does."

"Mom will never forgive me."

"She has forgiven you!"

"No, Sarah. You don't know! Sho was the good one! I'm just a screw-up. I feel it when she looks at me. She wishes...she wishes..."

"Don't say that, Mia. Your mom loves you. I've known her a lot longer than I've known you."

"She blames me! I was there! He said, 'Let's go to the beach!' and I said, 'Sure!' It was such a gorgeous day." Mia found her fingers tracing over the pale white streak of scar tissue under her clothes, where the feather-light tentacles had drifted across her skin, and exploded thousands of little microscopic barbed spears into her flesh. The sudden pain seared into her memory. She and Sho at the beach on a gorgeous summer afternoon, he with his baseball, wheedling her to play catch yet *again*, she with her beach towel and sunglasses and bikini that her mom didn't approve of, the skinny, gawky little girl pretending she was older than she was, too cool to hang out with her annoying brother, soaking up the warm sun, relaxing with the waves of the surf, drifting off into nap-land, then a thump next to her, spraying her with grit and bouncing something like a little fist into her ribs, feeling that surge of anger at the baseball-sized circle of sand on her well-oiled skin, growling as she picked up the baseball and threw it as hard as she could out into the waves. His angry cry of *Mi-aaa*! Sho was a good swimmer; he could go and get the baseball and leave her alone for a while. Sho running out into the surf after it, and Mia enjoying the silence, until the silence was ripped open by his gurgling scream of agony, and Mia flinging herself upright, seeing his tiny form screaming, crying, bobbing on the two-foot waves about a hundred feet out, running, splashing after him, reaching, grasping, her brain a tumult of wordless panic and confusion, hearing his screams swallowed by saltwater, a hand clutching the baseball rising from the water, the sand dropping away under feet, swimming to him, reaching for him. Then it hit her like a spray of infinitesimal shards of molten glass. Pain tearing across her arm, her body, stunning her in its shocking magnitude. Sho's face, screaming, screaming, screaming, choking, the vivid scarlet weals across his face, left there by the brush of invisible tentacles, trying to grab him, screaming for help, fighting through her own agonizing pain, his head disappearing under the surface, her own screaming, choking, trying to grab Sho and hold his face above water, losing him, brushing him, losing him to the toss of a wave, the plunging flailing presence of the lifeguard forever later, too late, and then nothing. She woke up in the hospital, and Sho was dead.

Mia sighed. "You know, I ride around in the car, around this city, and it seems like there's a church on every street, and I hear kids in school talking about it, and Mom and Dad never talked about religion much, and I hear people talk about God sometimes and I think, 'God, if you exist, you are such a *bastard*, because the only reason for that jellyfish to be in that spot on that day was because *you* put it there to take my brother away!' It was God, and Mom blames *me*."

"No, she doesn't, Mia."

"Yes, she does! *I* blame me. Two days ago was the day."

"I know. I wanted to call, but I was on a plane."

"Things haven't been the same since. Not even between Mom and Dad. They fought some, for a while. Mom's like a turtle, gone so deep in her shell, Dad can't reach her. I can't reach her."

"I'm here for a while. I'll help however I can."

"I hope you can. But I doubt it. Mom has to want to live, and I'm not sure she does."

"I had no idea."

"Sometimes I think I'm the only who knows. Dad has his job. He spends a lot of time there, especially lately. He pretends everything is okay now. When he comes home, she puts on the good face. But it's like she doesn't even know I'm there, so I get to see how she is the rest of the time."

Sarah pulled Mia close, and Mia wanted to pull away again, but Sarah was surprisingly strong, squeezing the tears out, and Mia let it happen.

Mia's cheek pressed against Sarah's chest. "Nate was my friend, but I was too stupid to realize it. Why do I care about him more now that he's dead than I did when I thought I would see him in class tomorrow?"

"That's just the way people are, Mia. We take people for granted sometimes."

"I'm a horrible friend." Her chest felt like a cold, empty hole. Where were the stupid gazelles? "I want to hug him."

Sarah sighed and squeezed her again for a moment.

Mia pulled away. "That's enough crying." She clasped her arms across her chest and walked on.

The next enclosure housed the okapis. Or at least it should have, but she didn't see any here either. "What is it, Animal Vacation Day or something?" she muttered.

"Mia, wait."

Mia turned.

"It's okay to be upset about your friend. It's okay to be upset about Sho."

"But I don't want to be. I just...It's just...I don't have that many friends at school, you know? We weren't even that close, but...maybe that's the problem. Why weren't we? I don't have any close friends, because every time I've ever had one, we've had to move. It's too hard to keep trying. I miss Nate now, but we didn't hang out that much. We talked sometimes in class, in the halls. Mostly he just wanted to talk about this crush he had on Tara. It just sounds stupid."

"It doesn't sound stupid at all."

Mia searched Sarah's eyes. Sarah cast her gaze to the ground. "When there's no one near you to care about, you feel alone. When someone is taken from you, even if you weren't that close, it makes that aloneness sharper, you know?"

The conviction in Sarah's voice poked a hole in Mia's self-pity party. "What happened?" Mia said.

"I lost some friends in Iraq, in Afghanistan, and other places I can't tell you about."

Mia fixed her with fresh interest. Suddenly she wanted to help Sarah, but didn't know how.

Sarah crossed her arms and leaned against the okapi fence. "Sorry, I'm supposed to be the one helping you."

"You just read my mind."

Sarah shrugged. "I'm pretty good with sort of thing. It's what I do."

"Where do you learn to do that? Does the military have a Psychic School or something?"

"The C.I.A. used to."

"You're kidding."

"I know all about it. I saw it in the Discovery Channel."

Mia crossed her arms. "I hate it when you do that."

"What?"

"Throw some little clue like you know cool secret stuff, then when I want the truth you mess with my head."

Sarah looked contrite. "Sorry. It's just habit."

Sarah's reply had been too easy. Mia crossed her arms. "So tell me the truth."

"Okay, if I can."

Mia stood up straight and paced before her like lawyers she had seen cross-examining witnesses on TV. She spoke in a deep voice, "Miss O'Reilly. If that *is* your real name."

Sarah snickered.

Mia spun to face her. "Do you have any personal knowledge of any sort of government school to train people with E.S.P.?"

Sarah gave her a strange smile. "Something like that."

"For real?"

"It's mostly instinct and intuition, but you can learn."

"Can you teach me?"

Sarah's strange smile held. "Sure. Some other time, though. It's not exactly something you pick up in a day. Some people have a talent for it."

Mia's eyes narrowed. "So what do you do anyway?"

Sarah walked past, toward the sable antelope paddock.

Mia followed her. "You're not in the military anymore."

"Not anymore."

"So then, what?"

"I can't tell you."

"Are you a spy?"

"I work in an office."

"What kind of office?"

"Mia."

"Okay, okay. Dad never tells me about his job either."

"Mostly it's just boring."

"What about when it's not?"

"You don't want to know."

"But I do!"

"Mia."

"Okay, okay." She sighed. "I was trying to take my mind off of stuff."

Sarah smiled again. Then she paused. The two of them now stood before the sable antelope placard on the fence. Sarah raised her nose into a gust of breeze, and her smile evaporated. Mia saw gooseflesh rise on her arms.

Mia touched Sarah's arm then recoiled. Sarah's pulse was practically bursting through her skin, hammering. "What is it?"

Sarah glanced quickly at Mia, then rubbed the gooseflesh down. "Nothing, just smelled something strange. That's all."

"An elephant fart? What was it?"

"I don't know."

Mia's brow crinkled. Sarah had answered that question a little too quickly.

Sarah turned toward the fence. "Where on Earth are all the animals?"

"They haven't put them away for winter yet I hope."

"Not yet, surely. It's only September."

"Maybe," Mia said, "And stop calling me 'Shirley'."

Sarah snickered again. "You're too young to be making *Airplane* references."

"Dad used to watch that movie all the time. He's such a dork."

Sarah threw back her head and laughed. "You have no idea, the depths of his dorkage! Here's a secret I can tell you. About your dad."

Mia grinned. "Lay it on me. I'll blackmail him with it."

"Your dad actually used to play *Dungeons and Dragons,* and he watched *anime*, when it was still called Japanese animation, and when he was a little kid he had a crush on Smurfette."

"Who's Smurfette?"

Sarah chuckled. "Better perhaps that you don't know."

A zookeeper pulled up nearby driving a camouflaged golf cart with a cargo bed full of boxes and bags.

Mia called out to him. "Hey, where are all the animals?"

The man slid of the car and pushed back his cap. "Well, the okapis and the gazelles are locked up for now, along with the deer and zebras."

"Why?"

"Last night there was some trouble..."

"What kind of trouble?"

"Some of the sable antelope are gone."

"Gone?"

"Um, yeah. As in killed. Something got in there with them. A predator."

Alarm filtered into Sarah's voice. "Did something escape?"

"No, no, nothing like that. All the predators are accounted for."

"What was it then?"

"We're still investigating."

Sarah's knuckles turned white. "Were the antelope devoured?"

"To the bone."

"No predator eats an entire antelope in one night, much less several antelope. Except an entire pride of lions maybe."

The zookeeper shrugged. "We're investigating, but that ain't my department."

"How many antelope did you lose?"

"Two."

"Have you warned the residential neighborhoods around here?"

"The police are on that, ma'am. But don't tell anybody I told you." His face reddened. "I could lose my job."

Sarah nodded. "Thanks. We were just curious."

He said, "Just don't spread it around, you know?"

Sarah nodded to him, then turned. "Come on, Mia. I want to check out the Bat Caves."

Mia made a face. "You're so weird."

"That's why you love me."

CHAPTER TWELVE

Mia and Sarah arrived home at dusk.

Mia's thoughts kept turning to the memory of the femur under her foot, the blood-smeared bones poking up through the fallen leaves. Had the bones really been gnawed or was her overactive mind creating the tooth marks in her memory?

The thought of Nate not only being dead, but perhaps eaten, turned her belly into a solid knot of cold, dry spaghetti, impenetrable and tangled.

Thoughts twisted together in a silent rhythm. *I'm a horrible friend. I have to do something.* Nate was dead, and she couldn't say goodbye.

Sarah was quiet on the ride home, too. Mia asked her a couple of times what she was thinking, just to get a break from her own increasingly annoying thought patterns, but Sarah brushed off the question with a lie. "Nothing," she said, but her face looked worried, pensive.

Mia had said, "I'll be fine. You don't have to worry about me."

Sarah reached over and squeezed her hand with fingers that felt like warm iron. "I know. It's not that."

"What then?"

Sarah gave her a smile that was a little too bright. "Oh, it's nothing. Maybe your mom will let me stay for dinner."

"More like she'll try to keep you prisoner."

Mia's mom was making dinner when they came into the house. The television in the living room was turned on, with the volume turned up so that it was audible in the kitchen. The local news was previewing stories about a wave of break-ins at local drugstores and a strange decrease in visitors at local homeless shelters.

They entered the kitchen, and her mom had both arms in the sink washing dishes. "Did you enjoy the zoo?"

Mia said, "It was weird."

"Yeah," Sarah said, "Something apparently got in and ate some of the antelope."

"Then watch the news. They mentioned a story about that coming up."

Mia walked into the living room and sat down beside Deuce on the couch. He rumbled and put his head in her lap to be scratched, which she dutifully did. She waited for the stories she didn't care about to pass by. The weather. A rash of missing cats and dogs.

Then a reporter appeared, standing before the entrance of the zoo with a microphone clenched in her fist. She tucked a few strands of wind-blown blonde hair behind her ear. "Zoo officials are reporting a possible attack. Last night two sable antelope were killed on the zoo grounds. An investigation today revealed that the antelope were killed by a large predator, possibly a mountain lion."

The scene cut to near the antelope enclosure where Mia and Sarah had stood earlier that day, with the reporter standing with a man in a zoo uniform. The reporter said, "What kind of animal could do something like this?"

The zoo official scratched his head. "Judging from the remains, possibly a mountain lion, a bear, or some sort of large canine."

"Large canine, do you mean like a coyote?"

"No, bigger than that, much bigger."

"Like a wolf?"

"Maybe, but we weren't not really following the wolf hypothesis. Wolves can't climb, and whatever got in came over the walls. More likely that it's something else."

"Were there any tracks left behind?"

"Yes, but not clear enough to identify the animal. Just that it was big enough to bring down an antelope."

"How do you explain losing two antelope?"

The man wiped his lips and looked away. "I can't."

The scene cut back to the reporter at the entrance. "Zoo officials are warning people citywide to keep their pets indoors, and if you see any unusual animal activity to call Animal Control or the police immediately. This is Christine Miller, Eyewitness News."

The anchorwoman appeared on-screen. "Thank you, Christine. We have here in the studio tonight a zoologist from the University of Nebraska, here to talk to us about large predators in Nebraska, Doctor David Kincaid. Welcome, Doctor."

A spare, bespectacled man sat beside her at the news desk. "A pleasure, Catherine."

"So there have been stories increasing for years about how mountain lions are migrating across Nebraska and the Great Plains from the Rockies eastward."

"It's true. They are expanding their territories. The Game and Parks Commission has numerous documented sightings. The Nebraska population of white tail deer is estimated at over a quarter million, with perhaps fifty thousand mule deer in the western part of the state, to say nothing of all the livestock statewide, so cougars have plenty of prey available to draw their territories eastward."

"But within the city of Omaha?"

"Many of the best-documented sightings have been in small towns where the animals venture in to forage from garbage cans. Somewhat of a rude awakening for someone to go outside thinking to chase the raccoons out of their garbage and finding something else."

"That's an understatement!"

"If the attacks on the zoo grounds were perpetrated by a cougar, the animal is likely still within the city. They are stealthy animals, and in spite of what you might think there are plenty of places for them to hide. Trees, undeveloped areas, waterways, parks, and so forth. People should keep in mind, though, that cougar attacks on humans are extremely rare. In the last one hundred and twenty years, there have been only ninety-three confirmed attacks on humans across all of North America."

"What can people do if they find themselves face-to-face with a mountain lion?"

"Don't run or try to play dead, because those things could stimulate its chase instinct. Face it, make eye contact, yell and scream at it, wave your arms, throw things. The key is to make yourself appear to be very aggressive. This will drive the cat away."

"Thank you, Doctor Kincaid." The anchorwoman turned back to the camera.

Mia turned off the television and went back into the kitchen. "Feels kind of funny not being at the top of the food chain."

Sarah sipped a cup of green tea. "People all over the world live with apex predators. They just have to be careful. Lions and leopards in Africa, tigers in Asia, jaguars in the Amazon, wolves coming back strong in the Rockies."

"And bears," Mia's mom said.

"But the biggest things we're supposed to have around here are raccoons!"

Sarah gave her a mock serious face. "You ever see a ticked off raccoon? Take your arm off."

Mia rolled her eyes.

Deuce started scratching at the garage door.

Mia sighed. "Looks like Goon-san needs to go out." Then she remembered the news broadcast saying to keep pets inside at night. "I'll take him for a ride."

"Be careful," her mom said.

"I'm not worried. Deuce could take down a mountain lion."

Deuce ruffed.

Mia said, "The mountain lion has a belly full of sable antelope anyway. It's probably sleeping, and the zoo is on the opposite side of town."

"Just be careful."

CHAPTER THIRTEEN

Mia made sure her cell phone was in her pocket as she mounted her bicycle and gripped Deuce's leash, then rolled out of the garage. Her mind went elsewhere as she pedaled down the street, Deuce loping along beside her.

Memory of that dream kiss floated back into her mind like a puff of cloud at sunset, but then storm clouds came along, bringing thoughts like *How am I going to get out of the house Saturday night?* She sighed. Maybe if she had had a chance to say goodbye to Nate, she would feel better. The police hadn't even identified the body yet, so who knew when a funeral might be. Funerals were for saying goodbye, her dad had told her when her grandmother had passed away. She didn't want to wait that long.

If she hurried, she could make it out there to the spot before her mother started to worry. Fifteen, twenty minutes tops. Ride out, say goodbye, ride back, done. Then maybe the cold, vibrating knot in her stomach would loosen. She turned her path to the trailhead, and within minutes she was pedaling fast down the trail.

The night was cool, the sunset fading against the rolling horizon. She shifted her bike into high gear and pedaled hard. Deuce ran easily alongside her, his loose skin lapping in waves across his hard-muscled frame, black-speckled tongue lolling from the corner of his mouth. His legs were short but he could keep up with a car passing through the neighborhood for a block or two. Her heart pounded, and her legs began to burn with the effort of sustaining that speed. Surely if she were only away for a little while, she wouldn't get into trouble.

She panted, "And stop calling me 'Shirley.'"

The site was just around the next bend. Wind rustled across the soybean leaves in the nearby field. By now the police must have finished with the crime scene. In the distance, a coyote yipped at the gathering darkness. A splash of yellow stripes criss-crossed a path-side bush.

A surge of sadness weakened her feet against the pedals, and a sob caught in her throat. Her eyes burned. She coasted the last fifty yards and braked beside the web of police tape.

His eyes saw infinitely fine yet clear shades of gray, with a few splashes of bright color. In the dusk, the girl's clothes gleamed like neon lights beside the slashes of yellow police tape. Her scent, fresh and clean and smelling vaguely of powdery strawberries, formed a trail that was like an undulating neon snake. Strangely, she didn't smell of fear.

Dusk was the most vulnerable time for humans. The sky was too bright for their meager night vision and too dark to see clearly. They relied too much on their eyesight. His companions were hiding nearby, watching her as well. They would follow his lead. But he only watched her. The evening air was a symphony of scents—earth and soybeans, wildflowers and night insects, a pheromone trail nearby blazed by a colony of ants, the tang of distant car exhaust and the rotting stench of the canal beyond the trees. And here, in this place, blood and death.

He kept low as he moved through the soybean rows. She wouldn't see him unless he raised his head, and he did not need to see her to follow.

She hummed to herself, a soft tuneless melody, as if trying to steady her mind against something amiss but not quite sensed. She was so soft. He or his companions could slaughter her at will, sate their hunger.

Her companion, the dog, sniffed the air. The dog was not so foolish as her.

A sigh shuddered out of her. She threw her leg off and laid the bike down, wrapped Deuce's leash around her hand again. He raised his nose into the wind, sniffing. A low growl rumbled out of his thick chest. Her heart thundered against her chest, and sweat cooled on her face and neck.

Mia stood before the low opening in the bushes, clearing her throat. "Okay, well, I don't know how to do this, but...Nate, if you can hear me or whatever, I'm sorry for what happened to you. You were my friend, and I liked you more than I let you know, even if you were a big goofball, and the sad part is that I didn't know it until you were gone. I'm sorry for that, too." Beads of starlight gathered in her falling tears and turned to sparkles on the leaves of the bushes. "God, I feel so stupid." She sniffed and wiped her nose. "I'm going to miss you, and I promise that I'll do whatever I can to help, the police, whatever. Okay?"

The wind whispered through the sumac.

"But if somehow Nate turns out to be okay and you're somebody else who died in there, I'm going to kill Nate for making me feel so crappy. I'll still feel bad for you, though."

She sighed again, cleared her throat again. "Okay, Goon-burger."

Moments later, she was back in the seat pedaling for home.

As she picked up speed, she wondered if she felt better. Maybe a little.

He listened to her speak, heard the regret in her voice. His curiosity aroused, he made sure to keep pace with her as she rode, but carefully. He did not wish to be seen. The dog looked strong, barrel-chested, muscular, loyal, an excellent representation of his cultured brethren. But the dog would stand as nothing against even one of them.

The moistness among the bean leaves tickled his nose as he trotted through the field after her, the leaves slapping against his face and chest.

She had accelerated to a good clip when goosebumps jumped up the back of her neck and down both arms, and they weren't the good kind of goosebumps. Something was moving through the soybean field behind her. Deuce heard it, too, and glanced back. Leaves rustled at the passage of something just hidden by the waist-high bean plants.

She pedaled faster, gripping the handlebars tighter. Her heart leaped against its cage, thumping, flopping.

Her legs started to burn from the effort.

Multiple shapes paced her. Big ones. Their breath pumped from deep lungs. Their heavy paws thumped on the bare earth of the bean field. Their shoulders charged through the leafy greenery. Canine. But they were huge dogs. No, not dogs. Wolves? Her throat clenched. Had the zoo lost some wolves and then lied about it? There were no wolves in the wild within five hundred miles of here. They had to be dogs.

She threw as much power as she could muster into the pedals, rising from the seat and leaning low over the handlebars, focusing her attention on the darkening path ahead, even as her ears tuned for sounds of her pursuit. Her tires buzzed on the concrete, and the rubber grips grew slick in her hands. Deuce pounded the pavement beside her, his breath heaving in and out of him, ears laid back, body tensed.

When she looked back, the dogs were gone. She slowed to regain her breath and slow her stampeding heart, coughing the ragged burn from her chest, wiping the tears from her cheeks.

A dark, hairy shape exploded out of the bushes toward her. White slavering fangs. Gray-brown streaks of fur.

Deuce snarled and jerked to interpose himself, snapping the leash taut. The hand that held the leash twisted the handlebar with it. Her tires scored black streaks on the concrete as the bicycle jackknifed and she flipped airborne over the handlebars, plowing a swath through the viny, leafy rows of soybeans, rolling to a halt, her breath bursting free so forcefully she could not catch it. Dirt filled her nose and mouth and eyes, sucked into her throat with each harsh gasp.

Deuce snarled and strained against his leash, jerking her arm taut.

A cacophony of barking snarls erupted around her, so loud she ducked and covered her head with one arm. Her arms and legs melted as the horrendous noise sent every nerve in her body into explosive overdrive.

Deuce's pulling jerked her onto her face again. Her tears melded into mud, and she tried to blink away the burning dirt, spitting, blowing it out of her nose. She hugged the ground in the beans, praying that whatever that thing was would not see her, like vainly hiding from a monster in a dream that she knew already saw her.

Teeth snapping, snarling, barking, Deuce roaring with frustration, as if he could not reach the real battle. His quivering muscles rippled down the leash into her arm. For an eternity, the catastrophic battle raged, and Mia huddled, trying to regain her meager senses. Then, just as quickly, it ended, as if a switch had been thrown. The last thing she heard was one or more somethings charging into the bushes. Deuce kept barking for long moments while she spat dirt and blew gobs of snotty mud from her nose.

And finally, silence.

Crickets.

A mourning dove in the distance.

Mia lifted her head and peeked out of the bean field. The path was empty.

Deuce stood beside her, his growls subsiding.

Her entire body felt like a feather vibrating in the gust of a fan. She picked up her bike and pushed into the path.

A wet spatter of blood droplets on the concrete was the only evidence that anything had happened. But blood from what? Deuce's frenzied scrambling had torn up a swath of bean field in his desperation to reach the path where the fight had been. He was covered with soil and moist leafy vines.

Then a voice came from the bushes across the path. "Hey, you okay?"

Deuce roared a challenge, jerking the leash taut, muscles quivering.

"Deuce! Hush!" she cried. A boy of about thirteen peered out of the bushes, his face a pale smear in the shadows. As Deuce's snarling diminished, Mia said, "I'm awesome. Why are you in the bushes?"

"Long story," he said. More rustling from behind him.

"Is someone with you?"

"Yeah, I got a couple of friends."

After what had happened, her nerves jittered like she had just pounded down four energy drinks. "Come out and let me see you."

"You sure about that?"

"Yes! Please! I'm kind of freaked out."

Three boys of comparable age half-emerged from the bushes.

They looked about thirteen.

Oh, god. The tallest one, silent, resembled—No, not now.

"So what the hell are you guys doing hiding in the...oh, my god are you *naked*?"

His voice was mostly calm, but with a quavering undercurrent. He held a leafy branch in front of his groin. "Yeah, sorry. Somebody stole our clothes. Part of the long story." His accent was different, maybe Southern. Bits of leaves sprinkled his close-cropped hair and smudges of dirt across a smattering of freckles. The two other boys stood on either side of him. Even in the dusk, she could see their faces redden as they tried to cover themselves with branches. But she saw something else on their faces, too. Their wide eyes flicked up and down the path, shoulders tense.

Deuce growled at them, straining against the leash. The tallest one kept scanning the trail, and fear tightened his face. The dark-skinned one kept his nakedness concealed behind a bush and looked away sheepishly. They all looked exceptionally muscular for kids that age. They also looked too afraid to be dangerous.

"Deuce! Cool it!" She rubbed his head to calm him down. "Look, you guys need to be careful. I saw wolves."

"Wolves? In Nebraska? You must have hit your head."

"I know what I saw. Something attacked me."

"It musta been a dog. 'Sides, your friend there looks like he could Rochambeau a grizzly. Musta chased off the other one. You ain't bit or nothin' are you?"

"No, just dirty..."

"Good," he said quickly.

Mia threw a leg over her bike. "You guys are weird. But you better get out of this area. It's not safe."

"Yeah," he said, looking up and down the path. "We'll be careful."

She put her foot and pedal and pushed off. Deuce followed her, watching the boys suspiciously. Her heart was only now slowing down, and her arms and legs were so wobbly she could barely control her bike.

She brushed the detritus off her clothes, her face, out of her hair, out of Deuce's coat before she took him in the garage.

Even so, her mom noticed. "*Why are you so filthy?*"

"Um, I had a little spill."

"I was about to call you!" Mia's mom said. She and Sarah were sitting in the kitchen. "*Are you all right?*"

"I'm okay. Sorry." Mia held the door open for Deuce as she slipped off her shoes.

Sarah said, "Your mom's just a little freaked out."

Mia met Sarah's gaze and saw something strange there. Sarah's eyes narrowed, fixed on Mia, and her nostrils flared. Mia said, "Hey, are you reading my mind again?"

"Not as far as you know."

Her mom said, "What are you talking about?"

Mia said, "Sarah told me today that she reads minds. Learned it in the K.G.B."

Sarah said something in a language Mia didn't know.

Mia crossed her arms. "What language was that, smarty-pants? Russian?"

Sarah held her gaze, smiling faintly. Mia tried to pry some meaning from Sarah's strange gaze, but nothing came loose.

Mia's mom asked, "That was Russian? Where did you learn Russian?"

"Defense Languages Institute in California." She winked at Mia. "You seriously have the coolest aunt ever."

Mia sighed, defeated. "Yeah, you're right. I seriously do. So I'm going to go to my room now and slit my wrists because I feel so inadequate. Deuce can come and feed on my corpse. Okay, Deuce?" She rubbed his head.

Deuce ruffed.

"Have fun with the suicide thing," Sarah said.

Mia headed upstairs, Deuce following her. Her mom said to Sarah, "*Her spirit is so dark sometimes.*"

Mia almost yelled back down the stairs, My *spirit is dark?*

Sarah laughed. "Hello, Little Miss Tokyo Goth!"

"That was just a phase."

"You still have the clothes? Do they still fit?"

Mia cocked her ear at the top of the stairs to listen. She pretended to open and close her bedroom door.

After the bedroom door closed, her mom whispered. "Yes, they still fit."

Sarah's rich laughter filled the house, and Mia slipped quietly into her room.

Mia's brain was too scattered for algebra to make any more sense than Hokkaido dialect. Even more than an hour after the attack, her hands were still shaky. She sat at the picnic table on the backyard deck, listening to the drone of the cicadas, textbook containing the mathematical secrets of the universe spread before her, and she could do nothing with them. The air had grown chilly but she barely felt it. Deuce occupied his customary place of slumber upstairs on Mia's bed. Her mother was somewhere within the house, probably in bed early, as usual.

A *psst!* brought her thoughts back to the world, seeking the source of the sound. A boy's head, a familiar one, peeked over the wooden gate into the backyard. He looked around. "Hey!"

"Hey, yourself. What are you doing here?"

"We followed you."

"Uh, I gathered that. And that's more than a little creepy. What do you want?"

"Well, you're nice, and we wanted to ask you something."

"What?"

"Um, you got any food you could spare? We ain't eaten nothin' in a couple of days is all."

Suddenly she felt like a complete jerk. Her mom's delicious pork buns, none of which she could bring herself to eat earlier, were still sitting in the steamer waiting for her dad to get home. "Hang on, I'll bring you some."

She went into the kitchen, opened up the steamer, and picked out three large buns, wrapped them in a paper towel and took them outside. "I hope you're not still naked," she said as she opened the gate. They weren't.

The boy said, "We found some clothes."

Their attire consisted of an ill-fitting mishmash of T-shirts, sweat pants and jeans. The leader didn't even have shoes. She looked at the tallest boy's hot pink sweatpants dappled with yellow flowers. "Somehow I don't think those are yours."

The boy's mortified look said it all.

She handed each of them a pork bun. "My mom made these. They're awesome."

"What are they?" Jace said.

"They're called *nikuman*. Steamed pork buns."

"They got meat inside?"

"Yeah."

"Weird."

The tallest boy said, "What the hell is this?"

The leader said, "You heard her. It's a nee-koo-mahn."

"This ain't no American food. You Chinese or something?"

Mia tensed. "No, I'm American. But my mom is Japanese."

The leader said, "Yeah, butthead. Can't you tell she's American? Now say you're sorry. She's sensitive."

The tallest boy said, "Sorry."

Mia said, "It's okay, I guess."

The leader's cheek bulged. "Thanks for the nee-koo-mahn."

"You're welcome."

"What's your name?" he said.

"Mia."

"I'm Jace." He pointed to the tall, thin boy with a shock of unruly blond hair that looked like it had been trimmed by beavers. "The rude one is Lee."

Lee looked away sheepishly. "Shut up. Sorry."

Jace pointed to the dark-skinned boy. "That's Malcolm."

The boy rubbed his close-cut curly hair. "Call me Mal. It's a pleasure to make your acquaintance, Mia."

"Nice to meet you, too."

"So, why did you follow me? If my dad wasn't inside, I might have called the cops on you." Her dad was not, in fact, home at all.

The boy glanced at his companions. "Well, like I said. You're nice, and we could use some help. See, someone's chasing us. We're trying to get away from them."

"Is this a joke?"

"No."

"You were a mile from town, *naked!*"

"Um, that's a long story...They took our clothes."

"Who?"

"Can you help us?"

Lee shuffled his feet and didn't know what to with his hands. Like Sho. She said, "Then you should call the police. They can help you and—"

"No! No police."

"What? Why? Are you guys in trouble or something?"

"No, nothin' like that."

"And I'm supposed to believe you."

"Yeah, sorry. I know it sounds a little strange."

"A little?"

"Someone's tryin' to hurt us."

"If someone is trying to hurt you, we should call the police."

"Please, don't."

"Give me one good reason I shouldn't go inside right now and call the police and tell them I saw three naked kids out along Spearhead Trail and now they're in my backyard wearing a bunch of stolen clothes."

"It's complicated. Ain't a good idea. The people after us might have told the cops we done some bad things. Please, we don't want to be no trouble—"

"So what do you want then? If you won't call the cops, you better get out of here." She edged away, back toward the steps to the deck. "My folks are inside."

Lee said, "Jace, listen."

The boy who was speaking cocked his ear and froze.

Mia opened her mouth, but he shushed her. All she heard was the rhythmic drone of cicadas, punctuated by crickets, maybe some frogs. And something else, a howling yipping barking that sounded like it was bouncing back and forth between distant hills. "Are those coyotes?"

"Shh!"

Mia thought back to the enormous fangs rocketing toward her face just a hour before. Nate's gnawed bone under her foot.

"We should go," Jace said. "It ain't safe."

"Yeah," she said, "You should go." Fear tightened her chest again, and her words trembled in a way she had never experienced before, but she didn't know why. "Be careful." Her voice caught behind her tongue. "A friend of mine...was killed on that trail a couple of nights ago."

Jace paled and swallowed hard. "How?"

"I don't know, but I found some bones."

The boys traded glances. "Thanks for the nee-koo-mahn," Jace said. And they faded into the darkness.

CHAPTER FOURTEEN

Mia walked into the kitchen and stacked up her useless home-work on the kitchen table. Her mom leaned against the cor-ner of the hallway, eyes dull and bloodshot.

"Geez, Mom, you look tired. You should go to bed."

"I've been trying."

"You want some tea or something?"

"No. Do you know what Tuesday was?"

How could Mia forget? She nodded, but the old ball of dread reformed in her stomach, along with an impulse to flee like a rabbit. She didn't know which way to go.

"He would have been such a good boy. Everyone loved him."

Mia tensed. "Yes, he would have. He was."

Her mother's eyes flicked toward Mia's homework and hardened. *"He was such a good student."*

Mia's throat clenched, and tears started to form. But she didn't have enough strength left tonight for this argument. "Yes, he was," was all she could say. She went outside. She didn't need to see her mother shuffle back upstairs and head toward the bathroom. She plopped down onto a tree stump in the backyard and let the tears come. The bathroom light switched on, and she heard the shower begin to flow.

Suddenly every hair on her head, her arms, her legs stood on end. She stood and scanned the darkness within the wooden perimeter. The only light came from streetlights filtering through branches surrounding the fence and from the feeble glow of the kitchen light. A deep, heavy snuffling puffed underneath the backyard gate. An animal, something, and a big one. Something hard like nails scratched faintly over the paving stones on the path to the gate. More snuffling, sniffing.

Then the latch on the gate began to rattle.

Her blood froze.

The latch clicked and the door began to swing slowly inward.

In less than a heartbeat, she threw herself behind the backyard shed, which lay closer than the back patio door.

The gate squeaked faintly.

Her trembling hands sought the latch on the shed door, tried to slide it ever so gently, silently. A click that sounded like thunder as the latch released and the door swung open. She ducked inside and ever so gently, silently, eased the latch closed. There were spiders in here. She never went in the shed for just that reason, but she did not dare think about that now, did not dare think about the webs that might inches from her flesh, or all the little creepy-crawlies that waited in the dark to suck the fluids of insects unlucky enough to be ensnared. The sharp tangy smells of gasoline and oil and lawn fertilizer overlay the scent of earth and dust.

Moments after the door closed, the puff of breath came under the door, sniffing, the kind of sniffing that comes from deep, cavernous lungs, lungs that were not human. The sound came from the rear corner of the shed, moved along the base of the wall toward the front. Only a thin sheet of wood separated her from whatever that was, and it had to be enormous.

Mia's trembling hands shifted gears to earthquake mode. Don't rattle the latch!

The heavy breathing moved to the corner of the shed, then back to the door, and a shadow obscured the bottom half of the light square around perimeter of the door. Nostrils moved to the bottom corner of the door, sniffing at the crack. Mia imagined the breaths as they found their way inside driving up little clouds of dust from the floor of the shed.

Something hard, unyielding clamped over the latch on the outside, like the grip of a pliers.

Then a powerful snarl erupted outside, and the grip on the latch was torn away. Mia held it as tight as she could. Growls and snarls, deep and savage, tore through her backyard for several long, stomach-wrenching seconds and then stopped as suddenly as they had started.

Silence again.

Her lower lip quivered, and the entire shed rattled with the ferocity of her grip on the door latch.

Maybe it was gone now, whatever it was. For several long minutes — she didn't know how many—she stood there clasping the latch.

Then she heard a whisper. "Psst! Hey, Mia! You can come out. It's okay now."

She opened the door to see the three boys standing before her.

Lee said, "We chased it off."

"Chased what off? What was it?"

"A big dog."

"You mean like the size of an elephant, right?"

"Not that big. It's dark. You're scared. We chased it off," Jace said.

Mia took a deep breath and let it out. "Anyway, thanks." She didn't want to think about how a dog had opened her backyard gate and then tried to open the shed door as well, but those thoughts were starting to gnaw at her ability to speak.

Jace jumped in, "Look, it's gone now. No big deal."

Her hands began to unclench, and she wiped them on her legs to restore feeling in her fingers.

"Thanks again, you guys. Look, I'm sorry about before."

"It's okay," Jace said. "We understand where you're comin' from."

"I know it's not much, but maybe you could stay here. Maybe I can talk my mom into letting you share the living room floor and—"

"No," Jace said. "I don't want your folks to know. If it's all the same to you, this shed will do just fine."

"Are you sure?"

All three of them nodded.

"Okay, I'll go bring you some blankets, and a sleeping bag if I can find it."

She went inside, and her mother had retired from the bathroom to the bedroom and the light was off. Mia needed to be quiet, but not sound like she was sneaking around. She gathered some spare blankets, found the sleeping bag in the basement and bundled it all out to the shed, where the boys now sat in the dark. As she arranged the blankets, she said, "Have you guys known each other a long time?"

Jace said, "A few years."

Mal said, "I came the latest."

"Came where?"

Jace's gaze flicked toward Mal in the dimness, and Mal went silent.

Mia shrugged. "Look, you don't have to tell me. Keep your secrets. I'm not going to hurt you or turn you in." Then she fixed a look on Jace. "Unless you do something bad."

Jace said. "We just don't know who to trust is all. We don't want to hurt *nobody*." He said the last word with a strange vehemence.

She said, "What are you going to do tomorrow?"

"I don't know yet. We just need to get out of sight for a while, let the heat go down."

"What did you guys do, anyway?"

All three voices rose together. "Nothing!"

Mia said, "Who's hurting you?"

"Let's not talk about it."

"Hey, if somebody is hurting kids, don't you think the police should know about it?"

"The police can't do nothing. They'll just take us back. We can't go back. If you try to turn us in, or send us back, we'll run. So if you're planning something like that, tell me now, and we'll save you the trouble."

"Send you back where?"

"Never mind that. But I mean what I say."

Mia raised a hand. "Okay, geez. Settle down."

Malcolm said, "The police cannot help us. They wouldn't understand. It is an utterly intractable conundrum."

Mia blinked.

Jace said, "Mal likes readin' the dictionary."

Mia's throat thickened. Maybe Mal would like H.P. Love-something-or-other.

Lee said, "Thinks he's some sort of scientist."

Malcolm snorted. "Who's the one wearing sweats with flowers on the buttocks?"

"Shut up!" Lee hung his head and muttered, "Egghead dork."

Malcolm ignored him. "I intend to be a scientist someday."

Mia nodded. "What kind?"

"A geneticist. Or a virologist."

"Cool. I like biology too. And chemistry." Mia noted Lee edging away from them, his hands thrust deep into his pockets, his shoulders slumped. "What about you, Lee? What subjects do you like in school?"

"I hate school."

"Well, you're not alone there. Lots of people hate school."

Malcolm said, "Lee hates school because he can't read."

Lee snarled and punched Malcolm on the shoulder. "I can too!"

The blow was so hard that it knocked Malcolm over. "Ow! You butthead!"

"Why you always gotta run me down, Mal!"

Malcolm clutched his shoulder. "Because you're an ignorant buffoon, Lee!"

"Screw you!"

Jace waved a hand between them. "Enough! Shut the hell up, both of you!" Jace looked at Mia apologetically. "Lee has trouble reading because he didn't have no school till he was ten. He's a little behind is all."

Mia wondered what kind of life Lee was born into that he had had no schooling. "Where you from, Lee?"

Lee turned his shoulder away from them. "Lots of places."

"Where?"

"Texas, Oklahoma, Arkansas. Nebraska had some kind of law about protecting kids or something so my mama had the bright idea to just leave me here." Bitterness dripped from his tongue like acid.

Mia said, "I'm from lots of places, too. Yokohama, Okinawa, Los Angeles, Guam. My dad was in the Air Force, until he retired."

"I ain't never heard of some of them places. They in California?"

"Japan." Perhaps best not to tell them that her dad was a special agent for the F.B.I.

Jace said, "Does this door have a lock?"

"Yes, but it's broken."

Lee said, "That's not very safe. Don't nobody steal anything around here?"

Mia said, "No, this is a pretty good neighborhood."

Lee sniffed. "Somebody ought to."

Mia stiffened.

Jace jumped up and stood over him. "Don't you even think it!"

"I wasn't! It's just that these people got it so good—"

"Right! 'Cause they got jobs and schooling and ain't strung out on meth!"

Lee cast his eyes down.

Jace stepped toward him. "I thought you said you wanted to be good! You didn't want to be like them people you was living with before! And you didn't want to be like *him*."

"I do! I don't!"

"Then you treat these people with some respect! We are going to be guests in Mia's home! Er...her backyard at least. You give a little respect, you might get a little. That's what my grandpa always said. Right, Mia?"

Mia blinked. "Uh, right."

"You cause any trouble, I'll send you back there myself and let *him* have you! 'Cause then you'll be no better than them! You get me?"

Lee stood straight and faced Jace, his face grim, shoulders square. "I get you."

"Good. Mal, quit teasing him."

"What did I—"

"Just quit it, all right?"

"All right."

Mia finished arranging their bedding. "I'm sorry, it's kind of crappy."

Jace said, "It's okay. It's better than being in the open."

Mia looked toward the house. Better to hang out in the backyard than go back inside with a chance of running into her mother. She pulled the shed door shut.

The boys situated themselves around the small interior. A thread of dim light filtered around the edges of the door again, but the interior of the shed was tar-black.

Malcolm spoke in a hushed voice. "Hey, here's a flashlight!" A pillar of dusty light speared toward the ceiling.

Mia blinked and covered her eyes. "How did you find that in the dark?"

"Uh, just lucky I guess."

"Turn it off," Lee said, "it hurts my eyes."

Mia said, "Hide the beam so it's not so bright. I want to be able to see."

Malcolm situated the flashlight under Mia's duffel bag, so that the bag glowed a vague white, enough for her to see their outlines and faces.

Then she heard more snuffling at the door, and her heart almost exploded into her throat. She clamped both hands over her mouth.

"It's okay," Jace said, "It's just your dog."

Mia opened the door and Deuce poked his head into the interior. He must have ventured outside through the dog door for his nightly constitutional.

She reached for him, pulling him inside and hugging him close.

Jace said, "What's your dog's name?"

"Deuce." Mia rubbed the dog's head, and he lay down beside her.

Lee said, "How come he's all wrinkly like that?"

"That's the breed. He's a shar-pei."

"Looks kinda silly. Like his skin is too big." Lee held out his hand.

Deuce raised his head for a quick sniff, found Lee tolerable, then relaxed again.

A waft of breeze came through the opening. Jace sniffed it. "You guys smell anything?"

Lee said, "I can't smell nothing 'cept what's in here."

"Hear anything?"

Lee said, "Your flappin' lip."

The only thing Mia could hear was breathing, hers, and the boys around her. But they were not just breathing. They were sniffing. Then, after a minute or so, they relaxed. What was it? Had that big dog—or whatever it was—come back?

Distant howling filtered through the shed walls.

"You should go inside, Mia," Jace said. "We'll be fine. And don't worry, we won't be here in the morning."

"Why?"

"We don't want to stay in one place too long."

CHAPTER FIFTEEN

She needed to get Deuce in the house, or else he would start howling and barking himself any second. She opened the patio door for him. "Come on, Maximus Goonicus."

He clattered inside with her. She squealed and jumped a foot into the air at the sight of a dark shape standing in the kitchen.

"Jumpy aren't we?" her dad said.

"You scared the crap out of me!"

"Clearly. You're going to need new pants now."

"One doesn't make poop jokes about girls, Dad."

He chuckled. "Are you hearing that outside?"

She put on her best mask of innocence. "Hear what?"

"Listen."

"The howling?"

"Yeah. I'd swear some of those voices are wolves, off in the distance. I know what a coyote sounds like, and those are not coyotes."

Barks and howls seemed to come from all directions.

Mia said, "The neighborhood dogs are going berserk."

"Listen, it's like they're all talking to each other."

"But there aren't any wolves in Nebraska. Except in the zoo."

"It would certainly be strange." He shrugged, then turned his attention to her. "How are you doing, sweetheart? With everything that's happened, I mean."

"I'm okay. It's been a day, though. I'm headed for bed."

He sighed. "It's been a day for me, too. Probably be another one tomorrow." Something in his voice told her there was a story there that he would never tell her. He clicked on the light overlooking the backyard and locked the patio door.

"Are you going to leave the backyard light on?"

"Yeah, for tonight. There's all the talk of a mountain lion or something escaping from the zoo. Whatever it is will probably want to stay away from the light."

"Why are you gone so much lately?"

His expression darkened. "Something serious is happening. I can't tell you about it, and you wouldn't want to know if I could. The field office needs every ounce of man-power they have."

"Mom and me have been fighting a lot lately."

"She told me."

"It's never about Sho, but that's what it's about, you know?"

He flinched at the name, fixing his gaze out into the night.

"Dad, nothing will ever be okay until we all let it go."

"I know, sweetheart. Someday."

"I don't know what to do."

He leaned his forearm against the glass, then his forehead on his arm. "You're smart, Mia. You're my daughter. Whatever it is, you'll figure it out."

She almost protested, pleaded *Help me!* But then she stopped, and just hugged him. "'Night, Dad."

"'Night." He kissed her on the cheek.

She shuffled upstairs doing her best exhaustion walk. Even with the windows closed, the cacophony filtered in. She tried to rub some persistent goose bumps flat across her arms.

She waited until her parents were likely to be asleep before she snuck downstairs and grabbed a good armful of leftovers from the refrigerator. On her way through the house, she wondered what she would tell her parents about the armfuls of blankets and the sleeping bag she last used when she was twelve on a camping trip to Yellowstone. If asked, she would tell them that Deuce had lain on the blankets and not only sullied them with muddy doggy prints but also his unique doggy B.O. She treaded softly in her rainbow-colored fuzzy socks, stepping carefully on the stairs to avoid creaks. Darkness filled the house, chased away from the windows by streetlamps piercing the living room blinds and the square of patio light shining across the dining room floor. When she opened the patio door, backyard darkness yawned before her. The shed seemed hundreds of yards away. Deeper shadows lurked behind everything. She returned to the kitchen junk drawer and took out the flashlight. Its beam was feeble, but better than darkness. Her heart started to pound as she headed for the shed, her ears poised for any sounds of movement.

She knocked on the shed door. A torrent of panicked whispers sifted through the door.

Jace said, "Don't come in."

"Why? Are you all naked again or something?" Mia said.

Scuffling, shuffling noises.

"What's up?" she said. A bolt of nervous vibration shot through her as she shined the flashlight around the yard.

Another short pause, then Jace's voice came. "Okay, you can open the door."

She opened the door and the three of them were sitting facing her, trying to look innocent and carefree. The swinging door drew out a waft of the scent inside. Now, along with the smells of gasoline and lawn fertilizer, came something else, a thick, coppery scent.

"What are you guys doing?" She pointed the flashlight around inside the shed.

Jace wiped his mouth. "What you got there? Food?"

"Yes." She handed him the plastic containers and foil-wrapped bundles.

Jace reached out for it, and his hand passed into the flashlight beam. Reddish stains painted his palm and fingers.

"Is that blood on your hand?" she said.

"Nah."

"You're lying. What happened?"

"Nothing."

"I hate it when people lie to my face. Especially when I'm trying to help them."

"Look, you don't want to know, all right?"

She played the beam around inside the shed. Tucked behind a can of lawnmower gasoline was a clump of grayish-brown fur with a white tuft and wet, red stains. A fresh rabbit skin. But without the rest of the rabbit.

Lee wiped his mouth. Malcolm sat on his hands.

Mia said, "Um, did you guys just eat a rabbit?"

"'Course not!" Jace said.

"Then what's that?" She pointed.

Jace deflated. "That's, uh, a rabbit skin. Okay, yeah, we, uh, just, uh, ate a rabbit."

"Ew! Sick!"

"I knew you wouldn't understand."

"If you were hungry, you could have told me sooner!"

"We, uh, we need a special kind of food."

"What? Why? Raw, dead bunny? Seriously?"

"I can't tell you any more."

"What is up with you guys?"

"Mia, please don't make me tell you."

"Then how can I help you?"

"Please, for now, just trust me. We ain't gonna cause you no more trouble. We ain't gonna hurt nobody, 'specially you. We just need to lay low for a couple more days. Mal here needs a little more time."

"Time for what?"

"He's, uh, he's sick. He needs a couple more days to get over it, and then he'll be okay."

"Then he should see a doctor. What's wrong, Mal?"

Mal shifted where he sat, and turned his gaze into the corner. "I'm fine."

"The cure isn't eating bunnies, is it?"

"No," Jace said. "Like I said before, no cops. No doctors neither. A doctor would call the cops."

"Where'd you get the rabbit?"

Jace said, "I caught it over there by the fence."

Cottontails could turn on speed like an F-16 going supersonic. "You caught it."

"I did, yeah."

"God, this is impossible!" She threw up her hands. "Fine! Fine! I'm going to bed now. I'm exhausted. Just don't eat the neighbors' cats or anything."

"Whatever you say."

"You want me to bring you some live mice for breakfast?"

"Nah, too squirmy. Not enough meat on 'em."

Malcolm and Lee snickered.

Mia's sarcasm picked up speed. "Raw steak maybe?"

The boys quit snickering.

Jace smiled. "That might be all right."

Mia sighed and went back in the house, her mind whirling, and didn't sleep for a long time. Something niggled at her mind, but her mind was too weary and shocked to grasp it.

CHAPTER SIXTEEN

Mia's mother called up the stairs, "Mia, no school today."
Mia shuffled out of her bedroom, rubbing her eyes,
already dressed but still half-asleep. Not only had she been
all but unable to fall asleep, she had awakened at an obscene hour for
no explicable reason. Her dreams had tumbled with visions of fangs and
fur, the taste of the banana split on Dalton's lips, Nate's thigh bone, all
in a sick, relentless mess that she couldn't shut off. "Huh?"

"School is canceled today."

"Why? Anything about Nate?"

"No, they didn't say."

Mia trudged downstairs. No school meant that she wouldn't get
to see Dalton today. Unless she called him. Maybe he would call her.
Weren't boys the ones supposed to do the calling?

Her mom had made breakfast for her, some miso soup, along with
a raw egg cracked over a bowl of steaming rice. She thought about how
to take some food outside for the boys without her mom's notice. Were
they still out there?

As she picked up the rice and mixed the egg around like she had
hundreds of times, the punctured yolk spreading ribbons of sunrise-
yellow through the rice, the egg white making the rice grains glisten like
tiny pearls, it occurred to her that this little egg could have become a
baby chicken. A chicken with blood, and bones, and a brain, however
small. And that even though the heat from the rice cooked the egg a
little, it was still mostly raw. She set the bowl and looked at it for a while.

"What's wrong?"

Mia picked up the miso soup and sipped at it. "Nothing. Just thinking about a lot of stuff."

Deuce pattered into the kitchen, headed for his water bowl in the corner, and slobbered up copious quantities. Then he stood straight, ears cocked.

Mia's cell phone was ringing in her bedroom. She ran to retrieve it and answered just in time. "Yo, Nicki, what's up?"

Nicki's voice shrilled through the receiver. "Omigod, Mia! Turn on Channel 4! Now!"

Mia hurried downstairs and turned on the television. A Channel 4 News reporter stood outside of a house, backgrounded by several police cruisers. "...again, the girl's parents report they were awakened by a loud noise coming from the bedroom at around 4:15 a.m. They found the bedroom window broken out and their daughter gone. There were apparently signs of a struggle but, so far, no indication of how any intruder was able to reach the second-story window. Police are still investigating the scene, and they are treating this as a kidnapping." A photo appeared on the screen beside the reporter, a photo of a blonde, smiling face. "Tara Anderson is a junior at West High School. She is five feet seven inches tall, medium length blonde hair, blue eyes. The police are asking anyone with any information to call this hotline." The number appeared on the screen.

Mia sank onto the couch. "What is going on?"

Her mom stood nearby. "We saw her at school yesterday. Do you know her?"

"She was a friend of Nate's."

"Strange."

"Uh huh. Too strange. There has to be a connection." Mia's heart started ka-lumping in her chest, and not in the nice Dalton-way.

"The police haven't confirmed that the body was your friend's have they?"

"No, but I know it was him. I just know it."

Her mom sat down beside her. "Mia, please be careful. If someone is going after students connected to this—"

"I know, Mom."

Her mom's hands started to wring each other like washcloths. "*Your father is worried, too.*"

"Does he know anything about Tara and Nate?"

"I don't know."

"It's not a serial killer or something is it? Terrorists?"

"I don't know."

A vehicle rolled into the driveway, and Deuce ran to the door to await the credentials of the incoming guest. Mia's mom got up and peered outside. "Sarah."

Mia relaxed like a deflated balloon. Had she really been so tense? Bad news lurked around every corner. And hiding in the shed were still three boys who liked to eat fresh bunny.

Sarah's face looked pinched and tight when she came in.

Mia hugged her, trying to squeeze some of Sarah's wiry strength into herself. "What's wrong?"

"Oh, nothing. Just came over to see how you're doing. I brought bagels." She held out a paper bag.

Mia's mom took the bag. "Mia's right. Something is bothering you."

"Well," Sarah took a deep breath and sighed, "I would love to tell you, but I can't. It involves work."

Mia said, "Nate's friend Tara was kidnapped last night."

Sarah froze, her brow knitting, her lips pursed. "That's strange."

"We've already covered that ground." Mia let enough frustration into her voice to show that she knew Sarah was holding back. Sarah *knew* something.

Sarah's gaze met hers for a long moment, searching, then she spun on her heel for the kitchen. "So let's have a bagel."

A bagel and cream cheese suddenly sounded better to Mia than a bowl of rice with scrambled unborn baby chicken. God, she hoped she wasn't becoming vegetarian. Mia followed Sarah, and as Sarah stood near the table, her nostrils flared, and she fixed her gaze on Mia again.

"So, Mia. Anything else...strange going on?"

The pressure of Sarah's gaze bored into her. "Um, I don't know what you mean. The last few days have been crazy."

Sarah sniffed again, crossed her arms, went to the patio door, slid it open. "It sure is a beautiful morning. Too nice for all this crazy stuff.

Might as well enjoy it."

"A great idea," Mia's mom said. "Let's sit outside and enjoy the morning." She took out a teacup for Sarah and carried the warm teapot outside to the picnic table on the patio.

Sarah stood at the head of the steps leading down to the grass, her gaze hard and piercing. "So, have you seen anything strange out here lately? No mountain lions or anything?" She cracked a half-smile.

Mia almost jumped. "Nope! Nothing!"

Her mom said, "Well, last night Marc thought he saw something out here. It was too dark to be sure, though."

"'Something?'"

Her mom shrugged. "He said it was too dark to see clearly."

Sarah descended the steps to the grass, lifting her nose.

Mia said, "What is it with the sniffing? You're not a dog."

Sarah said, "Just thought I smelled something unusual. Can't you smell it?"

"I can't smell anything except a bagel and cream cheese screaming my name. What about you? Do you want one?"

"Sure." Sarah's tone was distracted as she strolled, almost aimlessly, across the backyard, vaguely toward the shed.

Mia's mom called, "What are you doing?"

"Just looking around." Her arms were crossed. As she neared the shed, her attention turned toward the ground. A small patch of earth near the door of the shed was trampled bare of grass. She knelt over the patch of earth.

Mia's heart pounded against her ribcage. "Uh, what kind of bagel do you want?"

Sarah touched the earth. "You said Marc saw something. Was it around here?"

"Yes, by the shed, he said."

Even at this distance, Mia could see Sarah tense. Mia gulped for air. Sarah stood and reached for the shed's door handle.

"Don't go in there!" Mia cried.

Sarah turned toward her, puzzled.

Her mom said, "Mia, what is wrong with you?"

"I saw a spider over there the size your head yesterday! And it's...

really messy. Lots of sharp stuff everywhere." Mia sank into a chair, defeat filling her belly like lead bricks. What on Earth would she say when three sheepish boys shuffled out? Pretend she didn't know?

Sarah smiled and turned back to the door, but she opened it cautiously, standing aside as if expecting something to burst out.

The shed entrance stood at an angle from the patio deck, so Mia could not see inside.

Sarah looked in. "Wow."

Mia's stood up. "It's just that—!"

"You're right, Mia. It is messy in here." Sarah shut the door and started back toward the patio.

Mia's blood thundered in her ears. Her hands shook. She sank back into a chair, her vision fixated on the blueberry bagel in front of her, its bluish-purple veins swirling across the surface.

Sarah sat down across from her.

Mia's mom watched them both, the perplexity plain on her face.

"I'll have to tease Marc now for keeping such a messy shed," Sarah said, her gaze fixed on Mia.

Mia couldn't meet Sarah's gaze.

"After breakfast," Sarah said, "I have some errands to run. Why don't you come with me, Mia?"

Mia gulped. "Sure."

CHAPTER SEVENTEEN

M ia's hands were shaking as she shut the door of Sarah's Jeep. What had Sarah seen in the shed?

Sarah said nothing as she backed out of the driveway, shifted into Drive, and eased onto the gas.

Mia's cell phone rang. The caller ID said, "Pay Phone."

The unspoken questions hung between her and Sarah like thunderclouds roiling to cut loose. She answered the call, glad of the need to speak to someone else. "Hello?"

"Mia, it's Jace."

She tried to keep her voice neutral and friendly. "Um, where are you?"

"At the Quick Shop about four blocks from your house."

Relief flooded through her like a dash of warm water. "Thank god! Everything all right?"

"For now. Say, are you with your friend Sarah?"

"With my Aunt Sarah, yeah, we're running some errands."

"Something's up with her. You might be in danger."

"What? What are you talking about?"

"I can't explain, but something is definitely up with her. We were hiding under your patio while you guys had your bagels. Bring her someplace where you can talk to her and we can see you."

"Why?"

"Just trust me, okay?"

"*You* want to help *me* with math, Nicki? You haven't cracked a book all semester!"

"Just trust me."

"Well, I'm kind of in the car right now."

"Get a cup of coffee here at the Quick Shop or something."

Mia sighed. "I'll see what I can do." She hung up and gave Sarah a big grin that she hoped didn't look too fake. "So, where are we going?"

"I'm trying to decide whether I should take you to the police station or to the F.B.I. office to talk to your dad."

Mia's hair practically stood on end, and she spun to face Sarah. "What? What are you talking about?"

Sarah turned her sharp, steady gaze onto Mia. "I think there are some things you need to tell me."

Mia slumped into her seat.

"Mia, whatever it is, I need to know. This could be huge."

Mia sighed again. "Okay, but first take me to the Quick Shop. I need, uh, a cup of coffee." God, she hated lying.

"You drink coffee?"

"Uh, yeah. A nice frappaccino or something. My hands are shaking." And that was no lie.

As Mia and Sarah pulled up to the Quick Shop, she saw the boys inside through the plate glass window, sitting in one of the small booths set aside for coffee drinkers and donut eaters. Mia went inside to pretend to look for something to drink. She ignored the boys and they ignored her as she snatched two milk coffees from the cooler. Her stomach was twisted in knots so tight she could hardly breathe.

Back in the Jeep, she gave one of the coffees to Sarah, hoping her gesture of consideration might reduce the impact of what was coming. She fretted with her coffee, waiting for the six-hundred ton weight to land on her head.

Sarah's steady gaze was implacable, opaque, patient.

Maybe Mia could still keep the boys out of this, but then maybe Sarah would understand the difficult situation they were in. She was a very understanding person, but today she was acting strangely. This seriousness and tension were not like her at all.

Mia took a deep breath and then a drink to wet her parched mouth. "Our trip to the zoo yesterday got me thinking. I wanted to say goodbye to Nate, so I rode out there, and...something weird happened. There were these big dogs that chased me, then they disappeared."

"What did they look like?"

"Well, they were big, like really big. Like big Huskies."

"You mean, like wolves?"

Mia gulped again. Her mind had been dancing around that idea for some reason. "There aren't any wolves in Nebraska."

"So they say."

"So then, this other one jumped out of the bushes at me. Scared me off my bike."

"It attacked you?" Sarah's eyes bulged and began to search Mia's arms and skin. "Did it...hurt you?"

"No, I fell off my bike. There must have been some others there, and it sounded like his huge fight, and I just hid. Then they all disappeared. I got the hell out of there. I didn't say anything because I didn't want Mom and Dad to worry." Mia let her voice trail off, hoping Sarah wouldn't press her for more.

"You were incredibly lucky last night."

"I kind of figured that out already."

"So what was in the shed that you didn't want me to see?"

Mia shrugged.

"Mia."

"I know, I know. You can read minds. I can't tell you, though."

"Why not?"

Mia sighed and squeezed her can of coffee.

"Are you protecting someone?"

Mia nodded.

"From whom?"

"I...I don't know what to do. There's so much weird stuff happening, and it's freaking me out and...I don't know what to do."

Sarah ran her fingers through her hair. "Okay. Here's what I can tell you, and maybe you'll back me up. Last night, something came into your back yard. Something very big and very bad. Worse than you realize. And it might well come back."

"You mean a mountain lion?"

"I don't think so. The tracks I saw in the dirt near your shed were not feline."

"Do you know what it was?"

"Maybe. And you know more about it than you're telling me. Mia, this is serious. Something bad happened to your friend, and I'm sorry about that, but if this goes on, bad things will happen to a lot of people."

"You said, 'very bad'. What does that mean?"

"Something that could have—and likely would have—torn you into shreds without a second thought, and whoever else was hiding in that shed."

As Sarah's words sank in, Mia raised her gaze from the can of coffee to Sarah's face. "How did you know that?"

Sarah tapped her temple.

"Geez, I can't keep any secrets at all."

"There's something else. I'm going to be staying with you for a while."

"Really? Why?"

"Girl bonding." Sarah grinned.

Mia sighed. "Mom has been in a better mood since you've been here."

"That's good. And no, you're not going to be able to hide anything from me while I'm there, so you might as well come clean."

"Stop that!"

Sarah shrugged.

"When the dogs were chasing me." The wolves? "I met some kids." She was such a squealer. The sickness in her belly thickened. "Three boys. They were running from someone, someone who wanted to hurt them, they said. They asked me to help them." She felt the eyes of the boys upon her, even though they were studiously pretending not to watch. They couldn't hear her conversation with Sarah.

"Help them do what?"

"Just hide them for the night. Give them a place to sleep."

"So you put them in the shed."

"They were afraid Mom and Dad would have called the police."

"They were right about that. Why not call the police?"

"I think someone there is abusing them. They mentioned some guy that they're afraid of."

"Why are they inside?"

Mia's mouth dropped open.

"This is what I do, Mia. And I'm good at it."

"Remind me never to try to hide anything from you ever again."

Sarah smiled, reached over and patted Mia's hand. "No need to scare them off. Nothing is going to hurt them right now. Are they going back to your place?"

"I don't know."

Sarah pulled out her wallet, withdrew some cash, and handed it to Mia. "Go in and buy them some food. I'm going to pretend to go to the bathroom. Don't worry, I'm not going to let them know you ratted them out."

"Gee, thanks. I feel so much better."

Sarah squeezed her hand. "You did the right thing."

The boys tensed when Mia and Sarah went inside, but Sarah breezed by them on her way to the restroom, seemingly oblivious to their presence.

Mia did her best to act sneaky. She noticed that the boys' faces and hands looked clean now, their hair freshly combed. She didn't want to know where they got the sneakers. "Here, take this." She handed Jace the cash. "Get yourselves something to eat."

"Thanks. That your aunt?" His gaze was glued to the door of the women's restroom.

Mia nodded.

"You trust her?"

"Of course!"

Jace frowned. "She ain't been acting funny has she?"

Mia hesitated for only a instant. "No, why?"

"Never mind. Any grocery stores around here?"

Mia pointed down the street outside. "Supermarket eight or ten blocks that way."

"Okay, thanks. Let's go, men." The three of them started sliding out of the booth.

"Thank you, Mia," Malcolm said. His face was strangely pale, his cheeks drawn.

Mia said, "Mal, are you feeling all right?"

"I'll be utterly in capital condition soon. Right now, my stomach is indisposed."

Mia pulled out her purse and gave Jace all of her lunch money for the week. "Get Mal some medicine or something, too."

Jace pocketed the money. "He'll be okay."

Her mind went back to the image of Jace's bloody fingers and an empty rabbit skin. "When are you coming back?"

"After dark. We can lay low until then."

"What then?"

"We'll talk. We gotta hash out a plan." With that, he led the other two outside, where they disappeared around the corner of the store.

Moments later, Sarah came out of the restroom. "Are they gone?"

Mia nodded. "What now?"

"Now, we really do have a couple of errands to run. Things could get pretty hairy before this is over."

CHAPTER EIGHTEEN

S arah had gone into Guns and Ammo Unlimited, leaving Mia to wait in the Jeep, when Mia's cell phone chirped. The screen said, "Dalton."

She answered as nonchalantly as she could manage. "Hey."

"Hey, Lucy Liu."

Her voice grew cold. "Lucy Liu is Chinese." Was Dalton one of those small-minded Midwestern idiots who didn't know the difference between China and Japan? How many times had she been called a 'Chink' by that select group of high-school jackasses? Who was it that had first called her Moo-Goo-Gai-Pan, and how many times had she wished for fleas to infect that boy's crotch?

"I know that, but she was Japanese in *Kill Bill*, so there."

Her ears warmed like fuzzy muffs. "Oh."

"Pick a smokin' hot Japanese actress and maybe I'll compare you to her. It's been a pretty weird week, huh."

"You have no idea." How could she tell him she had almost been killed last night? Then again, maybe he would come running and be her knight in shining leather jacket. He had said *Smoking hot*.

"How are you doing?"

"I'm still here. No kidnapping or serial killers." She groaned internally; god, she sounded like such an idiot.

"I'm glad to hear you still have your sense of humor. So I've been thinking about Saturday."

Oh, no. Was he going to cancel? Her heart landed on the floor of the

Jeep, between her feet, and started to flop around like a fish in the bottom of a boat. She tried to keep her voice even. "What about Saturday?"

"Look, with all the stuff going on, I just wanted to make sure we're still on."

Her heart leaped like a golden salmon back up into her chest and started to glow like the sun. Her hands started shaking. *Breathe deep, let it out, relax, relax. Coolness. Calmitude.* "I suppose so. No more scary movies."

"I'll make sure to protect you from the werewolves."

"Right. And I'll bring the holy water."

"That's for vampires. Werewolves' weaknesses are silver bullets and wolfsbane."

Oh, yeah. Duh. She slapped her forehead.

His voice sounded hopeful. "So are you doing anything this afternoon?"

"This afternoon? You mean, um, today?"

He said, "Yeah. I'm going to Caffeine Dreams for a while. Want to come and hang out a while?"

"I'm, uh, indisposed at the moment, but I'll see what I can do. I'll make sure I forward this to my secretary."

"Okay, my people will call your people." He laughed. He had such a deep laugh.

After she hung up, it occurred to her that she hadn't yet manufactured a story about Saturday for her parents, much less been granted clearance for hanging out at a coffee shop with...somebody.

Sarah came out of the store, climbed into the Jeep, and tossed a bag onto Mia's lap. "A little protection. Put that in your pocket and leave it there until further notice."

Mia reached into the bag. "What is it?"

"You know those 180 decibel airhorns? The really painful ones?"

"Yeah, some joker blasted one of those in the girls' bathroom last semester. If I hadn't been in the bathroom already, I would've peed my pants." Mia took the innocuous black box with its single, ominous red button out of the packaging.

"This one only works on animals. It's ultrasonic."

"So humans can't hear it."

"Right. Just don't use it anywhere near Deuce or you're liable to turn him into a whimpering wreck."

Mia raised her thumb over the button to try it.

"Don't!" Sarah grabbed Mia's wrist.

"Ow! Nice grip!"

"Sorry. I mean, just only use it if you're danger. You know, mountain lions, big dogs."

The memory of the something big and deadly snuffling at the door of the shed tightened her fingers around the device. It was about the size of a cell phone, easy to shove into her pocket.

"And yes, I'm loading you up with weapons, but here." Sarah handed Mia an ominous black cylinder, the size of a small thermos, also with a big red button.

"What on Earth is 'Bear Spray'?"

"Never mind that. I want you to keep that on you until further notice. It's pepper spray, with a heavy dose and a thirty-five foot range. Backpackers use it. It'll stop a charging grizzly dead in his tracks."

"You're telling me there are bears around here?"

"You never know."

"And why on Earth do you have this?"

"Never mind that. And if you spray that in your own face, you'll be awfully damn sorry."

Mia dangled it gingerly between two fingers, like a large grenade that could go off in her hand. On one hand, she liked the idea of having some sort of self-defense, in light of everything that had happened, but on the other hand, she had never held anything the only purpose of which was to cause incapacitating pain. "I'm going to need a backpack for my arsenal. I'll bet you have grenades too."

"Put it in your backpack or your jacket pocket."

Mia sighed and acquiesced.

Jace's shoes were beginning to cramp his toes. All three boys walked with their faces pointed toward the sidewalk. The breeze wafted a chorus of scents into his nostrils. The chemical stench of cars and over-fertilized lawns, perfumes and colognes and hairsprays and mouthwashes drifting from the windows of homes and passing cars, the smell of the blood from a woman on her period, the sweat of a man who had just worked out, the smell of another man who must have eaten a whole can of beans, the presence of hundreds of little critters that lived just below the surface of human notice, squirrels, rabbits, raccoons, opossums, rats, mice, snakes, insects, the sharp tang of a swarming anthill, the smell of autumn coming, a slight nip in the air that he had never sensed back in Killeen, Texas. Someday, he would have all of this sorted out. It was the only way he would ever be able to own what had happened to him.

Lee's hands were thrust deep in his sweatpants pockets. "So, what are we gonna do?"

Jace had been thinking about Lee's question since they woke this morning just before dawn. "First, we're gonna get some food. We'll all feel better when we get some meat."

Malcolm sighed. "It's just so grotesque. I can't believe that I love it more than I used to love chocolate."

"It's like *he* said. We need it. If we don't get it, we get sick, at least in the beginning."

Lee snorted. "I thought you weren't gonna mention *him* anymore."

Malcolm said, "How long before you got over the shakes and queasiness, Jace?"

"About three weeks. Your body is changing."

Malcolm kicked a crack in the sidewalk. "Sometimes it feels like it doesn't belong to me anymore."

Lee said, "Yeah, and I just started growing hair on my junk, you know?"

Malcolm made a face. "God, T.M.I.!"

Jace laughed. "Ain't no call to be embarrassed, Mal. Everybody's got hair on their junk."

"I don't want any vision of Lee's junk anywhere inside my cranium."

"We ain't just boys no more," Jace said.

"No, we're something else, something not right," Lee said.

All three of them sighed at that and walked.

Lee said, "So what are we gonna do?"

Jace's teeth clenched. "Like I said, we're gonna get some meat and—"

"No, I mean after that. You want to be the leader, it's your job to come up with the plan, right? So what's the plan, leader?"

"I'm working on that."

"So how long you gonna work on it? Because you know damn well that *he's* got a plan. I say we just say screw it and get the hell out of town, jump a train or something."

Jace shoved his hands further in his pockets. "We got nowhere to go."

Malcolm said, "What if we run into more of *them*?"

Lee said, "We keep going. Anywhere else, far away, has got to be better."

Jace shook his head. "What if we could stop him? What if we could find someone who'll believe us? We have to tell somebody what's going on! Maybe somebody can stop him!"

Malcolm affected a terrible British accent. "An admirable position. That's why I signed up for this regiment, old chap. Someone has to serve him with a cease and desist."

Lee's face went sourer than normal. "Yeah, but why us?"

Jace said, "Who else?"

"There's a lot more of *them!*"

"I know that. I'm fixin' to come up with a plan. I'll let you know." The truth was that Jace was hoping something came to him. As long as he didn't think about things too hard, an idea always came to him when he needed it. But this time, the ideas were taking their awful sweet time about it. The weight of what was looking for them felt like hot breath on the nape of this neck.

"Yeah, you do that." The acid in Lee's voice twisted Jace's blood into anger.

Jace snarled and turned to face Lee. "Maybe you want to be the leader, ass face." His voice deepened. His hands clenched into fists, and the muscles of his arms coiled and bulged under his skin like living ropes, reconfiguring themselves. His shoulders swelled. His legs thickened, his feet elongating. His chest deepened, tightening his shirt. His nails gouged into his palms.

Lee swallowed hard, but he stiffened, meeting Jace's gaze with bone-hard tenacity.

Malcolm stuck a hand between them. "Not here, you guys, geez! It's daylight. We're trying to be surreptitious, remember?"

"What the hell does that mean?" Lee growled.

Jace snarled, "I think it means 'sneaky.'"

"Right," Mal said, "so can we please go back to being sneaky? If you want to fight a challenge, do it later, out of sight."

Jace edged closer to Lee. "Fine. Until then, what I say goes. Got it?"

Lee's teeth clenched. "Got it."

Jace stepped away and resumed his path down the sidewalk. The others followed. The towering sign for the supermarket came into view a couple of blocks ahead. His shoulders and arms slid back to their normal size, leaving him with that familiar tingling sensation as if a hundred little electric shocks had just wiggled through him. His heart slowed to its normal rhythm. He flexed his shoulders until his neck popped. Then he noticed that the sides of both shoes had split open. He sighed. "Damn it, Lee. There goes another pair of shoes."

CHAPTER NINETEEN

What was it about Dalton that turned Mia's entire body into the buzzer on a cell phone? She sat alone at a table in Caffeine Dreams, her gaze drifting around the abstract paintings that adorned the red-brick walls. She had convinced Sarah that she needed a little alone time. Sarah hadn't liked the idea, but Mia now had a dangerous bulge in her jeans pocket, the ultrasonic blaster, and bulky weight in her jacket pocket, the bear spray. They felt bulky and uncomfortable, but she found herself often fingering them.

To distract herself from the excitement of waiting for Dalton and all the other annoying junk going round and round in her head, she turned her attention to the music playing inside the shop. A song of almost unbearable melancholy filled the room with strange, unexpected chords and a deep, scratchy voice. Nearby, a man was typing on a laptop, and his face grew more anguished with each verse.

> I hurt myself today
> To see if I still feel
> I focus on the pain
> The only thing that's real

Each repeat of the chorus furrowed the man's brow deeper and deeper with the containment of some immense inner pain. His lips moved with the lyrics. When the song was finally over, he sniffed and poured fresh vigor into his fingers.

He looked to be about her dad's age, large build, with streaks of gray running through his goatee and sideburns. Her heart went out to him, because he didn't look creepy, only tortured. How often had she seen that look on her father's face? "Excuse me, sir. That song was pretty dark. What was it?"

He blinked as if shaken from a trance, then trained his haunted eyes on hers. "Johnny Cash. The song was 'Hurt.'"

"I'd say it was nice, but it's got to be one of the saddest songs I have ever heard." Nate's smiling face leaped into her mind, the image of him tossing a baseball. As far as she knew, Nate had never once touched a baseball.

The man wiped his lips and swallowed hard. "It's a Nine Inch Nails cover, but the Cash version is better."

"I haven't heard either version before."

He continued as if he had only barely heard her speak. "It's about finding yourself alone, and the pain we cause the people who love us. Sometimes something happens that you can't understand, couldn't see coming, but it changes everything."

"Tell me about it."

He went on, muttering as if he had not heard her. "You question what you have become, and don't understand why it happened. That line about everyone going away in the end just tears me up. Sorry." He flashed her a half-smile that could only sustain itself for a second. "I'm overloading you a little."

"It's okay. It's been a freaky few days. I lost a friend this week." For some reason, she wanted this stranger to listen.

"I have a daughter a little older than you." His eyes went to the laptop screen and the corner of his mouth quivered. "What are you, fourteen?"

She stood straighter. "Sixteen."

"Same age then. Too young to start losing friends."

"It sucks."

"There's going to be more of that."

Did he mean life in general or for her? His tone made her think he was alluding to something specific, something that went beyond the obvious platitude.

He continued, "I was writing something."

She blinked and stiffened. "You're not going to...um, kill yourself or anything are you?"

He smiled a heart-broken smile. "No, nothing that simple. You wouldn't understand, and neither will she. But I have to do it."

"I'm sure she would rather have her dad around. Are you getting divorced or something?" She pursed her lips then. Oh, sure, Mia, maybe you should just give him some paper cuts and squirt lemon juice on them.

He smiled wanly. "You're direct, aren't you." Then he folded up his laptop. "Again, considerably more complicated than that. Sometimes you have to do the right thing for your family even when it's the hardest thing you could possibly imagine. I see I'm creeping you out a little. Sorry. Time for me to go." He slipped the laptop into a case.

The thought of her own father suddenly walking out of her life brought a lump into her throat. "Maybe you can work it out. Whatever it is."

"Maybe someday somebody can. I can't." He stood up and tucked the laptop case under his arm. "I have to go, kiddo. Take care of yourself." He turned toward the door.

"You, too."

"No, I mean it." His eyes met hers with a deep, electric flicker. "Be careful." He hurried out.

Elsewhere around the shop, couples and friends chatted over mugs and chessboards, lounged on comfy-looking couches.

Mia's belly suddenly felt like a vast sour cave. Her chair had been comfortable only a few minutes ago. That was the most ominous thing anyone had ever said to her. She sipped her hot chocolate, trying to dispel the cold unpleasantness in her throat.

Her gaze turned outward through the front windows and tracked the man as he hurried toward his car. Three familiar boys emerged from an alley on the back side of the parking lot, ambling toward him. What on Earth were they doing here? Following her?

The man noticed the boys, and all four of them froze in place, eyes glued to each other. For several seconds they held their positions. Jace slid to the side and the other two followed him, maintaining their distance from the man. He turned with them. They were too far away for her to see the expressions on their faces, but the tension in their shoulders and stances was plain. The man side-stepped to his car, eased open the door, and slid inside, closing the door, roaring the engine, and squealing out of the parking lot. The boys watched him until the car disappeared down the street, then they spoke to each other furtively, puzzled expressions on their faces.

The front door tinkled as they entered. Jace spotted her immediately and approached.

Mia said, "What are you guys doing here? How did you know I was here?"

"We followed you."

"How? You don't have a car."

"Never mind that. We had to find you."

"What's up?"

"We were walking by Elm Creek Park. You know where that is?"

"Sure." She had spent several afternoons there over the summer, playing with Deuce or reading.

"The place was swarming with cops. I think they found another body."

"That's terrible, but I can't do anything about that right now. It's just, I'm supposed to meet a guy here and—"

Lee snickered. "Mia's got herself a boyfriend, Jace."

"He's not my boyfriend. Not yet. Er, well—"

Jace waved it off. "Whatever, we just had to tell you."

"Why?"

"'Cause the body was mostly just chewed up bones."

"How do you know that?"

"Heard them talking."

Could it be Tara? "Did they say who it was?"

"No. But it might have something to do with your friend. We should go back before the cops and gawkers spoil all the scent trails."

"Scent trails? What are you talking about?" Something in her brain clicked, but she couldn't believe it. Three dogs. No, three wolves. Three naked boys. No, impossible.

"Never mind. You coming or not?"

The door tinkled again, this time admitting a tall figure in a leather jacket.

Her chest tensed and her blood tingled. She waved to Dalton.

Dalton's eyes never left hers as he walked up. "Hey."

"Hi," Mia said.

He regarded the three boys. "What's up, little dudes."

Jace and Lee stiffened.

"Dalton," Mia said, "this is Jace, Lee, and Malcolm, kids from my neighborhood. Guys, this is Dalton."

Dalton held out his hand. Jace sniffed once and shook it with skepticism. Malcolm gave Dalton's hand a single authoritative shake. Lee just ignored Dalton's extended hand, nodded and muttered, "Hey."

Dalton said, "Nice to meet you all. I'm going to grab a drink. Be right back." He sauntered off toward the ball.

"Douche nozzle," Lee muttered.

"Hey!" Mia said. "That's not nice!"

Jace nodded. "Yeah, man. That's Mia's prospective squeeze."

Mia rolled her eyes. "You guys have to get out of here before you screw this up for me."

Jace sighed. "You're right. Just thought we had something important to tell you is all. You told your friend that you wanted to help."

"Sorry. Look, why don't you guys go back there. I'll catch up. I know where it is. I promise."

Jace considered this for a moment. "Whatever."

As they all turned to leave, their disappointment painted on their faces, Mia said, "Seriously. I promise."

Jace nodded, and they departed.

Dalton sat next to her and looked into her eyes. "Alone at last."

She giggled. "What about all these other people?"

"I don't see anybody else here."

Mia's face heated, and she took a drink. His gaze smoldered. She couldn't meet it for long. Then he leaned back in the chair, and she was able to relax, and for a few minutes they chatted about school and friends and all the strangeness of Nate's and Tara's disappearances. But she didn't discuss the strangeness of events in her backyard, or the niggling suspicion about the boys that her logical mind was so reluctant to accept. Because such things didn't exist. They couldn't. That was only scary movie stuff.

Dalton had been talking. "...And you're really not listening to me at all. Hello, Earth to Mia!"

She blinked, swept her suspicions under a nice thick rug. "Sorry. I was just thinking about going for a walk over to Elm Creek Park."

He gave her a crooked smile. "Sounds like fun. Let's go."

She pushed her bicycle, and he walked beside her. The day was warm and sunny, but the bite of impending autumn lingered in the air. Yellow streaked the curtain of leaves. She wished she didn't have her bike now so that she could walk closer to him.

Elm Creek Park was a square city block of trees and well-manicured grass. Elm Creek wandered along the backside of the park, high embankments protecting the park against floods. A playground occupied the center, and a carefully landscaped garden in the corner of the park was filled with sun-bright chrysanthemums, sprays of pink and purple asters, scattered blood droplets of roses.

A fleet of police cruisers with dazzling arrays of blue and red strobes had cordoned off the corner of the park around the garden. A crowd had formed on the sidewalk and spilled around the barriers. Three news vans with transmission booms reaching toward the sky sat parked across the street.

Dalton whistled. "Looks like a circus. Maybe we should just stay out of there."

Mia paused, scanning the crowd for the boys. She had to know what was going on.

"Where are you going?" Dalton said.

"I want to see." Part of her felt like a rubber-necking jerk, worried that Dalton would think she was, but she needed to know. She pushed her bike toward the news vans.

She recognized the woman reporter from the zoo broadcast. The reporter stood with a microphone in hand beside a van, preparing herself for a broadcast.

Mia continued closer, and Dalton followed. "Mia are you sure?"

The cameraman waved to the reporter, who tucked stray locks of blonde hair behind her ear. "Okay, all set. Ready in five, four..." He started counting down to zero on his fingers.

The reporter's face was earnest. "Christine Miller reporting from Elm Creek Park, where a neighborhood resident this morning discovered a half-buried collection of human remains, the second to be found within the Omaha Metro area in the past week. According to Joann Dawson, who was taking her dog for a walk at around 8 a.m., she discovered the remains located in the beautiful flower garden that Elm Creek Park is known for. The identity of the victim and the cause of death are under investigation. We'll remain on the scene for this developing story. This is Christine Miller, Eyewitness News."

The cameraman said, "Okay, we're out."

The reporter lowered her microphone. "Did you upload the interview with the witness?"

"Yup. Poor old lady. I think she just about keeled over."

Mia stepped forward. "Excuse me, um, I live right over there." She pointed vaguely toward some houses down the street. "I know Mrs. Dawson. Is she okay?"

The reporter gave her a sympathetic smile. "They took her to the hospital to calm her down."

"What did she see?"

"She said she found a bunch of bones hidden in one of the flower beds, or I should say the Shih Tzu found the bones."

"Do you think there's a connection between this and the zoo animals?"

The reporter's eyes widened.

Mia beamed a smile at her. "Yes, I saw the report you did."

The woman smiled back, blushing a little, then glanced around, lowering her voice. "Maybe. The bones were bloody and some of them were broken. The police won't say yet, but it could be an animal attack."

"So the bones were fresh?"

"I suppose so. You say you live around here?"

Mia nodded. Actually, she lived more than a mile from here.

"You see anything unusual? Any mountain lions?"

"No, but the other night all the dogs in the neighborhood went ballistic, all at the same time. That was weird I guess."

The reporter pursed her lips, losing interest. "Okay, well, give my regards to Mrs. Dawson."

"I will. Thanks!" Mia pushed her bike on down the street, and as she did, her cool, confident demeanor fell away, and her mouth fell open. She couldn't believe she had just done that! Suddenly she felt like a detective in a mystery story. It had been so easy!

Dalton sidled up to her. "So what was that all about? You don't live anywhere near here."

"Just getting a little information."

"What for?"

Mia shrugged. How could she explain it to him? So she changed the subject. "Hey, how do you know where I live?"

Dalton shrugged, then he pointed. "Hey, aren't they those kids from the coffee shop?"

Her gaze followed his finger to where the three boys were standing on the fringe of the crowd of onlookers. "Um, looks like they're curious, too." Then past them, she saw another familiar shape stalking toward the boys. She would never forget that short, stocky frame or those piercing blue eyes. His gaze speared the boys with recognition. He walked as quickly as he could without drawing too much attention, using the crowd to obscure his approach. They had not yet noticed him.

She opened her mouth to call out, but at that moment, Malcolm happened to spot Slade's approach. Malcolm yelped a warning. The other two spun. Then all three lunged away from the crowd, darting for an alley between two houses. Slade dropped the pretense of his casual approach and sped after them. His gym shorts hugged his hairy, rippling legs, and his Saint Sebastian's golf shirt made him look like a block of solid muscle.

"Oh, no!" Mia said. There were police officers everywhere, but none of them could help.

Dalton touched her shoulder. "What is it?"

She had to do something.

Slade disappeared down the alley after the boys. He was going to drag them back to Saint Sebastian's and abuse them or something. The terror on their faces had been plain.

Do something, Mia! She threw a leg over her bike, and as she did, the hard cylinder of bear spray bumping into her ribs. She knew what to do.

"What are you doing?"

She looked up at Dalton, her gaze lingering on his lips, her scalp tingling. The urge to kiss him plowed through her, just like in the movies, and then she would ride off to save the day. Until she became acutely aware that she was just a sixteen-year-old girl on a bicycle. Not exactly Angelina Jolie. "I'll explain later." Then she jumped on the pedals and surged away from him.

She picked up speed with every rotation of the pedals, weaving through the fringes of the throng, past the news vans and down the alley. She expected to see Slade's back running down the alley after the boys— he had entered the alley only a few seconds ago—but he was gone. Her legs bore down on the pedals, and her fists clutched the grips. Gravel crunched under her tires. The alley quickly came to the intersection of another alley that passed behind the rows of backyards on both sides, forming a '+' sign in the center of the block. The alley was bordered by wooden fences, chain link fences, open grass yards, old garages and sheds. The boys could have darted anywhere out of sight.

A pile of discarded cloth lay beside the gravel path, the royal blue immediately familiar. She skidded to a stop beside it. The wrinkled, torn cloth exposed the Saint Sebastian's emblem on what had been a golf shirt.

Impossibilities snapped into her brain again.

Then she caught a glimpse, straight down the alley leading through the next block, of a pair of pink sweatpants disappearing around a distant corner.

She charged forward again, her feet spinning the pedals like crazy. Her bike bounced out of the alley into the next crossing street and bumped over the pavement leading into the next alley.

Out of nowhere, a black and silver bulk rocketed into her, bowling her off her bike onto the ground. Gravel tore through her shoulder. Hot, fetid breath swept over her cheek. Rocks and claws raked her arms and leg. The breath whooshed from her lungs. Thick, hot fur brushed her arm, and she looked up into slavering red jaws that bristled with yellow fangs. Searing blue eyes blazed into hers. Two massive paws pressed her against the earth, grinding her into the gravel as if she were a lump of chewed gum.

She screamed and struggled to scramble out from the under the massive beast, her legs flailing. Her hand shoved into her pants pocket and clamped around the smooth plastic lump inside.

The huge wolf's eyes glittered with intelligence, and its snarl almost looked like a smile.

It lunged down upon her, jaws snapping.

Her finger jammed into the button of the ultrasonic blaster.

She heard no sound, but more felt the presence of something powerful all around her, pressing against her with invisible waves. Her finger pressed harder into the button. Instantly the beast's eyes squeezed shut, and its head turned aside. Its jaws clashed on empty air. Its claws tore furrows in her jacket and shirt. Dogs began to bark from all directions.

The beast shook its head in pain and retreated a few steps, backing away from her. It snorted and spewed slaver, eyes burning with fresh rage. Its blue eyes burned with a feral hatred she had only ever seen in a movie, erasing everything else except its forest of fangs from her mind.

She jerked the blaster out of her pocket and shoved the speaker cone toward the wolf. It retreated three more steps, snarling, spitting, fangs gnashing.

Dogs howled and yiked and yipped and cried, and the invisible, inaudible power roared in her hand like a dental drill from hell.

The wolf gave her one last glare of sheer, pulsating hatred, then turned and fled, throwing every ounce of its incredible strength into a lightning-fast retreat.

Sobs of terror and rage boiled out of her, and she spewed a torrent of words that she had never used before. Dogs continued to howl and cry all around her. She took her finger off the button, and the silent scream disappeared. The yowling and whimpering began to subside.

How long she stood there, gasping for breath, tamping down the sobs, she didn't know, but the neighborhood had gone silent again, and the beast was still gone.

She picked up her bike, but her hand would not relinquish the blaster. Her legs felt like stacked-up jell-o molds, and her hands shook so badly she could hardly grip the handlebars. There was no way she could find the boys now. Hopefully they had had enough time to get away.

Her mind tried to correlate the contents of what she had just experienced. There could be only one explanation, but it defied the real world.

A minute or two later, she emerged onto the street near the news vans. The crowd was still there. The police were still there. No one paid her any attention. Her jacket sleeve was sticking to her arm. Blood had soaked through the ragged tears and turned cold and sticky. Jacket insulation drooled from the tear on her chest. Blood trickled down her shin. She limped.

She couldn't see Dalton anywhere.

"Mia?"

She turned.

Her father strode up to her, his eyes concealed by impenetrable sunglasses. "What in god's name are you doing here? Are you okay?" He looked so scary, and yet she wanted to hug him and melt into his embrace like a little girl. But she couldn't make her hands let go of the handlebars. He would never believe her. "Just a...just a...just little bike wreck."

Anger mixed with concern flickered across his face like alternating traffic lights. He wasn't happy to see her. Dalton walked up a few paces behind him, his face looking sheepish.

"Dad, I—"

His face was tight. "Come on, let's get you patched up. Then you can tell me what the hell you're doing here."

CHAPTER TWENTY

An ambulance waited to take the bones to the morgue. Mia's dad talked the paramedics into patching up her gravel scrapes and the claw marks that raked her right arm.

Her dad eyed the claw marks. "A bike wreck?"

She nodded.

His brow furrowed and his lips tightened as he crossed his arms.

"How come you're here?" she asked.

"I'll explain that when we get home. We have some things to talk about." He gazed pointedly at Dalton.

Dalton cleared his throat and thrust his hands deeper into his pockets.

The paramedic finished taping the gauze over the scratches on Mia's arm. "All set, Mia."

"Thanks," she said. "It feels better already."

Her dad turned to the paramedic. "Thanks again." He turned to Dalton and extended his hand, his eyes sharp. "It was nice to meet you, Dalton."

Dalton smiled and shook it. "Sure thing, Mister O'Reilly. You, too."

"Just remember, I can call in air strikes."

Dalton's face blanched.

"Dad!"

Mia's mom sat across the kitchen table. Her dad leaned against the counter, arms crossed. He was silent the entire drive home. Mia squirmed like an earthworm in the sunspot of a magnifying glass. Sarah stood in the open patio door, leaning against the jamb.

"Geez," Mia said. "I feel like I'm going to jail or something."

Her father cleared his throat. "First things first. What on Earth were you doing at a crime scene?"

"Well, I—"

"Secondly, I saw you take off on your bike. Where were you going so fast?"

"See, I—"

"*And* thirdly, when were you going to mention this Dalton guy? Do we need to have That Talk?"

Mia sighed, the pattern of the tablecloth fuzzing through her vision. The thought of having The Sex Talk with either of her parents turned her insides to sour milk. She already knew all of that stuff anyway from biology class and books. "Dalton wants me to go to a movie with him Saturday night. Is that okay?" Oh, good lord, had she just told the *truth*?

"You're starting in the wrong order, young lady."

"Yes, but Dalton is the easy part."

"We'll table that request until the end, if you're not grounded. Go on."

Mia gulped. Her mouth felt like fine-grit sandpaper. "See, there's been some weird stuff going on, and it's all tied up with Nate and Tara and..."

Sarah turned toward her, eyes narrow and focused.

Mia sighed. "You won't believe me."

"Try us."

"I don't believe it myself."

Her dad stood up straighter.

Her mom said, "Mia-chan, just tell us. We're more likely to get angry if you hide things."

Mia carefully restrained her retort. "Oh, yeah? We've all been hiding everything for two years!"

Her words hung in the silence for almost a minute. No one looked at anyone.

Her dad said, "Spill it, then we'll sort it out."

So Mia told them about her promise to Nate to help find out the truth, about the three dogs, no, the three wolves, about the attack, about the boys and how they were running from Slade, about how she agreed to help them, about the boys' night in the shed and their strange hunger for raw meat, about the boys telling her another body had been found, about how Slade chased the boys today, about how she found Slade's shredded clothes in the alley, and the massive wolf that attacked her.

As she talked, she studied each of them, trying to determine just how badly screwed she was. Her dad listened intently, clutching his chin with the end of his fist. Her mom stared in outright astonishment, mouth open. Sarah swallowed hard, over and over, her eyes glistening, lip quivering, unable to look at Mia, apparently studying the shady patterns the afternoon sun spattered through the leaves across the backyard.

Mia kept it together until she spoke of the attack today. The memory of the sheer power of the wolf's relentless ferocity blazed fresh in her mind, all bunches of hair and muscle, the scent of musky fur and horrible breath, its searing blue eyes and deadly jaws. Her voice cracked. "It was Slade. I know it was."

Her mom squeezed her hands in front of her. "*What?*"

Her dad sighed.

"See! I knew you wouldn't believe me!"

Sarah sniffled, clutching her shoulders.

"It knew me, Mom! I could see it in its eyes! I recognized its eyes! And it was going to kill me. Look, I know you guys don't believe me. *I* don't believe me! And now I'm sorry I said anything because you all think I'm a liar."

Her mom stood up. "Mia, this is not funny."

Mia stood up, too. "I know! It's freakin' terrifying! I just want to have a boyfriend! Or friends in general. And go to school and not suck at it! And I wish Nate wasn't dead and that I never met those kids. And most of all, I wish I didn't believe they're all freaking werewolves!"

There. She said it.

Werewolves.

As soon as she did, her mind starting working through the possibilities that she had denied before. What was the real situation between Slade and the boys? She had thought they ran away because they were being abused, but now, if they were all werewolves...

Mia slumped back into her chair. "God, I'm going crazy. I swear."

Sarah gave Mia's dad a pointed stare.

Her dad nodded slowly, keeping his voice steady, controlled. "Mia, you've been through a lot this week. Fighting off that dog or wolf or whatever it was had to be terrifying." He circled the table, hugged her, and kissed her hair.

"I know you don't believe me."

"It's a pretty wild story, but I saw the scratches on your arm. Those were not from a bike wreck. You're safe now. No werewolves here."

The thought of how the thing in the backyard might have been Slade—and how easily it could have broken through the shed door, or the patio door—sent a spike of ice through her.

Her mom said, "We should call the animal control people."

Sarah turned her face into the breeze, breathing deeply. "It won't matter. Whatever it was is long gone now."

Her mom said, "How can you be sure?"

Mia said, "A dog catcher wouldn't have a chance against that thing, even if they found it. And Sarah's right, it's gone. It's too smart to hang around for long. *He's* too smart."

Her dad said, "We still have a lot to talk about. Mia, go on up to your room."

"I'm grounded, huh."

"Not yet."

A warm, fuzzy head poked between her knees and licked her hand. She slid off her chair and went upstairs.

Sarah took a deep breath and tried to calm down. The sour taste of fear was in her mouth, and her throat felt tight for all the terrible things Mia experienced today. This situation was far worse than she thought. Far, far worse. Mia had no idea what she was up against.

Kyoko said, "I can't believe that she would lie."

Marcus rubbed his forehead and ran his fingers over his bristly military cut. "I don't think she's lying."

Kyoko's eyes bulged. "Werewolves! Marcus! Seriously!"

"I'm not saying what she saw was a werewolf. But when I saw her come out of that alley, she was clearly hurt and traumatized. She has four scratches." He raked his fingers across his bicep. "Something clawed her. Even it was just a huge dog, a husky or wolf mix, or even a wolf on the loose, she was lucky. You don't have that kind of look on your face unless you've just fought for your life." He turned to Sarah. "So, why did you buy her an ultrasonic blaster?"

Sarah couldn't meet her brother's gaze. "Mountain lion scare on the news."

Her brother's gaze bored into her. "No. Do you know something?"

Sarah shook her head. "She told you everything that I know. And then some. She told me some of this earlier today."

"No, that's not it. You know something."

"Don't make me play the 'That's Classified' Card."

"Are you kidding?"

"I'm not kidding."

"Are you saying you're involved with something here?"

"Dammit, Marc, you know as well as I do that when something's classified, it's freaking classified!"

"You know I have top secret clearance."

"It's code-word clearance."

Marcus's eyes widened, and he whistled.

Sarah couldn't tell her brother what she knew because it was classified above top secret, requiring a code word to which only a few individuals were privy.

Kyoko wrung her hands. "Are you saying that Mia is involved with something top secret? She's really in danger?"

Sarah nodded slowly.

Kyoko said, "What about those poor boys? If someone is trying to hurt them, they need to be kept safe!"

"Yes, they need help," Sarah said, "but I took a look at them. They're tough kids." And none of them were exactly normal any longer. If they managed to lay low for a while, they would be fine. "However, if this Slade is truly after those boys, he has help. There is no chance whatever that he's working alone."

"How do you—? Never mind. You just know."

Sarah nodded. "But you can tell me what *you* know. I have top secret clearance, too."

Marcus scratched his head. "True."

They both looked at Kyoko.

Kyoko's eyes narrowed. "Oh, that's just rude! My daughter is in trouble, and you're keeping secrets from me!"

"Honey, you know we have to." Marcus's eyes softened and he reached for her.

Kyoko edged away. "I know! Screw you both! *Right now, I would rather go to jail!*" She crossed her arms.

"Honey, go see if Mia is okay. She needs you. Sarah and I will compare some notes."

Kyoko sighed. "Sometimes I hate all this military government secret crap! Just hate it!" She spun on her heel and went upstairs.

Sarah waited for Kyoko to be out of earshot, then looked her brother in the eye. "Kyoko says you've been putting in an unusual amount of time at work and you're stressed out."

"Something is going on here in town, maybe across the state. It's like there's a flu outbreak or something. Lots of absenteeism from jobs all over town. Hospitals, too, Omaha P.D. I even see it at the F.B.I. office. It was like when the swine flu hit. Except that this...phenomenon has been going under the radar for about the last two months. No one is going to the hospital with any kind of new or unusual sickness. People just disappear for a while. And then they come back...What?"

"Hmm?"

"You just got all tense when I said that."

"Did I?"

"Oh, for god's sake, Sarah, give me some credit!"

"Sorry, it's just habit, you know? So, what are they like when they come back?"

"Reclusive. Their personalities are changed. Friends don't want to be around them anymore. A buddy at work, Charlie, he went on medical leave for a month, but he never went to a see a doctor, and he never told me what the problem was. When he came back, he would barely speak to me. Being around him makes me nervous somehow."

"So, why are you spending all the extra time at work?"

"Thirty-seven people have been reported missing over the last two months. Omaha P.D. freaked out and called us in at ten. We've managed to keep it out of the media, but I don't know how long that will be. If we're dealing with a serial killer, or several serial killers working together, we don't want to alert them to the investigation."

"Thirty-seven!"

"That we know of. There are rumors that the number of homeless people has dropped sharply, but so far we haven't gotten any of them to talk to us, at least anyone with brains that aren't scrambled by meth or Mad Dog 20/20. Plus the C.D.C. is investigating all the absenteeism. And if a missing person comes back on his own, there's not much for the F.B.I. to investigate, is there?"

"The Center for Disease Control? For missing persons cases?"

"Hospitals don't know what is going on. The same thing is showing up in pockets all over the U.S. A rash of disappearances, people who *don't* come back. O.P.D., State Patrol, and the local sheriffs' offices swamped. We're thinking this is bigger, and growing." He looked her in the eyes again. "Does any of this click with you?"

She squeezed her biceps. "Let's just say we're in the same ballpark."

"But what the hell is it? If it's a disease, why is it being kept secret? An unauthorized bio-weapon? A terrorist germ weapon? A new strain of swine flu or something? Typically when people get really sick, they go to the freaking doctor! But they're not. And if the missing people are dead, their bodies are not in their homes."

Sarah lied, "I don't know. But I'm going to try and find out."

"What does this have to do with Slade and those boys?"

Sarah lied again. "I don't know. You just keep a close eye on Mia, and I'll do the same. How about that?"

"Agreed."

"So, speaking of keeping a close eye on Mia..." Sarah gave her brother a little smirk. "What about this Dalton guy?"

Marcus sighed. "The day has finally come. I have to worry about boys. What am I saying? I've been worrying about boys since she turned twelve."

"I'll wager you put the fear of god into him."

"I did." He grinned devilishly.

"What did you say to him?"

"I said that I have the ability to call in air strikes."

Sarah chuckled. "'Air strikes,' that's good. You been saving that one?"

"Since the day she was born."

"Was he properly cowed?"

His grin widened. "Terrified, in fact."

They laughed together for a moment, a laugh that ended with shared looks of serious worry.

CHAPTER TWENTY-ONE

Mia's mother sat beside her on the bed, her face tight. She was still simmering. "I'm not lying."

Her mom sighed. "It's just such a crazy story. But everything will clear up eventually."

"You don't believe me."

"I don't believe in werewolves, but I believe that something terrible happened to you. And I'm proud of you for wanting to help those boys."

Mia blushed. She couldn't remember a time when she received so much praise from her mom. It felt...weird. At the same time, it was scary, because that meant that this situation was serious. "Are Dad and Sarah talking about top secret stuff that involves me?"

Her mom nodded gravely.

Mia's arms went a little weak.

The sun slanted through her bedroom window and splashed across her legs, warming them. "Um, what about Saturday?"

Her mom stiffened. "Your father and I haven't talked about it."

"But what do *you* say? Please, Mom! He's a great guy and—"

"Who are his parents?"

"I don't know. I've never met them."

"Does he have a car?"

"I think so."

Her mom stiffened more.

"What movie?"

"Uh, I don't know."

"You're not old enough for rated-R movie."

Mia sighed. Images of London's werewolf and the ensuing film carnage splattered into her memory. "He didn't say what movie." Her phone chimed and relief flooded her. She picked it up from the nightstand. The screen said, "Pay Phone."

She answered it. "Hello?"

"Hey, Mia," came Jace's voice.

She clutched the phone tighter. "Oh, god, are you guys all okay?"

"Yeah, we're all good. We got away." He took a deep breath. "We're glad you're okay, too."

"Where are you?"

"See that's the thing. Might be better if I didn't tell you. You been real nice and all, but—"

"Listen, you have to let me help you."

"You already done a lot. We don't want you to get hurt."

"I'm already in this. Slade tried to kill me today."

Silence hung over the line.

Jace let out a long breath. "He did?"

"Yeah. And when he's a wolf, he's got black and silver fur, and nasty blue eyes."

Dead silence.

"Well?" she said.

After another long pause, he said, "Seems like we need to have a talk."

"Seems like. Where are you?"

"We're in a storage area next to the interstate."

"What's the name?"

"Husker Bob's Storage."

"Okay, stay there. We'll come to get you."

"Hold on a minute! Who's 'we'?"

"I don't know yet. Me and somebody who can drive, I suppose." Mia gave her mother a questioning look.

His voice rose out of the ear-speaker. "You said you wouldn't tell nobody!"

"Sorry, Jace, that promise went out the window when I had wolf jaws snapping in my face. It's okay. They want to help you, too, and if you say, 'no police' then there won't be any police."

Jace's voice went dark, like a shadow crossing the moon. "Slade knows where you live, Mia. You ain't safe there. Not no more. You gotta stay out of there until all this blows over. Your family, too. You don't know what he'll do, especially after dark."

"But—"

"Just believe me, all right?"

"Why does it matter being in the dark? He was a wolf today, during the day."

"Humans can't see in the dark, Mia. Not like...he can."

The hair on the back of her neck stood straight. "Oh." The savage blue eyes of that wolf this afternoon jumped into her memory like a fun-house frightener. "Okay, where will we find you?"

"There's a rusted out red van next to the front gate. We'll be around there. How long you gonna be?"

"Maybe half an hour."

"All right then." The line went dead.

Mia turned to her mother. "Mom, we have to go and get them."

Her mom gave Mia a long look. Mia saw the flicker of refusal cross her mom's expression, the impulse to call her dad, or Sarah. Her mom nodded. "All right."

The two of them went downstairs, Deuce following.

Sarah's Jeep engine roared to life in the driveway.

Mia's dad said, "Good, you're just in time. Sarah and I have just had a very disturbing talk."

Mia said, "And?"

"I have to go back to the office and do some investigating." He picked up his car keys from kitchen counter.

Mia's mother asked, "Where's Sarah going?"

"To do the same."

The Jeep swung out of the driveway, and Sarah gunned it away down the street.

"Dad, Jace just called. Mom and I are going to get the boys."

"And do what with them? Bring them here? No, I'll send some agents."

"Those agents wouldn't find them in a million years. It has to be me. We're not going to bring them here. Jace said that would not be a good idea. Slade knows where we live."

Her dad considered this. "Okay, bring them to the office. We have a room with some cots for the night. You two will have a safe place to sleep too."

"I don't know if they'll go for that."

"Be persuasive. They might need medical attention, tests."

"They might not go for that either."

"We'll worry about that when the time comes. Let's get moving."

Mia stood at the door of the minivan. "Come on, Goonoid."

His tail wagged and his ears perked up, as if to say, *Once more into the jaws of death, dear friend.*

She closed the door and her mom started it up. Minutes later, they were on their way. A quick search on her smart phone—bow to the internet and G.P.S. gods—gave her the address of the storage place and directions. As they drove down the freeway from the suburbs toward the industrial area where the storage lot was located, a strange exhilaration pumped through her in escalating bursts.

The sun was just touching the horizon when her mother pulled off the major through-streets into the looping dead-end drives of the industrial park. Mia's smart phone and G.P.S. led them easily to the empty parking lot of Husker Bob's Storage. Mia's mom pulled the minivan into a parking space. The engine hummed quietly.

The time was after six o'clock, and the office was dark. The main building was an old structure with walls covered in ugly greenish-gray corrugated steel. Waist-high wild grasses reached up the walls of the building, up the chain-link fence, snarled with creeping-jenny vines, topped by barbed wire. A gravel drive led back into a matrix of red-doored storage compartments. A padlocked chain-link gate stood closed before them, and beside the gate stood a decrepit Volkswagen microbus, its red paint fading to gray in patches. A faded peace sign was painted next to a white 'N'.

Mia's eyes scanned the tall grass for any movement, any lupine shapes. She pulled the ultrasonic blaster out of her pocket.

Deuce stood up on the back seat. A low growl emanated from his throat.

The setting sun turned the nearby trees into black silhouettes, the neighboring warehouses, roofing companies, and auto-body shops into dense black boxes, all deserted now after the end of the workday. Long grassy shadows spilled across the asphalt parking lot. The grimy windows of the rusted red van looked opaque, like frosted glass. Mia rolled her window down and listened. The air had cooled with the coming of night. Smells of fresh wild grass, pollen from the jungle of goldenrod and sweet clover mixed with the smells of grease and paint and chemicals from the nearby businesses. A mourning dove cooed from a stand of cottonwoods on the far side of the building.

Mia called out, "Jace?"

A robin sang.

Deuce's growl continued to rumble behind her.

"You guys here? Deuce, hush! I can't hear."

Something rustled through the grass on the opposite side of the red van.

Her mom said, "Do you see them?"

"Jace? Are you over there?"

An enormous wolf leaped onto the roof the old red van, a hulking shape of hunched muscle and fur.

Mia yelped something incoherent and rolled up her window. With the sun behind the wolf, she couldn't discern the color of its fur. Another wolf stepped around the front of the minivan, this one lean and black. Its tongue lolled as its yellow-green eyes scrutinized Mia through the uncomfortably thin glass of her window. The intelligence in those eyes was plain, making her feel like a worm squirming on the end of a fishhook.

"Are those wolves...them?" her mom asked.

Another wolf stepped out from behind the van, a tall, lanky gray one. Could that one be Lee?

"I don't know, Mom. Are you saying you believe me now?"

"Yes, Mia, I believe you now." Her mom kept her voice even, but cracks emerged in her veneer of calm.

Mia tried to discern more about the big wolf on top of the van, but the details were too obscured by dusk. Was that one Jace?

A fourth wolf stepped out from behind the van and trotted out toward the minivan. Its lips pulled back from its fangs, and its eyes blazed.

Mia's voice croaked. "Oh. No."

Her mom cried out, pointing out her own side window toward three other wolves standing on the edge of the parking lot.

Deuce snarled a challenge.

A flicker of movement in the rearview mirror caught Mia's attention. Four more wolves stood tense and expectant on the verge of the grassy roadside sward behind them.

"Mom, we need to get out of here."

The wolves threw their noses toward the sky and howled. Mia's blood turned to ice.

Her mom gulped for air, muttering, "*Yes. Yes.*"

The wolves charged.

They slammed themselves into the windows with such force that Mia was shocked that the glass didn't break. Snarling, teeth gnashing, spraying slaver across the glass. Green and yellow eyes blazed in with hatred and hunger. The minivan rocked as the heavy bodies threw themselves against it. A wolf launched itself up the hood, onto the roof, where its claws scratched against the paint like nails on a chalkboard. Dagger-filled snouts thumped against the glass. Howls and snarls poured into the minivan, spurring Deuce's challenges into a deafening roar.

Mia's mom screamed.

Mia gripped the ultrasonic blaster. Would it work through the glass?

Her fingers felt like overcooked macaroni as she tried to work the window. The glass came open two inches, and instantly a gnashing muzzle thrust itself through the opening. She raised the blaster to the opening the squeezed the button.

A high-pitched squeal of anguish ripped from Deuce's throat, and he dove behind the seat, his claws tearing across the cloth and vinyl. Several of the wolves peeled away from the windows, thrashing their heads, their tails dropping between their legs. Deuce continued to yike in a frenzy of pain. The wolves howled and snarled, casting spears of hatred at the minivan from several paces distant.

Mia's mom threw the minivan into reverse.

"Mom! What about the boys?"

From the opposite corner of the main building a voice called out, "Hey, you freaks! You looking for me?" It was Jace.

Her mom hit the brakes.

The wolves turned toward Jace.

Another voice called from the roof of the main building. "What about me, you boneheads!" Lee stood there twenty feet off the ground.

A fist-sized chunk of concrete skittered across the pavement in front of the minivan. "Over here, slimeballs!" Malcolm slung another chunk that thumped against the side of one of the wolves with a sound like hitting soft wood.

The wolves stood confused, three directions to go.

Jace turned and disappeared behind the office. Several of the wolves charged after him. Several others ran toward Malcolm, who turned and darted away into the tall grass. Two wolves charged Lee. In less than a heartbeat, they reached the foot of the wall. In another heartbeat, they leaped twenty feet straight upward, a leap no normal wolf had ever made. Their front paws scrabbled for purchase at the lip of the roof as they tried to heave themselves up after Lee.

Lee laughed at them. "You guys suck! Should I just hang out until you make it?"

One of the wolves dropped to the ground, backed up several paces, then launched itself again, and this time, landed all four feet on the roof. Lee's taunting smile evaporated, and he ran. The other wolf leaped over the chain link fence in one bound, and chased after them along the side of the main building.

The wolves were gone, and the sounds of pursuit diminished.

Mia took her finger off the ultrasonic blaster button.

Deuce's yiking diminished to an anguished whimper.

"We have to call the police!" Mia's mom said. "Those boys are being attacked by wolves!"

"The wolves aren't going to kill them."

"What are they going to do?"

"Capture them, punish them for running away, I don't know. But they'll be long gone before the police get here."

"We have to do s—!"

Her mom's side window exploded inward, spraying them both with razor-like pellets of glass. A dagger-filled snout and blazing blue eyes, an enormous black and silver head.

Mia and her mother screamed in chorus.

Mia jammed the blaster button again. Deuce howled. The invading beast barely flinched.

The huge jaws clamped onto her mom's shoulder belt and tore through it with a loud rip. Her mom threw herself away from the window, but the wolf lunged deeper and its teeth snapped down on her shoulder, tearing into her flesh. Her scream shrilled, ragged with pain.

The wolf hauled her through the shattered window out onto the asphalt, lap belt flapping loose. Her arm and legs flailed, and her mouth opened into a wider scream.

"Mom!"

With her mom's foot removed from the brake, the minivan began to creep backward, still in reverse.

The beast threw one last look of calculated malevolence at Mia. With its lips still clamped around her mom's shoulder, it smiled. Then it turned and ran, carrying Mia's mother away as if she weighed no more than a rabbit. The hulking shape and its screaming burden disappeared into the tall grass.

All Mia could do was watch it go.

"Mom!" she sobbed, but her voice disappeared into the deafening silence, and the minivan rolled backwards.

CHAPTER TWENTY-TWO

Mia unbuckled her seat belt and threw her legs over the console so she could climb behind the wheel. Bits of shattered glass ground into her hands and legs as she slid into the seat. The window yawned, and the cool evening breeze wafted into her face. She grabbed the steering wheel and stomped her foot down onto the brake pedal. The minivan jerked to a stop. She lurched against her seat.

"Mom!" she cried out the window. *"Mom!"*

A distant cry receded into the grass and darkness.

Deuce slunk out from under the seat and jumped up into the passenger seat, his eyes scanning the gathering dusk. He ruffed softly in the direction the wolf had dragged Mia's mom.

Mia had never driven before. She had been pressing her parents to teach her how to drive, to let her at least get a Learner's Permit, but without much success. She looked at the gauges, felt the pressure of the brake pedal against her foot. The engine idled.

The boys had scattered. Her mom was lost in the grass, dragged away by a monster. If she went after them on foot, the pack of werewolves would bring her down like a rabbit. She had the blaster, but she didn't know how long the batteries would last, and it had had no effect on Slade. She had the bear spray, too, but she was uncertain how effective it would be on a werewolf. Normal wolves could not make a twenty-foot standing vertical leap. Normal wolves could not smash out a car window.

She pulled out her cell phone and thumbed her dad's number by feel and memory; her eyes scanned the movement of every blade of grass, every shifting shadow. Her dad's phone rang. And rang. And rang. Then went to voice mail. That meant he was at work. When he was in his office in the sub-basement, cell phone signals couldn't get through. There was a landline to his office, but she never used it—couldn't remember the number.

Her hand trembled so badly she could hardly hold the phone. "Dad! The wolves just took Mom! They dragged her away! There are at least—" How many were there? "—Uh, eight or nine of them! I'm okay, but I don't know what to do!" But she didn't break down. She kept her voice even.

She hung up and dialed Sarah.

Sarah picked up on the first ring. Her voice was taut, clipped, with traffic noise in the background. "What's up?"

The story spilled out of Mia in a frenzied rush. She gripped the steering wheel to steady her voice.

When Mia was finished, Sarah cursed under her breath, then said, "Mia, get out of there."

"I've never driven before!"

"Do the best you can, but get out of there, drive a few blocks away and stop, just go. I'm going to call the police. They'll at least give the wolves something else to think about for the time being."

Could the wolves really think? "What about Mom?"

"One thing at a time."

"What about the boys?"

"One thing at a time, girl. I'll be there in fifteen minutes."

"They're really werewolves, aren't they."

"Yes, Mia."

"And you know something about this, don't you."

"Yes, Mia."

"And you're going to tell me about it, aren't you."

A long pause. "I think I have to."

"Okay, I'll call you again when I manage to get out of the parking lot."

"Be careful."

The connection went dead, and she put the phone on the console.

Talking to Sarah had steadied her nerves. She took a deep breath and let it out, gripping the steering wheel with both hands. "Okay, Goonaramus. Emergency driving lesson for Mia."

Deuce blinked at her as if to say, Cheerio, then, mistress. Tally-ho.

Foot on brake. Heart slamming her breastbone like a piston. Slide the shifting lever to "D". Foot off the brake, minivan easing forward.

Something heavy slammed against the sliding door. Mia screamed and her foot reflexively smashed the brake pedal. The minivan's tires squeaked as it jerked to a stop.

Malcolm's face and hands were plastered against the glass. "Mia! It's me! Wait!"

"Get in!"

His hand fumbled with the outer latch. "It's locked!"

She fumbled with the door lock switch. All the doors unlocked simultaneously. He threw the sliding door open and dove inside.

She lifted her foot off the brake. "Where are the others?"

A distant voice sounded through the open door. "Right here!" Jace and Lee burst out of the grass at a dead run.

She slammed on the brake again. Deuce piled into the dash nose-first.

In moments Jace and Lee threw themselves through the open door, and Lee slammed it shut. Their shoes were missing and their clothes were torn, stretched as if in unnatural ways. Grass seeds, burrs, and pollen clung to their clothes and hair.

Jace gasped, "You got maybe twenty seconds to get the hell out of here!"

Mia jammed her finger on the door lock switch, sucked a deep breath and stomped on the gas pedal. The minivan surged forward with a squeal of tires, throwing them all back against their seats. Mia's foot lifted from the pedal, and the van slowed, throwing them all forward.

"Geez!" Lee yelled. "Don't you know how to drive?"

"It's my first time!" Her hands felt like she could bend the steering wheel into a taco.

Like an inchworm, the minivan lurched toward the street.

A howl echoed through her open window, close by. A chorus of howls rose from out of sight around the minivan, growing louder.

"Mia," Jace said.

"I know!"

"Mia!"

"I know!"

Concentrate, Mia. She eased her foot onto the gas pedal, and the minivan eased forward, gathering speed, heading for the street. She pressed harder. The wheels bounced over the corner of the curb. She peeled into the street. A long, straight road lay before her, and she gunned the engine. The parking lot receded in the rearview mirror. She half-expected a pack of lupine shapes to fall into pursuit behind her, but there was nothing, only empty street and deepening dusk.

Jace leaned forward. "Mia, where's your mom?"

A stab went through her heart. The words would barely come. "Slade took her." The torn end of the seat belt flapped in the wind of the open window.

A chorus of protests rose from the back seats.

Mia said, "Are they going to kill her?"

Jace said, "I don't know. Maybe."

Malcolm said, "That's why we left, why we're trying to get away."

"Why's that?"

Malcolm gulped. "They eat...people."

Jace said, "Slade tried to make us."

Malcolm said, "We couldn't."

Lee said, "Yeah, screw that noise."

"So, you guys are werewolves."

"Yeah, but it ain't like in the movies. It ain't got nothing to do with the full moon or such like."

"Why is he after you?"

Malcolm said, "He wants us back in the pack."

Lee said, "He didn't take kindly to us going off on our own."

Jace said, "We left, when he tried to make us eat..."

"Who?" Nate's face flashed in her mind.

"I don't remember. When we're wolfed up, some things don't make the connection. It's hard to explain."

Malcolm said, "We are aware and in control—"

Lee said, "Mostly."

"Yes, mostly in control. But parts of our intellect get lost somehow. Or at least, they're transmogrified."

"Good word," Jace said.

Malcolm grinned. "Slade tried to preach to us about 'survival of the fittest' and becoming the world's new 'apex predator.'"

"Hell," Lee said, "I don't even know what that means."

Mia said, "It means being at the top of the food chain. So he thinks that werewolves—you guys—should just eat humans, keep them as food?"

Jace said, "That's the idea."

"That's insane."

Malcolm said, "Perhaps trying to teach science to middle-schoolers makes one's grip on reality tenuous."

"He's a science teacher?"

Jace said, "Used to be a good one, Eric said."

"Who's Eric?"

"One of the pack. Slade's favorite."

"So they're going to eat my mom?" Mia's voice cracked, but she tightened her grip on the steering wheel. Still nothing in the rearview mirror. She could drive all the way to Kansas and it wouldn't be far enough to feel safe.

Jace said, "Was she still alive when he took her?"

"Yes. I heard her..." Screaming.

Malcolm laid a tentative hand on her shoulder. "They're probably not going to eat her right now."

"Yeah," Lee said. "Maybe they're saving her for later."

A peep of anguish slipped from Mia's lips.

Jace punched Lee hard on the shoulder. "God, dude, you are such an ass-douche sometimes!"

Lee's voice rose quickly. "I just meant that Slade might have a plan for her! That guy's a schemer."

Jace shook his head. "You're still a jackass."

Mia's confidence with control of the minivan had grown. Keeping the vehicle between the ditches—check. Keeping a constant speed—okay, reasonably constant—check. No werewolves in hot pursuit—check. "We need to tell someone about this!"

Jace said, "Who's gonna believe us?"

"Well, can't you change or something and show them?"

Lee snorted, "Yeah, and they'll lock us up like lab rats. Besides, I could barely shift enough to get away from Jeremy."

"What do you mean?"

Lee rubbed his stomach. "Hungry."

Mia could hear it growling over the engine noise. "Sorry, I didn't bring any food."

Lee said, "You ain't got the kind of food we need."

Jace said, "We need raw meat, the fresher the better."

"Oh."

Lee said, "Something in the raw meat. Slade said that raw meat has a mean old acid or proteins or something, I don't know, gives us fuel to shift."

Malcolm rolled his eyes. "It's 'amino acid,' idiot."

"Shut up! Anyway, that's why we...ate the rabbit."

"So to change into wolves, you need to eat raw meat?"

"And to change back."

"Eww!"

Lee said, "It ain't bad once you get used to it."

Mia twisted her face. "Again, eww!"

Flashing red and blue lights came into view several blocks ahead of them. Four police cars pulled onto the street and sped toward them. The boys ducked low. Sirens blared and gained volume, headlights spearing into Mia's vision. She practically froze to the seat, her arms locked in place.

Malcolm said, "Um, I think when you see emergency vehicles, you're supposed to pull to the side of the road."

"Right." Her heart thumped again. She took her foot off the gas and eased the minivan to the right.

Seconds later, the parade of police cars rocketed past her.

The storage area lay perhaps half a mile behind them, so she pulled into the small, deserted parking lot in front of Rodriguez Roofing.

Jace said, "This ain't far enough. They can still track us by scent."

"Then keep your eyes open. Noses, too." Mia thumbed Sarah's number.

Sarah answered and said, "Almost there. Four minutes."

"I got away. We're stopped right now."

"We?"

"I have the boys with me."

Mia's phone beeped. There was a call waiting, from an unavailable number. An invisible shadow of dread descended over her. "Hang on, Sarah." She clicked over to the other call. "Hello?"

Slade's hoarse voice drove a spike of ice through her belly. "Hello, Mia."

CHAPTER TWENTY-THREE

Mia could barely squeeze out the words. "What did you do with my mom?"

Slade cleared his throat, but his voice was still hoarse, strangely distorted. "I want those boys, Mia."

"They don't belong to you!"

"Oh, yes, they do. They're my children. I made them. They belong with me."

"Leave them out of this! Is my mom alive? Are you going to eat her, you sicko freak?"

"She's alive. For the time being."

"So you want to exchange her for the boys, I guess, huh?"

"You're a smart girl. Bravo."

"And if I don't go for it, you'll eat her, is that it?"

"Use your imagination."

"When and where?" The coldness in her belly congealed into an icy chip of hatred.

The boys shifted in the seats behind her.

"I'll be in touch. Don't go too far, Mia. You don't have a driver's license, and you can't hide from us. Not many people working at Rodriguez Roofing this time of the evening. Tell me where the boys are, and I'll let your mother—"

The scrabble of pads and claws on asphalt was her only warning. A snarling gray face darted through the open window. Teeth tore into her forearm and jaws clamped tight. Pain shot up her arm and flared into her brain. Green eyes blazed. The jaws pulled her hand off the steering wheel. Deuce lunged across her lap from the passenger seat, a hurtling block of bristling muscle and fangs. Frothing jaws, slashing teeth, spraying spittle, Deuce's claws heavy, pressing into her legs, scrabbling for purchase as his teeth tore into the wolf's face. The smell of blood. The terrible squeezing, piercing pressure on her forearm disappeared. The two powerful beasts tore into each other inches from her face, spraying warm droplets. A furry muzzle slammed into her chin, clapping her teeth together. Pain blazed into her vision.

Jace came from behind her, over her, yelling, shoving, punching, clawing. The side door slid open. Footsteps jumped out and circled the van. Two more voices roared. The wolf's head jerked out of the window. Its snarl turned to a whimper. Deuce tried to scrabble over her, past her, out the window, but she caught his collar. A tearing sound, like soft velvet being ripped asunder, like a turkey drumstick wrenched from a warm bird. The whimper shrilled to a shriek. A sour, wet, metallic stench wafted through the window. Something splatted against pavement.

Mia's head swam. Her vision blurred. Her arm hurt. Blood plastered her sleeve to her arm. She coughed and rubbed her eyes. Sounds were coming out of her mouth, but she couldn't gather them into words.

The shrieking stopped and silence fell.

Cicadas in the trees.

The engine purred.

Malcolm and Lee stood beside her door, looking down at something, chests heaving.

Jace's arm still reached across her. He eased back.

Deuce peered down over the edge of the window. Mia didn't look. Instead she hugged Deuce with her good arm and kissed his bloody, stubbly face. He licked her face, and she smelled blood again. Then with a last kiss she shoved him back into the passenger seat.

She said, "Get in."

Malcolm and Lee glanced at each other then ran back around and dove through the sliding door. Their arms looked thicker, knotty, shoulders hunched, drenched in blood up to their elbows. Their nails were long and black.

Mia gunned the minivan out of the parking lot, heading down the street, only barely glancing at the crimson, shapeless, glistening mass strewn across the pavement behind her.

Jace said, "He's gonna be pissed."

Both of them said in chorus, "Mm-hmm."

"That was Caleb."

Lee said, "Yeah."

Mia tried to ignore the throbbing pain in her arm, the puddle of blood dripping onto her leg. "You know them?"

"We know them all," Jace said.

Malcolm's voice cracked. "We go—went to school with them."

Lee sniffed. "Son of a bitch used to steal my comic books."

Mia's skin felt like a blanket of ice. "You just killed somebody."

Malcolm started to cry.

Jace laid a hand on his shoulder. "Settle down, buddy. It's okay. We had to."

Malcolm's voice dripped with sorrow. "No, it's not! I've never killed anyone before!"

Lee said, "He was gonna kill Mia. We couldn't let that happen."

"I know! But...I lost control of the wolf part of me! That's never happened before!"

"It happens sometimes." Jace's voice was soothing. "Caleb knew what he was doing. So does Slade. And it's wrong! And that's why we're here and not with them!"

"But now we're no better than them!"

Three heavy sighs.

The gashes in Mia's arm throbbed and burned. "No, you're wrong. You saved my life."

They looked at her.

"Thank you. All of you."

Lee said, "You're welcome."

Malcolm let out a long, shuddering breath. "Yes, you're quite welcome, Mia."

Jace said, "We have to do something with your arm."

"I'm okay for now."

Jace looked at Lee's arms, sinewy and long, swathed in blood and tipped with lethal black claws. "Hey, aren't you gonna shift back?"

"I can't. I'm done until I get some meat."

Malcolm said, "I as well." His arms were no longer human arms.

The smell coming from both of them turned her stomach into a queasy mess. Thick, rich, coppery blood, a meatiness like raw steak, but also an acidic sourness, almost like vomit. The smell of the things their claws had raked through, deep inside.

Mia tried not to look at them, turning her attention instead to the rear view mirrors. "How fast can you guys sprint when you're shifted?"

Jace said, "Fast."

Malcolm said, "I would estimate forty miles per hour."

"How long can you keep up that speed?"

"I dunno," Jace said. "A couple of miles maybe."

"How far can you run?"

"Never tested that. Probably a real long ways. Why?"

She was running out of empty industrial park roads. She had no choice. She would have to take the highway, join the endless flow of other cars. The distant lights of the police cars behind her looked like strobing jewels of red and blue. Howls echoed from somewhere behind her, closer than the police cars. "You guys put your seatbelts on."

Jace said, "What about yours?"

Hers was useless, shredded by Slade's teeth. Mia shrugged with false bravado. Inwardly, however, she was so accustomed to wearing a seatbelt that she felt naked without it. The fresh scrabble of feet on gravel and asphalt behind her grabbed her attention. Two massive furry shapes fell into pursuit, red tongues lolling, yellow-green eyes burning into hers, deep breaths puffing.

She gunned the engine, but there was a stop sign coming. She shook her head. Not a chance. The minivan zoomed through. Two blocks ahead hung the traffic light that led onto a major street.

The wolves kept pace. The speedometer said thirty-five miles per hour. To her, behind the wheel for the first time, it felt like a hundred. Her injured arm trembled, and her left hand felt as weak as a sodden dish rag.

A pair of headlights swung around the corner ahead of them, coming fast. Sarah's Jeep.

In seconds, the Jeep zoomed past the minivan and swerved into the oncoming wolves. The Jeep careened sideways with tires squealing, plowing into the two lupine bodies. The wolves went flying amid wails of pain as if swatted by an enormous hand. The wolves sprawled somewhere in the tall grass beside the street. The Jeep bounced up onto the curb, the lights went out, and Sarah jumped out, waving.

Mia hit the brakes.

With lightning speed, shocking speed, Sarah ran alongside the minivan to the driver's door. "Move over!"

Mia shoved the transmission into Park and rolled out of the driver's seat across the console into the back with the boys. Sarah slid inside, tossing a small satchel onto the floor between her feet.

Mia looked for signs of the wolves. "Did you kill them?"

Sarah jerked the minivan into gear and the tires squealed. "I doubt it. Hang on."

The minivan surged ahead again. Sarah ignored the red traffic light, roaring out onto the highway. Car horns blared.

Lee whooped. "You drive like a crazy woman! I like it!"

Sarah kept her eyes on the road, her jaw tight. "Mia, what happened to your arm?"

Mia clutched Sarah's shoulder. "Never mind, just a scratch. Slade called me. He wants to trade Mom for the boys."

Sarah's eyes teared up, and she clamped a hand over her mouth, then a deep breath as she clutched the steering wheel with both hands again. The plastic creaked under the force of her grip. "How do you know she's alive?"

"I didn't think of that! I should have asked to talk to her!"

"So, what now?"

"He said he'd be in touch."

Mia didn't like the look of mounting horror on Sarah's face.

CHAPTER TWENTY-FOUR

The small Japanese woman's eyes glistened with terror. Slade could smell it roiling off her like waves of delicious mist. Fear and struggle tenderized the meat, from the build-up of lactic acid in the muscles. Most Americans were already so fat and tender from their lifestyles that they made excellent food. Hardy immigrants, however, used to working in packing plants, bean fields, and construction crews, were less palatable, stringy and tough. After letting them struggle or flee for an extended period, they made much better meals. The homeless made easy hunting, living on the fringes of human society, having no one to miss them, but their flesh was often so steeped in alcohol and drugs that it was barely edible. Nevertheless, it was the way of nature that the weak would be those first lost to predators.

The woman drew her knees to her chest, leaning against the concrete pile of the railroad bridge, her face wet with tears. Blood soaked her shoulder from the bite.

Slade's pack encircled her, those who had not gone off in pursuit. Nine young wolves sat on their haunches, resting, tongues lolling, eyeing their next meal. They would not eat before he did. He was the Alpha. They were his children; he had made them all.

All of them were larger than normal wolves, Slade in particular. The Law of Conservation of Mass dictated that they weighed the same in wolf form as in human form. He weighed two-twenty-five, and had managed to keep the fat off even before the change. Two-twenty-five made a damn big wolf.

The trestle was hemmed by foliage and far from any witnesses, except the occasional locomotive, shielded by the bridge from eyes in the sky. In the distance, perhaps four hundred yards away, police radios relayed useless messages among helpless, hopeless police officers. The police could not catch them. Indeed, he had sensed that there were some on the police force who now *would* not catch them. They had joined the Pack, as Slade had come to call it, the secret spread of New Becoming.

Of course, all of these words, no matter how grandiose, lost much of their meaning in the human world. The human world might understand the Pack as a concept, an abstraction, a scientific curiosity. The wolf felt the Pack in his heart, in his bones, in the deepest core of his D.N.A. The Pack was family, brethren, race, and religion, all threaded together into a weave that *meant* something. Little in the human world carried such meaning that people felt it in their viscera. Except perhaps, parents' attachment to their children. Add that devotion to the pure, stark, primal emotions of a wolf, now there was meaning.

His children had gone astray, part of *his* Pack.

He had not always understood such things, until that night camping on a sandbar beside the Niobrara River last autumn, leaning against a gnarled log that had been stripped white by river and sun, beside his tent, staring into the campfire. His Winchester .30-30 leaned against the log beside him. Its blue steel and well-worn wooden stock gleamed in the light of the flames. A long day of deer hunting had chilled him, and the fire felt good. He had had a good shot at a mature buck, and missed. If he had mounted a scope to his rifle, it would have been an easy kill, but he liked open sights. The Corps had turned him into a marksman, and keeping up practice reminded him of better days, when things were simpler.

He tried not to think about Connie's final letter to him, the hurtful words she had called him as she packed up their two beautiful daughters, loaded them into *his* truck, and drove out of his life for good.

All that bullshit that she worried about—cars and clothes and credit cards and whether he said "I love you" every goddamn day—meant nothing, not a crying damn thing, when a bullet could take off the top of your buddy's head on any given day, or take your best friend in the throat and he lay in the god-forsaken desert sand next to you with his blood spurting all over your leg and you could do nothing except watch him gag and choke for breath as he bled out for a solid minute and a half as his eyes stared up into yours, begging you to help him, reaching out with bloody fingers, and you finally drag him back under cover and clamp your fingers over the hot, ragged *hole* in him to stop the blood and you feel it all—blood, breath, life—just...stop. And by that time, his eyes aren't looking at you anymore.

Screw her, telling him that he had *issues*.

Eight years out of the Corps and he was doing just fine. The night terrors ceased a long time ago, the insomnia, the rages. What else could a man do when he had seen how the universe really worked?

The last pictures of Megan and Emily were so gorgeous. Their mom's blonde hair and full lips, and his cheekbones. Connie would want a man around—if for no other reason than to fend off the boys. He hoped his girls didn't become sluts like their mother. He wished he knew where they lived so he could check in on them from time to time.

Maybe he hadn't always been the most attentive father, or the most romantic husband. But they were *family*. Family hadn't meant anything to *her*.

The bourbon helped sometimes to wash such thoughts away, or at least that's what he told himself. It burned away the pain gathering in his throat on its way down. The crackle of the fire, the mutter of the river lulled him. He breathed deep and let it out. The half-empty bottle of Jim Beam was warm between his legs, as it slipped out of his fingers, as he nodded off.

His old sixth sense that had warned him of danger so many times in the close-packed hell-streets of Baghdad, fighting house to house, when half an inch, give or take, meant the difference between life and death, dragged him out of his stupor just in time to see yellow eyes and fangs surging toward his throat. He got his arm up and the fangs tore into his wrist. Rage and curses boiled out of him as his wrist bones shattered and ligaments tore out of him like leathery spaghetti.

The massive wolf jerked so hard his shoulder popped, and he thought his arm might come off at the shoulder. He kicked at the wolf's body, without effect. His left hand flailed for the rifle. The wolf's haunches danced through the dying fire as it spun him, scattering sparks, heedless of the orange-hot coals.

Heavy steel and wood in his grip. Cocking the lever-action with his left hand. Levering the barrel around as his body was jerked around like doll. The bones in his forearm snapped like twigs and his forearm bent in the middle like a grinding hinge.

The muzzle blast knocked the wolf's body sideways, off his arm. It almost fell over, one front leg collapsing under it. Its eyes squeezed shut in pain. He kicked it away from him. It lunged at him again, but with only three legs and with blood pouring in a deluge from the fist-sized exit wound in its ribcage, its strength had diminished.

But not as much as he expected.

It bowled him backwards across the log, slavering jaws going for his throat like a last gasp. He raised the rifle just high enough. Its teeth clamped around wood and steel, grinding, snapping. His right arm was useless flopping meat, but he hooked his right thumb into the lever and cocked the rifle. Agony seared up through shattered bones, ravaged flesh, and shredded tendons. Somehow he braced himself against the log and shoved away from it, kicked the wolf off him, lowered muzzle and pulled the trigger with the remains of a finger.

The wolf's eyes bulged and it dropped at his feet like a pole-axed water buffalo.

It was a four-mile walk back to his truck, a long way with a bleeding, splinted arm and the knowledge that wolves always moved in packs. Morning had found him passed out beside the door of the truck, a night free of the familiar nightmares. The doctor at the emergency room in Valentine was surprised that the attack had happened only hours before, amazed that his skin and muscle were already healing. Within a week, he had taken off the cast.

That was only the beginning. The coming weeks brought him abilities he had only seen imagined in comic books and movies. And the hunger. Much of the last year had been one long experiment. He was a science teacher. He had made sense of things in Iraq—the utter senseless depravity of the universe—with science. Science was logical. It was consistent. One might not know all the rules, but there were always rules. The few legitimate-seeming books on lycanthropy he had found were nothing more than a load of mystical, woo-woo bullshit. Science would explain what had happened to him, not God, or religion, or alchemy, or legends of Native American skinwalkers.

Each boy was an experiment. In those experiments, he found his home again.

Depending on the immune system of the victim, the virus—and he had come to believe that it was, in fact, a virus—transferred from a bite could lead to transformation in from one to ten days. All it took to transmit infection was a bite delivered in wolf form, presumably when the lycanthrope virus was most active. He tracked how long from infection to the initial stages of transformation, to full transformation, and how long before the immune system subdued the virus and forced the wolf side back into hiding, allowing the human side to reassert itself. When he tried to turn Latrelle, the virus ran amok and killed the boy. The thing that finally expired was neither wolf nor boy.

He was not even remotely interested in finding a cure. His aim was to understand what he had become, and embrace it. These boys, his Pack, his family, helped him. And he had given them all a gift greater than any parent ever could.

He turned toward the approaching sound of padded feet and ragged breaths. Two of his children limped painfully toward the pack circle. Bloody cuts streaked their faces. Jimmy hobbled on one front paw. One of DaShante's eyes was swollen shut and several of his teeth were missing or broken.

Slade said, "What happened?"

The two stopped at his feet and nuzzled his naked legs. Their bodies tensed and quivered as they initiated the shift back into human form so that they could speak. Muscles bunched and writhed under furry skin, bones grew or compressed, organs slid and shifted, patches of fur sloughed and fell from fresh skin. The two soon resembled naked boys kneeling at his feet, one white and one black.

"They got away, Mister Slade," Jimmy said, his voice distorted by a receding snout, a morphing nasal cavity, tongue, and palate.

"Yeah, somebody hit us with a car," DaShante said. "Sorry, Mister Slade."

"Where's Caleb?"

Jimmy sniffled. "He...he..."

"Come on, spit it out."

Jimmy wiped his nose with his forearm. "He's dead, Mister Slade."

"They killed him," DaShante said.

Slade snarled and roared. In an instant, his claws snapped out clean, his neck thickened, and his muzzle sprang out from his face with a gritty, wet crackling. The dim blur of dusk turned sharp and gray as his eyes became those of a wolf. He howled at the underside of the bridge.

His pack cowered, their heads slumping, tails tucked between their legs. He paced back and forth, his lips peeling back from teeth that stretched and sharpened. He had gotten used to the pain. When his teeth shifted, it felt like a mouthful of dental drills without anesthetic, and the elongation of his snout felt like a punch in the nose every single time. He snarled and spat and paced on two legs. He had learned to arrest the change, and now howled in a half-human, half-wolfen voice.

The woman cried and curled into a ball.

He let the waves of rage and sorrow wash through him, until he could steady himself with breathing, enough that he could suppress the wolf and bring his face back to a shape where he could speak. His breath heaved in and out. His legs quivered with the compulsion to run and leap. His mouth watered with the desire to taste hot flesh and warm blood. He looked at the woman and stood before her, his claws digging into the leathery pads of his palms.

He swallowed the last of his rage and said, "Eric, Garrett, Juan, go find Caleb's body. Bring it back here before someone finds it." He didn't want to give the human world anything to examine, even if they would not think to necropsy a wolf carcass. Unlike werewolves from all the old movies, once one of the Pack was dead, the body did not shift back to human form. The natural processes that caused the changes ceased to function, just like everything else. Unless a coroner looked at the body at the cellular level, its human origins were masked.

The three boys turned out of the circle and loped off into the dusk.

Slade knelt and laid his hands on Jimmy and DaShante. "Are you both okay?"

Jimmy sighed and leaned against Slade's leg. "I think my leg—er, my arm's broken."

DaShante's voice was pained and thick with swelling. "I lost some teeth, Mister Slade. And I think some ribs is broke."

"You'll heal. I'm glad you're okay, boys. As for letting them go..." He snarled and cuffed each of them hard across the side of the head.

They yowled, sprawling from the force of the blows. He jumped after Jimmy and landed a hard kick to the boy's stomach. Then he turned and sent DaShante flying with another such kick. The boys lay on their backs, gasping for breath, crying, gagging, whimpering. Their bodies would heal soon enough. A day or so of pain and they would be back to normal. Their broken bones would take a few more days, but with enough raw meat and fresh bone marrow, those would heal, too.

He looked at the woman again. She was strangely alluring in her terror, with finely sculpted cheekbones, dainty build, beautiful dark hair and almond eyes. If he allowed her to live long enough for the virus to take hold, she might make a fine mate. But the little girl didn't need to know that her mother had already been irrevocably changed. If he allowed the woman to live, his bite would make ultimately make her Pack.

He walked to where he had left his clothes piled against the concrete wall, placed there before he changed. He picked up his cell phone from where it lay atop the pile.

CHAPTER TWENTY-FIVE

Mia's eyes bulged, and a sick, cold dread settled into her stomach after the explanation Sarah had just given her. "So now I'm going to want to eat *bunnies?*"

Jace said, "They're good, actually."

"Strangely tasty," Malcolm said. "Reminiscent of chicken."

"Oh, my god, I'm going to be sick." Mia covered her mouth.

Sarah guided the minivan through rush hour traffic, her face grim. "You're not necessarily infected, Mia. There's a chance the virus wasn't transmitted."

"How much chance?"

"I don't know."

"So when will I know?"

"Maybe within twenty-four hours."

Lee said, "It was three days for me."

Malcolm said, "A week for me."

Jace said, "Same here, but I felt sick for three days beforehand."

Mia clamped her teeth shut and squeezed away the tears, looking out over the rolling, corn-field-covered hills interspersed with residential subdivisions. "How do you know all this stuff, Sarah?"

"I've been researching this phenomenon for a few months. It's worldwide. That's why I went to Japan this last time. Some scientists are doing research that was...intriguing. We've known something has been happening for a while, but it's so...unbelievable that no one in the upper echelons has listened to us."

"But it's a virus, right? Where did it come from?"

Sarah shrugged. "Could be one of ours, could be the Russians, the Chinese, could even be the British."

Mia sat back in her chair, trying to wrap her mind around the enormity of what could be happening. The entire world? A werewolf plague?

Malcolm said, "If you begin to change, Mia, we'll assist you. It's less traumatic if you have someone to hospice you."

All three boys glanced at each other and nodded.

"Hospice!"

Sarah smiled, "You might want to recheck the dictionary on that one. Mia, you're not dying. I think he means that it's easier to make the transition if you have someone there to help you.

"Um, right," Malcolm said. "It's just kind of *like* dying."

"Well, isn't that a relief!" Mia swallowed back tears. "What's the first sign?"

Jace said, "A hunger that you can't put your finger on."

Sarah nodded. "That's the virus forcing the body to crave what it needs to make the necessary changes. Raw meat and bone marrow."

Cars and semis slid past outside, lights flashing in the deepening night. All those people, so unsuspecting. Mia said, "It's going to get worse, isn't it."

Sarah changed lanes and headed for the off-ramp. "It could get a lot worse."

Mia leaned her head back against the seat. "I'm not going to eat anyone." She didn't even like steak; she couldn't imagine herself craving raw steak. Her mind drifted. The scope of what was happening was so enormous and complex she could scarcely fathom its dimensions.

Jace said, "Even if they're gonna eat you?"

Mia bit her lip. What had Mrs. Johnson said the other day during algebra class? They were looking at a tremendously complex equation on the board. Looking at the equation gave Mia a headache. Mrs. Johnson cautioned against looking at such a complex problem as a whole. Instead, start small, approach systematically at the most manageable level. She spent the entire class period on that one equation, going through a number of simple steps, all of which Mia understood. When it was finished, all the variables and common factors canceled, the result was astonishing in its simplicity. 1 + 1 = 2.

So, first step, keep it simple. She couldn't stop a worldwide werewolf epidemic. She couldn't stop herself from becoming a werewolf; if the bite had infected her, it was already too late. But she could try to save her mother, and she could help stop Slade. Everything else would have to wait.

Except.

"Oh, no!" Mia said. "Mom was bitten, too!"

Sarah's hands twisted steering wheel cover.

Jace said, "If she changes, he won't eat her. He doesn't believe in eating our own kind."

Mia rolled her eyes. "That's great news."

Lee said, "But he might kill her if she disobeys him."

Mia laughed in spite of herself, feeling a sudden rush of hysteria. Her mom's only hope right now was to become a werewolf or else for Mia to turn the boys over to Slade.

Sarah said, "If we give the boys to Slade, he'll likely try to kill us anyway. He can't have witnesses. There are still laws. There are still police. There's still a government."

Mia's phone chirped. She pulled it out. The screen said, "Dalton."

She groaned. The phone went back into her pocket. He would never speak to her again if he knew. Would he speak to her again anyway if she kept ducking him? How could she ever see him again if at any moment she could wolf out and kill him? And *eat* him.

Her stomach heaved. "Stop stop stop!" she cried.

Sarah slammed on the brakes and slid to the shoulder. Mia threw open the door and vomited, spewing acid and bile onto the road. Her eyes streamed with fresh tears. When the heaving subsided, she wept.

Then she felt stupid. She wiped her mouth, wiped her eyes, smoothed her hair, sat up straight in the chair. She sniffed once. It was time to be strong. Her mom was kidnapped, possibly infected. Mia could be infected herself. She had three young werewolves in the seat behind her, and an entire pack of them on her tail. Time to quit acting like a baby. Dalton would have to wait. She closed the door. "I'm okay now. I'm fine."

Their destination, a long building of pale concrete and dark glass was just visible several blocks distant—the F.B.I. field office.

Mia's phone rang, and her stomach clenched. She pulled it out. The incoming call was "Unavailable." She said, "I think it's him."

Sarah said, "Put it on speaker. Boys, don't say anything."

Mia pushed the speakerphone button and answered. "Hello?"

Slade's voice rumbled out of the speaker. "Hello, Mia." The boys froze in their seats. "Where are you?"

"Wouldn't you like to know."

"I have no intention of chasing you. I expect you will come to me. Bring all three boys to the intersection of Bennington Road and 198th Street."

Lee leaped forward. "Screw you, Coach!"

Slade's voice growled. "Is that Lee I hear? How are you, son? It's time to come home, for your own good."

Lee's voice rose with fear. "Don't listen to him! He's going to kill us!"

"Son, I have no intention of killing you. You're one of us. You belong here. Do you want Mia's mother to die because of you?"

Lee swallowed hard, and his posture softened.

"Mia, you have thirty minutes. No tricks, no police, or your mother dies, and then I *will* come after you.

Mia said, "Let me talk to Mom."

"Certainly. I am a...creature of my word."

Moments later, her mother's voice came from the speaker. "*Mia, I'm okay for now! Don't listen to him! He'll—!*"

The phone was wrenched out of her hand. "Now, now, Kyoko. No spoiling the arrangements. Mia, are your instructions clear?"

"Bennington Road and 198th Street, thirty minutes. Got it."

"Good girl."

The connection went dead.

Mia said, "I have no idea where that is."

Sarah said, "It's about thirty miles from here. Northwest of the city."

"We don't have time to find Dad, do we."

"No."

"Then let's go. We'll barely make it in thirty minutes."

Sarah made a U-turn and drove back the way they came.

Mia felt the tension boiling in the back seat. It was an impossible choice. Three lives for one. "We can't do this, Sarah. We can't just turn them over."

"It's okay, Mia," Jace said. "This is our problem. Right, guys? We don't want your mom to die."

Lee and Malcolm nodded.

Sarah floored the minivan down the freeway. Cool wind whipped through the shattered window. She asked the boys to bandage Mia's injured arm. Jace tore a strip of cloth from the hem of his T-shirt and tied it carefully over the torn flesh. Mia could hardly look at it. The bleeding had stopped, but the gashes were deep.

"We could fight them," Lee said.

Malcolm snorted. "Yeah and get our asses trounced. Excuse my language, ladies."

"No," Lee said, "we could fight them long enough for Mia to get her Mom back, then we could run again. Slade can't keep us there against our will for long."

Malcolm snickered. "Yeah, Jace'll just come up with another escape plan anyway, then we're gone again. We'll pretend to be good pack mates for a while."

Jace rubbed his eyes. "I don't think that's what he aims to do."

Mia said, "You said he wants you back in the Pack."

"Maybe. But something's been eating at me. When a leader of the pack is challenged, there's always a fight. The loser gets a good beatdown. Ain't no way I'm ever gonna let him break me, and he knows it. He knows I'll try to get away again. Mal, would you have run away on your own?"

"Maybe...I don't know."

"What about you, Lee?"

Lee pursed his lips. "Probably...Maybe."

"To keep you guys, he needs me gone. Two for the price of one."

"You saying he's gonna kill you?"

"He needs to make an example. He can't very well have the rest of the pack getting their own ideas neither, you know?"

Mia said, "None of you are going back! Sarah, what if we just call the police? The F.B.I.! Report it as a kidnapping."

Sarah said, "Wolves know how to signal each other about prey or danger, even over great distances. A lot of information goes into a wolf howl. These are wolves who think almost like humans. They'll know the police are coming."

Mia threw her hands up. "We can't just give them over, Sarah!"

Sarah frowned. "We don't have a choice. Sometimes you have to play the game."

"Play the game?"

"We're trapped, and he knows it. But he doesn't know everything."

They drove in silence toward the inevitable. They did not dare to miss the meeting, and they did not dare to go through with the exchange. As the minutes and freeway slid past, Sarah's face grew harder and harder, her mouth drawing into a thin line. Eventually they left the freeway and headed northwest through residential neighborhoods that grew ever more sparse. Night had since fallen, and streetlights grew farther and farther between until the lights disappeared altogether. They turned onto a dark gravel road.

Mia couldn't bear the thought of turning the boys over to Slade any more than she could bear the thought of a pack of wolves eating her mother, even the dark hole of sucking depression that her mother was. Maybe she could talk to Slade. Maybe he could take Mia in exchange. She still had the ultrasonic blaster and the bear spray in her pocket. She envisioned using the ultrasonic blaster to incapacitate the werewolves while dashing out and spiriting her mother to safety. However, the blaster had not worked on Slade the second time. Somehow he must have devised a way to block its effects.

Sarah said, "This is Bennington Road. A couple of miles to go."

Hope plummeted in Mia's chest. "What are you going to do?"

"I'm going to...talk to him."

The hope sputtered and died completely. "Talk to him? Sarah, I'm sure you're very charming with all that spy mojo, but do you think a werewolf is going to let you talk him out of his evil plan?"

"I can be very persuasive."

Mia sat up straighter. "So you have mind-control powers, too?"

"Afraid not."

"Look," Jace said, "just let me fight him. You three can get away. We can heal pretty fast. Maybe I'll survive. Then the three of us can figure out what to do later."

Lee said, "We could just up and skedaddle. Make 'em chase us again."

"No!" Sarah said. "You boys are not to get out of this car. Unless my 'talk' doesn't work."

Mia said, "What if your 'talk' doesn't work?"

"It has to. It will."

Lee piped up, "We just passed 192nd Street."

"Mia," Sarah said. "Trust me. I've been in situations like this before. There's something I want you to do, though. If you get the chance to take your mom, do it, and don't look back. Don't look back."

"What are you talking about?"

"Just tell me you'll do it. You'll be ready."

Mia swallowed hard. "I'll be ready."

"Good girl." Sarah reached over and squeezed Mia's hand.

"That's what Slade said to me."

"Sorry. You know I love you, right?"

"I love you, too, and you're scaring me."

"It's okay to be scared. Fear can be useful. Just don't let it freeze you up. We're here."

CHAPTER TWENTY-SIX

Sarah slowed the minivan and brought it to a halt in the lonely intersection of Bennington Road and 198th Street, two gravel roads with tall, dense thatches of mature corn growing in all directions.

Another set of headlights flooded through the night about fifty yards up 198th Street. A black silhouette appeared in the headlights, a figure walking toward them.

Sarah got out of the minivan and walked toward the lights.

Slade's voice came from the silhouette. "So. You're the...aunt." Mia strained her ears to listen. "Does she know?"

"Where's Kyoko?" Sarah said.

Slade raised his arm and made a signal. A slim, unsteady figure appeared in the headlights, flanked by two taller shapes.

Mia got out of the van.

A chorus of whispered warnings came from the three boys.

She started walking toward her mother.

Sarah eyes went wide. "Mia, what are you doing?"

Mia clenched her fists. "I'm going to get my mom," she said to Sarah. Then she glared into Slade's eyes and walked past. Her insides turned to cold pudding. A small smile played across Slade's lips. Mia kept walking.

Slade said, "Where are my boys?"

"In the van," Sarah said. "They're not coming with you."

Mia flinched and almost stopped, but she forced her feet to keep moving. Her knees felt wobbly.

Slade made another signal, and the taller shapes grabbed the middle figure by the arms.

Mia's mother cried out.

Slade said to Sarah, "So you're breaking the deal?"

Mia walked up to the two young men standing in the headlight beams and holding her mother by the arms. The headlight beams spilled from the snout of a white full-size van. The young men were clean-shaven, a year or two older than Mia, both naked except for gym shorts. One of them towered over her with his piercing blue eyes. He had arms and shoulders like a competitive swimmer, lithe and muscular.

Mia looked up at him. "What's your name?"

She vaguely heard Slade's voice behind her. "...ending this woman's life?"

The young man met her gaze. "I'm Eric."

"I would smile and shake your hand, Eric, but you're holding my mom prisoner. Kind of hard to be friends this way."

Her mom looked dazed, barely able to stand. Blood soaked her shoulder, stained the front of her shirt. "Mia," she whispered, "*what are you doing?*"

"I'm taking you home, Mom." She turned her gaze up at Eric again. "Please let my mom go."

The other young man grinned at her. "You got yourself some *cojones,* little girl."

Mia tried to hear what Sarah was saying, but she did not dare look away from these two. Raw, animalistic power radiated off them in waves.

Sarah said to Slade, "I wanted to give you one last chance to talk things over like rational human beings. You're a rational man. You're training is in science. You should know the value of logic, of *reason.* You should know that you don't have to behave this way. You can control the bestial side."

Eric said to Mia, "Jace and the guys okay?"

Mia poked him in chest. "Except for being hungry and terrified, they're fine. Better with me than with you.

Eric nodded, unable to meet her gaze. "Good."

Mia looked up into his face. "What are you doing? Let her go. Please. She needs a doctor. And I need somebody to make my lunch for school tomorrow."

The other young man laughed. "Seriously?"

Slade laughed. "You think *this* is my bestial side? Oh, honey, this is the rational side! This is about discovering the truth. This is the scientific method itself! I intend nothing less than to get to the bottom of this... gift, and turn it to full advantage."

Sarah inched closer to Slade. "We are still civilized human beings. We still have laws, morality—"

"Those laws were written by humans. Can human ethics be applied to a pride of lions on the hunt? To sharks?"

"But what you're doing is evil!"

"Of course it's evil! Just like gazelles must see lions as evil, or mice see house cats as evil—or maybe how cattle, pigs, sheep, chickens must see humans as evil. Even as humans we eat creatures with brains and heartbeats and feelings. Food must always see its predator as evil. Nature simply doesn't care!"

"You're insane!"

"No, *you're* insane if you think all this—" He slapped his chest with one hand and gestured toward the wolves with the other. "—isn't going to change *everything*! This is about restructuring the Earth's entire food chain! Humans are about to lose their place at the top of it. Morality has no place in science, or in the law of the wild. Human ethics certainly had no hand in creating this virus!"

Mia stood closer to Eric, almost close enough for her breasts to touch him. Alas, her queendom for bigger boobs! Even so, their closeness to Eric's powerful rippling body sparked tingles throughout her body. His nostrils flared, and he licked his lips. She took her mother's hand and gazed up into Eric's eyes, then laid a gentle hand on his iron-hard wrist. "Please, Eric."

His grip loosened, and she slipped her mom's arm away.

The other young man said, "What are you doing, man?"

Eric whispered, "Let her go."

"What?"

"Just do it, man, she's hurt!"

Mia looked up at him, trying to contain her shock. "Thank you," she whispered, trying to hold her voice steady. She threw her mom's good arm over her shoulder and hurried her back toward the minivan. Seven silent lupine shapes lined both sides of the road, a gauntlet.

Sarah's voice rose. "This is still nice, safe, Heartland Nebraska. You know, go Huskers! This is still the United States!"

Slade's voice remained neutral. "You obviously know something about what's going on here. How quickly do you think this virus will spread? How long before the entire population of the United States becomes either predator or prey? How long do you think our two-hundred-year-old institutions will last against forces of nature that are older than mankind? How long do you think civilization itself will stand? There's a war coming. And your side won't know who the enemy is."

Mia and her mom passed Sarah and Slade. Two wolves fell into pace beside her, one on either side, tongues lolling, heads cocked at curious angles, their breath forming puffs of steam in the headlight beams.

Sarah inched still closer to Slade. "Laws still exist, and you do still look human most of the time; therefore, I think pretty much any cop would arrest you for kidnapping, attempted murder, assault, child abuse, and umpteen other charges. As for charges against the wolf side, those might be a bit hard to prove. You know all this as well as I do, however much the bloodlust has seeped into your brain. We know your name and where you work. How can you possibly expect that we believe you'll let us go?"

The wolves on either side of Mia started to growl.

Slade cracked his knuckles. "If you're so certain I'm going to kill you, then why are you here?"

Mia looked over her shoulder.

Faster than sight, Sarah lashed out, her open hand appearing to stroke Slade's throat. Slade staggered back, clutching his throat, gagging, gasping for air. Instantly she was behind him, on him, one arm looped around his throat, the other locking it place. Slade's eyes bulged. His corded hands and muscular arms clawed at her slim white forearm.

Sarah cranked her arm tighter. "To challenge you for the pack!"

The wolves snarled and turned away from Mia, rushing toward the sudden grapple.

Mia dashed toward the minivan, half-dragging her mom. The side door stood open and she shoved her mom inside. Deuce still sat on the front seat, and he looked at her as if to say *What on Earth are you doing? Are you deranged?*

Seven wolves encircled to two struggling figures in the headlight beams. Slade's face turned red, and a lupine muzzle thrust itself out from his nose and mouth, razor-sharp teeth gleaming. His shoulders and arms thickened from within, meaty pops and slitherings. Claws sprang from his fingertips and slashed at her, tearing gashes across her shoulders.

Mia stood transfixed by the melee. "Sarah!"

Sarah kept her eyes on Slade. "Go, Mia! Now! Go!"

The wolves edged closer around the fight.

Sarah's legs hooked around Slade's torso, and the force of her pull cranked his back into a painful arch. How could she be so strong? Slade thrashed and struggled, but her arms corded like two steel cables intertwined. His efforts were losing strength.

But her face didn't look right anymore.

His breath came in ragged gasps. Then his body fell onto all fours, an enormous black and silver shape, and then onto his side with Sarah still holding on. Slade the wolf thrashed up puffs of road dust.

The pack edged closer, their eyes fixed on the melee, six of them now, all awaiting the outcome.

Mia ran around the minivan and threw herself into the driver's seat. The three boys hunched forward, their faces almost against the windshield. Mia gripped the steering wheel with one hand, the other paused over the shifting lever. She couldn't just leave Sarah like this. "What does she think she's doing?"

Jace's eyes shone. "She's *challenging*."

"You mean she's trying to take over the pack? But can't only wolves..."

Sarah's clothes were ripped now, and the growls merged into a cacophony of snarls. Slade's struggles diminished.

Lee pumped a fist. "C'mon, Sarah, tear his freakin' head off!"

Malcolm whooped in agreement.

The circle of wolves drew closer to the melee, obscuring Mia's view. Mia had never wished harm on another human being before, but she wanted Slade dead. But how could Sarah kill a werewolf, even with all the military hand-to-hand and martial arts training in the world?

A broad splash of silvery white fur appeared in the melee. Sarah's shredded shirt flew. A flurry of movement drove the circle of wolves back a few steps, revealing a white wolf with its powerful jaws clamped around the throat of the black and silver beast. The white wolf's torso was wrapped in a strange black suit that left only white furry legs and head exposed. The black suit gleamed dully in the headlight beams.

"What is she wearing?" Jace said.

Malcolm said, "It appears to be a wetsuit."

Lee snorted. "A werewolf in a wetsuit? How many thousand miles is it to the ocean?"

Slade's body twisted, and its claws raked the white wolf's underbelly, but no gashes appeared in the black suit. The white wolf tore at Slade's throat, and blood stained the white muzzle. With a tremendous heave the black and silver wolf finally threw the white wolf aside, breaking the grip of its jaws.

The two monsters faced each other, circling, snarling, teeth snapping in challenge.

"Sarah!" Mia cried, then clamped her hands over her mouth.

The white wolf glanced away from Slade toward the minivan. In that instant, Slade attacked, lunging forward, driven by the tremendous power of his massive shoulders and sinewy legs. His teeth slashed across Sarah's face. Their teeth clashed with a loud snap, like cracking two thick sticks together. Blood sprayed across the road, but Mia couldn't tell from which. The two shapes thrashed and slashed and snapped, faster than Mia could follow, darting, falling back, feinting, rage and bloodlust gleaming in their feral eyes. Slade's muzzle clamped around Sarah's throat. Her hind claws bunched and tore into his underbelly. Red ribbons of flesh spattered blood across the dirt. Sarah's eyes squeezed shut. Mia couldn't see how it happened, but suddenly Sarah was free. Her white throat and muzzle and claws were stained deep red as she spun and leaped over the circle of wolves, out of the headlight beams into the ditch, half disappearing in the tall grass. A streak of white arced over the barb wire fence into the corn field. Slade roared with rage and charged after her. The other wolves fell into pursuit.

"Sarah!" Mia peeped.

Jace clasped her shoulder. "Let's get out of here!"

"But—!"

"Don't you think she can take care of herself? She's leading them away!"

Mia swallowed hard and nodded. Her mom lay unconscious on the back seat. Mia threw the minivan into gear, turned down 198th Street, away from the other vehicle, and smashed the gas pedal against the floor. The tires spewed gravel and left a plume of thick dust gathering moonlight behind them.

CHAPTER TWENTY-SEVEN

The emergency room at Immanuel Hospital was like a morgue. Only one nurse on duty sitting behind the admittance desk, and only one patient, an old man who lay on an examination table with an oxygen mask over his face and his elderly wife who sat beside him, quietly weeping. Mia and Jace helped her mom inside.

Jace wrinkled his nose. "Cripes, it stinks in here!"

Mia sniffed. Alcohol, urine, and other chemical smells she could not identify.

The nurse saw the blood covering Mia and her mother, and hurried around the counter to help them, ushering them into the E.R. Even as they eased Mia's mom onto a bed, Mia sensed Jace's nervousness.

His gaze flicked here and there, over his shoulder as if expecting a cop to attempt to cuff him at any moment. He whispered, "I gotta go."

"You're not leaving are you?"

"No, I'll get the guys and we'll wait out front. I hate hospitals."

The E.R. doctor was older than her father, bald as a billiard ball, but with a face cragged by untold years of witnessing anguish and death on a daily basis. His voice was gruff, terse. "What happened?"

Another nurse, hefty and flinty-eyed, pulled her mother's shirt up over her head.

Mia slid into her carefully prepared story. "We were attacked by a really big dog. Really big. It bit her."

"Where?"

"Walking on a bike path. Spearhead Trail."

The doctor's gaze flicked toward her for a moment.

The nurse sponged the ragged wound and wiped away the blood. Mia's mother was awake but with glazed eyes, sitting up on the examination table. Blood still leaked from the deepest gashes.

The doctor said, "What happened to the dog?"

"I chased it away." Mia squirmed under the force of his gaze.

"You chased it away." A hairless eyebrow rose.

"With this." She pulled the ultrasonic blaster out of her pocket and showed it to him.

He nodded vaguely and scribbled something on his clipboard. "Was the animal frothing at the mouth?"

"Not that I saw."

"What kind of dog was it? You should report this to Animal Control. That dog could attack someone else."

"It looked like a wolf."

He stopped scribbling and fixed his gaze on her. "A wolf. You sure it wasn't a coyote or something?"

The nurse measured the bite with her hand. "Too big to be a coyote, Doctor. This bite is from a large animal."

He turned his skepticism on the nurse. "How do you know this?"

Her voice dripped with disdain. "I watch *C.S.I.* And my boyfriend has a Great Dane and a pit bull. I know dog jaws. This is a Great Dane size bite. The jaws clamped over her entire shoulder." She demonstrated with her surgical-gloved hand. The torn flesh around the gashes was as pale as the nurse's gloves.

The doctor glanced at the wound again and sniffed strangely, then put down his clipboard. He lightly fingered the flesh around the wound, scrutinizing the depth and damage on both sides. "Get me a nineteen gauge needle and some normal saline so I can irrigate this." The nurse brought him a plastic bag filled with clear liquid and poured it into a small stainless steel basin, then a large syringe, which she filled with saline. For the next several minutes, the doctor gently squirted saline into the gashes, catching the bloody salt-water with sterile gauze pads. As he did so, he peered closely at the internal tissue. "There's a bit of damage to the tendons, but none severed, nothing permanent. You're not going to lose any function. A bit of nerve damage, though. You'll have some numb spots."

The nurse said, "Scalpel for debridement?"

He turned to the nurse long enough to give her a withering stare. "Yes, that will be next."

Mia blanched. "You're going to cut her?"

The doctor's attention fixed back onto the gashes. "Have to."

The nurse rolled her eyes at the doctor's cold tone. "Don't worry, hon. It's just to cut away the tissue that's too damaged to heal properly. It'll heal better with clean cuts."

"Oh. Will it hurt?" Mia found her gaze drawn to the pale skin marred by ragged holes. It all hung loosely over what looked like raw steak.

"No, we'll use some anesthetic."

"Oh. That's good."

"If you're going to question everything," the doctor said, "perhaps you should go out to the waiting room."

The nurse gave Mia a kind smile and shook her head. Mia sighed and tried to relax.

The doctor stepped back. "Apply the topical. I'll be back in a few minutes to debride. Then we'll send you on your way with some oral antibiotics. I'm going to call animal control and tell them to look for the dog. If they can catch it, it should be tested for rabies. You may need to get rabies shots."

The nurse nodded, and the doctor strode away. When he was out of earshot, the nurse glanced after him. "He didn't used to be such an ass."

Something in the nurse's tone raised Mia's short hairs. "No?"

"He goes on vacation or sabbatical or some such for like a month, comes back, and seems to have lost his bedside manner entirely. But you didn't hear me say that." She winked at Mia.

Mia smiled weakly.

"We're so short-handed lately, he can't afford to tick anybody off." The nurse touched Mia's injured arm. "That dog get you, too? You okay, hon?"

"Yeah, it did. A little."

"Take that dirty bandage off and let me have a look at it. Sit down here." She gestured to one of the empty E.R. beds.

"Okay."

The nurse peeled away the bandage made from Jace's T-shirt, and

Mia's heart jumped at how raw and painful the gashes looked. Fresh pain burned up through her arm.

"You okay, hon?" The nurse set to cleaning the wound.

"I'm okay. Just scared."

"It'll be okay. This bite isn't so bad. Some antiseptic and bandages and you'll be fine." With practiced efficiency, the nurse picked up the syringe and saline solution and began to clean the wound, similar to how the doctor had irrigated her mother's. The nurse pointed to the bandages from Slade's attack earlier that day. "What's this one?"

"Bike wreck."

"You've had a rough day."

"You have no idea."

As if awakening from a daze, her mom laid a cold hand on Mia's forearm and squeezed gently. *"Has your father called?"*

Mia almost answered in English, but then she remembered the nurse's comments about the doctor. "No. I called him when...when they took you. But he didn't answer. I called him again on the way here."

"It's not like him not to check his messages for so long."

"I know." Another sting.

The nurse went to a nearby cabinet and began to gather more packages and bottles on a stainless steel tray.

"Where's Sarah?" Her mom's voice grew weak, wavering. "I remember something strange. She was fighting..."

"She got away."

"I...don't remember that. She had him in a headlock, then..."

"Don't worry about Sarah now, Mom. She's fine." Sarah's cell phone was still in the minivan. Even if she was alive, even if she had reverted to human form, Mia had no way to contact her now. All she could do now was wait.

The nurse daubed ointment onto the gashes, then wrapped Mia's forearm in gauze and secured it with tape.

"I'm starting to look like a war victim."

The nurse smiled. "Just keep it clean and you'll be fine. Let me change that other dressing for you." Dried blood had seeped through the gauze. Mia gritted her teeth as the nurse peeled the tape from her skin, revealing the deep scratches Slade's claws had left.

"That doesn't look like a bike wreck to me."

"Uh, there was a dog involved with that one too."

The nurse leaned back. "Girl, you don't have to tell me, but I don't appreciate being lied to."

"Sorry. I'd just rather not. It's been a hard day."

The nurse frowned as she replaced the paramedic's bandage with a clean one.

Mia smiled and clasped her hand over it. "Thanks."

The nurse glanced over Mia's shoulder. "Looks like there's somebody over there wants to talk to you."

Jace hovered in the emergency room entrance.

She slid off the bed and approached him.

He glanced past Mia and around the E.R., searching for something or someone. "Your mom okay?"

"So far, so good."

"We'll know if she starts to change. Her wound will heal real fast. That's how it happened with me."

"Where are the other two?"

"Sitting outside. Their arms are still...you know. And they hate hospitals, too. Too many powerful smells that cover up important stuff."

A pair of orderlies wheeled a gurney into the E.R. and lifted the old man onto it, gathering the I.V. pole and detaching the monitor cables.

Mia said, "What are you looking for?"

"That doctor."

"Why?"

"I can smell one around here."

"One what? Oh."

"We give off a scent that ain't quite human. Sometimes it can be covered up, but...With enough time we can always tell."

Mia sniffed the air and her hackles rose. Was her olfactory sense getting stronger, too? Did she want it to? "Is it in the emergency room?"

The orderlies wheeled the old man out of the emergency room, and his elderly wife did her best to follow. The doors swung shut behind them.

"I can't tell. Too many chemicals."

Her phone buzzed against her leg, and she whipped it out, hoping to see her father's name. She was elated and disappointed at the same time to see a text message from Dalton. "HEY GORJUS. U OK? WORRIED ABOUT U. NASTY SCENE 2DAY."

A tingle of pleasure wafted through her, quickly followed by twin stabs of sorrow and fear. How could she ever have a boyfriend if she was a werewolf? If she ever had kids, would they look like puppies? She thumbed a text back. "I'M OK. LONG HARD DAY. HAD TO TAKE MOM TO DOCTOR. AND THX FOR ASKING. *~ SMILE ~*"

She looked at Jace. "What if you come in with me again? Maybe you can spot it."

"Trouble is, whoever it is will have just as much chance of spotting me, too."

"It couldn't be...Mom, could it? Or me?"

"Too soon, I think."

Another text came from Dalton. "GLAD UR OK. HOW'S ARM?"

She fingered into a reply, "PAINFUL. IT NEEDS A KISS." What was she doing flirting at a time like this? Her finger hovered over the send button for only an instant before launching the missile that opened her up to getting shot down.

Jace shoved his hands in the pockets of his sweat pants. "You know, if it turns out..."

"What?" She shook her head at her own audacity with Dalton and turned her attention back to Jace.

"If it turns out you and your mom...you know."

Mia sighed and nodded.

"You'll be different, but...you'll still be yourself, you know?"

Mia imagined herself eating raw flesh and felt her gorge rise. She covered her mouth.

A new text came in: "HAPPY 2 OBLIGE. WHERE R U?"

The memory of the amazing dream-kiss flooded her mind like warm chicken soup, the smell of him, the taste of him. God, she wanted him... Here! She wanted him *here*. Something. A warm touch. Anything. She texted back: "IMMANUEL HOSPITAL."

Jace said, "I mean, you ain't gonna turn into a monster or anything. You don't have to."

She thought about Lee and Malcolm's grotesque arms, their blood-soaked black claws. Were they monsters? The enormous black and silver wolf that had dragged her mother away like a bloody rag doll. "*He* became a monster."

"He made choices. He let the animal take over, and then he talked himself into how that was okay."

"Do you wish you could be normal again?"

"Sometimes. But it ain't all horrible. I'm still me. And I know the kind of things I ain't ever gonna do again, either normal or wolfed up."

"What times do you wish you could be normal again?"

He blushed a little. "When I meet a cute girl who ain't one of us." He cleared his throat and looked at the floor. "When I think about how the other kids in Slade's pack are losing themselves, too, like he is."

"Like Eric."

"Yeah, Eric is a good guy. He used to be. Awesome wrestler, captain of the team, made All-State last year, the only guy from Saint S's to make it in almost ten years. He always thought Slade was an awesome teacher. I suppose he might have been, before."

Her phone buzzed with a new message from Dalton: "OMW." A thrill shot through her. She wanted somebody to take care of her, and right now, there was no one else.

She thought back to Eric again, and the way he looked so...normal, a cute guy just a little older than her, someone she could have had a crush on if he went to West High School. And didn't eat people. "Maybe something can change their minds. Turn them away from the Dark Side or something."

He shrugged. "Not as long as Slade's in charge. He's the alpha."

"What happens if they give in to the wolf for a long time? Does it get harder to control it?"

"It gets easier to control the physical stuff, but it gets hard to remember what it's like not liking raw meat, not being able to run like a freaked out antelope, not being stronger than normal people, not being able to know people by scent. It gets hard to not look down on normal people. They're weaker."

The sound of movement turned her around. The doctor approached her mother and sat down next to the nurse, glanced at Mia and Jace, then set his bright blue coffee cup down on a nearby cart.

The doctor glanced at Jace again, reaching for the scalpel. Then he stopped. Something passed over the doctor's face, like a flicker that left his expression strangely changed. He cleared his throat and turned to the nurse. "I forgot something. I'll be right back." He stood and walked out of the E.R., just a little too quickly.

Jace's eyes narrowed.

"Could it be him?" Mia said.

"Real hard to say unless I got close and smelled him. Most people think that's kinda rude." He smirked at her.

She smiled back.

A man's voice came over the P.A. system in the emergency room. "Rhonda to I.C.U., please. Rhonda to I.C.U."

The nurse sighed. "Shoot." To Mia's mom, she said, "You just lay back and relax, honey. I'll be back shortly." She eased the wounded woman back onto the elevated bed and covered her up. Then the nurse hurried out of the E.R.

Mia crossed the empty E.R. to her mom's bedside. The shoulder gashes still looked ragged and raw, but the bleeding had stopped. Jace came and stood nearby.

Her mom smiled at her with half-lidded eyes. "It's okay not to worry, Mia. I'm all right. I'm just so tired..."

Jace said, "Thanks for coming to help us, ma'am. I'm real sorry you got hurt."

A tear trickled down her mom's cheek. "You're a good boy."

"Not really, ma'am, but thanks all the same." Jace looked around the E.R. The silence was broken only by the hum and beep of machines and the whisper of the ventilation system. The cold, pale glow of the fluorescent lights turned her mom's pale skin into the flesh of a ghost. "I'm gonna go see what the guys are doing." He headed for the door, glancing around as he went.

Her mom said, "He's such a nervous boy."

Jace pushed through the swinging doors to the waiting room and disappeared.

Mia squeezed her mom's hand. Her gaze fell upon the coffee cup the doctor had placed on the cart. It was royal blue, and read SAINT SEBASTIAN'S WRESTLING BOOSTER CLUB.

Mia gasped.

A sharp yelp sounded from the waiting room.

CHAPTER TWENTY-EIGHT

Mia ran to the swinging doors and stopped to peer through the window into the waiting room. The doctor clutched Jace's body with one arm, and in the other a syringe stuck in the boy's neck. Jace's eyes blazed with fear and rage as he struggled against the doctor's grip. The doctor's face was devoid of emotion as he pulled out the syringe and tossed it away, holding Jace tight until the boy's struggles weakened and his body began to sag.

Mia ducked below the window. Her entire body felt like a quivering water balloon that had just been emptied. From across the room in bed, her mom stared at her. Mia ran back to her side. "We have to get out of here! Right now!"

"But—"

"The doctor is one of them! Come on, Mom! We have to go."

Her mom swung her legs off the bed and tried to stand.

"Can you run?"

"I can walk."

Mia spotted some packages that said STERILE BANDAGE on the nearby cart. She snatched them and stuffed them into her back pocket, then spotted the scalpel, its blade safely sheathed in plastic. She took that too. "Come on."

"Wait, I have to get dressed," her mom said. Mia had forgotten that she was only wearing her jeans, shoes, and a bra. Her shirt lay on a tray, torn up and soaked with dried blood. Mia stripped a blanket off the bed, threw it over her mom's shoulders, and took her hand. They hurried toward the doors that led deeper into the hospital.

The clock on the wall said: 9:30. Her dad should have called by now. She hurried through the doors into a long, deserted hallway. More doors dotted both sides of the hallway, bearing plaques with medical-sounding words she didn't understand. She pulled out her cell phone and called her dad again. The phone rang and rang in her ear as they rounded a corner, passing an arrowed sign that said LOBBY. The call went once again to her dad's voice mail. She hung up.

Her mom said, "Maybe we should call the police."

"What are we going to tell them? Werewolves are coming to get us? The doctor gave Jace a shot to knock him out. That doctor can tell the police anything he wants, and he knows Slade. I saw the coffee cup."

Her mom clutched the blanket tighter around her shoulders. A semi-brisk walk was the fastest she could manage.

A young nurse rounded the corner ahead of them. She smiled. "Hi. Can I help you?"

Mia smiled back, a big beaming grin that felt cracked at the edges. "Just going for a little walk. Looking for the lobby."

The nurse thumbed over her shoulder. "You're headed the right direction."

"Great! Thanks!" When the nurse had rounded another corner behind them, she whispered, "We have to get out of sight." She noticed a plaque next to a nearby door. PRIVATE FAMILY WAITING ROOM. It was unlocked. She threw open the door to the dark room beyond, felt for the light switch, and ushered her mom inside. A click of the switch revealed a comfortably appointed room with a couch, several soft chairs, a coffee maker, tiny microwave, a small faucet and sink, a telephone, and a television. She eased the door closed, checking the hallway. All clear. Then she shoved one of the chairs under the door latch.

Her mom sank onto the couch and sprawled back. "Ah, my head hurts. I feel so dizzy."

"Do you want some tea?" A small tray beside the coffee maker held tea bags and sugar packets. Maybe some caffeine would help wake her up.

"Thirsty..."

Mia's hands shook as she filled a cup with water, stuck it in the tiny microwave, and waited. The minute ticked by to the microwave's steady buzz. Why hadn't her father called her back? Was Sarah okay? She needed to get her mom to a different hospital, one on the other side of town, far away from this doctor, farther away from Slade. She needed to tell her dad what was happening. And she needed to help the boys. But how?

Her dad had told her a couple of times the name of the department where he worked, but she couldn't remember. It sounded like so much F.B.I. mumbo-jumbo, just like all the military stuff she had lived with her entire life, and she was tired of hearing it. Now, she would give anything to remember. The microwave dinged. "Mom, do you have Dad's phone number, the land line?"

"I don't remember it, but it's in my cell phone."

"Where's your cell phone?"

Her mom's eyes glimmered with hope. "In my purse."

"Where's your purse?"

The glimmer diminished. "In the van."

Moments passed in silence.

Her mom said, "I'll be fine. Not everyone in this hospital is a werewolf."

"How do you know?" Mia gave her mom a long look. Then she slid the chair aside. Then she spotted the number of the phone on the coffee table. "Wait." She thumbed the number into her phone and saved it, in case she might need to call this room.

"Be careful."

"I'll be back."

As she stepped out in the hallway, it occurred to her that the doctor might have alerted hospital security or even the police to be on the lookout for a little Asian girl and her injured mother. Would he be so bold? He was the one with something to hide, after all. Would he dare draw that much attention to himself? Then again, perhaps he was crafty enough to hide in plain sight. The cops would certainly believe anything a doctor had to say, at least initially, long enough to put the boys firmly back into Slade's clutches, perhaps even have Mia and her family arrested for harboring fugitives. She hoped Sarah was okay. All these thoughts gave her pause, but only a pause.

She strode purposefully down the hallway. The best attitude would be to act as if she was supposed to be there. Just a little Asian girl doing her own thing. Nothing suspicious at all. Nothing to see here. Don't see me. Don't notice me. Smile at the nice lady doctor.

The nice lady doctor stopped. "Are you okay?"

Mia's heart leaped into her throat. She slowed her pace. "I'm perfectly fine, actually. Perfectly. Why?"

"You have blood on your shirt."

Mia looked down and noticed the blood spatters all over her shirt, from when Deuce and the werewolf had clashed inches from her face, from the bite on her arm. "Oh, that! It's okay. It's not mine. I'm fine really. My mom was in an accident, but everything is okay now."

"Are you sure? You look a little shaken up."

Mia gulped. "Really. I'm okay. Just going to get, um...some juice. Vending machines this way?" She pointed down the hallway. Please let the vending machines be that direction. Her heart hammered against her throat like a fish trying to jump out of a bait cooler.

"Yes, that way." The doctor gave her a worried smile. "Here, I'll show you."

"That's okay. You don't have to."

"It's no trouble." The doctor led her down the hallway.

They rounded another corner. Mia stifled a gasp as she came face-to-face with two tall, broad-shouldered police officers.

The doctor said, "Excuse us."

The officers hurried past on either side, hands on their sidearms, heading in the direction of the emergency room.

Mia cleared her throat feebly. "They looked like they were in a hurry."

"Sometimes patients in the E.R. cause trouble. No big deal. Happens all the time." But the wrinkle of concern on her otherwise smooth brow told a different story.

Through the plate glass windows of the hospital gift shop, Mia could now see the lobby, a brightly lit expanse dotted with islands of chairs that looked only semi-comfortable, and beyond that another wall of plate glass that surveyed the front parking lot. In a small nook beside the gift shop, a handful of vending machines offered drinks and snacks, none of which Mia found remotely appealing.

She smiled anyway. "Thanks, Doctor."

"You're quite welcome. And take care. Hope you have a better night."

Mia breathed relief as the doctor resumed her trek to wherever she was going. When the doctor was out of sight, Mia surveyed the lobby for any security guards or police. None in sight. She hurried around the gift shop and made a beeline for the revolving front doors, doing her best to move quickly but not too quickly. Two men slept in their chairs; a woman watched a news report on television about a rash of missing persons cases. The information desk was unoccupied. No one paid her any attention. The revolving doors started to move at her approach.

Moments later she stood breathing the cool fresh scents of the outside air, exhilaration flickering through her that she had gotten this far. The minivan was parked near the emergency room entrance, at the rear of the hospital. She had to circle the building. In the open, under the streetlights. Better again to act like she belonged there than to act suspicious, so she turned nonchalantly and started the long walk around the enormous building.

Bugs swarmed in the light-pools of buzzing street lamps. The dark beetle-shells of cars gleamed dully, scattered around the sprawling parking lot. Crickets and frogs creaked in the grass.

A car approached, headlights washing over her. She kept walking. The car tires squealed to a stop.

CHAPTER TWENTY-NINE

A familiar voice issued from the driver's window. "Mia? Is that you?"

A peculiar mixture of elation and horror burst through her. Dalton smiled at her from behind the wheel. "Hey."

Her legs felt like pillars of rotten wood strapped together with rubber bands. "Hi!" She tried to smile, but it didn't quite work.

"Where you off to? Walking home?"

She smiled. God, he was cute. "No, silly. Just headed to the back parking lot."

"Why?"

"Get my mom's cell phone out of the car."

"Why are you walking around the entire building?"

"Wanted some fresh air." Why was it so easy to lie?

"How about I give you a ride back there? It's gotta be a quarter mile around this building."

In Dalton's car, she could remain hidden longer, stay less visible. "Okay." She shrugged, but there wasn't a single cell in her body that felt casual. She was acutely aware of his eyes on her as she passed through the pool of headlights. He swiped a pile of wrappers off the passenger seat. His car was older than either of them, with a few minor dents and a line of rust that skirted the lower edges of all four doors like a brown lace fringe. The door creaked open for her, and she slid inside. The interior smelled like stale burgers and fries. A plastic skull with flashing red eyes hung from the rearview mirror, and a bumper sticker was stuck to the ceiling. I'M THE PRODUCT OF A SECRET GOVERNMENT PROJECT. A glance in the backseat revealed a morass of crumpled McDonald's, Taco John's, and Runza bags and paper cups.

"Yeah," he said, "my car is a mess, I know." He eased the car forward and began to turn around.

She threw herself across the console and flung her arms around his neck.

The tires squeaked as he stomped the brake and shifted himself to return her embrace. "My, this is a surprise." His breath was warm against her neck, her face.

No, she would not tell him how happy she was that he was there. "I have to keep you guessing. It's part of my allure of mystery."

He chuckled, and turned her face to his, and kissed her. Her world exploded, and in the molten aftershock, her body melted against his like warm butter. His left hand slid across the small of her back, just under the hem of her shirt, warm and soft and strong all at the same time. A wave of heat surged over her from her toes to the top of her head, pounding in her ears. His tongue flicked against hers, deftly, not intrusively. Their lips molded as if they had never been separate, and every part of her flesh from her nipples to her belly button on down began to tingle and melt with exquisite ripples. She pressed her lips against his with a sudden wanton animal yearning. His warm hand crept up the skin of her back, sending little lightning bolts up and down her spine, short circuiting her brain, which was somehow amidst this chaos of sensation pinging at her like an alarm klaxon.

With a gasp, she pulled her lips away from his. His hand slid down to her hip, over her jeans.

Three inches apart, their eyes locked.

Pulling her lips away had severed the short circuit, and the alarm klaxon blared, killing the sensations like a bucket of ice water.

Mia whispered, "Whoa."

Dalton whispered, "Whoa."

She eased herself away from him, sliding back into her own seat, acutely aware of the quickening of her breath, the after-surges of warm blood spreading throughout her body, her skin vibrating, still yearning to be touched. She cleared her throat and tucked some stray hairs behind her ear. "Emergency room is in back."

"Gotcha." He took and deep breath and resituated himself in his seat, adjusting his jeans.

Mia's eyes were wide as she looked out in the dark and a thundering silence hovered between them. She tried to put some reins on the speed of her heartbeat. Her hands trembled as she laid them over her chest. What *was* that? She could live the rest of her life, and never forget that moment. She had French-kissed some gawky band geek back in L.A. at a spin-the-bottle party, right before her family had moved. He had groped her clumsily, over her bra, in the backyard of Kate's house. It wasn't awful, and she had allowed it, but nothing like this. Nothing had ever felt like this. That yearning, aching, tingling had turned off her rational brain like a switch, and some kind of animal had taken over.

What would have happened if she had not been able to control that animal?

She knew exactly what would have happened. Every twinge of curiosity she had ever felt, every meandering moment of romantic reverie, all would have been satisfied.

Then she would have immediately felt like a slut. A cold gobbet of guilt congealed in her belly, collecting all those pleasant tingles in her body like a bath tub drain, disappearing. How many conversations had she had with Nicki and other girls about when it was okay to do this or that? First base, second base, third base, and then the Big One. It seemed that sex, and the infinite gradations of it, were the only topic of conversation sometimes. Girl A was a tease because she had been dating Boy B for six months and the poor sod couldn't get past second base. Girl X was a slut because she let Boy Y round all the bases and high-five his buddies as he crossed the plate. Rumors churning, recriminations burning.

But that moment had been real—and utterly beyond her control. Not just guilt now, but fear, too. She had wanted to throw him down and...

Dalton's voice intruded. "... So how's your mom?"

"Hmm?"

"How's your mom?"

"Too serious for a band-aid but not serious enough to stay overnight. Make sense?"

"Enough."

"I *really* have to call my dad. She has his number."

A high-pitched whine impinged upon her consciousness. A siren, incoming. Ambulance or police car?

"So, what happened to your mom?"

"I'll explain later, I promise. It's a really long story. Right now, I just need to call Dad."

Dad certainly would not approve of the thoughts swirling in his little girl's brain, of the things her body wanted to do just a minute ago. And it had *wanted* to do them. She squirmed a little in her seat.

Flashing red and blue lights appeared on the distant street leading to the hospital. She hoped Lee and Malcolm were still free. She hoped Deuce was okay. He was still a little freaked out when they had arrived at the hospital, whining in the front seat as they had gone inside without him.

A minute later, Dalton made the turn leading toward the small parking lot near the emergency room entrance. An ambulance stood with its rear doors open at the hospital entrance.

"Stop!" Mia clutched his arm.

The flashing lights of three police cars, parked near the emergency room entrance.

Dalton slowed the car. "What? Why?"

"Uh, just do it, okay?"

"Whatever." He braked to a stop about fifty yards from the police cars. Mia searched for the officers.

The minivan was the only other car in the parking lot. She saw no heads in the windows. "Pull up beside the van," she said.

Dalton eased the car forward.

"On the side away from the cop cars."

He turned a strange expression on her.

"Just trust me. It's been a weird day."

He smirked. "Don't mind me. This is just getting interesting." He slid the car into the parking space hidden from the police cars by the van. Mia jumped out and circled to the van, shielded her face to peer through the side window. No sign of Lee and Malcolm.

Deuce jumped up on the seat and ruffed at her, his tail wagging furiously. She opened the door, crawled in, and squeezed him in her arms. A warm wet tongue slid up the side of her face, and her eyes teared up. A stampede of experiences came like a herd of bison through her mind, thundering, so much crammed into so little time. It was then that she realized that some of the blood crusting his face and chest was his. Several wet gashes wept blood across his muzzle. One ear was torn and limp, one eye swollen. His body quivered with weariness. How could she have not noticed?

She kissed him on top of his bristly head. "Oh, god, I'm so sorry! We need to get you cleaned up!" But there was no way to do that now. She hugged him again, and he licked her. "Oh, I'm so sorry! You have to stay here a bit longer."

No officers were visible, but two silhouettes sat in the backseat of one of the cruisers. Lee and Malcolm. Their heads hung heavily, motionless. Had the officers seen the boys' shapeshifted arms? Had they managed to shift back?

Her mom's purse lay nestled against the side of the driver's seat. Mia grabbed it, gave Deuce's head one last rub, then shut the van door. She found herself walking around the van toward the cruiser that held the boys, ducking low. Her voice came out in a hoarse whisper as she asked herself, "Mia, what are you doing?" She slid around the trunk toward the rear door on the opposite side from the hospital entrance. Could it be this easy? She lifted the handle.

The door popped open. Gasps of surprise burst from within. Lee and Malcolm stared. She swung the door wide. "Come on!" she whispered.

The boys lunged out, gratitude and fear painted thick on their faces.

She left the door hanging open and led the boys back around the van toward Dalton's car.

Lee said, "One of *them* grabbed Jace. He looked like a doctor."

Mia said, "He *is* a doctor."

They came alongside Dalton's car. Dalton cracked a grin. "Now, this is really getting interesting. Jump in the back."

Lee opened the back door and crawled over the piles of old fast-food containers like a crackling avalanche. "Holy crap! Dumpster much?"

Malcolm said, "There are about ten proverbs that would advise you to shut the frak up, Lee."

"What's a proverb?"

Claws scraped against the side window of the minivan, and a sigh of resignation escaped Mia. She couldn't leave Deuce here alone. She didn't know when anyone would be coming back. Moments later, Deuce had joined them, his tail whishing invisible 'Z's in the air. He jumped into her lap, a massive chunk of bristly muscle pressing her deeper into the seat.

Mia said, "Let's go."

Dalton put the car in gear. "You're going to explain all this to me, right?"

"As soon as I can. First, get us out of here."

"By thy command, Lady."

Mia's eyes refused to turn away from the emergency entrance. If one of the officers came outside before they could drive away... "Not too fast."

He grinned at her. "Relaxeth, thee. Thou art looking at the King of Subtle."

Mia smiled back. "Somebody's been reading Yeats again."

Lee said, "Why you talking so weird?"

Malcolm said, "Because he's trying to impress her, dummy."

"Shut up." Lee punched him on the shoulder, and wrappers crackled as the boys shifted on top of them.

Dalton glanced in the rear view mirror. "Jesus! What's up with you guys' hands?"

Mia laid a hand on his. "That's part of that explanation that's coming."

"This gets more interesting by the minute."

Mia's ears warmed, and she stifled her own grin. "Duck down, you guys."

The boys obeyed.

Dalton tooled the car nonchalantly out of the parking lot. As soon as he reached the service road, he gunned it back toward the front of the hospital.

Mia's heart slowed down. She hadn't realized it had been racing.

Dalton cleared his throat and gave her an imploring look.

"I promise I'll explain. First, I have to call Dad." She pulled out her mom's cell phone and started thumbing through the contact list.

There it was! The number of his land line. Send.

Ring tones.

"Come on, pick it up."

Ring tones.

Click. A female recording spoke with maddeningly neutral tones. "You've reached the desk of the Special Intelligence Services. Please leave a message. If this is an emergency, press five to page."

She pressed five.

"Page sent. Your call will be returned as soon as possible."

Her teeth clenched. "Grrrr! Where is he?" She called the number again, and this time left a message: "Dad! Call me! This is an emergency! Mom is hurt, Sarah is missing. We're at Immanuel Hospital right now, but we're going to get out of here. There are—" She glanced at Dalton and cleared her throat. "There are werewolves here, Dad. This is really, really bad! Call me on Mom's cell or mine."

Dalton stopped the car in front of the hospital. "'Werewolves.' Is that some kind of secret military codeword?"

"No," she said, "there really are werewolves there. At least one, that doctor."

Lee said, "Two counting Jace."

Malcolm giggled. "Four counting us."

Dalton grinned half-heartedly. "You're messing with me."

The words caught just behind Mia's lips.

He shrugged. "It's okay. If nothing else, it's fun. Now what?"

Mia cleared her throat. "Park the car way over there and wait for me to come back out. We're taking my mom to another hospital."

Malcolm said, "What about Jace?"

"The cops probably have him."

Dalton said, "If the cops have him, they'll probably take him home, unless he's in trouble for something. You guys in trouble?"

Lee snorted. "You might say."

"What'd you do?"

"We didn't do nothing 'cept get out of a bad way!"

Malcolm said, "We didn't commit any crime, if that's what you're asking."

Dalton said, "If there's no warrant for Jace's arrest, the cops'll just take him straight home, probably. Where is that?"

Mia said, "Saint Sebastian's. How do you know so much about all this?"

Dalton smirked. "Let's just say I've had some experience with this kinda thing."

Lee groaned. "That means the cops are going to call *him*."

Mia sighed. "First things first. I have to get Mom. When I come back out, flash your lights and come pick us up."

Dalton nodded. "Sure thing."

Mia opened the door to the family waiting room.

Her mom sat up from her slump in one of the easy chairs. "Did you find it?"

"I got it. And I called Dad. No answer, though. I left him a message."

Her mom's worry wrinkle appeared between her brows, the one that had grown so much deeper in the last two years.

Mia checked the hallway. "Come on, let's go."

She took her mom's hand and led her down the hallway back toward the front lobby. Running through the hospital at breakneck speed was all that her legs wanted to do, but she held back to a brisk walk. The cops wouldn't be guarding the front entrance would they? Even though she had only walked through there a couple of minutes prior, she envisioned getting trapped by a sudden police blockade.

The front lobby looked as empty and uninteresting as it had the first time she passed through. Her mom's gait was wobbly.

Mia supported her by one arm. *"Does it hurt?"*

"It's mostly numb, but it aches deep down."

As they passed through the revolving entrance doors, Mia let her breath out and wondered when she had managed to tie her shoulder muscles into such knots. Standing on the sidewalk out front, she scanned the dark parking lot for Dalton's car.

Another set of headlights came up the drive and turned toward the emergency room entrance. A white full-size van.

"Slade's here." Mia squeezed her mom's arm. Here to get Jace. What would he do to him?

And a more pressing question: where was Dalton?

CHAPTER THIRTY

Jace's eyes snapped open. He was lying on a white-sheeted bed, surrounded by a flowery curtain. The scents around him were like the noise of a crowd. Where was that doctor? Fortunately, the doctor didn't seem to be aware of a few things, such as how their animal nature revved up their healing ability, not to mention how it boosted their resistance to certain types of drugs. Wherever this virus came from, it was like a red Corvette with all the cool options. Too bad Corvettes sucked gas by the barrel. He tried to sit up and found his arms and legs strapped down with thick leather restraints.

He let his head fall back onto the pillow. How stupid was that doctor anyway? Didn't he know that all Jace had to do was shift? These restraints weren't sized for a wolf's legs.

He stared up at the fluorescent fixture above the bed and took a deep breath. Among the raucous noise of the smells of cleaning chemicals and sick people, he detected the tang of gun oil and the pheromone musk of Pack. There were cops nearby. What were the chances of simply getting shot if he wolfed out and tried to run out of here? He doubted he would die from a bullet wound, except maybe one to the head or directly to the heart, but it might slow him down enough for them to catch him again. It would certainly hurt like the bejeezus.

He held his breath and listened. The door muffled some male voices.

"...called Saint Sebastian's. They're sending someone over to pick him up."

The doctor's voice dripped with lies. "The poor kid just went crazy.

We can help physical problems here, and some of the mental, but what that boy needs is a good home. I feel sorry for him."

"Yeah, it's always the hard cases. Since he doesn't have any parents and you're not going to press charges, Child Services said to just send him back to Saint S."

"I can't imagine the life that boy has had. I just hope this is the right thing for him."

"We see this kind of thing every day, Doctor. It never gets easier to watch. Even perfectly good kids just implode sometimes."

Jace rolled his eyes. He hated it when jerks felt sorry for him—or worse, pretended to—looked down on him because he didn't have a mom and dad. He had had parents once, but they had been gone a long time. And he was ten times smarter than that stupid doctor.

The door and the room's other bed were obscured by a curtain. Blinds blocked the view through the room's single window. The window had a latch and crank to open it. He wondered which floor this was. Immanuel Hospital had eight floors. Could he survive a plunge out the window?

He could try wolfing out a little and see if his increased strength could break the restraints. But the cops would likely hear that.

Perhaps he should just wait for Slade to show up. With the police watching, Slade would have to take Jace back to Saint Sebastian, although he'd probably lock Jace in the Cooler, the room where they put the kids who lost control for a while.

How could Father McManus not know that Slade was no longer what he claimed to be—human? The priest who ran Saint Sebastian's was a good man, if a little too good sometimes. He treated every kid, no matter how hardcore, no matter how bad a seed someone became, with kindness. His respect had to be earned, but he did treat the kids with kindness. Perhaps he was able to run a place like Saint S's because he refused to let the darkness control people. Perhaps that made it easy for him to ignore the fact that Slade was behaving strangely for going on a year. Hiding the activities of an entire pack of werewolves had to be a full-time job. Unless Father McManus had become one of the Pack during the boys' absence, too. That would be convenient.

Slade would take Jace back there, and Father McManus would

kindly lock Jace up for a few days "for his own good." Slade would bring him plenty of cereal and cooked food, and eventually Jace would lose his ability to wolf out. But the hunger would not go away. It would be agony, and Slade would know just how agonizing it would be. He would do it anyway, just to prove to Jace he was the Alpha, to control Jace's ability to shift, just like he wanted to control every aspect of his pack's lives. Jace's hunger could only be fully satisfied by raw meat, and with a belly full of raw meat, the wolf would be able to howl again. Then Slade would let him out, and there would be a fight. Jace would lose.

The door opened, and footsteps came in.

The curtain whisked to the side, and the bald doctor stood there next to Slade, with two cops standing behind and looking suitably (but not terribly) sympathetic.

Jace pulled at his bonds. If he wolfed out now, he would definitely get shot. A surge of wolfish urges pulsed through Jace's body. The familiar tingle shot through his muscles. All he had to do was release it, and he would begin to change.

Slade said, "Settle down, son, or these officers here will put you in handcuffs."

"I'd rather go to jail."

"Juvenile detention is no place for you, son."

Jace sighed. "Fine. I'll go with you. But you have to leave Lee and Malcolm alone."

Slade's voice became almost kind and fatherly. "We'll worry about them later. But I'm taking you home."

On the far end of the parking lot, a car flashed its headlights twice. Mia took her mom's arm and led her across the driveway toward the distant car. As they stepped off the sidewalk, the car eased out of its stall and approached. Mia felt a moment of doubt about whether it was, in fact, Dalton's car, but when it came closer, she saw that it was.

She placed her mom in the front seat and then piled in the back with Deuce, Lee, and Malcolm. She tried not to think about what might be in the carpet of fast food sacks scrunching flat underneath her. "Slade is here. I saw his van."

Malcolm and Lee groaned.

Lee said, "He's gonna take Jace back to Saint S."

"Then what?"

"I don't know. Probably lock him up for a while. Or else kill him."

Dalton said, "Did you say 'kill'?"

Mia's mom said, "How could he get away with that?

Lee shrugged. "Kids try to run away from Saint S all the time. Some of them don't come back."

Mia's mom wrung her hands. "We can't let that happen."

Mia squeezed her mom's uninjured shoulder. "First we have to get you to a different hospital."

"Then take me to the Air Force hospital near the base."

Mia nodded. "By the way, Mom, uh, this is Dalton. Dalton, this is my mom."

Dalton reached over and offered his hand. "Nice to meet you, Mia's mom."

Her mom gave Dalton a long look, then shook his hand. "Kyoko."

Dalton spoke the next syllables slowly. "Do-zo yo-ro-shi-ku."

Her mom smiled. "You speak Japanese!"

He glanced at Mia. "I've been practicing."

Mia's cheeks heated again, and parts of her started to tingle in ways that her mom would not approve.

CHAPTER THIRTY-ONE

The sounds of happy chewing and slurping echoed through the car, and the pungent aroma of raw beef wafted from the back seat. Discarded cellophane and styrofoam meat packages lay in Mia's lap, along with two packages still unopened. Each boy clenched a massive sirloin steak in both hands, and tore out great bites with strong white teeth. They grinned and wiped the reddish moistness from their mouths with the backs of their now human-looking hands.

Lee was the first to finish. He leaned back with a moist burp. "Boy, good call on the supermarket! That hit the spot. Ain't had that much meat in a while."

"Glad you liked it," Dalton said, "You guys owe me a couple of weeks worth of lunch."

Lee smirked. "After this is over, I'll bring you a whole deer. How 'bout that?"

Mia studied Dalton's face. "You're awfully calm about having three werewolves in the back seat."

"Calm?" Dalton said. "I have an alien ready to explode out of my chest. I guess I'm okay right now because I'm pretty sure they don't want to eat me. And this pretty much makes me the coolest guy in school, bar none." He winked at her.

Her face flushed.

The boys tore into their second helpings of raw meat with equal relish, and when it was all finally gone, they leaned back against the seat and patted their bellies with contented sighs.

The rest of the ride to Bergquist Hospital, which was situated near Offutt Air Force Base, passed in silence. Mia's mom fell asleep with her head against the window. Mia let the night breeze wash across her face. She breathed deep of it, savoring the fresh coolness, noticing nuances of scent that she had never experienced before. The smells of the city giving way to the smells of the country, as the military base was placed on the far southern fringe of the metro area, where suburbs became interspersed with corn and soybean fields.

"So, you remember Yeats?" Dalton's voice.

"Hmm?" Mia emerged slowly from her reverie.

"That Yeats poem." Big brown eyes looked at her in the rearview mirror.

"I remember." She tried not to look at him.

She somehow sensed the heat of the blush rising in his face.

He sniffed. "Pretty goofy, huh."

"Pretty sweet, actually," she said. "And a little unexpected from a guy with such a bad reputation."

"Bad reputation?"

"I hear things."

His voice lost its levity. "What things?"

"M.I.P.?"

He shrugged. "Guilty. Vince put together a party down on the river, a little prom night hoe-down for underclassmen and those of us less interested in conforming. We had some beer and cheap ass wine. We got a little loud. The cops busted us. Everyone ran. I got caught."

"What about the fight?"

"What fight?"

"With the kid from North?"

"Oh, that fight." He silently for while. "My buddy Adam and I snuck into a show at a bar. It was this band he really liked. Some drunk douche bag starts calling Adam a faggot. Adam is gay, but he's only come out to me. He doesn't want anybody else to know. Adam wants to get out of there, but I'm kind of liking the band, too, and this asshole is spoiling it. I tell him to back off. He doesn't. He takes a swing, I kick him in the stomach. He pulls a knife and comes at me. I block it, and he stabs himself in the thigh. He looked so surprised, standing there with a switchblade sticking out of his leg."

"You kicked a guy in the stomach and blocked a knife?"

"Brown belt in tae kwon do in middle school. We beat it out of there. For all I know, no one ever called the police. He was a minor, too, in a twenty-one-and-over show. I suppose he just pulled the knife out and limped home. Some people saw this, thought I stabbed him. Dumbass."

His eyes lingered on her in the mirror, and she saw in them a universe of life, practically none of which she was privy to. Passions buried or slain. Who had broken his heart back then? Another urge to go kick that girl's ass, whoever it was. Then take him for herself, of course.

She thought back to that torrid moment in the Immanuel Hospital parking lot, not an hour ago. If they lived through this, Nicki and rest of the Crowd of Judgment could go hang. She didn't want to die a virgin. She'd be waving Dalton around second base, maybe even hitting a Grand Slam or two herself.

Her mom sighed in her sleep in the seat ahead.

Mia cleared her throat and shuddered those thoughts away. Bad, Mia! Slutty, Mia! Guilt and fear came back and danced a tango in her belly. Tango was *hot*.

She must not forget that her mom could probably read minds like Sarah, just because she was Mom and even when she was asleep, and then transmit those thoughts telepathically to her dad, who would then send out an F.B.I. task force to lock Mia into an electrified chastity belt with G.P.S. tracking.

Yes, no thinking about sex. Put that stuff away.

Dalton's musky *maleness* sitting over there, so close she could touch it. No, Mia, stop it!

But the warmth remained, even as she reached out with her perceptions to the strange, powerful chorus of smells pouring through the crack in her window. So many, so sharp, so deep, cutting into her. Thoughts about what that meant for her niggled at the corner of her brain like a little fish nibbling at bait. She pushed that little fish away and just enjoyed trying to identify the smells.

She had to push it away often.

The more she tried not to think about it, the more her skin tingled, itched. The lights seemed brighter. The thrum of the engine and the tires on the road vibrated through her. Her stomach rumbled, and she wondered if, when she next had the opportunity to put something in it, the only thing it would want would be raw meat.

Her mother's cell phone felt like a hot, dead lump in her hands. She checked the signal display incessantly to make sure it was receiving. If it had a good signal, why were there no calls coming? What was her Dad doing? Had something happened to him? Part of her was growing angry at him. What could be more important that this? The world had gone crazy, and he had disappeared down a hole. Or maybe it was Mia and her mom and the boys who had disappeared down a hole, like the rabbit hole to Wonderland. Which world was real: the one with werewolves and death and evil conspiracies, or the one with loving family and suburbs? Maybe the worlds were too different for a cell phone signal to bridge. Maybe she had already gone crazy.

Bergquist Hospital admitted her mom quickly. Mia refrained from telling them about their experiences at Immanuel. As far as they needed to know, the attack had just happened. The E.R. nurse noted how clean the wound already looked, but Mia glossed over that fact with a tale of how thoroughly she had cleaned the wound before bringing her mother to the hospital.

Lee and Malcolm, their arms and hands shifted back to normal, kept their noses alert for any signs of Pack, but they appeared relaxed. Dalton paced back and forth with them in the waiting room of the E.R.

When the female E.R. doctor picked up the scalpel to debride her mom's ragged wound, Mia turned away and bit down on her finger.

Just then the cell phone, still clutched in her fist, sounded its ring. Relief gushed through her, so strong she almost dropped the phone.

Her hand trembled as she thumbed the button. "Hello?"

"Mia, what the hell is going on?" The sound of her father's voice brought a fresh torrent of tears.

"Hang on, Dad. Somebody else needs to hear this, too, and I don't think I can tell it more than once." She left her mom's side and went out to the waiting room, approached Dalton. His curiosity was evident, and then she took his hand in hers. Their eyes met, and then it all came out in a tumbling rush, the last several hours of flight and pursuit and fear.

Werewolves, car chases, lonely country roads, pack challenges, Sarah's flight, death and threats of death. He remained silent for the length of it, and so did her father. When her tale finally wound down, she said, "Are you there?"

"Yeah, hon, I'm here."

She looked into Dalton's eyes. "Please. Say something."

Dalton's normally flush cheeks had gone pale, and she couldn't read his eyes.

Her father's voice was carefully neutral. "Mia, it's a crazy story. Is your mom there?"

Mia's voice grew shrill. "Yeah, in the E.R.! You need her to back me up?"

"No, I believe you. It's just that I can't talk right now. Just know for now that I love you."

Her anger rose again. "What do you mean you can't talk now!"

"I have to talk to your mom."

Mia nearly wept. "Okay. Dad, and I'm scared."

"I know, hon. Put your mom on."

Mia sighed, released Dalton's hand, and went back into the E.R., where she handed the phone to her mom. Her mom listened with her typical stoicism and an occasional "*Hai.*" Then her eyes started to glisten with tears, lips quivering. "*Okay, dear,*" was all she said. Then she hung up.

Mia clasped her hands to her chest. "What did he say?"

Her mom glanced at the doctor. "*He said he received a strange message from Sarah a couple of hours ago. The call was dropped. It was very mysterious.*"

"*Was it before or after the fight?*"

"*He didn't know.*"

"*What did she say?*"

"*It was all classified. He couldn't say much.*"

Mia was starting to hate, *hate, HATE* rules. Screw national security!

"*He also said that we should stay here. He's sending a couple of agents to protect us until he gets here. All he would say is that he's in the middle of something very important.*"

Mia rolled her eyes.

"*He also said to check the television news. Something is happening.*"

Mia swallowed hard and sank back onto the waiting room sofa. A chill breathed up the back of her neck. Lee and Malcolm sat on either side of her. Dalton stood nearby, arms crossed. The waiting room was otherwise empty and quiet.

The blonde anchorwoman's voice betrayed her surprise and confusion through the frame of the TV screen. "Again, for reasons yet undisclosed, the State Patrol, Douglas and Sarpy County Sheriffs' offices, and metro area police are now blocking any and all traffic into and out of the Omaha metro area. All roads, highways, and interstate traffic are being diverted at the Douglas and Sarpy county lines. Traffic on I-80, both eastbound and westbound, is now backed up for miles. I-29 is open but jammed with confused drivers and their vehicles. Flights from Eppley Airfield have been canceled, and inbound flights are being diverted to Kansas City, Des Moines, and Denver. Authorities request that citizens remain in their homes. As yet, no explanation has been given for this action. The governor has scheduled a news conference in thirty minutes, at which time he will presumably explain this sudden situation. Eyewitness News will be there. Stay tuned for further information as it becomes available."

The news broadcast went to a commercial about seed corn.

"Wow," Mia said.

Lee and Malcolm spoke in chorus. "Wow."

Malcolm said, "You don't suppose the authorities are getting involved to stop the virus or something?"

Mia said, "It sounds like a quarantine. I've never even heard of something like this happening before, except in movies."

Dalton cleared his throat. "That would be the Center for Disease Control. So, this werewolf stuff is from a virus? It's not a magical curse or anything?"

Mia glanced up at him sheepishly. "Afraid so."

"So you needed the meat to change. Some kind of biological requirement."

Malcolm and Lee explained it to him, and Dalton sat down and put his elbows on his knees, running fingers through his hair.

Malcolm said, "So what is our course of action?"

Mia said, "My dad said to wait here."

Lee frowned. "What about Jace? Slade might just decide to kill him, and who'd be the wiser?"

Malcolm said, "We'd know."

Lee snorted. "Yeah, and then what? Who'll believe us?"

Mia turned to him. "You have a few people on your side now, Lee. You think he can kill us all?"

"His pack could easily kill us. All of us. One time, he had us run down almost an entire herd of deer. We separated each of the deer and brought them down one by one. That's how wolves roll. The pack would do the same to us. Separate and kill."

Dalton said, "Then we have to stay together. And we have to stay here, where it's safe. A pack of werewolves is not going to charge into a hospital."

Lee looked him in the eye. "Who says? Who'll stop 'em? A pack of us could charge in here and kill everyone in this hospital before anyone knew what was happening, much less stop it. Then we would just skedaddle, fade away."

Dalton's face turned paler, his features taut. He clasped his elbows tight. "You sound like you have experience with this."

Lee said, "Slade talked about this stuff sometimes. He used to be in the Marines. He talked a lot about surprise and violence, how they go together for...Mal, what was the word he used?"

"For assaults. He said that surprise and extreme violence were the keys to a successful assault."

"'Assault,' yeah, that word."

Malcolm hugged his knees. "So we have to stop him somehow."

Lee nodded. "We got to get Jace out of there."

Mia said, "The law still exists. There are still police. We have to expose Slade as a murderer, regardless of the form he was in when he did it."

"If we take Slade out, the pack will be done for," Lee said.

"Yes, but how?" Malcolm said.

Mia thought about her mom being bandaged up in the emergency room, about the agents coming from the F.B.I. office to guard them.

The presence of federal agents would put a slight crimp in any plans to help Jace. They could not call the police. Every officer in the metro area was out on roadblocks, and the police department probably wouldn't believe the story anyway.

Mia stood up. "We have to go."

Dalton said, "Come on, Mia. Settle down. What about your mom?"

Her skin felt hot, as if she were feverish. The fine hairs on her arms crawled. "Mom will be safe. The agents will be here in a few minutes. We have to go before they get here."

CHAPTER THIRTY-TWO

This was the first time Jace had ever been in the holding room at Saint Sebastian's, the Cooler as it was known. The room was perhaps ten feet by ten feet, with a single narrow window near the ceiling. Faint light from one of the grounds lights filtered through the dingy, wire-reinforced glass. The place smelled like disinfectant, mildew, and fear. The only furnishings were a single gray steel chair and a small bed. He sat on the bed, leaning against the red brick wall. A crisp white sheet and green woolen blanket covered the ancient mattress. The mattress smelled of must and old urine. A fluorescent light fixture flickered colorless light onto the floor. The door was heavy steel, with thick, wire-reinforced glass like the outer windows; there was no knob or latch on the inside. How many boys had been locked in here for misbehavior, when the teachers or even Father McManus simply couldn't decide what to do with them?

Jace had been in a couple of juvenile detention facilities before he came to Saint Sebastian's. A kid just had to eat, but sometimes store managers didn't look the other way. Compared to those places, the Cooler was fairly low security, just a room where they locked kids up for a while, but the feel of this place was darker, oppressive. It was below ground level, dank, old, in the basement of what used to be the original Saint Sebastian's orphanage. In the hundred years since the orphanage was built, the grounds had expanded ten-fold, with many newer buildings, a gymnasium, classrooms, quarters for the nuns and Father McManus. But this building felt its age in every crack in the mortar, every warp of ancient plaster, borne down by the weight of a thousand stories of suffering and redemption from the children who came before.

A shadow appeared on the window, keys rattled, and the lock clacked. The door swung in, and Slade's shadow fell across the floor. He stepped inside, carrying a tray of food and a bottle of water.

Jace's belly roared, and his mouth watered—until he saw the tray carried a bowl of oatmeal, some toast, and an apple. The wolf inside growled in frustration.

Slade set the tray on the floor and turned his gaze upon Jace, his eyes fierce and smoldering blue. "You must be hungry."

Jace turned away.

"We'll talk more soon. We have some things to resolve, don't we. Meanwhile, eat up. You're a growing boy."

Slade's mouth turned into a smirk as he backed out of the room and locked the door behind him.

Jace sighed and looked at the food. The boy in him still needed it; the wolf would just have to go hungry for now.

"It's all over the radio, too," Mia said, pressing the scan button over and over on Dalton's car radio. Every radio station was broadcasting special reports about the metro area quarantine. Streets and roads within the city were open, but when Dalton checked the highway leading south out of the suburbs, they found it blocked by police barricades. Now, they were on the freeway, crossing town toward Saint Sebastian's. Traffic was all but nonexistent. The incessant train of semi-tractors that usually choked the interstate was gone, blocked at the outskirts or diverted. Lee and Malcolm and Deuce sat in the back seat. The boys took turns scratching the dog's ears. Whenever they stopped, Deuce poked one of their hands with his nose.

"Wait," Dalton said, "the last two stations have had the same thing."

Mia stopping clicking the button. The broadcast had been identical on the last two stations.

"...asking everyone to please stay inside as much as possible. Officials from the Center for Disease Control are en route, and I have mobilized the Nebraska National Guard to offer assistance to the State Patrol, metro area police departments, and to the sheriffs' departments of Douglas and Sarpy County. Again, no one will be allowed into or out of the Douglas and Sarpy County area until the C.D.C. has given us the all clear. STRATCOM is on high alert, due to the nature of this possible contagion, which has yet to be determined..."

Lee snorted. "Gee, and all we have to do to get out is wolf up and run across a corn field or two. That's all stupid."

Dalton said, "Maybe it's something else."

"...national, state, and local authorities are working in collaboration to ensure public safety. We ask that people stay indoors, and furthermore to avoid contact with all wild animals..."

Dalton grimaced. "I guess not."

"...Rest assured, this matter will be resolved as soon as possible, and we can all go back to normal, but right now, public safely is our primary concern. Now, we will take a few questions." Cameras snapped in the background, and a general muted uproar arose from the reporters in the room.

A man's voice from the crowd of reporters, "Governor Carlson, what is the connection to wild animals? Is this some form of rabies? Swine flu? Bird flu?"

"We have no information on that. We're not even sure at this point about the nature of the possible contagion."

"Is it a virus?"

"We don't know."

A different man said, "What kind of animals?"

"At this point, we believe that coyotes, dogs, and foxes should be avoided."

"What about family dogs?"

"We're advising that family pets be kept indoors, as well as isolated from family contact."

Mia rubbed Deuce's head, "Hey, Goonalicious, maybe you can be a were-human or something."

Deuce gave her a thoughtful look.

A woman's voice. "Is this contagion life-threatening?"

"I want to make this very clear. This is a serious situation. There are doctors investigating that possibility as we speak."

Another woman's voice, one Mia recognized as belonging to the reporter she had spoken to at the park. "Is there any connection to the bizarre animal deaths at the zoo earlier this week?"

The governor cleared his throat. "We know of no connection between these events."

The same reporter said, "Then what led to this drastic action? This kind of quarantine is unprecedented. If there is no clear contagion, how can you quarantine two counties and over six hundred thousand people?"

"We're investigating right now, with the help of the Omaha field office of the F.B.I. and the State Patrol. We'll inform the public of the results of that investigation as soon as we have something substantive. Thank you for your questions."

A chorus of voices rose, and the radio announcer's voice spoke. "This has been a special press conference with Governor Dave Carlson, regarding the quarantine of the Omaha metro area. Stay tuned to KLIF for more information as it becomes available. And now, back to Delilah."

The audio switched to a mournful, heartful love song. Mia leaned back into her seat. Three days ago, she would have died to be sitting in Dalton's car with him listening to a sappy love song. Now, she just felt numb.

His warm hand touched her arm. "It's going to be okay."

And what if she wolfed out and tore him to pieces for his bone marrow? But she didn't say that. She just nodded.

Malcolm said, "So how are we going to stop Slade when we find him?"

"I don't know," Mia said. "Any ideas?"

"We need to get the F.B.I. to listen to us," Dalton said.

"We need proof," Malcolm said.

"Proof," Mia said. Then she smiled. "My house first."

CHAPTER THIRTY-THREE

"There's my house." Mia eyes scanned the dark, deserted street for any sign of Slade's white van. Closed garages kept cars protected within. Closed shutters and drapes kept in the light and the lives. Silence hung like a pall. "Pull up. Stay on the street." It would be easier to flee if they didn't have to back out of the driveway first. "I'll just be a minute. I think I know where to find it."

"Mia, wait a sec—" Dalton said.

"You're the getaway driver. I'll just be a minute."

She took out her keys and ran to the front door. Why did she feel like a thief going into her own house? The door opened under the practically automatic ministrations of her hands and key, and she flipped on the foyer light; the rest of the house was dark. The air in the house was cooler than normal.

She hurried toward the stairs and up to her parents' bedroom. They kept the video camera in a bag in the closet. Flick on the light, fling open the slatted closet door. Now where was the camera bag?

Something registered in her brain. Had the patio door been ajar?

The hairs on the nape of her neck spiked. She spun.

Two furry shapes slunk toward the bedroom door, their yellow eyes glinting in the darkness of the hallway. They moved with utter silence, as if they were mere shadows of the strength and sinew and fangs they truly were. She glanced at the window. How badly would she hurt herself if she smashed through it? Badly. "Hey, guys, how's it going?"

The wolves padded into the room, faint growls emanating from their throats.

Mia flung herself into the closet. The wolves lunged. She pulled the door shut after her. A massive weight slammed into the door. The louvered wooden slats cracked and splintered.

She heard a harsh, guttural slur from a throat that wasn't human. "Come out, Mia. Let's play."

A hard, hairy snout punched into the weakened slats, splintered two of them free. Hot breath huffed into her face.

Mia screamed and clutched the door knob with both hands. Hard teeth and powerful jaws clamped around it on the other side, grinding into the metal, twisting, wrenching. Mia's hands gave her a surer grip. She acutely felt the hard lump of the ultrasonic blaster in her jeans pocket, but she didn't dare take her hands off the doorknob to pull it out, or the bear spray in her jacket.

Another snout tore into the opening between the slats. Teeth clamped and tore the hole larger. Claws raked the wood, and the door shuddered and creaked. With every crackle of splintering wood, Mia thought the door might be torn from its hinges. The door knob twisted in her grip.

Then came the sound of a savage snarl and two muscled bodies colliding. The teeth tearing at the slats were wrenched away. She caught a glimpse of a lithe black shape flying past. The torque on the door knob disappeared. Mia seized the chance to pull out her pepper spray. If she used the blaster, her allies might be incapacitated, too. The bear spray was a stout black cylinder with a no-nonsense red plunger. She placed her thumb over the plunger, and then took a moment to cast about for the camera bag. She wasn't going to leave without it. There it was, on the upper shelf.

Snarls of rage turned her blood to ice. Open, fingers, one by one, release the doorknob and grab the camera bag. The bad guys have forgotten you for just a few seconds. She dropped it to the floor and ripped open the zipper. The camera was inside, battery, minidiscs. Everything she needed. Heavy bodies thrashed, plowing into the bed, the nightstand, the dresser. Glass cracked and tinkled. More wood crashed and crackled. Howls of pain erupted. She zipped up the bag and slung it over her shoulder.

Dalton's voice. "Come get some...you..."

Mia's stomach clenched. Those wolves could tear him to pieces.

She flung open the closet door, bear spray brandished.

Shreds of bedspread flew as two wolves tore into each other atop the bed. Two more rolled in a ball on the floor between her and Dalton. Dalton stood in the doorway, eyes bulging, mouth slack, an aluminum baseball bat sagging in his grip.

Deuce charged between Dalton's legs, his lips peeled back. He leaped onto the bed and buried his fangs into the haunches of one of the wolves. Mia had only a vague notion of who was whom. The two beasts on the bed looked so similar she couldn't distinguish which one was Lee. The black-furred one between her and Dalton was Malcolm. She knew that for certain. Blood and spittle and hair flew in every direction. She aimed her bear spray at Malcolm's adversary.

"Malcolm!" she cried. "Look out!"

The black wolf's ensanguined jaws released his prey, and he bounded back. Mia rushed forward and jammed the plunger of the bear spray with her thumb. The cylinder bucked slightly with the release of pressure, sending a narrow cone of mist squarely into the other wolf's face. Its howl of agony deafened her. It sprang away, eyes squeezed shut, its face contorted with rage and pain. Great gashes in its coat trailed blood behind it. It thrashed its head, howling and whining.

Dalton broke his stupefaction, seized the bat in both hands, rushed forward and laid a tremendous blow against the side of the wolf's head. The clang of the aluminum rang with the crunch of shattered bone and teeth. The wolf's legs buckled, like pistons with the internal pressure suddenly released, but it didn't go down. Dalton cocked for another blow, but the wolf lunged at him, startling him back a step. The wolf slammed into his chest, knocking him onto his back, then it bounded over him and through the door.

The enemy wolf on the bed spun its body and flung Deuce in an arc that tore loose his grip. The dog skittered off the bed and thumped onto the floor. Then the wolf gathered its powerful sinews and launched itself toward the bedroom window, slamming against the drapes and the glass beyond. The glass shattered, and the wolf's body disappeared into the curtain of night.

Cool night air fluttered the drapes.

Downstairs, claws scrabbled on the kitchen tile, and the patio door rattled with the passage of the wolf's flight.

The five of them stood in the silent vacuum of the wolves' departure. The harsh, stinging stench of the bear spray wafted throughout and made Mia's nose start to run, her eyes to water. Her parents' bedroom was a disaster of savaged bedding, cracked furniture, and spattered droplets of blood. The closet door was gouged and splintered. But they had what they came for.

A pang of despair lanced through her. She hoped her parents would get to sleep in that bed again soon.

Dalton's face was pale, his hands shaking, and his voice as hoarse and dry as crumpled newspaper. "Come on. We have to go."

CHAPTER THIRTY-FOUR

Slade sat down behind his desk. The yellow light from the old hanging fixture cast a jaundiced glare over the room. Bookshelves lined with science books, a few about the biology and behavior of wolves, books on military history and tactics, a scrapbook that Connie had made for him of his time in the Corps, the only thing of hers that still remained in his life. On his ancient steel desk, everything was as he had left it: biology exams neatly stacked (yet to be graded, thanks to this troublesome mess), the green-hooded desk lamp, pens neatly ensconced in his Saint Sebastian's desk caddy.

His encounter with the little girl's aunt had left him with a few scratches. He took off his shirt. Gashes crisscrossed his chest and ribcage like scabrous cornrows. His throat still felt bruised. That woman was a trained fighter, someone to be reckoned with. He opened the drawer of his desk, took out a box of gauze pads, tape, and antiseptic ointment. The gashes would heal quickly, but in the meantime, bleeding through clothes tended to draw unwanted attention. Too bad she had gotten away.

Somewhere in the old brick walls, a cricket chirped its song, unobtrusive but mournful, lonely. It had no Pack. He could remember what it was like to be a pure human, alone, with no one to call his Brother, and he didn't miss it, not in the least. The metamorphosis had been profound. He wondered if the butterfly remembered its days as a caterpillar.

Human relationships were so shallow, even marriages, as Connie had so pointedly shown him. The closest thing he had ever experienced to the Brotherhood of the Pack was his time in the Marine Corps. Men who trained together, ate together, slept together, fought together, faced death together, created a bond of closeness that other human beings could not imagine; only the bonds created by war and death were remotely akin to the connection with his Pack. They were *his* boys. His. He would do anything to keep them safe, anything to keep them in the Pack, because the Pack was where they belonged. With the government coming down on him, it was more important than ever to maintain pack integrity. He might have to take them away from here, go wild for a while, find a new place. The Feds had no means of tracking a single wolf pack, much less a single wolf.

He just needed a little more time. It took the new ones time to adjust; he had to allow for that, give them time to come around. They would; he would make sure of that. The instincts of the wolf ran strong and would take over soon enough. They would seek out a pack naturally; he just had to make sure it was his. It was the only way he could teach them properly, the only way they would reach their full potential.

If he let them continue in the human world, clinging to its values, the things it saw as virtues, things that held no meaning to the wolf, they would turn weak, shallow, and callous. They would forget the things that really mattered to the wolf: community, brotherhood, hierarchy, mutual survival, and for the strong, a mate.

He took his old bayonet out of his desk drawer and used the point to clean the grime and dried blood from under his nails. Best to let Jace stew for a while. Given enough time, the hunger would help soften the boy's resolve to get away. Few things in life were more acutely motivating than hunger. Starving people would do almost anything, eat almost anything, to put something in their bellies. He'd seen that in a few Third World cesspits.

Human beings were cruel to each other, heartless. They didn't give a damn if the person next to them had a scrap of food to eat, or shoes to wear, or a roof that wasn't shot full of holes over their heads. They blew each other up in the name of religion, tortured each other in the name of justice, experimented on each other in the name of science, and ignored each other in the name of their own selfishness. Wolves, on the other hand, took care of their own. When a member of the pack was sick, they fed her. Pack mates cared for each other's pups, shared their food—all in proper order of hierarchy, of course—worked together for the survival of all, and shared bonds that among humans only veteran soldiers could come close to imagining.

Wolves were superior beings, and now that their best instincts and their incredible strengths had been merged with the resourcefulness and invention of human intellect, the new race of wolf-men would be immensely superior. And thus, rightfully, they sat at the new apex of the food chain. Eventually, inevitably, pure human beings would diminish as masters of planet Earth, to be supplanted by those who were superior. Pure humans would become cattle, food for the new masters of the Earth, or servants.

A knock came at the door.

"It's open."

The door swung inward, and Eric followed it in.

Slade scowled.

"You wanted to see me, sir?"

Slade fixed him with a cold gaze. "Sit."

The young man swallowed hard and sat down on the spare metal chair before the desk.

Slade stood and circled the desk, stopping before Eric, two feet away, crossing his arms. "What should I do about you, Eric?"

Eric's gaze fell to the floor. His shoulders slumped and his head turned aside to expose his jugular.

Slade's anger simmered, tightening his jaw. "You let her go. Why the hell would you do that?"

"Because...it seemed like the right thing to do. Sir."

"Was it because the little girl is cute?"

"No, sir."

"Big brown eyes and you thought you might break off a little piece if you gave in to her? Going to give her a call are you? Ask her out on a date? See if she'll show you her belly? Put her haunches in the air?"

"No! Sir."

"Let me make one more thing perfectly clear, son. Nobody in this pack, and I mean nobody, gets anything, from any female, without my say-so. You hear me?"

"Yes, sir."

"Look at me."

The young man's eyes turned upward, but couldn't quite meet Slade's gaze.

"Look at me!" The young man's eyes turned sheepishly upward, and Slade drilled his gaze into them, backed by twenty years of Marine Corps blood and steel and leather, combat tours, drill instructors he both hated and respected with every fiber of his being, and the sight of death at its most heinous, most gruesome. "You know what happens when somebody steps out of line."

Beads of sweat trickled down Eric's face. His shallow breaths quavered as he nodded.

"Good. I'm glad to hear there are some things you haven't forgotten. See, I'm going to let you make this up to me, to your pack mates."

Eric gulped, his eyes hopeful. "Anything, sir."

"Anything is right. You and Jace were buddies before the change, right?"

"Well, sort of."

"He looks up to you."

"I guess so."

"So you can see why what you did is not the least bit acceptable."

"Yes, sir."

"That's why you're going to be the one to put him in his place."

"Me, sir? I thought you would want to do that, sir."

"Normally, I would. It normally falls to Alpha to enforce the Law. But here's where the human side makes the wolf side even better. I can delegate. That's why you're going to do it."

After only a moment's hesitation, Eric nodded. "I'll do it, sir. When, sir?"

"Tomorrow morning. Early." He didn't want to sit on this too long. Best to get things over with. Thanks to Eric's age, experience, and physical strength, he had become Slade's lieutenant. But Eric had disobeyed. It was time to make him pay, to bring both boys back into ranks. But Jace was a tough kid, and becoming a wolf evened the playing field somewhat. There was a chance that he could actually beat Eric. Either result was fine; the stronger would win. If Jace won, Slade would have a new lieutenant, a superior one. If Eric won, Jace would get the beat-down of his life. Sometimes challenges did get out of hand, and in this case, Slade would not be particularly inclined to call things off early. If Jace won and still refused to submit, then Slade would have no choice but to assert his authority in the harshest way possible.

It was a stroke of luck that Doctor Reinhardt, Tony to his friends, was the E.R. doctor tonight at Immanuel Hospital, or else those boys might have gotten away. Slade and the good doctor had met in a field hospital in Kuwait during Gulf One. A decade or so passed, during which they had no contact, but a few years ago they had reconnected when one of his boys had to be rushed to the emergency room for passing out during wrestling practice. Once a Marine, always a Marine. Tony was more than a little 'surprised' at the news of Jack's sudden change in...lifestyle. Especially when Jack transformed and then bit him. Some people were worthy to join the Pack, others were not. Tony was a warrior *and* a healer, and smart as hell. The scientist in Tony didn't take long to come around to Jack's way of thinking.

Eric gulped. "I won't let you down, sir."

"That's right. You won't let me down *again*."

"Not again, sir."

"Now go and get some rest. Oh, here." He circled the desk to the small refrigerator in the corner and pulled out a package wrapped in butcher's paper. "Have a nice pork roast." He tossed it, and Eric caught it.

"Thank you, sir! I'm really hungry, sir."

"Thought you might be. Garrett and Max are patrolling the grounds. Make sure the others are all bunked up. Let me know if Russell and Brad come back."

"Yes, sir." Eric stood up and left the room, package tucked under his arm.

As the young man's footsteps receded down the hallway, Eric's voice echoed back to Slade's office. "Hello, Father."

An old man's scratchy voice followed. "Good evening, Eric. I hope you're doing well."

"Very well, Father."

"Good, good. Glad to know it. But you know you're up past curfew."

"Um, I've been working on something with Coach Slade."

"Ah, I see. Well, I was just coming to talk to Coach Slade about something. Good night, my son."

"Good night, Father." Eric's footsteps started to recede again.

A few moments later, a wizened old man shuffled into Slade's office, hands thrust in his black trouser pockets, his priest's collar the only splash of non-black in his attire. His silvery white hair was combed back, but a few unruly strands frizzed out on the top and sides. His cheeks were narrow and high-boned, sunken with age, framing a sharp, aquiline nose and two rheumy gray eyes. His lips were wet and spotted with age, his hands gnarled with veins and arthritis. "Good evening, Jack."

Slade leaned back against the desk, clearing his throat. "Good evening, Father."

"Heard you had a bit of trouble with Jace."

"I did, but it's under control now. He's back home."

"Good, good. You know, sometimes I think the Lord makes boys so difficult simply to test the faith and patience of their elders."

"Absolutely, Father."

Father McManus sighed and sat down in the chair. "You still have that good Scotch?"

Slade smiled. "Of course. It's been a rough day. I could use a belt myself." The old priest did love the whiskey, but the truth was, since the change, Slade could no longer stomach it. It was an indulgence of the human world that he occasionally missed, but it was a small price to pay for the biological gift he was given. He pulled the bottle of Johnny Walker Green and two tumblers from his file cabinet drawer, poured a couple of fingers into each, and offered one to Father McManus.

Slade pretended to drink. The sharp, layered aromas of the Scotch—smoke, peat, malt—were even more pungent to his sensitive nose, but his stomach rejected the alcohol.

The priest took a sip and closed his eyes in appreciation. "You know there are no bad boys. None of them want to be bad. But there are so many boys from bad homes, bad circumstances, bad experiences."

Slade nodded and refrained from rolling his eyes. He had heard this speech many, many times.

"I know you'll take good care of him, do what's necessary."

"I fully intend to. I care for that boy like he's my own son."

Father McManus nodded with appreciation. "Any race that doesn't take care of its young cannot survive."

"Amen to that, Father."

"I'll check on him tomorrow after morning prayers, let him know that he hasn't been forgotten."

"I think that would be a great idea, Father. He needs to know that people love him, want to do right by him."

"There's this other matter, Jack. It concerns me..." The priest cleared his throat.

"Other matter?"

"You've been taking the boys out on these excursions. You know, after hours. After lights out."

Slade stiffened. "I have, yes."

"It doesn't look good, Jack. It doesn't look good. And, of course, it's getting around. It makes all the other boys wonder what's going on. We can't appear to have favorites, you know, any more than we can afford to punish anyone unfairly. We must be fair in all respects."

"I understand that, Father."

"So..."

"So?"

"It's going to have to stop. No more extracurricular activities of that nature. And I've been very good about letting you have your space in that regard, but—"

"Stop right there."

"Excuse me?"

"I said, 'stop'. You're not going to dictate to me what I do on my own time."

"Perhaps I should remind you who is in charge here—"

"Perhaps I should remind you who you're talking to. I'm the guy who practically runs this place. Hell, you could wander off and disappear and this place would still run like a Rolex because I'm doing all the work."

"Now, I'll grant that I've given you a lot of responsibility but—"

Slade stood up and let the wolf emerge just enough to deepen his voice, bulk up his limbs. "No one, *no one*, is going to tell me how to do my job. This place is my life, just as much as it is yours."

Father McManus cleared his throat and tugged at his collar. Sweat beaded his wrinkled forehead. He stood up and edged away. "I know it is, Jack. You've done such good work here and—"

"And I'm training those boys. Training them hard, and they love it, every one of them. Taking it away from them now would do them an awful disservice."

"Training them for what?"

"To be fighters! You want them to win State again, don't you? You want them to become strong, honorable young men, don't you? Pushing those boys a little harder is just the guidance they need. The wrestling and the training helps them control their aggression, channel it."

"You're right, they do need guidance." Father McManus tipped up the tumbler of Scotch in a trembling hand and drained it. "Even in their free time. It'll turn them into better men."

"Absolutely, Father. I'm doing God's work."

"Yes, yes. Good." He cleared his throat and put the tumbler down on the chair. "Now, I, uh, I must be going. I have some reading to do yet tonight. Bless you, Jack, I'll see you tomorrow."

"Of course, Father. Good night."

"Good night." The old priest turned and left the office quickly, his footsteps picking up speed as he walked down the hallway.

Slade smiled. Yes, he was definitely doing God's work, teaching those boys the Laws of Nature that he himself created. He would be damned if some foolish old priest was going to get in his way. The old and the weak were always the first to be taken down. It was the first Law of Nature. The old priest's days were certainly numbered—a man didn't reach that age and not know that truth—but Father McManus didn't know how numbered they were.

CHAPTER THIRTY-FIVE

"Maybe this isn't a good idea," Dalton said. The streetlights of the deserted freeway washed over them in rhythmic waves. He hadn't spoken since leaving Mia's house. Throughout the drive, his hands had clutched the steering wheel hard, his eyes haunted and wide.

Mia found herself less traumatized by the fight in the bedroom than she would have expected. The quivering, electric sensation in her belly had faded to a fluttery haze. Too many life-or-death battles in one day. Perhaps she was getting used to it. She had already gotten used to the idea of werewolves as real flesh and blood things. Dalton had not. "Of course it's not a good idea."

Malcolm leaned forward. "Our efforts are probably the epitome of lunacy."

Mia said, "But it's the only idea we have."

"Yeah," Lee said, "Jace could be dead by morning. And the cops won't help us. Ain't none of 'em care about no delinquent orphan kid from Saint Sebastian's. They're trying to save y'all rich white folks."

Mia squirmed at Lee's pronouncement. His voice held the conviction of hard experience. "It won't be that hard," Mia said. "We'll just wait until late, late at night. Then we'll sneak in, get Jace out, and be gone before anyone knows we were there. We have the video camera to record everything."

Dalton kept his eyes steadfastly on the road. "Are you sure it's wise to record us breaking in? We could get in trouble for that."

Mia nodded. "Yes, but if we get Jace out, then everything is okay. We don't need the video."

"And if they catch us, they'll just destroy the video anyway."

"Well, maybe one of us will get away. We'll go to the F.B.I. field office, and Dad will help us. There's no sense hiding anything now. If we run into Slade or his puppies, Lee and Malcolm do their thing, on camera, and Slade will have no choice but to react, all on camera."

"You think you're going to be able to run a video camera if we're running for our lives?"

"God, you're such a downer!" She gave him an exaggerated eye roll. "But seriously. A recording device can record sound even if the camera is flying everywhere."

Malcolm burped, and it smelled of raw meat. "And we are fully prepared."

Dalton said, "What if we get all this on tape and then he eats all of us?"

Mia pursed her lips. Of course that was a possibility.

Lee snickered. "What if'n we rub hot sauce all over ourselves? Kinda like your pepper spray." He pronounced it like 'spry'. "We'll be too spicy."

They laughed.

Malcolm smirked. "Perhaps we might just acquire some barbeque sauce and smear it all over you."

Lee blinked once, then narrowed his eyes. "Hey, shut up! Y'all ain't making me into no main course!"

They laughed all the harder. Mia found the laughter pouring out of her, building as it filled the car, as if it all assembled and fed into something funnier than it actually was.

The phone in her jacket pocket rang. She left her mom's phone at the hospital with her, but not without first saving her father's land-line number into her own phone. The incoming number was RESTRICTED, but she answered it anyway. "Hello?"

"Mia." Mixed swirls of fear and relief surged through her at the sound of her dad's voice.

"Hey, Dad." She couldn't help the sheepishness in her voice.

"Hey nothing, little girl. What on Earth are you doing? The agents got to the hospital, then called back here and said you had left."

"Yeah, about that. Mom's going to be okay, right?"

"So they say, but I made the hospital keep her overnight for observation. With everything going on, they thought it was a good idea."

"Good."

"So spill it. This is not the time for screwing around."

"I know. Trust me, I'm not screwing around."

"Mia, you have no idea how dangerous it is to be out tonight, and—"

"Actually, Dad, I pretty much do. The quarantine is about containing a werewolf plague, right? Somehow, somewhere, someone probably saw something. Enough someones saw some things, scary things. Maybe somebody got eaten. Maybe somebody saw a werewolf shifting. Or maybe this has been building up for a while, and this is what you've been spending so much time on, and now it just all exploded. Sarah's involved. You're involved. The entire government is involved. The whole state could be quarantined by tomorrow night. They're trying to keep it from spreading. Am I anywhere near the mark?"

The earpiece hung silent for a minute before he spoke again. "Yeah, that's it in a nutshell." Was that a moment of pride in her that she had heard in his voice?

"So, every cop within fifty miles is out on roadblocks, shutting down the interstate, and all that and—"

"Mia, what are you doing?"

"Dad, we're going to get Jace."

"What!"

"If we don't, Slade and his pack will probably kill him."

"Slade and his pack will kill *you!*"

"We'll be careful. I have two werewolves here on my side. And Deuce." She tried to make it sound light, utterly nonchalant. "And you know Deuce is a total badass." The thought that she might become one of them still hovered in the back of her mind about two inches below every conscious thought. The fact she could smell Deuce sitting two feet away from her—and distinguish his scent from Lee's and Malcolm's—did not help dispel those thoughts.

Her father couldn't help but chuckle once before his voice turned stern again. "This is no time for joking around."

"Well, I'm not really. You should have seen him take a bite out of this wolf's butt." Probably best to save the story about the fight in the bedroom until later. Boy, were her parents in for a rude awakening when they got home.

Deuce's tail started to wag, and he raised his head, sensing that he was being discussed. She reached back and rubbed his stubbly head.

"Mia, I'm going to call the police."

"Good idea. Maybe they'll listen to you. They won't listen to me or any of these boys if we start telling them werewolf stories. Maybe the cops will actually get there before we do and pull Jace out. If Jace is safe, we'll come back to the hospital, hang out with Mom, and everything will be okay." She let the tone in her voice convey what she thought about the likelihood of these events. Her voice choked up. "I love you, Dad. I have to go now."

The weight of helplessness came through in his sigh. "Mia, don't you—!"

As she thumbed the disconnect button, she realized she had never felt more alone in her entire life.

They called it 'the Cooler' for a reason. As the night deepened, the air got colder, and since there was no heat in the room, Jace could see his breath. He wrapped the spare green blanket around him as he sat on the bed, knees pulled up to his chest. The food Slade had brought him had fed the human side, but the wolf inside still hungered. He had eaten enough meat recently to feed the wolf for one more transformation, but the wolf would be weak; he didn't know if he would be able to change back. Whatever Slade had in store for him certainly would include a challenge, and if Jace's wolf side was not at full strength, he would probably lose.

A shadow appeared on the window along with the shuffle of footsteps.

The hour had to be too late for it to be anybody but Slade.

Keys jangled, the lock clacked, and the door opened.

It wasn't Slade.

Jace said, "What are you doing here?"

Eric held up a crumpled up package of blood-tinged butcher's paper. "I thought you might be hungry." He tossed the package across the room, and Jace caught it like a football, like one of the many times he and Eric had tossed the football back and forth during noon break.

Jace smelled the raw pork the moment it smacked into his grip. "Does he know you're here?"

"No. We're going to fight tomorrow, you and me, in the morning."

"You know, you could just let me go."

"If I did that, he would rip my throat out. I'm lucky to be alive now. At least in a challenge, we both have a chance to survive."

Jace unwrapped the package. He breathed deep of the succulent scent of blood and flesh. It was a pork roast, already half eaten, but he wasn't going to complain. He picked it up in both hands and tore off a chunk with his teeth.

Eric sensed the unspoken question hanging between them. "It's going to be unfair enough as it is without you being hungry."

Jace chomped and chewed, smacking his lips. "What are you talking about? I'm gonna whup you."

Eric cracked a dark grin. "I guess we'll see."

CHAPTER THIRTY-SIX

D odge Street shot like an arrow through the center of the city, toward the Missouri River in the east and toward small towns and farm land in the west. Saint Sebastian's lay on the far west fringe of the city, surrounded by farmland and sparsely placed suburbs. Dalton turned his car off the freeway and headed west on Dodge.

"Weird," Mia said after a while. "Like twenty blocks and we haven't seen a car."

"I didn't think they had locked the entire city down."

"It's like we're in a foreign country or something." Every radio station was broadcasting endless rehashes and commentary on the governor's press conference. Listening to music when the night was so still and dead would have felt so surreal anyway.

Thirty seconds later, a dazzling wall of strobing red and blue came into view. A solid barricade of police cars filled the biggest intersection in the center of the city.

Lee and Malcolm sank lower in the seat.

Mia said, "Turn off of Dodge. We need to find a way around. They might be looking for us."

Dalton downshifted, carefully hit his turn signal, and turned off the thoroughfare onto a dark, curving residential street. "Good call. That many cops in one place just freaks me out anyway."

Mia smirked at him. "Why? Have you been naughty?"

He smirked back. "That's a good word for it. Let's just say we don't want to come across any K-9 units."

Lee piped up, "Yeah, dude. How much weed *do* you have in the glove box?"

Dalton cleared his throat. "Just a tiny little bit. Couple blunts is all."

"Oh, god," Mia groaned, "I knew you were too good to be true."

"More like I just choose to behave most of the time." Dalton winked at her.

A week ago, knowing that Dalton smoked weed would have felt like a catastrophic red flag. The drug of peace perhaps, but she hated the way it shut off people's minds. She had known too many stoner military brats with their brains turned off. But hey, stoner versus ravening flesh-eating monster seemed like a minor bump. Did werewolves who smoked weed get the munchies and eat more people?

The houses in this neighborhood were old brick structures, fraught with climbing ivy and well-trimmed hedges. Old stately trees—oak, elm, box elder—cut deep shadows through the meager pools of street light. The street curved and recurved, branched, turned.

Mia said, "Are we still going the right direction?"

"Uh, I think so."

"Look out!"

Dalton stomped the brakes as a large gray shape darted from a steep driveway into the street. Too late. The car's front bumper struck the wolf on the haunches, spinning it around. It leaped back to its feet and faced them with lips peeled back and eyes blazing, fur bristling, shoulders hunched to spring.

Dalton laid on the horn. "Fuck you!"

The wolf glared at them for several long seconds. The car windows were up. Lee and Malcolm edged forward in their seats, ready to act.

The wolf leaped over the car and disappeared. Mia spun to look for the wolf, but it was gone.

Dalton took his hand off the horn.

Mia almost laughed. The Toyota's horn sounded about as intimidating as a four-year-old's squeaky toy. "Potty mouth."

"Burn your ears with that harsh language, Snow White?"

Her ears were warm, but that wasn't why.

A chorus of howls erupted like a series of discordant pipe organs for blocks around.

"Oh. My. God," Dalton said.

The howls comingled into two separate choruses, two groups, the sounds melding to form a strange ululating conversation, the meaning of which danced around the perimeter of her understanding. The harmonies came and went, danced and clashed.

Mia cracked her window just a little to hear. "What are they saying?"

After a few moments of listening, Malcolm said, "They're arguing, or getting ready to challenge. Like what happens when one pack moves into another's territory."

"What are they fighting about?"

Lee said, "Territory. Ain't no wolf pack lets another horn in on its space."

Malcolm said, "That's part of it. But there's more, and I can't quite put my finger on it. Sometimes words aren't enough."

Dalton said, "We're in the middle of werewolf turf war?"

Lee's voice was quiet. "We need to get the hell outta this neighborhood."

Malcolm nodded. "I concur."

Dalton hit the gas and sped up the street, around the oncoming curves. The Toyota whined in protest.

Lee laughed, "Whup them hamsters, dawg!"

Dalton's lips drew tight into a grim smile, both hands clenching the wheel.

A flurry of furry activity emerged in the pool of headlights. A mass of lupine shapes, from lithe wiry coyote-sized to massive hulking shapes of gray and brown, black and white.

Mia breathed. "They're...beautiful!"

She clamped a hand over her mouth. Had she really meant that? Majestic, savage, powerful, yes—and more intelligent, each and every one, than any wolf ever born.

The pack was gathered around something near a parked car at the side of the road. Three of the wolves turned toward them from the group, their snouts dripping red in the white headlights. Their movement revealed that which lay on the street. Shreds of turquoise and yellow jogging suit soaked with crimson. A severed stump of human ankle emerging from a blood-smeared Nike. Flaccid, bulging ropes of ensanguined entrails spilled across the pavement. A flash of white bone shone amid crimson wetness.

An incoherent noise gurgled from Dalton's throat.

The other wolves noticed the car and ceased feeding. Ten of them fanned out across the road, eleven. Twelve.

Lee whispered, "We are so dead."

One of them howled in triumph and this time Mia understood. *More food here.*

The wolves padded closer to the car, fanning out to encircle it.

Mia whispered, "Go!"

Dalton's voice was choked. "Where?"

"Forward or back! Pick one!"

Dalton slammed the gear shift into reverse and gunned it. He looked back over his shoulder, trying to steer as the car picked up speed.

The wolves loped along in pursuit, their eyes flashing with feral hunger, some with malevolent, ravenous glee. Some of them *loved* this. Like Slade.

The Toyota engine roared, and the car still felt as if it were moving at a crawl. The wolves picked up speed, drawing closer. Dalton kept glancing forward. Each time he saw that they were closer, he stamped harder on the gas, but the poor little car could do no more. The headlights swam back and forth over the approaching wolf pack as he tried to negotiate the curved street while roaring backwards, dodging curbs and parked cars.

Mia saw it coming in the side view mirror. "Look out!"

Crash.

The car sideswiped a parked pickup truck and ground to a halt against the fender.

Dalton swore. Dark blue door panel filled Mia's window. Fortunately, the glass had not broken.

The wolves closed within a few paces and prepared to charge.

Another chorus of howls from what sounded like a few blocks away. Many howls. There had to be more than ten, sustained, challenging.

The pack paused, many of them turning toward the new voices.

The chorus was coming closer.

Some of the pack flinched as if to run. Tails dropped from rigidly aggressive to fearful, submissive. The largest of the pack, a huge pale-furred male, snarled at his pack mates. He howled back a furious challenge. In an instant, all of them dashed off into the night toward their oncoming enemies.

The Toyota idled quietly. Inside the car, no one breathed.

It could have been a couple of seconds or a couple of minutes before Mia finally said, "Go, Dalton. Go now."

He swallowed hard and blinked away tears, then slammed the car back into drive and tore up the street.

As they sped away, the howling, roaring cacophony of a massive lupine melee echoed through the dark streets as if savage violence had become a living beast stalking the night.

CHAPTER THIRTY-SEVEN

Mia flipped around and around both the AM and FM radio stations. There was no mention of anything besides the quarantine.

"I don't get it," Mia said. "People are being eaten in the streets, and the news is not covering it?"

Dalton said, "Think about it. If you were on the receiving end of that call, at one of the TV stations, and someone told you that they had just seen a pack of wolves outside, or that you had seen someone change into an animal, or that your daddy disappeared and hasn't been right lately, how would you react?"

"I see your point."

"Even if by some chance the person on the phone is convincing, and the guy at the station doesn't hang up snickering—maybe he even passes the story along—would the station send out a reporter to cover such a thing? What reporter would head out at this time of night to check out a werewolf story? Other news organizations would laugh them off the planet!"

Mia groaned, "People are so stupid sometimes."

"Yeah, everybody's attention is on the quarantine. Nothing like this has ever happened anywhere. It's too bad they don't realize the virus moves pretty fast on four legs, and has brains behind it."

Malcolm snickered, "Except for Lee."

"Shut *up!*" Lee elbowed him.

"But there's no human brains behind running amok in the street!" Mia said. "What is going on?"

Malcolm said, "We keep varying degrees of our human intellect and moral codes. When you first begin to transform, the urge is powerful to just run, to become the animal for a while."

Dalton said, "It's like a coming out party. And we're the *hors d'oeuvres.*"

The car was as silent as a casket for the rest of the drive. They had to take side streets once more to avoid another police roadblock.

A cornfield bordered the grounds of Saint Sebastian's School for Children, and at this time of year the corn stood mature and starting to brown as it ripened, a forest of stalks seven to eight feet tall, perfect for concealing a late-night approach. The school was situated at the outskirts of the city on the crest of a low hill, with a major highway passing along one side and surrounded by fields on all the others. Spearhead Trail lay perhaps a mile distant. At Malcolm's suggestion, Dalton parked the car along a lonely gravel road on the opposite side of the cornfield.

Malcolm said, "There's a security guard. Nice guy."

Lee added, "But mostly a doofus. Probably asleep by this time of night."

Mia checked the battery on the video camera and shot some test footage to make sure it was working. Then they left the car behind and waded into the ditch grass.

Dalton peered into the shadows under the corn stalks. "Looks dark in there."

The darkness hung dense under the starlight. Mia nodded. It looked like the kind of darkness that would swallow a teen-age girl and never spit her out.

Lee and Malcolm stood behind the car, tossing their clothes into the back seat. Malcolm called out, "Don't look, we're changing!" They took deep breaths, their bodies tensed, and they hunched down behind the fenders out of sight. Ten seconds later, two lean wolf shapes padded out from behind the car.

Dalton whistled in awe. "Holy crap."

The wolves leaped from the road, over the barb wire fence, disappearing into the corn. They made a twenty-foot leap look effortless.

Mia took a deep breath herself and crossed the fence. She parted the curtain of leaves and slipped into the shadows.

Two steps within, her face passed full into a gauzy veil of spider web. A scream tore out of her, and she slapped frantically at her face, jumping up and down, spitting and sobbing incoherent syllables.

Dalton was at her side instantly. "What? What is it?"

"Spiders!"

She sensed him suppress a snicker, but he clasped her shoulder and pulled her close. "It's okay, they won't hurt you. You're okay."

The casual strength of his arm thrilled her to the marrow of her bones, even as she felt like an idiot for freaking out. After what she had been through today, she was scared of *spiders*? There were werewolves about, and she was scared of spiders. She breathed deep several times, and Dalton's voice calmed her. Finally, she said, "Okay, I'm okay."

"You sure?"

She nodded. If she ran into any more webs, she would not do this again. She was stronger than that. She could not afford to make any noise like that again, especially when they were closer to Saint Sebastian's. For all she knew, werewolves had super-hearing and she had just rung the dinner bell. "Let's go."

They made their way through the cornfield toward the grounds, following the ruler-straight rows. The shadows under the stalks and leaves hung dense under the starlight. The moon was absent, but Mia found that she had no trouble seeing. The starlight turned the world into sharp silvery-grays, like brilliant sparkles of star-powder on a tapestry more vibrant than she had ever seen before. The leaves crackled at their passage, and she winced at the noise, but it couldn't be helped. Crickets and grasshoppers chirped a rhythmic symphony around them that went silent as they approached and resumed behind them. Dalton, despite his efforts to be quiet, sounded like a herd of bison tearing through the cornstalks.

Lee and Malcolm slunk along on either side of the two humans, gliding silently under the leaves. Deuce padded just ahead, his nose lifted, ever sniffing the air, but his breath was growing ever more ragged. The rich, earthy smell of the soil, the sweetness of the corn, the sharp tang of the weeds that managed to survive among the corn rows, and strangely, the scent of moisture in the air. The sky was cloudless, but Mia smelled rain. Mia found herself so entranced by this new world of scents that she all but forgot the video camera she carried and the threat of more spider webs in her face.

The traverse of the cornfield was perhaps three hundred yards, and as they reached the crosscutting end rows, they eased through them to view Saint Sebastian's. A chain link fence surrounded the grounds. Nothing about the place looked remotely modern, save for the new scoreboard standing above the end of the football field. The buildings were dark brick structures, two- and three-storied, with tall, narrow-paned windows. The spire of the cathedral bell tower stood like a black spiky silhouette against the star glow. The hedges and lawns were well-trimmed. The profusion of lights would make a shadowed approach difficult. The dormitories loomed dark and blockish, with only the yellow lights of their entrance ways shining in the night.

Lee and Malcolm crouched at the edge of the cornfield, noses raised.

Mia breathed deep, trying to dissect the plethora of scents. Lawn chemicals. Greenery. Flowers. Something warm and alive that didn't smell like wolf, dog, or human. She rotated her head to pinpoint the source of the smell, finding it when she spotted a dark, roundish bump and two yellowish eyes glinting at her from near one of the hedges. A raccoon.

A sick dread settled atop her heart. She had just smelled a raccoon at fifty yards. She took a deep breath and let it out, swallowed the sob that almost came. Her fists clenched the invisible spike of fear. Time enough to worry about turning into a freak later. Now was not the time.

Lee and Malcolm had drawn a map on a fast-food napkin and described the main classroom building where Jace was likely being kept. The Cooler was in the basement of that building. The doors were supposed to be locked at night, but since Slade had taken to his late night excursions with his pack, he usually left the door propped open so he could get back into his office. It was kind of hard for a wolf to carry a set of keys around, except in its mouth. The main building was the oldest on the campus, built with architecture from a century before Mia's time. Along with the cathedral, it dominated the center of campus. The gymnasium and the dormitories, grounds shack, and visitor center encircled the two central edifices. The massive I-beams of the water tower stood on a thick concrete foundation at the near-left corner of the campus, and the huge tank loomed black against the sky, shaped vaguely like an old coffee pot.

Lee and Malcolm crept out of the cornfield but kept their bodies low in the grass, still sniffing. Then each with a single bound cleared the chain link fence and landed inside. They darted for the shadows of the nearest hedge.

Mia crept out, and Dalton and Deuce followed her. As she faced the eight-foot chain link barrier, she thought about how to get Deuce over it.

Dalton pointed to a small concrete culvert that passed under the fence about thirty yards away. She led Deuce there and pointed through it. He huffed in agreement and thrust his barrel-chested body into the aperture. Mia hadn't climbed a chain link fence since sixth grade. Nevertheless, she jumped up, hooked her fingers in the links and climbed. It was easier than she had anticipated. A strange lightness, an energy and alacrity she hadn't felt since she was a little kid, crackled through her at the effort. Throwing her leg over the top and jumping down felt as easy as walking, as if her body was as light as thistledown.

Deuce wriggled out of the drain and stood beside her, beslimed with muck, detritus clinging to the bloody gashes on his face and chest. His face was weary but resolute.

Dalton jumped down from the top of the fence, and the three of them rushed toward the shadows where Lee and Malcolm waited.

Mia checked her watch. Two a.m. She could see two lights inside the main building, one coming from a window on the second floor, another from a basement level window along the side of the building. That window was probably the Cooler, and she would bet any money that the light on the second floor was Slade's office. Who else would be awake at this hour? The blinds were open, and from this angle all she could see was the ceiling fan and its shadow.

She switched on the video camera, opened up the screen and started shooting. The window, the entrance, her companions, and herself. She looked into the lens and whispered, "This is Mia O'Reilly, daughter of Marcus and Kyoko O'Reilly, and I'm filming this because our friend Jace is being held prisoner inside this building by Jack Slade. Jack Slade is...not what he appears to be. Um...I hope we don't die."

The whites of Dalton's eyes practically glowed. "Nice, Mia. Just what I needed to hear."

"If you want to go back to the car, now's the time."

"Are you kidding? This is the coolest thing I've ever done. Except for almost getting killed twice so far, that is."

She cocked her head and mouthed the words, "Then let's go." She darted into the open and headed for the door of the main building. A young man, a dog, and two wolves ghosted in her wake. Did that make her pack leader? As she drew nearer the front door, she hoped Malcolm's guess that the door would be open would prove correct. A smile crossed her features when she saw that the door was ajar, propped open by the fold of the foyer rug. Standing bathed in the light of the entry lamp, she felt a sudden chill at being exposed. The curving brass door handle, probably predating the 20th century, felt cold in her grip as she eased the door open, held it for Dalton and the three quadrupeds, and then slipped inside after them.

The foyer door was unlocked, as the boys had predicted, and soon they all stood in the hallway that felt as old as another century, built with lots of dark, heavy wood, floor tiles that looked like a grim, gray honeycomb, and white plaster walls. Rows of plaques and black-and-white photographs lined the walls, cases filled with dusty trophies, a hallway darkened for the night, illuminated only by a single hooded-glass fixture at each end. A long wooden stairway paralleled the hallway, leading up to the second floor.

Mia took a deep breath and sneaked down the hallway toward the door at the far end, the one that Malcolm had said led to the basement, the eye of the camera held before her. Her sneakers moved as silently as a ninja's *tabi* across the tiles. Lee hung back, watching the rear, his yellow-green eyes glowing like lamps in shadows, nose raised for any hint of threatening scent. Deuce's claws clicked on the floor as he padded at Mia's side, legs half crouched, ready to spring at the first sign of danger. Her skin felt electrified, super-sensitive, and her hands were quivering. She pulled out her bear spray and clutched it in her other fist.

She imagined that she could sense Slade in his office just above, burning the midnight oil, doing whatever things evil werewolf wrestling coaches did at 2:00 a.m., perhaps with a nice raw leg-of-lamb in front of him, or leg-of-human perhaps.

She hoped she would never, ever want to eat a bunny.

The door to the stairwell was a fire door, with its heavy thumb latch, horizontal bar, and massive *ka-chunk* sound that would give them away instantly. But there was no choice. Dalton grasped the latch in both hands and squeezed it down. It opened with barely a click. He eased the door open and then propped it open with a small wooden wedge sitting nearby for just that purpose. Down the stairs to the basement they went, with Malcolm's dark shade ghosting in the lead and Lee bringing up the rear. The stairs led down into a hallway. Just past the foot of the stairs, a narrow door hung ajar, with a little sign that read STORAGE. Down another long hallway, where the air smelled like earth, dust, cleaning chemicals, and old wood. Doors to classrooms opened on both walls to dark rooms filled with dark wooden desks and slate blackboards. Starlight filtered through a few age-clouded windows.

They rounded a corner, and Malcolm trotted ahead to stop beside a steel door with an opaque glass window. His tongue lolled as he gestured with his head.

Mia knocked on the door, quietly. "Jace! Are you in there?"

Startled movement inside, then Jace's voice. "Yeah!"

The door had a solid handle, but no latch. It was held closed by a key-lock above the handle. She looked at Malcolm plaintively. "No key!" she whispered.

Malcolm lowered his head and opened his mouth. Sounds came out, horribly distorted by a mouth not made for human speech. Each syllable sounded like a struggle. "Uff sturrs. Off iss."

"You mean Slade's office upstairs."

Malcolm nodded. It was strange to see a wolf nod.

Her heart sank. How could they possibly get the key from Slade's office? She hadn't considered the possibility that Jace would be kept in a locked room like a jail cell.

Dalton said, "Let me see that." He stepped up and examined the lock, then pulled out a pocket knife. He worked the blade down into the crack between the door and the door frame.

"You know how to do that?"

"Doesn't every high school kid know how to open things they're not supposed to?" He gave her a smirk.

She kept the camera on him. "Delinquent."

"You love it." He worked the door in and out with one hand and jimmied the latch with the knife in the other. "Got it."

He pulled the door open and Jace stood there, practically bouncing with excitement. "Thanks, you guys!"

Mia's eyes teared. A boy a few years her junior, bouncing with excitement. Something in her heart settled into place. No matter what happened to her after this, she had done the right thing. "We have to get out of here. Where's Slade?"

"I ain't seen him in a couple hours." He threw his blanket back onto the bed, and his face turned serious, his eyes shadowed. The wolf rose nearer the surface. In a few heartbeats, he had gone from frightened boy to restrained predator, ready to fight for his life.

Mia said, "Come on." Then she led them back down the hallway toward the stairwell. Her ears crackled with every tiny sound, the shuffle of their feet, the whisper of their clothing, the buzzing whine of the video camera, their breathing, sniffing, and the echoes of those sounds. Again, Malcolm took the lead. In the stairwell, each step felt like an eternity, each step closer to the front door, and freedom for all of them. How could they make so much racket even when trying to be quiet?

Malcolm stopped in the fire door and checked the hallway, then moved into it. Mia and the others followed close behind. She kept the video camera trained before them, finding it hard to concentrate on stealth at the same time. In the viewfinder, the window glass from the entry way at the far end of the hallway formed black rectangles.

A globe of light danced against the glass. "Uh-oh," Dalton said.

The globe became a flashlight beam.

Jace whispered, "It's Harvey!"

"What now?" Mia whispered.

The beam coalesced and a uniformed figure appeared behind. A security badge glinted on a paunchy jacket. The security guard spotted them in the hallway instantly. "Hey! What are you doing in here?"

Mia hissed, "What do we do?"

The security guard yelled, fumbling with his keys. "Don't move or I'll the call the police!"

Two pairs of fireflies floated into the glass rectangles, glimmering orbs, hovering just behind him.

Jace called, "Look out, Harvey!"

One pair of orbs darted toward the security guard. His feet were snatched back from under him, his face smashing against the door as a he fell. He screamed, a blood-curdling shriek of terror and agony, diminishing as his flailing arms disappeared into the night.

The screaming stopped.

Then the orbs appeared in the glass again, moving toward the gap where the front door hung propped open. A dark, blood-spattered muzzle thrust into the crack and wedged the door open, and the rest of the furry, brownish-gray body shouldered into the foyer, eyes fixed on them.

CHAPTER THIRTY-EIGHT

The wolf's gaze drilled into Mia. She met its gaze, and surges of fear and anger tore through her.

Malcolm charged. Lee vaulted over all of them in a single leap to join him.

The wolf in the foyer snarled and snapped its teeth.

Jace started peeling off his clothes. "Bring these along would you?"

Dalton snatched them from Jace's hand.

In a flash, Lee and Malcolm faced the wolf through the door glass. The second wolf outside shoved into the foyer. The four of them created a savage ruckus of snarling and growling.

Deuce hugged against Mia's leg, reluctant to leave her side, even though every muscle in his body was as taut and quivering as a bridge cable in an earthquake. She ran to Lee and Malcolm, averting her eyes from Jace as he denuded himself of clothing.

From behind and above her, a voice echoed down, quiet and menacing. "Why, Mia, how nice of you to bring everyone."

She gasped and spun. Slade stood at the top of the stairs, backlit by the feeble light fixture. His eyes burned yellow, and her heart quailed.

They were the eyes of a beast within looking out through the eye sockets of a human skull.

He leaped. Mia thought vaguely that she should turn the camera onto him, but her mind froze between infinitely narrow slices of time. Slade alit beside her and snatched at the camera. She jerked it away.

Deuce lunged and buried his teeth in Slade's naked knee. Slade's face twisted in pain. Jace's wolf form flew past Mia's shoulder like an arc of quicksilver and plowed into Slade. Teeth flashed and crimson jaws gnashed. Slade stumbled back against the wall, dragging Deuce with him. She raised her bear spray and camera together, but couldn't get a clear shot to land the spray in Slade's face. Slade's body started to shift, limbs changing, bones realigning.

The four wolves still faced off through the glass, roaring, none of them able to manipulate the door latch.

Dalton grabbed Mia's shoulder. "Downstairs! Maybe there's a back way out!"

Slade struggled to protect his face from Jace's snapping jaws and his leg kicked at Deuce to dislodge the dog's tenacious grip. Deuce's head jerked and tore at Slade.

Dalton yelled, "Come on!"

Lee and Malcolm heard Dalton's cry and backed away from the door.

"Come on!" he cried again.

Mia tossed him the video camera. She rushed forward and grabbed Deuce's collar. "No, Deuce! Come on!" Deuce relinquished his grip and allowed himself to be pulled away, his lips stained with blood. In that instant, Slade's fist lashed out, propelled by a thick, hairy arm, and smashed into the side of Deuce's head. A horrible yipe of surprise and pain exploded from him. The force of the blow wrenched Deuce's collar out of Mia's grip and sent the dog spinning through the air. His body smacked into a row of photographs on the far wall, smashing frames and glass. He hit the floor as limp and motionless as a piece of steak.

A tiny squeak peeped out of Mia's throat. She willed Deuce to get up and shake himself. But he didn't. A gobbet of cold lead rose in her throat.

One of the wolves outside stepped back and launched itself into the glass, head lowered. A long, spider-webbed crack appeared.

Dalton snatched her arm again. "Let's go!" Mia allowed herself to be pulled away. Dalton yelled as they ran. "Jace!"

Jace bounded back, away from Slade. In another flash, he stood between Lee and Malcolm, three wolves standing between the humans and certain death.

Mia and Dalton ran for the fire door. The three wolf-boys raced after them.

The door glass exploded inward with a flying brownish-gray body. The wolf landed at the foot of the steps in a cascade of glass shards. Slade's massive, black and silver wolf form slunk around the balustrade of the stairway past the other wolf, limping from the massive gashes on his rear leg, and his face was criss-crossed with scarlet gouges. The third wolf jumped through the empty window frame.

Slade charged, the other two wolves close on his heels.

Dalton kicked the wooden wedge free as Mia dove through the fire door. The wolf-boys lunged in after. Dalton slammed the steel door shut. The door shuddered as Slade's massive weight plowed into the other side. Dalton and Mia clutched the heavy horizontal bar and held the door closed. Teeth ground and snapped against the door's thumb latch on the opposite side.

Dalton's knuckles turned white as he clutched the bar. "We need to jam it somehow!"

Mia cast her attention over her shoulder and spotted the open storage closet. "Hold on!" She leaped down the steps five at a time, flung open the door, yanked the pull-string hanging from a naked light bulb. Pale yellow light spilled over an assortment of buckets, mops, brooms, and cleaning supplies.

The fire door shuddered and creaked. Claws ground and scratched in the furious assault on the opposite side.

She shoved the pepper spray into her pocket, grabbed an armful of mops and brooms, and then spotted a screwdriver in an open toolbox on a shelf. She snatched that too and ran back up the steps.

A raw, bloodcurdling voice, thick with wolfen distortion, found its way through the thick door. "Can't hide long, Mia! Can't hide ever!"

Dalton glanced at everything she was carrying. "Screwdriver." She offered it. He snatched it out of her hand and jammed it into the door latch mechanism. The raucous pounding, snarling, and clawing continued. "Nothing is going to open that door anytime soon until somebody pulls that out."

"What about these?" Mia said, offering the mops and brooms.

"I don't think we have time to clean."

She smirked and thrust the handles behind the horizontal door latch, positioning them to hold the latch in place and bar the door. "Let's go, jerk."

They ran down the steps and found the three young wolves already waiting at the far end of the hallway. Jace yipped to urge greater speed.

Mia reached them ten steps ahead of Dalton. "Is there a back way out?"

Jace surged ahead. Past the empty Cooler, down two more hallways to a glowing red EXIT sign above another fire door. Through that door, they found themselves in a cavernous room that smelled of wood and tools and machines. Workbenches lined the room, and a rack of raw boards stood along one wall. Power saws and tools that Mia found incomprehensible filled the spaces between the benches; racks of hand tools covered the walls. Another red EXIT sign glowed dully on the opposite side of the shop beside a garage door. They dashed toward it. From a box of scrap wood Dalton snatched up a stout piece about the size and thickness of a baseball bat. Jace threw his body against the exit door and let his weight carry the door open. The five of them spilled out into the fresh air of night.

Mia's heart hammered in her chest as she scanned the glistening gray dark for pursuit. The can of bear spray was slick and warm in one hand, and her fingers ached from clutching the camera in the other. Somewhere in the distance, a howl echoed. Jace and others stopped to listen. She shoved the bear spray back into her pocket.

Another howl answered, closer, from the direction of the auditorium. Their eyes followed the sound.

The shape of another wolf appeared at the edge of the auditorium roof, silhouetted against the stars. Eyes flashed in the darkness.

Dalton tugged Mia toward the nearest perimeter fence. "Let's go!"

A choking sob rose in her throat. "But Deuce! What about Deuce?" How could she just leave him here?

"Do you want to die?"

Her eyes burned with tears, but she allowed him to pull her toward the fence. If they could get enough of a head start to reach the car, they might yet escape. The wolves could track them by scent, so it would only be a matter of time before Slade and his minions were on the escapees' trail.

The wolf atop the auditorium was gone. Jace paused and looked in that direction, his head cocked at a puzzled angle.

Mia checked the video camera. Still recording, battery still good. The video would be awful, but hopefully something on it would be usable to incriminate Slade and show the authorities the truth.

As they sprinted toward the fence, Mia felt greater speed building in her legs. She hit the gas. Her feet flew, and she instantly left Dalton behind. In a twinkling she reached the fence, and with one leap she was halfway up, clinging to the chain links with her free hand. One quick snatch at the top bar, a swinging jump, and she was over. The wolves sailed over as if they had wings, landing with a snapping crush of cornstalks.

Another howl off in the cornfield, to be answered by a snarling cacophony of rage from within the Saint Sebastian grounds.

The understanding of those howls danced around Mia's consciousness. The first howl had sounded like...a challenge. The challenge was answered by the second. And somehow, Mia understood.

Dalton landed on the wild grass beside her. "Don't wait for me! Go!"

The howls held her in place. The single howl sounded again, this time from farther away.

Dalton took her by the shoulders and gazed into her eyes. "We. Need. To go."

Her knees weakened as his glimmering eyes pricked her heart. But then into her mind's eye burst another image of Deuce's body smashing into the wall, the horrid, meaty sound of it. She swallowed her tears and nodded.

Through the pitch black cornfield they ran. Thick storm clouds climbed from the western horizon, veiling more than half of the tapestry of stars. Lightning flickered within the veil of clouds. The direction of the corn rows pointed toward the car. Raspy leaves slapped and tore at Mia's face and arms.

Distant howls continued to reverberate, sounding alternatively nearer then farther away, like ghosts that ignored distance. Suddenly another howl sounded from within the cornfield, shockingly close.

Mia burst from the cornrows into the grassy ditch between the field and the gravel road, and her heart leaped. They were almost free. She hurdled the barb wire fence in a single bound and reached the road in two more, casting her gaze back and forth in search of the car. The three young wolves surrounded her, their sharp eyes scanning the dark for threats.

Ice-water drenched her spine. "Where's the freaking car?"

CHAPTER THIRTY-NINE

Dalton crashed through the cornstalks behind her.

"Where is the car?" she cried again.

The three silent wolf shapes around her sniffed the night and looked up and down the road.

Was this the right road? Its undulations and fences looked unfamiliar somehow. Had they gotten themselves turned around in the night?

Dalton burst from the field, stopped at the barb wire fence, and gingerly crossed over. Mia felt a moment of pity for him at leaving him so far behind. He lurched up out of the ditch, his breath heaving from the dead run.

"Where's the car?" she said.

Dalton tried to catch his breath and looked up and down the road. He pointed. "I think it's over that little hill."

The road rose and disappeared over a small hillock perhaps a hundred yards away.

"Are you sure?"

"Pretty sure."

A howl of pursuit sounded, so near that she could have hit the pursuer with a thrown rock had she been able to see the source.

She snatched Dalton's arm. "Run!"

They ran.

Gravel skittered and crunched underfoot. The night wind whistled in Mia's ears. The video camera was hot and slick in her right hand. Had it not been strapped to her palm, she would have lost it long ago. She practically dragged Dalton with her. He stumbled alongside as if his feet were mired in a cold tar.

The pursuer's howl sounded again, this time unmuffled by the cornstalks. Directly behind them. Mia hazarded a glance over her shoulder.

A pale lupine shape surged out of the tall ditch grass and charged after them. Before the wolf boys could turn to face the pursuer, it leaped.

Its leap carried it full onto Dalton's back. He cried out, stumbled, and sprawled face first onto the gravel with an expulsion of painful breath. The wolf tumbled off him, turned and spread its jaws, lunged forward. Dalton rolled onto his back, his face bleeding and contorted with pain. The wolf-boys skidded to a halt and spun to fall upon the attacker.

The wolf, its fur gleaming like a ghost in the moonlight, bore him down, front paws on his chest, slavering into his face, pale blue eyes boring into him. It froze. Then its raw savagery seemed to begin draining away. Its tail started to wag, almost imperceptibly. It looked at Mia, then in turn at each of the three snarling wolves that now surrounded it. It lowered its eyes, tucked its tail against its leg, and stepped off Dalton's chest.

The wolf-boys stalked closer, cautious. The pale wolf kept its head low, submissive. Its shoulders quivered. It turned its gaze toward Mia, its eyes full of such profound sadness and regret that a pang of sympathy shot through Mia's heart.

Jace stood over the wolf, snarling, ears laid back, teeth bared. The pale wolf placidly kept its head low, shoulders slumped.

Dalton slid back, away from it. "Holy wow. Did one of them just come over to our side?"

"I think so," Mia said.

Dalton stood and backed away, brushing himself off.

The pale wolf edged closer to Jace, with its head lowered. A silent exchange passed between them, sniffing, nuzzling. The other two wolf-boys padded closer, wary.

Dalton approached Mia. "I've never seen anyone run like that before. You got some wheels."

She smiled. "Thanks."

"No, I mean I've never seen a human run like that before."

Their eyes met, and a splinter of fear went through her at the wall that had appeared behind his eyes.

He said, "You're going to become one of them aren't you."

Her mouth opened but wouldn't work. Inside she screamed the silent word *NO!* But some deep part of her knew that was a lie.

As their gazes locked them together, time disappeared in a swirl. An eternity of realizations in a single second. Part of her wept for loss, a loss that would last forever. Part of her reveled in it. She could run, she could leap, she could see things, *smell* things, *do* things. Maybe one day soon, she might even change into a wolf.

But she would never, ever, eat a bunny.

She reached out to touch his arm, yearning to kiss him again, to kiss the fear out of him, out of herself.

He turned away from her. "We have to get out of here."

Her heart shrank into soft, mumbling words. "We have to find the car."

"That way I think."

"Yeah, that way."

They ran that way. The four wolves ceased their hierarchical rituals and followed. A hundred yards later, cresting the hill, Mia spotted the lone dark shape of Dalton's car, perhaps fifty yards farther, right where they had left it. A smile spread across her face. They raced toward it. Almost immediately Dalton fell behind. Mia reached the car in a flash and threw open the door, gesticulating for the wolf-boys to jump in. Lee dove in, followed by Malcolm.

Dalton skidded to a stop beside the driver's door. His breath sucked in with a hiss. "Mia."

The tone of his voice called back the fear. "What is it?"

"Look inside."

She peered into the car. The steering wheel was gone, wrenched from the end of the steering column, leaving only a few shreds of ragged metal and splintered plastic.

Something large moved through nearby cornstalks. Several large somethings.

A massive black and silver wolf stalked out of the cornfield and leaped over the fence. The twisted, mangled steering wheel dangled from Slade's jaws.

Lightning silhouetted the Saint Sebastian's water tower. Thunder rumbled close on its heels, low and threatening. A fresh breeze ruffled the corn stalks, and the air of the late-summer night suddenly chilled, as if they all had just entered an air-conditioned room.

Four lupine shapes emerged from the cornfield behind Slade.

Mia dragged her bear spray out of her pocket.

Slade dropped the steering wheel in the grass beside the road. His gaze drilled into her like the points of yellow-hot awls.

The hairs on the back of her neck spiked, and her jaw clenched. Her knees started quivering, but anger began to boil in her chest. "Leave us alone!" She lowered the camera to her side, but held it so that the lens was trained on Slade and his minions.

Slade stood at the edge of the gravel, his three subordinates flanking him. He took a deep breath and held it. His back arched. His legs began to change length and position, his dark fur to fall out in clumps, his snout blunted, shortened, his ears sliding down toward the sides of his head, rounding. He stood. His thick wolf-like shoulders became thick human shoulders. In the chill air, the sweat from his naked flesh began to steam. His voice was still hoarse, barely human as he spoke. "There is only one way to end this."

"Yeah!" Mia shouted. "Let us be!"

"Only one way."

"You know the police are on their way, right?"

"The police mean nothing to me. They are a human construct, soon to be meaningless. The Wolf Pack will spread, and soon all human civilization will be become wolf civilization."

"There's no such thing as wolf civilization!"

"Exactly. The Way of the Wild will reassert itself, and it will endure forever."

"You're insane!"

"No, Mia, I am the sanest person you have ever met. You still cling to the human civilization that is destroying this planet, destroying its wilderness, its creatures, and even slowly but surely destroying human beings. We have created a society that is destroying ourselves. In believing we can tame the world, we have turned ourselves into weak, fat parasites. Humans give back nothing, only take. There is no harmony, no balance. But that will change. *Everything* is changing. You can either embrace the change or be swept under and drowned by it."

"You sound like some sort of tree-hugging terrorist! Like those guys that torpedo whaling ships."

"Embrace the change, Mia. It seems my bite has taken hold in you. You smell different now."

Mia glanced at Dalton. He stood silent, his club sagging toward the ground. Even in the dark, she could see that the color had drained from his face. "I'll never join you."

Steam rose from Slade's shoulders, and his eyes glimmered like red-eye in a photo. "I'll make you a deal. One contest. One challenge for all the bowling balls. How about that? But if you or any of these others try to run, I'll kill you all. Sound fair?"

"Not particularly. You like beating up on little boys, you freak?"

"Oh, not me. I'm going to leave it to Eric to show Jace the way."

Jace's hackles rose, and he growled a challenge.

Slade's strong white teeth gleamed. "That's the spirit!" Then he fixed his gaze on the pale wolf standing next to Dalton. "I'll even let Tara live, even though she betrayed my trust."

The pale wolf whined.

"It's not too late," Slade said. "We can all survive this. You, me, all of us."

Mia pointed her bear spray at his face. "Yeah, and be your slaves!"

"If Jace wins, you'll all walk away, and I'll let you."

"I don't believe you. We know who you are! What you are! And you know we'll send the cops after you! The C.D.C., the entire F.B.I., the National Guard!"

"I think they're going to have their hands full for a while, don't you?" He cupped an ear at the sound of another distant wolf howl. "Besides, they'll never find me. Ever. The Great Plains is a mighty big place. I could be in Kansas by this time tomorrow night. Or almost to Colorado. How will they find a single wolf pack in thousands of square miles of prairie? Or a single wolf? I could be in Canada within the week and start a whole new life. Mexico. With all of humanity's gadgets and technology, no human being can hide anymore, not for long. But a wolf can. Then maybe someday, when you're least expecting it, after you've gotten yourself all comfortable, and forgotten all about me, maybe I'll pay you a little visit, or maybe your mother, or your father. Wouldn't you like that?"

"Bastard!"

Slade turned to his pack. "Boys, it's time to play. Eric."

A lean brown wolf stepped forward, almost as tall as Slade's wolf-form, but lankier, lithe. Its eyes blazed with determination.

CHAPTER FORTY

The moist smell of rain wafted on a zephyr, stroking the crests of the cornstalks like invisible fingers, harbinger of a storm.

The three wolf-boys hung together, their bodies crouching against the gravel. Muscles bunched and flexed under their thick coats. White teeth flashed, and iridescent eyes glowed like marbles lit from within. The burgeoning wind caught the rising chorus of snarls, dampened them, carrying them away across the fields.

Mia clutched Dalton's wrist and tugged him away from the growling lupines. His arm quivered in her hand, but he stepped in front of her, makeshift wooden club rising in his other hand. A smattering of dust borne on the wind peppered Mia's face through her swirling black hair. Tara slunk backward with Mia and Dalton, wary.

Eric padded forward.

Slade stood behind him with narrowed eyes, his lips drawn into a tight line. His bristly salt-and-pepper curls fluttered, prairie grass rhythmically brushing his knees.

Eric and Jace faced each other. Lee and Malcolm edged away. The other wolves padded into a vague circle with the two combatants at the nucleus. Hackles rose. Snarls crescendoed. Sinews tensed.

Jace and Eric blurred toward each other and struck with the clash of teeth and the thud of heavy bodies. Jace weighed perhaps one-fifty, a big wolf, but Eric had at least a thirty-pound advantage in sheer muscle.

The circled wolves raised their faces to the tumultuous sky and howled, trumpeting the challenge's beginning. Mia felt the exultation of the howl, the joy and freedom of the wild and the hunt bursting within her chest, and a chill exploded up the back of her neck as she recognized this. And it didn't feel strange. It felt as if she had known it all along, as if it was part of her, as natural as her favorite pair of shoes, as comforting as the warmth of her family. She let go of Dalton's arm and sighed quietly, swallowing the lump in her throat.

The two wolves thrashed and tore at each other. Tufts of fur floated into the wind. Lightning strobed closer, and thunder crackled in its afterimage.

The larger wolf bore the smaller down with power and fury. Jace scrambled back and leaped over the edge of the circle, alighting on the roof of Dalton's car. From his vantage point, he turned to face Eric, ears laid back, teeth bared, eyes glittering. Dark, wet patches stained his fur.

Eric leaped after him. Jace slid over the side of the roof, and Eric sailed over the car, dragging his claws across the paint, landing twenty feet past the hood, claws scrabbling in the gravel. While Eric scrambled, off balance, Jace leaped for him, grazing him, slashing his teeth across Eric's flank. Jace slid to a halt twenty feet beyond and spun, spitting out a mouthful of bloody fur.

Eric's rear leg buckled for an instant. He glanced at Slade. Slade's eyes were cold and hard. Determination flared in Eric's eyes, and he lunged again. Jace jumped adroitly to the side. Eric flew past and landed chin first on the gravel, haunches in the air, skidding to a halt. He leaped up, eyes blazing, shoulders shaking with fury and frustration.

Eric leaped again, and Jace danced toward the car, out of reach. Eric leaped again, and Jace dodged away, but not before Eric's claw tore across Jace's ribcage. Eric flew into the ditch, disappearing for a moment into the tall grass.

Jace crouched before the car's front bumper, waiting. Eric stalked out of the ditch, fifteen feet away, his body quivering with rage, chest heaving with exertion. He faced Jace. The two young beasts traded snarls. Jace braced himself. Eric dug in his claws for another leap.

Slade jumped atop the roof of the car with single leap, his eyes glittering like hailstones.

The scent of rain strengthened. Mia's face cooled with the oncoming moisture. The pattering susurration of rain on leaves, drifting nearer across the cornfield.

Jace poised to meet Eric's charge.

Eric leaped, his jaws yawned wide, a forest of dagger-like teeth.

Jace jumped straight up into the air, out of Eric's path.

Eric's face smashed into the bumper with the crash of shattering plastic and the crunch of collapsing metal. His powerful momentum threw his haunches straight up, then flopped his stunned, limp body up onto the hood.

Jace alit, spun, leaped, and latched his teeth onto Eric's jugular. A heartbeat later, Eric's dazed eyes blinked with returning recognition. Jace jerked him by the throat onto the road, where he fell like a slab of meat. Jace could have torn out Eric's throat, but he did not. He simply held Eric's life in his teeth, squeezing off his air, and he growled.

Eric whined through the constriction of his windpipe. Jace dug his teeth dangerously deeper. Eric's whine choked away.

Slade grinned like a crocodile. "Welcome back to the pack, Jace. You're my Executive Officer now. But first you have to kill him. There is no place for weakness."

Blood dripped from Jace's wounds. His eyes reflected the flickers of lightning.

Slade said, "Do it."

Jace's growl softened.

"Kill him."

Mia clutched her mouth. "Don't do it, Jace! You're not like them!"

Jace released Eric's throat and backed away, turning defiant eyes up toward Slade.

Eric rolled onto his belly, panting, whimpering, one eye bloody and swelling shut, blood leaking from his nose.

Jace backed away.

Lightning glimmered again, highlighting the harsh ridges of Slade's face. "Do it!"

Jace shook his head.

Slade's face hardened like concrete. He sighed up at the sky. His three minions watched him expectantly. With a snarl, he leaped toward Mia. Dalton moved to interpose, but Slade's heavy knuckles, aided by the momentum of his descent, crashed down into Dalton's face. The young man dropped like a sack of boneless steaks. Dark blood spewed from his nose. Slade reached for Mia, his face springing outward as it became a toothy snout. Claws sprang from his grasping fingers, ripping through her jacket and shoulder.

Hot rage exploded in her. She dropped the camera and raised the bear spray, blasting it toward his face. His incredible celerity let him dodge the brunt of the spray cone, but it still caught the side of his face. He roared with pain, his skin darkening, sprouting fur. His massive paw swiped the bear spray out of her grip and sent it flying into the depths of the dark weeds.

Rain pattered the road around them, heavy drops brushing Mia's hair and shoulders.

The other paw swiped at her throat, a dark blur. The black, razor-pointed claw tips would have torn her head almost clean off, but she dodged back from the wind of the claw's passing.

The first paw swept back. She saw it coming in just enough time to raise her arm to protect her head. The blow hammered into her arm and knocked her sprawling. She scrambled away on all fours, her fingers tearing at grass and gravel. He lunged after her.

A chorus of rage and aggression filled the air as the two packs of wolves, one large and one small, threw themselves at each other in frenzies of attack.

An iron-hard paw pummeled her hip and flipped her onto her back. She scrambled backward on her hands and feet like a crab, Slade's wolf jaws snapping toward her face. Hot spittle spattered her cheeks.

CHAPTER FORTY-ONE

Something hard and sharp dug into Mia's butt as she scooted backwards, something in her pocket. The scalpel from the hospital. Slade's legs straddled her, and his jaws snapped shut an inch from her nose. She collapsed onto her back and dug the scalpel from her back pocket. Slade loomed over her, rearing back for a final bite. The stainless steel was smooth and warm as she tightened her fist around it. She stabbed upward into Slade's chest. Fur and flesh parted like butter at the thrust and slice of the surgical-sharp blade. Something hot gushed over Mia's fingers. Slade's eyes bulged in surprise.

She stabbed again. "You killed my dog, you son of a bitch!"

Slade jerked away, but his retreat pulled the scalpel's point out and drew the edge across his rib cage, leaving a deep dark gash behind. He lunched at her hand, faster than sight, and his jaws clamped onto her scalpel-wrist like a vise made of grinding needles. Her bones ground together and crunched, and white-hot pain tore up through her arm. She screamed. The scalpel fell from fingers that had stopped working. He was going to bite off her hand.

A ghost exploded out of the cornfield, streaked into Slade with a heavy thud and bore him sideways off Mia into the ditch. The two shapes tumbled together into a snarling pile of surprise and rage.

A flash of white, wolfen face lunged for Slade's throat. As the two forms thrashed and spun, she spied the white wolf's black wet-suit-like garment. A thrill of joy burst through her. But Slade's wolf-form was so much bigger and more powerful than Sarah. Even wounded, his teeth and claws were still lethal.

Mia's fingers were sticky with Slade's blood, and tufts of fur clung to her fingers. The scalpel lay within reach, and she snatched it up in her left hand, hugging her ravaged right hand to her chest.

The frequency of the raindrops intensified. The leading edge of a veil of rain advanced across the fields, obscuring the dark cornstalks behind it.

Jace, Lee, and Malcolm lay at the center of a horrible melee. The snarling, roaring cacophony of surging wolf bodies rose to meet the incoming storm. The wolves dashed and snapped and feinted and retreated and lunged and tore, all too quickly for Mia to follow. Dalton lay unconscious a few steps away. Her heart pounded in her chest, and every tiny scent burst like a packet of firecrackers in her nose, each with a unique identifiable signature. Her skin seethed with what felt like electricity, and the power in her legs and arms pulsed like a contained explosion. She wanted to help the boys, but if Slade hurt Sarah—or killed her—he would win, and then, without question, they would all be dead. If Mia jumped into the fight, it would be violating the law of the challenge—somehow she knew this.

But she wasn't a wolf, at least not yet, and someone she loved was fighting for her life. Righteous rage boiled up like hot liquid in her throat, dissipating the cold fear that kept her feet nailed to the ground. One of *her* pack was in danger.

Slade's teeth snapped down upon Sarah's shoulder, tearing into the black material that swathed her shoulders, torso, and haunches. Sarah's body pulled away, and the strange material seemed to slough off Slade's toothy grip and remain whole.

Mia sprang toward him.

When she landed on his back, he felt like a writhing, furry brick. She jammed the scalpel into his shoulder. He howled, more in anger than pain, snapping back at the sudden weight on his back. Mia snaked her bloody wrist around his neck. Her fingers would not work to clutch a handful of fur. He spun and whirled, flailing her legs. The force of the spin tore the scalpel from her grip, and she glimpsed the spinning splinter of silver before it disappeared into the depths of the ditch grass with her bear spray. She was flung off, tumbling through the air. Slade lunged after her, jaws gaping toward her face, eyes blazing like feral coals.

Sarah's teeth, buried in his haunches, jerked his advance to a halt as if he had reached the end of a chain. Stuck between two adversaries, Slade hesitated a moment before spinning back toward Sarah. Sarah danced out of his reach, maintaining her vise-like grip on his haunch. Mia burned with the urge to *attack*.

The tips of her fingers tingled with fiery slivers.

She normally kept her nails modestly trimmed and painted, but suddenly they sprang into fearsome inch-long points. Now, she had all the weapons she needed. She dived toward Slade again, raking the claws of her good hand across his eyes. One of his eyes was shot through with blood, the side she had blasted with pepper spray. A week ago, the sensation of her nails tearing through fur and flesh would have sickened her, but now it felt right, satisfying. His bloody eye disintegrated under her claw like an over-ripe grape. His body flung itself blindly into her like a battering ram, throwing her into the air toward the cornfield. The barb-wire fence caught her like a spiked clothesline. The wire tore gouges across her back, then snapped under her weight. She landed on her back among the cornstalks, then rolled back into a crouch and squeezed a handful of moistening field soil between her fingers. Her severed bra straps hung limp across her back. Warmth spread across her shoulder blades and down her backbone. Strangely, her brain registered no pain. Her teeth clamped tighter and felt thick behind her lips, as if she was wearing a football mouthpiece. A flick of her tongue told her they were sharper now, larger.

The sky fell open. A wind-driven deluge of rain lashed over them like a fire hose. She flung the handful of soil at Slade. It splatted against his side, unheeded. She screamed at him, "Hey, asshole! Over here!" Maybe if Mia could distract him again, Sarah could find an opening and finish him off. Mia snatched up a handful of mud and flung it, repeating her cry. Slade concentrated on trying to dislodge Sarah's teeth from his hindquarters. Something about his movements—perhaps a little slower—told Mia that his strength was flagging. Perhaps his accumulation of wounds was beginning to take its toll.

Thunder burst overhead. Wind drove the rain into a pounding torrent, waves of it lashing over them. A tremendous rhythmic beating filled the air, joining with the wind and rain like a succession of close-packed slaps.

With a tremendous surge and kick, Slade tore free of Sarah's jaws, pulling her off balance. She stumbled forward, giving Slade the moment he needed to spin on her with speed that denied human sight. With a roar, he snatched the side of her neck in his teeth and bunched himself to rip out her throat once and for all.

"No!" Mia threw herself into Slade with all her strength. She dug her claws into Slade's head, tearing at his ears and cheeks and lips, twisting, throwing a leg over his shoulders, trying to pull his head away from Sarah's vulnerable throat. In a single, lightning fast movement, Slade tore out Sarah's throat and clamped his teeth onto Mia's wounded hand again, crushing her meat and bones in his jaws.

Mia saw the ghastly scarlet gash open up in Sarah's throat as Sarah's body flopped away from Slade.

Again, Mia felt only a vague sensation of discomfort in her hand, and a fleeting thought that the wound would hurt a lot more later, if she lived, but the sight of Sarah falling away with a terrible red stain spreading across her the white fur of her throat crushed Mia's heart like the gravity of a black hole.

Slade jerked Mia off his back, propelling her with a heavy thump against the ground, directly under him. Her breath whooshed from her lungs as if she had been hammered by a small elephant. Her strength evaporated, along with the rest of her power to fight.

CHAPTER FORTY-TWO

A blazing white light slashed down through the curtains of rain. The *whop!-whop!-whop!* of helicopter blades drove the raindrops like hailstones against Mia's face. Mud squished into the back of her neck, into the barb-wire gouges across her back.

Slade looked back over his shoulder toward the light. Mia caught the silhouette of the aircraft descending through the tempest, circling, struggling against the wind.

Something struck the ground not far away. She looked toward the sound and saw a heavy stainless steel dart embedded into the earth.

A dart struck Slade, and he staggered, roaring in defiance.

He turned away from Mia and leaped toward the field, but his leap did not carry him as far as he seemed to expect. He landed against a fence post. His legs collapsed under him, but he surged forward again. If he disappeared into the cornstalks, he might escape.

Mia leaped for him, snagged his tail with her good hand and pulled with all her might. His claws tore deep into the soft wet sod, but with a surge of shocking strength, Mia dragged him back into full view. She caught another glimpse of steel as another dart speared into his back. He stumbled again, snapped weakly at her, but she yanked hard again on his tail, pulling his rump toward her.

Another dart snicked into his shoulder.

His movements wound down like a clockwork toy, grinding to a halt. His legs trembled. His massive chest heaved deep with exertion. Blood dripped from a dozen gashes, flaps of furry skin hanging open like drooling crimson mouths, one eye a pulped bloody mess.

Another dart.

His nose sagged toward the ground, shoulders slumping.

The melee of wolves halted, their attention turning toward Slade. The wolf-boys all backed away from each other, their attention warily divided between their adversaries and Slade.

Mia screamed at Slade, "Go down!"

The helicopter hovered lower. Two men in the open side door trained what looked like rifles downward. One of the other wolves yipped in surprise as a hissing dart lanced into it.

A silvery wolf sprang off the road toward the cornfield, followed by two others, a dark one and a striped one. Another of the wolves went down, brought low by a dart.

Slade's knees wobbled. He looked at Mia with his remaining eye, filled with hatred so pure that it turned her blood to slush. He stalked toward her, step by agonizing step. Then one final dart speared into his neck, and he fell with a ragged sigh.

Mia did not know how long she stared at Slade's unconscious body. Part of her, the wolf part, wanted to dash forward and kill him while he was helpless, so that he would never be a threat to anyone ever again. But the wolf part was just an urge. She recognized it, and knew that even after all he had done, she couldn't just kill him in cold blood. Had Sarah managed to kill him during the fight, however, Mia would have cheered.

Sarah's furry white form lay still in the grass, rain and blood soaking her fur and glistening like jewels in the harsh glare of the helicopter's spotlights. Mia wanted to run to her, but she could not bear the thought of seeing Sarah dead. The gob of anguish rising in her throat nailed her feet to the earth.

Jace, Lee, and Malcolm disappeared into the cornfields as the aircraft settled to earth. Tara and two other wolves had been brought down by darts. Eric lay where he fell, licking his wounds, his head hanging low like a beaten, sodden dog. Dalton lay on the road, as still as a corpse. She couldn't see his face.

Soldiers with guns leaped out of the chopper, covering the area.

Looking down the cavernous bore of the barrel of a gun, Mia threw up her arms. "Don't shoot! I'm the good guys!"

A tall dark shape, wearing black combat fatigues emblazoned with "F.B.I.", emerged from the helicopter. The figure approached her, squishing across the thickening mud, heedless of the pounding rain. Raindrops gleamed like heavy falling jewels in the blazing searchlights. The figure picked up speed, coming to her. Before she knew it, powerful arms threw themselves around her, pulling her tight against a strong chest. Her father's scent.

Marcus O'Reilly kissed her head and squeezed her like a bear. "I'm so glad you're okay."

"Hi, Dad." Tears burst free and stampeded down her cheeks.

They stood and held each for several long moments. Finally Mia said, "Is Mom okay?"

He nodded. "She's fine."

"Is she...infected?"

His face darkened. "It's too soon to say. The C.D.C. people are working on a test."

She swallowed hard. "If she is...can they...cure her?"

"I don't know."

"How did you find us?"

"G.P.S. in your cell phone. You know, I can't even begin to tell you how much trouble you'd be in. Under normal circumstances, that is."

"I know. I'm sorry for all that. I just...had to."

"I know. It's going to take some time to sort all this out."

One of the agents knelt and felt Dalton's neck for a pulse. "Medic!" Another leaped out of the helicopter carrying a med-kit.

Her dad noticed the ragged bloody mess that was her right hand. "Jesus, let me look at that!" He took her right wrist gently in his hand. Her shirt was soaked with blood, hers and Slade's. And so were her lethal inch-long claws. "Oh, my god! Mia!"

The pain in his voice almost made her cry, but she bit it back, and just shrugged. "It's been a long day."

He swallowed hard. "Can you move your fingers?"

She shook her head.

"Medic!" he cried.

The agent with the med-kit looked at him.

Her dad called to him, "When you're done there!"

The agent nodded.

Mia remembered the sensation of her claws extending. She smelled her father's day-old aftershave, and the shampoo he showered with that morning, and the coffee he drank at some point, and the stench of fear-sweat that the bravado in his voice tried to mask. The terrible gashes in her flesh made her queasy, but some part of her expected now that her wounds would heal just fine.

"Where are the boys?" he said.

Mia sniffled. "They ran off. Chopper scared them. I think they'll be back sometime though."

The agents kept their dart guns trained on Eric, who simply lowered his head and whined. Headlights appeared over a rise in the road, and moments later, a panel truck that looked like a S.W.A.T. van, but with F.B.I. markings, rumbled to a stop next to Dalton's car. More agents rushed out carrying submachine guns, deploying in close disciplined order.

Mia's dad hugged her close, interposing himself. Two men in dark jackets emblazoned with "C.D.C." in big yellow letters stepped tentatively out of the truck and approached the tranquilized werewolves. After a cursory examination, they pulled out walkie-talkies and began to report into them.

"Dad." Mia choked on the words. "Sarah—" She raised a trembling hand to point at where the white wolf lay dead.

But the shape was not a wolf anymore. It was long, lithe, pale limbs, curled. Moving.

Mia dashed to Sarah's side.

Sarah rolled onto her back. Droplets of rain spattered against the horrible crimson gash in her throat. Scratches and teeth marks crisscrossed her limbs. Her lip and cheek were swollen, her eye blackened, her hair clotted with blood over one ear.

Mia clasped her hand over the wound, feeling the warmth seep through her fingers. "You're alive! Hold on!"

Her father's voice roared over the din of helicopter engine, rain, and thunder. "Man down! Man down!" He threw himself down at Sarah's side. "Stupid sister, don't you die on me or I'll have to kick your ass."

Seconds later, the medic was there.

Sarah croaked and gasped. "Looks...worse than it is. He caught... part of my suit...missed jugular..."

Mia's eyes fell to the gruesome gaping hole with things moving where the skin should be.

Sarah's warm hand fell across Mia's shoulder, and a fierce squeeze told Mia that Sarah's strength was not gone. Mia hugged her, lifted her, squeezed her like iron clamps. Sobs burst forth.

The medic pressed a bandage over the wound, took Mia's hand and placed it there. "Hold this." Mia held it there with every ounce of her will, willing no more blood to come, while the medic gave Sarah an injection.

The strange black garment hugged Sarah's torso like a wet suit but with a tough, fibrous texture. And now, this close, Mia could smell the Wild in her; she smelled the kinship, the comfort of a close packmate.

CHAPTER FORTY-THREE

Morning slanted through the blinds, across the white sheets of the hospital bed. Mia blinked and sat up. The feeling of a lead weight on her wrist reminded her of the plaster cast. Birds twittered in the trees below her window. Traffic droned on the distant street. Human beings bustled about the halls outside. Across the room, in another bed, her mother slept. The air reeked of harsh chemicals, antiseptics, cleaning liquids, air fresheners masking the olfactory mess like a band-aid over a severed limb. A sea of scents, with humans drifting through it oblivious to the richness of the multilayered currents. The scent of her father lingered; he had been here recently. An I.V. needle was taped to her other arm, dripping clear fluid into her blood.

Her muscles hurt. Her wounds hurt. Before the doctors had knocked her out with dose of painkiller, the pain had built into a conflagration that a week ago she would not have been able to manage. Her body was a dissonant chorus of overlapping pains, from the multitude of bites, bruises, scratches, contusions, and the wrist that Slade had crushed in his jaws. What amazed her was how little pain she had felt at the time.

She sighed and leaned back onto the pillow. Her feet slid back and forth under the covers, and she realized they were seeking the comfort of a thick, warm bulk that always slept near her feet. Tears burst into her eyes. She clasped her good hand over her eyes and sobbed once. The I.V. tube lay against her cheek, dull and lifeless.

A tiny current of air moved aside for the door as it eased open. Mia wiped her tears.

Sarah whispered, "How you doing?" She was dressed in a hospital gown and robe. The swatch of bandage at her throat peeked up over the collar.

Mia's heart leaped at the sight of her, but then almost fell into a sobbing pile at the sight of all her bruises and bandages. "I'm alive."

Sarah slipped in and shut the door quietly behind her. "Me, too."

"Thank god."

"Thought you'd want to know what I've been hearing."

"Come on in. I'll whip us up some nice raw steak while you tell me all about it." Mia's voice quavered, and she pursed her lips against more tears.

"I'll pass. The thought of blood right now does not sit well. Doctor says that with some time to heal you'll be okay." Sarah sat down beside the bed and squeezed Mia's arm.

Mia sighed again. Would her entire life ever be okay again?

Sarah's face turned even more serious, and her warm gaze settled over Mia like a protective blanket. "So, do you have any...cravings?"

"A banana split."

Sarah cracked a short smile. "Good." Then serious again. "I saw what you did, what happened."

"The claws."

"And the speed, the agility."

"Yeah." Mia rolled her eyes. "That was *so* much fun." She intended her words to sound ironic, but maybe they were not. She wished she could decide how she felt about it. Being able to run and leap like a superhero was exhilarating. But at what cost for the rest of her life?

Sarah licked her split lip. "I have a question for you."

"Shoot."

"How'd you do it?"

"What?"

"How did you do it?"

"I don't know. It just happened." Mia narrowed her eyes and fixed them on Sarah. "Why do you ask how I did it? Isn't that all part of the package?"

"I mean, how did you do it without wolfing out completely? That kind of thing is not possible until after the infection has matured. Even then, only with experience, practice."

"What does that mean?"

"It means that the virus could be acting with you in a way we haven't seen before."

"Who's 'we?'"

"The C.D.C. and...other people looking into this."

"It's not cool when your favorite aunt in the whole word is a werewolf and doesn't tell you, you know."

"You're right. It's not. But there's a lot about that isn't cool for anyone. I can tell you that I've been studying this ever since...ever since it happened to me. I've been working with the government to figure out where it came from, what it does, how it works. It all came to a head here, last night. The quarantine is still on, and the media is building a tornado all around the country. Omaha is cut off. If there are a lot of people infected—and we think there may be dozens, maybe hundreds, in Omaha alone—there is no way this will be kept quiet. Videos are popping up all over the internet. Twitter, Facebook, blogs are going crazy. The government is trying to stem a nationwide panic. But that's not my problem. My problem is you."

"I'm just a problem child. Have you heard from the boys?"

"Not a word."

"What about Dalton?"

"He has a broken nose and cheekbone. He's in surgery."

"Surgery!"

"A broken cheekbone can be pretty bad. They have to put his nose and cheek and maybe his eye-socket back together."

Mia clenched her good fist. Fresh tears burst out. "I didn't want anyone to get hurt." Especially Dalton. She glanced across the room at her mother, still sleeping soundly.

"Of course you didn't. But Slade's a bad customer and he had time to practice the wolf side."

Mia swallowed hard, imagining Dalton with a face full of tubes, and knives coming at his skin. "How does the virus spread?"

"It's passed mainly through saliva and blood."

"Can you pass it by...kissing?"

"We don't know yet. Until then I would not recommend any long deep wet kisses."

The memory of the Dalton's kiss leaped into her mind. That

incredible moment in the car when she had almost surrendered her self-control. Mia's throat felt full, and she tried to sigh the feeling away.

Sarah forced a grin. "The good news for you is that you're going to heal quickly. The physical pain won't last long. It's apparently built into the package."

"I'm glad you specified the physical."

Sarah leaned toward her with a stricken expression. "Mia, I'm not going to lie to you. Becoming...*this* is not easy. As your body changes, it will create more fear, self-loathing, and emotional distress than you've imagined before."

"You mean like puberty?"

Sarah chuckled in spite of the earnestness of her expression. "Yeah, like puberty on crack. But you're a smart, tough little chick and I'll be here to help you."

"Maybe we can go chase cars together. But first you have to get me one of those black wet suits."

Sarah grinned. "Bio-engineered spider silk. Stronger than Kevlar, and stretchy too. Saves me those awkward moments when I have to change back into human form."

"I'll take two. One in white."

Sarah laughed. "That would probably require Congressional approval, wipe out the country's entire black ops budget."

"I have the coolest aunt ever."

"You do indeed."

"So, Miss Know-It-All, why, if the virus is linked to wolf D.N.A., does it make you heal faster? Wolves can't do that. Wolves don't have a twenty-foot vertical leap."

"We know this much. It's not just wolf D.N.A. There's other D.N.A. that we haven't identified. A kind of hyper-wolf. It's definitely engineered. We just don't know where it came from."

"Is Mom going to get it?"

Another voice sounded from the doorway. "That's what I'm here to talk about." A doctor in a white lab coat stepped inside and closed the door behind him. He was a tall, spindly man with a crew cut and goatee that made the sharp angles of his face even more pronounced. His voice was dry and deep like a desert cave. "Hello, Mia. I'm Doctor Weissman. Sarah."

Sarah nodded to him. "Good morning, Jim."

Mia's mom stirred and opened her eyes, rubbed her face sleepily.

Doctor Weissman said, "Good morning, Mrs. O'Reilly. How are you feeling?"

Mia's mom answered in Japanese. "My head hurts. And my tongue tastes like a mouse died in my mouth."

The doctor said, "What did she say?"

Sarah smirked. "She said her head hurts, and she could use some mouthwash."

The doctor poured a cup of water from the decanter on a nearby tray. He offered it to her.

Mia's mom scooted into a sitting position and took the water. "Thank you." As she took a sip, she looked at the doctor expectantly, as if waiting to shoulder the weight of bad news.

"I have good news for you, Mrs. O'Reilly. We've checked your blood for the virus, and it appears that you have not been infected."

Mia's mother practically deflated with relief. "Really...? *Yokatta! Sugoi!* That's great news!"

"The strange thing, however, is that your wound appears to have been thoroughly exposed to the virus through the wolf's saliva. So the question becomes, why were you not infected? The virus was certainly present, but it's not affecting you. We've compared your blood sample from Immanuel Hospital to one we took a couple of hours ago. In the first one, the virus *was* present in your blood. In the second, it was not." He glanced around the room at three puzzled expressions.

Sarah crossed the room and took her friend's hand. "What does that mean, Jim?"

"It means that she was exposed, but the virus did not affect her. It appears to have died out in her system. This seems to corroborate some of your findings, Sarah."

Mia said, "What findings?"

Sarah wiped her lips. "I'm not a scientist. I was infected about eight months ago. I was...in Asia at the time. After it happened, I did some checking and discovered rumors. A few vague posts on internet forums, strange news stories, that kind of thing. A Japanese scientist claimed to have information about this, so I went to Japan."

Mia's mom sat up straight. "That's why you were gone so long!"

"The scientist said that he had seen evidence that a few people of Asian descent had exhibited immunity to the virus. He said it could be similar to H.I.V."

Mia gasped. "H.I.V.!"

Doctor Weissman cleared his throat. "There is a genetic mutation prevalent in a small segment of people of Scandinavian descent that appears to make them immune to H.I.V. The recessive genetic code that causes sickle cell anemia, prevalent in people of African descent, makes them immune to malaria. Our current hypothesis, based on the work of the Japanese scientist and on what is happening with you and your mother, is that a portion of people of Asian descent, particularly Japanese people, might be immune to the lycanthrope virus."

Mia's mother asked, "Why Japanese?"

"Japan is an island country, with a history of isolation. Recessive genetic traits, like blue eyes and blond hair in Scandinavian people, become more pronounced in isolated populations. Mutations are more likely to be passed on. Some kind of mutation specific to those of Japanese ethnicity might make them immune to this virus. But again, this is all speculation at this point. The good news, Mrs. O'Reilly, is that you're going to be fine."

Mia's gaze fixed on the white lumps of her feet under the covers.

Doctor Weissman turned. "Which brings us to Mia."

"I know," Mia said. "I'm already showing my hairy side."

Mia's mom gasped, and her eyes became dark glistening orbs. Her voice cracked. "No, Mia."

Mia could not bear to see her mother's stricken expression, so she closed her eyes. Her mother slid her legs out of the bed, wobbling as she stood, and crossed the room to Mia's bed. She sat next to Mia, hugged her, kissed her on the cheek. Her mother's cheek was warm against hers, with a drop of coolness that spread like another kiss across the surface of contact. How long had it been since her mother had really hugged her, kissed her? Mia melted into her mother's embrace and wept. Two-year-old walls crumbled and dispersed in the deluge of tears.

After several moments, the doctor blinked at this display of emotion. "You're joking, right?"

Mia sniffled and wiped at her eyes. "Don't mess with me, Doctor. Especially when we're having a moment."

Sarah stood up. "Jim, what are you saying? Mia changed. I saw it."

"Do you mean she made a complete transformation?"

Mia shook her head. "No, just claws and teeth."

Sarah said, "Plus superhuman speed, strength, and agility. There's no question."

The doctor rubbed his pointed chin. "Then I must say I'm confused. The blood sample we took from you an hour ago shows no trace of the virus."

Mia sat up straight. "How can that be?"

"Frankly, at this point I have no idea. No one has ever contracted the virus and then overcome it, at least not to our knowledge."

"Does that mean I'm cured?" A sparkle of hope began to glimmer in the depths of Mia's gloom. As soon as Dalton was awake, she was *so* going to kiss him.

The doctor took a long, deep breath. "I can't answer that question without more tests. I'm going to have to schedule a full battery of blood work, D.N.A. testing, brain scans—"

If she was cured, why could she still smell everything like a wolf?

The door swung open, and Mia's father leaned in. "Everybody up?" Then glancing around, his eyes narrowed slightly. "Am I interrupting something important? You all look like somebody just dropped a bomb."

"Special Agent O'Reilly," Doctor Weissman said, "I came in here with good news for your family, but Mia seems to have thrown me a curve ball."

A curve ball that would bring any rounding of Mia's romantic bases to a shrieking halt.

Mia's father glanced around the room again. Sarah quickly recounted the conversation. He absorbed the information with a stoic expression, then said, "So Mia may or may not be infected."

"That's right," the doctor said. "We'll have to run more tests right away."

Mia's father stiffened, and his voice turned hard. "We'll see about that. I think she's had enough needles in her for one day."

The doctor squeezed his clipboard. "Of course, all in good time."

"You can experiment on Slade all you want. He won't be leaving custody anytime soon."

"How long can you hold him?" Sarah asked.

He smirked. "As far as the civilian authorities are concerned, we have a very dangerous wolf in custody. Wolves don't have the same rights people do. Can't very well put a wolf in jail, can we. I figure we'll let him stay in wolf form until we're sure what to do with him."

Mia said, "He can't change back?"

"He's pretty weak from all the punishment he took. I have a great big bag of Puppy Chow that says he won't be getting any raw meat for a while."

Mia said, "What about his pack?"

"Those are some abused, terrified, traumatized teenagers. We're going to keep them in custody for a little while, so we can let the doctor here do some tests on them. It's likely they'll be released back to their parents."

Mia said, "What if they don't have parents?" She thought about Eric lying wounded and half-unconscious in his wolf form, and the fear in his eyes when he looked at Slade.

"We're working on that. There might be other alternatives to putting them back on the street."

"Jail?" Strangely, Mia felt no ill will toward the young members of Slade's pack. They were simply following the will of their Alpha, and Slade had been a powerful Alpha. With Slade out of the picture, they would be lost for a while, vulnerable, until they found a new pack.

"Not jail. Something else. We'll see. Any word from Jace and his friends?"

Mia shook her head. Her cell phone had been silent for hours.

A knock came at the door, and a woman wearing a prominent F.B.I. badge on a lanyard around her neck poked her head inside. "Marcus, I have your um...package here."

His face brightened. "Excellent, Maggie! Bring it in."

The woman wheeled a cart through the door. On the cart sat a large pet carrier.

A black beady eye peered through the front grate. A familiar eye. The other was covered by the thick bandage.

Mia gasped.

Deuce raised his head from his paws, and his groggy, forlorn gaze nearly broke Mia's heart. "Can we let him out?"

Her father shrugged. "I don't see why not." He opened the front of the carrier. Deuce tried to stand, but the heavy cast on his leg prevented him. "Dad, help him out!"

Her father eased the dog out of the carrier, grunting at the weight, and onto the bed at Mia's feet. "He's awfully loopy right now."

Deuce lay down with a sigh, and suddenly Mia's feet were warm. Mia said, "He looks terrible."

Deuce looked at her as if to say, *Speak for yourself.*

Her father said, "If he weren't built like an Abrams tank, he'd be dead. Broken leg, dislocated shoulder, cracked skull, three broken teeth. He's on better painkillers than yours. Like I said, pretty loopy right now."

She reached over and stroked Deuce's bristly hide. He lay on his side, and his tail began to thump placidly against the bed.

CHAPTER FORTY-FOUR

A couple of days later, Mia was sick beyond measure of tests, of needles, of tubes, of being in the hospital, period. The bed across from her had been empty since the previous afternoon when her mother went home. The doctor, nurses, and lab techs had barely given Mia more than a ten-minute respite, but that did little to assuage the loneliness of the empty room. She still felt the warmth and love of her mother's good-bye kiss on her forehead. Mia couldn't remember the last time she looked forward to seeing her mother at home.

The television flickered silently near the ceiling, the small speaker attached to her bed muted against the incessant tide of the same irritating commercials.

A knock on the door preceded Sarah's voice. "Hey, Fido."

"What's up, Spot?" Mia said. "Want to play fetch?"

Sarah came in and sat on the bed. "Thought I'd let you know that they're kicking you out of here this afternoon. No more tests. Doctor Weissman said something about a follow-up exam in a few days."

"Thank god. I'm going to go stir crazy. Or else scratch my skin off." Her itching wounds were driving her nuts.

"That's the healing."

Mia held up her cast. "It's like even my bones itch. Is that possible?"

"You'll probably be able to take that thing off in a week or two."

"Awesome. Then you can show me how to dig for bones and hunt wildebeest."

Sarah sighed, and laid her hand on Mia's. "I'll help you. Anytime."

"Yeah, except the next time you disappear to Timbuktu for six months."

"We'll see about that, too."

Mia rubbed her growling stomach. "Did you see anyone out there with a food cart? I'm starving for green jell-o and mystery vegetables."

"No raw steak?"

Mia made a face. "Not yet, thank god. Oh, I had a question. Does raw fish count for the raw meat thing?"

"I don't know. Why?"

"I half-Japanese. Sashimi anyone? I could eat raw fish until cows come home and you think anyone would notice?"

Sarah laughed. "Clever."

The local noon news broadcast appeared on the television. A prominent yellow Biohazard symbol appeared above "QUARANTINE" on the screen next to the anchor-woman. Mia turned up the volume.

"...Officials from the C.D.C. announced this morning that the quarantine of the Omaha metro area will be lifted by the end of the week. They claim to have identified the nature of the outbreak and are taking steps to contain it. They are calling the virus Super-Rabies 1. It is transmitted through contact with infected animals, particularly through their saliva. Anyone bitten by an animal within the last week is strongly urged to report to a hospital for testing and treatment."

The video cut to a bald, professional-looking man in wire-rimmed spectacles and a bowtie. "We cannot stress strongly enough the dangerous nature of this infection. We all know how dangerous rabies is, and this strain is particularly virulent and fast-acting. If you've been bitten, go to the nearest hospital now. Right now. We have developed a test that is 99% effective in detecting the virus. We're working right now to determine how far the virus has spread through the local human and animal populations."

A voice from the forest of microphones said, "What about the local animal population and family pets?"

"They should be tested as well."

"Is there a cure or a vaccine?"

The scientist's face tensed. "We're working on that."

Mia glowered at the screen. "That's such crap."

Sarah said, "Do you really think that we can tell people that we're in the midst of a werewolf plague?"

"How can we not? People need to know so they can protect themselves!"

The anchor-woman returned, beside a photograph of a man in a hunter's cap. "A local citizens' group has taken a proactive approach to protecting themselves and the public. Led by local resident Jim Phelps, a group calling themselves 'The Freedom Hunters' has organized several teams that are combing the city and countryside."

The video cut to Jim Phelps wearing a camouflage suit, high-powered rifle slung over one shoulder, standing next to a battered pickup truck in hand-painted camouflage.

The reporter held the microphone to his face. "So the Freedom Hunters are out there looking for stray dogs and other animals that might be infected?"

Phelps stood straighter. "That's right. I figure it's our duty to help however we can. The government can't be everywhere. We got to protect the public. We got a right to protect our families."

"What are you doing with the animals?"

"Well, we're putting them down, of course."

The video cut to the truck's box, which was filled to the brim with scores of bloody carcasses. Meat hooks, caked with blood and matted fur, hung from the sides of the pickup. Coyotes, dogs of a dozen different breeds and mongrels alike. And the large, muscled bulks of wolves.

Mia gripped her mouth, choking.

The reporter said, "Are those wolves?"

"They sure are."

"Wolves aren't native to Nebraska."

"Tell that to them. We shot eleven wolves last night. They go down awful hard, too, unless you shoot 'em in the head. We ain't violating any hunting laws either. We got special permits from Game and Parks for wolves and coyotes. They're even offering a bounty."

"A bounty? You're going to make money on this?"

Phelps grinned at the camera. "All proceeds go the Nebraska Humane Society. It's our way of giving back."

"And the dogs?"

"If they're loose, they're a hazard. Fair game." He gestured to the pile of carcasses, an undulating sea of bloody fur, seeping wounds, lolling tongues, glazed eyes.

Among the morass of tawny brown, gray, black, and white, Mia looked for wolf carcasses that might resemble three in particular, but the pile was too deep and haphazard for her to see. She wished she could pause the broadcast and scan the video.

Phelps continued, "This is just our group. We got three more teams."

The reporter said, "Have any of you been attacked?"

"Some of the wolves, they want to fight when we got 'em cornered, but Marlene here..." He patted his rifle. "She speaks pretty well at a distance."

"Isn't it dangerous to the public for all of you to be out here with guns blazing all night long?"

Phelps stiffened. "We're all experienced hunters. We don't allow no crackpots. Would you rather have us or a bunch of rabid wolves in the streets? You wouldn't believe some of the crazy stories people have told us. People *changing*. Like some sort of werewolf apocalypse. Can you believe that?"

The video cut back to the anchor woman in the studio. "The C.D.C. is still warning residents to remain indoors unless absolutely necessary and avoid all contact with animals. Now, over to Jim Cantrell with today's forecast..."

Sarah said, "I'm sure the boys are laying low. They're too smart to get themselves shot by a bunch of rednecks."

Mia swallowed hard. "Freedom Hunters. Now *there's* a creative name."

"People like that aren't known for their imagination."

"I hate to say it, but maybe Slade was right."

"What about?"

"He said there was a war coming. I think it's here. It's going to be a fight for the top of the food chain."

Sarah gave Mia a long, searching look. "Maybe. But maybe it doesn't have to be."

"Why not? If werewolves are superior, then what's to stop them from taking over? Turning humans into cattle, like Slade said."

"Maybe we don't have to eat *people*. Maybe we can control the wolf side. I'm still a human being. So are you. We can choose."

Mia muted the television. "Maybe."

CHAPTER FORTY-FIVE

Mia leaned back against her locker and stared at the ceiling panels, dreading the imminent sound of the morning bell. How was she ever going to get caught up with her classes? She had not been in school in over three weeks. Even though the school had been shut down for a week because of the quarantine, she was still two weeks behind in her classes. Her parents had kept her out of school until they were sure that the window for any spontaneous transformations had passed. Doctor Weissman had brought her back for innumerable blood tests, D.N.A. analyses, CT scans, and MRIs. They had removed her cast a week ago.

She had tried to keep up with some of her homework simply to alleviate the incessant boredom, but when that didn't work she watched CNN and the local news. The military and the C.D.C. had tried to minimize public hysteria through a concentrated media blitz. They had concocted a completely fictitious yet convincing background for the origin and nature of Super Rabies 1, complete with 'experts' shipped in to reassure people through endless talk shows and news reports, all of them spewing carefully shaped lies. Everyone was safe. The threat had been averted. The quarantine was lifted. Werewolves in Omaha? An epidemic of lycanthropy? That was just crazy talk.

Nevertheless, the lists of missing people grew longer.

In between binges of television news, she combed YouTube for videos that might be related to this. It didn't take her long to find several videos of wolf attacks, or wolves prowling through backyards, or wolf howls in the distance, along with creeped-out commentary that there weren't supposed to be any wolves in Nebraska. She even found a video that purported to be a person transforming into a wolf. It looked pretty real to her, and the woman in the video, the woman changing, was absolutely terrified by what was happening to her. The comments on the video ranged from, "Wow! Cool!" to "What a ridiculous @$%&ing hoax! You can do better CGI than that with Photoshop!" Two days later, the video had disappeared as if it had never been.

Mia had considered sending her video tape to the reporter she had met. She watched it, assuring herself that if a viewer could avoid motion sickness, there was plenty on the tape to prove everything. But ultimately decided against it. Slade was already behind bars—or in a titanium kennel. There was no reason to implicate herself or any of her friends in any wrongdoing at Saint Sebastian's.

Hospital staff talked of hearing pockets of wolf calls late in the night, here and there across town, what sounded like wolfen battles. Blood was found sometimes, but no bodies. So many people were missing. The local news flashed endless successions of photos of missing people. How many had become prey and how many had become predator?

On one such broadcast, she recognized three young faces in the succession of still photos. She had heard nothing from the boys in three weeks.

On another broadcast, she recognized the photo of one James Matthews, the mournful Johnny Cash fan that night in the coffee shop. She hoped he was okay.

There was also a news story about the huge increase in government-organized animal control efforts. 'Dog-catchers' scoured the city en masse. Over fifteen hundred feral cats and five hundred stray dogs were captured and put down in the last three weeks, which was sad enough. So had a huge portion of the city's pet population because of fear of infection. Activist groups like P.E.T.A. and the Humane Society were going batshit crazy over the slaughter, but no one was listening. Dogs, cats, even birds, all were being euthanized, as if people were afraid the virus was some bizarre form of crazy bird flu.

All to support a carefully crafted lie.

There was now little mention of wolves.

Mia shook her head in disgust at these reports. Sometimes humans were so stupid, so reactionary. Maybe the next great plague would be were-finches and were-parakeets. She caught herself thinking of humans as separate from herself, removed from her. And weren't they?

A week ago, Sarah drove Mia to the park with Deuce, and on the way, Sarah pointed to a plain white van with a ladder on the roof. "Look."

Mia was immersed in her own gloom. "At what?"

"Government surveillance van."

"Really? How can you tell?"

"It's made not to be noticed and it's brand new. See how shiny it is?"

"Why are you telling me this? Isn't it supposed to be a secret?"

"Because we've passed four of them since we got off the freeway."

"Really?"

"This city is absolutely crawling with surveillance. No one believes this has gone away. Not really. Besides, the C.D.C. estimates there could be several hundred infected in the Omaha area alone. Those are the non-public numbers. The 'Freedom Hunters' aren't smart enough to have killed them all. The wolves are staying hidden for now, but that's a lot of them. But that's not the scary part."

"Comforting."

"The scary part is that it's not just here, and we have no idea how widespread it is. There are pockets of this lycanthropy virus worldwide, and I'm betting you could find stories about in the international news media, if you know what to look for."

"But that's just it. Why here? Why not L.A. or New York or Washington?"

"Viruses always spread in ways that can't be predicted. It could be the result of a biological attack, or an accidental release. But the virus is man-made, without question. There's a major military base here, one that controls much of our most powerful arsenal. The Missouri is a major river, and the Platte comes all the way from the Rockies. Wolves can follow the river valleys undetected, and there's plenty of game, both wild and domesticated, deer, cattle—"

"Domesticated humans."

Mia's offhand comment silenced Sarah for a long moment, and they shared a long look between them.

Then Sarah sighed and continued. "Anyway, this quarantine is going to dominate the U.S. media for a few more weeks, unless something worse happens, like a pop singer dies or something. The government doesn't have the resources to watch every area for signs of growing werewolf populations. We just don't."

"So, what then?"

"We have to find a cure."

"Slade wouldn't have wanted a cure. There are more people out there like him. Eating fresh bunnies is a small price to pay for superpowers. At least for some people who are not me. So how will the people know where they are?"

"We can keep a lookout for things similar to what happened here. A wave of missing persons, animal attacks..." Sarah let her voice sound mock-scary. "Howlings in the night! Anyway, there will be signs, and now we know what to look for."

"So you're going to teach me your spy tricks now?"

Sarah smiled. "Maybe."

"Well, I have Tuesdays and Thursdays free for lessons. Midnight work for you?"

Sarah clicked her tongue. "Those are school nights."

"I'm getting used to staying up late."

"We'll see."

Now, on her first day back at school, Mia had not seen Sarah since that drive a week ago. She figured Sarah was off saving the world. And Mia still hadn't seen Jace, Lee, or Malcolm.

A blond girl with a sheepish expression approached through the crowds of students in the hallway, clutching an armful of books.

Mia smiled at her. "Hi."

"Hi," Tara said.

"I'm surprised to see you. I thought they would have kept you locked in some dungeon or something."

"I was, for a while. They let me go a few days ago, after they lifted the quarantine."

"Do your parents know?"

Tara shuffled back and forth. She looked like the old Tara, the pre-werewolf Tara, not the haggard, tortured ghost Mia had seen the last time she encountered human Tara in the school halls. "They know I have a disease."

"But not the whole truth?"

"How could I tell them the whole truth? My mom would just die. My dad would start drinking again. The C.D.C. told them that the disease is in remission." Tara looked at the floor, unspoken words hovering around her. "Mia, I..." Her big blue orbs looked into Mia's, glistening with contrition. "I have a confession."

Mia's first thought was that it might be about Nate. She braced herself. "What is it?"

"It wasn't Chelsea who put that slut picture on your locker. It was me." Tara bit back tears of regret.

Mia crossed her arms, hardening. "Oh, really."

"Chelsea told me to do something to you, but I didn't have to. I did it because...because I had seen Dalton looking at you. I mean, really checking you out, a couple of days before all this started. And I...I didn't like it. I've felt awful about it ever since. I'm sorry, Mia." Tara sniffed and wiped a tear.

Mia found herself strangely calm. "Well, thanks for the confession—"

High heels came running toward Mia and Tara. "*Omigodomigod!* You're here!" Nicki skidded to a halt and threw her arms around Mia's neck. "Where have you been, G.F.?"

Mia accepted the hug and patted Nicki's back. "In the hospital."

"I've been so worried about you!"

Strange that Nicki's name had never once appeared on Mia's phone as an incoming call or text. Mia gave her a neutral smile. "I'm rockin'."

"Awesome! I've been going crazy without you! Algebra is *killing* me. You've missed so much, we *gotta* catch up. Have you heard about Dalton? He got messed up in this car accident!"

"I heard." A familiar lead weight settled atop her heart. He had tried to call her three times. She hadn't answered. Tara's eyes remained downcast.

Nicki continued unabated, "I saw him yesterday. He doesn't look bad after having surgery on his face and stuff. And the homecoming dance is Saturday." Nicki's face was carefully neutral as she glanced back and forth between Mia and Tara. The homecoming game and dance were rescheduled after the deaths and the quarantine. The weight in Mia's chest grew, along with the sudden urge to let claws spring out. Nicki waited for some sort of reaction, but none was forthcoming. "Anyway, it's so great you're back. Let's get together soon."

Mia nodded. "Surely." Not.

"*Ciao!*" Nicki flounced away.

Mia and Tara exchanged smirks.

Then two tall girls appeared next to them. "Tara!" Chelsea said, "What are you doing? Come with us. We need to catch up." She glanced at Mia. Brittany Matthews stood in her shadow, her face downcast, lacking the usual overabundance of make-up and hair-care products.

Tara's eyes flashed with anger.

Mia looked at Tara and shrugged.

Tara said, "Mia and I are talking about something important, Chelsea. You wouldn't understand."

Chelsea loomed over Mia with a tight-lipped frown.

Mia squared her shoulders and speared her gaze up into Chelsea's eyes. Her teeth clenched. Aggression rose in her throat like hot breath, waiting to be set loose. Just one wrong word...

Chelsea blinked and swallowed hard. A moment later she took a step back.

Mia took another step closer, holding Chelsea's gaze. "You wouldn't understand, Chelsea." Her voice was low, quiet, even.

Brittany gripped Chelsea's arm. "C'mon, Chels. Let's go."

Chelsea backed away, looking smaller now somehow.

"Mia-chan!" Kenji's voice echoed over the general din of students milling the hall.

Mia blinked and looked for him. He wound around the pockets of students, his face plastered with an enormous grin. "*O-hisashiburi!* Long time no see!"

Mia bowed to him. "*O-hisashiburi. Genki?* How are you?"

"I'm great!" Then he looked at Tara. His eyes grew wide, and his mouth fell open. "Wow."

Tara smiled.

"Kenji, this is Tara. Tara, Kenji."

Kenji bowed and extended his hand. "Please to meet you."

Tara shook his hand and smiled back. "Hi."

Kenji breathed with admiration bordering on reverence. *"She has such beautiful hair!"*

Mia rolled her eyes.

Tara smiled at Kenji. "You're kind of cute."

Kenji's eyes grew even bigger. "Really?"

Another voice approached, a deep one. "Hey, you two." Dalton's hand fell on Mia's shoulder and a tingling rush shot through her like a shower of warm glitter. His other hand rested on Tara's shoulder. "Kenji, how you doing, man?"

Kenji deflated like a punctured beach ball. "Hello."

Mia could barely make herself look at Dalton. His handsome face was still marred by the faint remnants of heavy bruising around his eyes and nose, and the imprint of stitches was still visible below his eye. But his smile and his eyes were bright and fixed on Mia. Tara swallowed hard and sighed a little. Mia edged away from his touch, even though she wanted nothing more than to collapse into it. His smile dimmed, and he removed his hand.

"Ladies," he said, "We need to get together and talk about things."

Mia nodded.

Tara squeezed her books harder.

Kenji said, "Dalton, you are too cool for me." He sighed and turned away.

"What? No way, man. We need to hang out sometime."

"Really?"

"Yeah, you can teach me Japanese. Let's watch some *Cowboy Bebop* or something."

Kenji beamed. "Great! I like *Samurai X*, too!"

The first bell finally rang, and the tension in Mia's shoulders made a *sproing!* sensation.

"Cool. Mia, Tara, after school?"

The girls nodded.

The afternoon sun turned the aluminum bleachers into massive butt warmers. Mia and Tara sat together, pretending to watch the football team scrimmage. Helmets gleamed in the sun, and the smell of boy-sweat and maleness wafted across the field.

"It's funny," Tara said.

"What is?"

"A month ago, this world was everything to me."

"You mean high school?"

"Yeah, all of it. Football, the cross-country team, who I wanted to date. Who was dating who, and who was fighting with who. Social media and cell phones and now..."

Mia said, "Now it's all garbage. None of it matters."

"None of it."

Mia nodded. That was not entirely true. Her cell phone still felt like a lifeline to the world...the human world. Part of her, however, longed to head into the country and just run.

"The thing is," Tara continued. "I used to be a pretty good cross-country runner. Not spectacular, but, hey, good enough. Now, I can run for miles and barely break a sweat. I can run circles around all of them. And because I can do that, I get to eat like a starving horse."

Mia grinned. "Or a wolf."

"Or a wolf. And my ass looks amazing!"

They laughed together for a moment, then Tara sighed, "Staying on the team now would be like competing against first graders."

"Sounds kind of cocky."

"But we both know it's true, and I don't want to draw any more attention. I keep thinking about how Slade turned into the way he was. He preached that humans were no longer the top of the food chain. They no longer mattered. They were *prey*. Is this what he was talking about? This arrogance? I *am* better than everybody else. And I know it. I can...kill them, so easily, if I want to. And part of me is okay with that."

"Makes it hard to not look down on people. You just have the urge to eat a few raw steaks now and then." Strangely Mia did not have that urge, although she did find meat more appetizing these days. She had noticed that her muscles looked more toned. Her soft skinniness had shifted in the last three weeks to a lithe muscularity that looked kind of hot. Except for the tiny boobs, that is. But at least they didn't get in her way.

Tara nodded. "I manage to hide that from my parents. So far, anyway. They're so clueless. They got my bedroom window fixed. They were frantic that night. I really did a number on my room. Lost control and busted out of there. I told them this wild story about how I don't remember anything, just found myself alone on the side of the road. They had me checked for rape and S.T.D.s and all this crazy stuff. It was pretty demeaning actually."

"Did they believe you?"

"I don't know. But I remember I just had to get out of there and run. They have no idea what their daughter has become. They don't know who I am at all."

"Mine know. Well, not all of it. The problem is that *I* don't know what I am." Mia raised her hand and extended her fingers. She took a deep breath and focused her will. Her heart sped up like an accelerating locomotive. Her fingertips tingled until a terrible, frightening tearing sensation hissed through them. Two-inch black claws tore from beneath her human nails, glinting dully in the sun.

"Wow! I can't do that."

"So they tell me. The doctors still say I'm virus-negative, but I can still do these things. Some viruses hide, so that they're practically impossible to detect."

"Like herpes."

Mia stuck out her tongue. "Yes, I'm like an S.T.D. Nice analogy, Miss Happiness and Sunshine. But yeah, like that. Part of me wants to wolf out, like it's in there clawing to get out sometimes, but I just...tell it 'no.' Part of me wonders if I can go all the way. But it scares me."

Dalton's scent crept over the breeze into her nostrils, his aftershave, his maleness, his sweat, the tinges of nervousness in it, sending an electric thrill and a melting warmth through Mia's body.

Tara said, "It's been three weeks. You haven't wolfed out yet?"

Mia shook her head.

"I never had a choice the first time," Tara said. "It just happened.

Now I can control it a little, but when I get angry it's hard."

"Sometimes Mom and Dad look at me like they're afraid of me. Like if I get mad I'll wolf out and eat them or something."

"Sometimes I feel like eating my little brother."

"Really?"

Tara snickered and elbowed her. "No, not really, you dork! I love my brother."

Mia chuckled.

The football players crashed together in an avalanche of helmets grunts. Coaches' whistles shrilled.

Mia wrung her hands. "Now that we're all self-confessed wolf-sisters and everything, I need to ask you something."

Tara held her breath. "Shoot."

"Did you kill Nate?"

Tara blanched. Fresh tears glistened. After a long pause, her voice was neutral, carefully controlled. "No, but I can understand why you need to know."

"Were you there?"

Tara swallowed hard. "Yes."

"What happened?"

"I saw Caleb in the bushes. He was naked. He asked me to help him with some clothes. They jumped me." She touched her throat. "Bit down on my windpipe so I couldn't scream. Then poor Nate...He came along and...they chased him, brought him down, dragged him back. He was screaming and begging them and crying and...they made me watch..." Her composure crumbled, and sobs poured out. She collapsed against Mia's shoulder. Mia put her arm around Tara and hugged, and she let her own grief pour forth in tears and sobs. For several minutes they cried together.

Dalton stood at the foot of the bleachers, pretending not to watch.

CHAPTER FORTY-SIX

Her blood heated and sweet tingles washed over her skin. She wanted his strong arms around her, but they weren't so strong anymore. She wanted to kiss him again. Maybe she should make him a werewolf so that they could be together. He would make a spectacular wolf, powerful and lean, yet sensitive and sweet...

No.

How could he forgive her if she turned him into a monster? How could she forgive herself?

Not much point in having a boyfriend if she couldn't even kiss him. Even now, the wanting was a kind of aching torture. The moment in the car, the utter abandonment to desire. The guilt. She wanted him. What if she wolfed out and hurt him? She would never forgive herself for that either. The wishing that she was still just a normal girl formed a splinter in her heart, and she cried for that too. Before long, the wishing for the impossible became mourning for what she had lost.

But there was something else, too, something she couldn't quite grasp. A different urge, an instinct to...seek? What that was, she could not say, but it was there, like an invisible thread tugging her in a direction she could not identify.

Tears burned her eyes as she watched Dalton. He waited with his back turned, until the two girls were finished bawling their eyes out.

Mia sniffled, then called to him. "Okay, silly boy. We're done." They wiped their faces. Mia's claws had retracted, reabsorbed into her flesh.

Dalton climbed the bleachers and sat beside Mia.

Mia took his hand and squeezed, for what was probably the last time. "I think we're going to be good friends, Dalton."

He met her gaze, and the expression on his face burst into hope, then faded into realization, then disappointment. Hurt.

Mia took Tara's hand, too. "All of us."

Dalton cracked a grin, but it was just a mask. "All right! I'm dating the two hottest girls in school! Let's all go to homecoming together! Glad to hear you two don't mind sharing."

Never give all the heart. Mia let him keep his mask on. She punched him on the shoulder and laughed.

"Ow." Dalton rubbed his shoulder.

A fresh breeze wafted over them from across the football field, bearing with it the sweetness of cut grass and the stench of sweat, mixed with a light tang of blood.

And something else.

Mia jumped up with a gasp.

Three boys stood beside the chain link fence on the far side of the field.

Tara jumped up and waved. The boys waved back. She took a few long steps down the bleachers and looked back. "You coming?" Tara said. She left the invitation open to Dalton, but they all knew it was for Mia alone.

"Not yet," Mia said.

Tara nodded and started around the football field to join the boys.

Dalton snatched Mia's hand. "'Friends', my ass."

"Dalton, I—"

"Look, I've been going crazy since I was conscious enough to pick up a phone and get blown off."

"I'm sorry."

"The last thing I remember was this huge fight exploding with monsters and all kinds of crazy shit, and then I wake up in Recovery and the only girl I want to talk to is nowhere to be found." He leaned toward her. She could smell him, feel his heat. His thundering pulse throbbed into her hand.

"Dalton, please—" Should she tell him that she *had* been there, but had to leave before he woke up because she couldn't bear to see him suffering because of her?

"And when all the bandages start coming off, enough for me to talk and see and think, she won't even answer my calls."

A wave of emotion shattered her and she threw her arms around his neck and hid her tears in his hair. Her blood seethed with liquid fire. He tried to turn his head to kiss her, and she twisted away from it, shaking her head. "No," she whispered.

"Why not?"

"I don't know what'll happen if I kiss you."

"I don't know what'll happen either." His hand slid down her back, pulling her belly close to him. She felt as light as a doll in his arms.

Her belly warmed, her body thrummed, wanting him, wanting his touch. "No, I mean if I kiss you, I could give you the virus!"

No hesitation. "I'll take the chance."

She pulled herself away and wiped at tears with her sleeves. "No, I can't be responsible for turning you into a monster."

"You're not a monster."

"I don't know what I am!" And until she did, there wouldn't be any kissing, much less anything else. She stood up and stepped back and each inch widened the crack in her heart. She looked across the field, where the boys stood. The pull... "I have to go."

"How long are you going to be?"

She looked into his eyes for a long time. "I don't know."

He nodded, sniffing, and his face hardened. He stood up, quickly, turned his back, and walked away. "See you around, Mia."

Jace unhooked his fingers from the chain links. "Geez, took you long enough."

Mia hugged them all together. "Where have you been?"

Jace smirked. "School. Where else?"

"Really? Where?"

"Saint Sebastian's."

Mia's shock must have been evident on her face.

Jace sniffed. "It wasn't such a bad place except for Slade. We ran as wolves for a few days, until the heat died down and Malcolm and Lee needed a video game fix."

Malcolm grinned. "Werewolves brought out of hiding for a hit of *Halo*."

Tara stood beside Jace, close. "It's so great to see you!"

Jace's face flushed. He gave her a nonchalant head-tip. "How *you* doing?"

Understanding snapped into focus in Mia's mind. On that lonely road, Tara had submitted herself to Jace's pack. He was now her Alpha Male. The Alpha Male had his choice of pack females. What did that make Mia? Was she even part of this pack?

Jace continued, "Father McManus knows all about us now."

Malcolm said, "He believes that he can redeem us from our satanic beast-natures."

Lee said, "He's full o' crap, but he's a good sort. Besides, sleeping in a bed is better than sleeping in a bush."

Malcolm grinned at him. "At least most of the time. Plus, I think he's using the Church's political influence to deflect some of the umpteen bazillion investigations. About Slade."

Lee's face darkened. "And Caleb."

Mia squeezed her left forearm, where there was scar from the bite that had infected her. From the wolf—the boy—that Lee and Malcolm had torn to pieces in the parking lot of Rodriguez Roofing. Her right hand had long since healed, leaving only a few faint pink scars.

Jace grimaced. "Haven't seen Eric, DaShante, and Jimmy since that night either. Father McManus says he doesn't know what happened to them."

Mia was sworn to secrecy but the government still had them. She put her hands on her hips. "Why did you wait so long to find me, you buttheads? I've been worried to death."

Jace rubbed the fine down of pale beard on his chin. "Needed things to settle down. Needed to think about some things for a while."

"Come up with any answers?"

"Nope, just that sometimes you need to run."

Mia understood that urge now.

Tara grinned, "Sounds like a great idea."

Jace grinned back. "You down?"

Tara said, "You know it."

"Let's go." Jace took off his shirt. "See if you all can keep up."

Lee and Malcolm grinned and jumped up and down. A wooded

drainage canal snaked across the back of the football field. No one would see them go.

A sudden pull exploded in Mia's chest. An urge. Her fists clenched. The air smelled sharp and sweet and full of time. Without thinking, she stripped off her shirt. Standing half-naked she looked back toward the bleachers. Dalton was long gone.

The boys faded into the woods, Tara close behind them.

Mia's limbs began to shift, her muscles to slither under her skin. Exhilaration swept through her. She dropped to all fours, shrugged off her remaining human clothes, and followed her pack into the woods.

Stay tuned for the next slam-bang thrill ride...

Volume II
of the
Lycanthrope Trilogy...

DAWN OF THE DEADLY FANG

ABOUT THE AUTHOR

T. James Logan writes a lot of different kinds of things, from science fiction, fantasy, and horror to working on roleplaying games and screenplays. In this persona, he loves to recapture bits of childhood, those times when a glimpse of a werewolf on television kept him up at night, those times when crushes were crushing, and those moments of youthful exuberance when the world was all possibilities. He lives in Denver, Colorado, with his family, plus a dog and a cat, neither of which are lycanthropes—at least he's pretty sure.

CPSIA information can be obtained
at www.ICGtesting.com
Printed in the USA
FFOW02n2241300418
46414142-48223FF

9 781622 254187